Bound by the Dark Side of Passion

"Father said to tell you that he would consent to our marriage—when you've made a million dollars."

"Good God!"

"You can do it, Pride." Esther put her arms around his neck. "I'll help you. I'll find out things and . . . Please say you will."

"All right." Pride groaned inside his heart, knowing he was really caught in the net of his own greed, beyond any chance of escaping.

Esther smiled. "Once we're married, you'll never want anyone else. I'll drive you insane. I'm bad," she whispered. *"I'm very bad. . . ."*

"A LUSTY STORY!"
—*The Kirkus Reviews*

FRANK YERBY

PRIDE'S CASTLE

A DELL BOOK

For Jacques, Nikki and Faune

Published by
DELL PUBLISHING CO., INC.
1 Dag Hammarskjold Plaza
New York, New York 10017

Dell ® TM 681510, Dell Publishing Co., Inc.
Reprinted by arrangement with
The Dial Press.
Printed in the United States of America
Previous Dell Edition #7108
New Dell Edition
First printing—August 1975

PROLOGUE: THE TIME WAS RIPE

THE MIDDLE YEARS—the eighteen-seventies, 'eighties, 'nineties—were a time of moral bankruptcy when men stole millions by a stroke of the pen or by the simple expedient of printing tons of worthless paper. Name the names—the list is endless: the Tweed Ring, the Crédit Mobilier Swindles, the Belknap Scandals—these were the measure of our good, golden days, when the relatives of Presidents waxed fat on the Federal payroll, when Rutherford B. Hayes sat in the White House by the dubious virtue of an election signed, sealed and delivered by sheer fraud.

These things the middle years were, and more. They were Jim Fisk dead on the steps of the Broadway Central Hotel, shot down by his fair Josie's lover; they were Jay Gould rowing across the Hudson with six million dollars in stolen money in a little black bag; they were old Commodore Vanderbilt spitting through his teeth: "The law! To hell with the law, hain't I got the power?" And William, his son, exploding, "The public be damned!"

They were the little children who never saw daylight, except as it filtered through the grimy windows of the factories; the women in the sweatshops; the miners dying in their eternal darkness. They were the grinding misery of the poor, and the plush and gilt and mauve and fine horses of the rich.

They were the years of terrible riots and bloody strikes: Haymarket in Chicago; Pittsburgh half-destroyed in '77; Martinsburg; St. Louis and Homestead where the Pinkertons stood and fired and fired again with strikers lying dead and wounded on the sooty earth. And they were Karl Marx in London, thundering: "Workers of the world, unite! You have nothing to lose but your chains!" and finding such fertile soil for the seeds of his religion of envy and discon-

5

tent that we, today, may presently have to strike down its pestilential growth.

A time of change and discontent, a time of order and stability, too, these days were—and a time of progress, with the coming of the electric light, the telephone, and later still the horseless carriage. A time of ferment. . . .

No wonder then that big Pride Dawson, crossing from Jersey on the ferry and seeing New York for the first time, could turn to Tim McCarthy and say:

"It's mine, Tim! The whole kit and caboodle! I'm going to be top dog here—I'm going up. Just you watch!"

And Tim, seeing the city low and dirty beyond the spars and masts of the shipping, could believe him. The time was ripe.

CHAPTER ONE—1870

THEY WERE NOT CITY MEN—anyone could see that at a glance. But it was not their dress that betrayed them. If anything, Pride Dawson and Tim McCarthy were better dressed than the New Yorkers who thronged about them. Their gray derbies with the wide silk bands were oppressively new, and their wing collars were starched into knife-blade sharpness above the rich watered silk of their scarves, which were tied in the fashionable Ascot puff and held by glittering stickpins. In everything they wore they were identical, from the loose-fitting black English sack coats with self-vests, and the contrasting striped trousers, down to their patent-leather Congress shoes with sides which gave comfortably with every step.

No, it was not their clothes. Rather, it was something in the way they wore them—as though they were unaccustomed to so much finery. A suit can be made to fit a man in a matter of days, but it takes years to fit a man for the casual wearing of finely tailored clothes. And yet it was more than merely their faint suggestion of awkwardness—it was the men themselves. Tim McCarthy, wide-shouldered and thick-limbed, built as square as a box, dwarfed the smaller city men in breadth if not always in height; but Pride Dawson dwarfed even him.

Tim was red-faced and rugged, with grave gray eyes and reddish hair; but Pride Dawson was a sight to see. He stood six foot four in his bare feet, and his face, beneath his coarse black hair, looked as though it had been blasted out of granite, leaving features of elemental strength. His mouth was big, with a touch of wry humor about it; and his eyes were as black as his hair. His nose looked as though it had been broken, which, as a matter of fact, it had been on several occasions in gargantuan tavern brawls; his chin was jutting and square. Point by point these oddly assorted features should have added up to plain ugliness; but strangely enough they did not. Perhaps it was his eyes, normally filled with gleeful mockery, which could change in half a heart-beat to ferocious savagery; or his mouth, always half-smiling, as if he were secretly amused at himself and the world.

There is a certain atavistic strain in women—and often in men, too—that makes them admire physical bigness and easy strength. That was part of his attraction. At any rate, to the end of his days, men and women alike described Pride Dawson as handsome. They were, all things considered, not entirely wrong.

He stood in the sunlight on the Bowery, and watched the scurrying crowds. He grinned at them quietly, complacently, and his hand moved, tossing an object into the air and catching it deftly. As it rose and fell, it glittered in the sunlight.

Tim knew what it was: a nugget of pure gold, polished into rounded smoothness and attached to a small chain. On it a jeweler in San Francisco had engraved: *Pride Dawson— His Luck!*

Luck, Tim thought, we'll need luck now. Only got three hundred and fifty of the stake we came East on. Sold that mine for nearly five thousand—and now look at us. Fine duds and empty pockets. And every saloon and bawdy house between here and 'Frisco's got rich off Pride. I shouldn't have loaned him any of mine. He swears he'll pay it back, and he will, too—that's one thing Pride's honest about. But now I've got to wait. Can't send for Lucy and the kid. Oh, well—I've waited this long—a little longer won't hurt. . . .

The crowds did not merely move along the Bowery, they swarmed. The street was a river of humanity, surging forward, piling up momentarily at the corners as a carriage or a horse-car blocked its way, then eddying around the obstacles, to plunge onward again. The air was alive with sounds: the rustle and swish of the women's skirts sweeping the sidewalks, the rumble of a ten-horse brewery wagon, snatches of greetings tossed back over a shoulder in passing, the cries of the hawkers, even music of a sort, echoing thinly from the opened door of a concert saloon.

Tim McCarthy looked up at Pride Dawson.

"Well," he growled, "we're here."

Pride did not answer. He pushed his new derby to the very back of his big head and, taking out a cigar, stuck it into the corner of his mouth. Then his hand moved out slowly and scraped the match with some deliberation down the thigh of the wooden Indian in front of a cigar store. He drew in upon the cigar, inhaling the fragrant smoke deep into his lungs, then letting it trail in twin blue-gray streamers from his nostrils. It moved upward, veiling his face. Like a cloud, Tim thought suddenly, like a cloud around a hang of rock on top of a mountain.

Pride's black eyes, luminous through the cigar smoke, darted over the crowds, and under the edge of his thick mustache the corners of his mouth moved slowly upward.

"Some town, eh, Tim?" he said.

"Chicago suited me fine," Tim complained. "Or, for that matter, San Francisco wasn't too bad. I still don't see why we had to come all the way back East."

Pride looked at Tim, his big, rugged face filled with amused contempt.

"I saw in the paper last night," he rumbled, "where there are more people in one square mile of this burg than in all of Chicago, Cincinnati and St. Louis. Hell, there are more people in sight right now than in all of San Francisco."

"People!" Tim snorted. "What have people got to do with it?"

Pride gazed out over the crowds, seeing the men clinging to the outside of the horse-cars, the horses laboring under the load, so that the driver was forced to use his whip. As he watched, the team of a light delivery wagon and that of an ironmonger's cart became entangled. One of the enormous policemen of the "strongarm squad" hurried out into the street and seized the reins of the bucking, squealing animals, while the drivers brandished their whips and screeched obscenities at each other. Pride raised his head and laughed aloud. Like everything about him, his laughter was big: belly-deep, bass-booming.

He stuck a playful thumb into Tim's ribs.

"My town, Tim," he said. "It's my town, every inch of it!"

Tim stared at him.

"Could be," he grunted, "but it seems to me that a heap of other people are going to have something to say about that."

9

"People, Tim. Where there's people there's money. Lots of money. I aim to get my share."

"Knowing you," Tim said, "I'd bet my last red copper you aim to get a hell of a lot more'n your share. Reckon you'll get it, too. You have before. Getting money ain't your problem. Keeping it, is where you fall down."

Pride frowned, his big face becoming for the moment serious. "I'm going to keep it this time," he said. "See if I don't."

They moved off through the crowds, Pride towering above the city men. There was more music now, for they were passing a row of concert saloons. Occasionally they could catch a verse or two. Pride's grin broadened. The verses were bawdy. My town, he thought, damned if it isn't!

Out of the concert saloons and the endless bars shuffled a slow stream of derelicts, filthy and in rags, their trembling fingers clutching the precious bottles they somehow had managed to obtain. Tim stared at them pityingly, but Pride gave them scarcely a glance. He was gazing with unconcealed pleasure at the thinly clad girls who darted occasionally from the side entrances of the saloons, and raced up the stairs into one of the shabby houses. Inside, they were awaited, Pride had no doubt. My town! he chuckled, my town!

On the edge of the sidewalk, the three-card monte operators and the artists of the shell game were unfolding their little tables. Next to them sat other men before exactly similar tables. Yet these men were entirely different: their dress was quieter, and they had an air of genteel shabbiness about them which hinted of better days. Pride stared at them. The tinhorn gamblers he had seen before, in the West from which he had so lately come, where they were even more of an institution than in the East; but these obviously well-bred men, who were just as obviously on the verge of starvation, were something new. As Pride watched, they opened their small boxes and brought out steel pens and stiff white showcard papers. Then they bent over their tasks, the pens swirling into elaborate flourishes, torturing the letters into the shapes of birds and flowers, filling up the paper with a network of exquisitely drawn lines and words of beautiful Spencerian script.

These they exhibited upon the tables to attract customers. Pride moved closer, still watching. The crowds milled around them. Pride straightened. Plainly a man could not make a living as a greeting-card writer. He was about to turn his attention to another of the varied sights of his new city, when one of the elderly writers was approached by a young woman.

Pride moved closer again, with Tim at his heels. He was bending over to see the old man's dexterity put to a real test, when the girl spoke.

"Will you write a small showcard for me?" she said.

Something in her voice moved Pride deeply. It was, he realized, a beautiful voice, with a great deal of natural music in it. He brought his gaze up slowly from the little table to the girl's face, and there his scrutiny lingered. For the life of him, he didn't know why. The girl was thin and pale, and her nose was freckled. Her mouth was wide—especially for so thin a face—and her nose turned up at the tip. Yet, somehow, the whole face was pleasing.

Pride let his glance stray downward over the girl's figure. Her body was as thin as her face. Good lines though, Pride thought. Hell, thoroughbreds aren't fat. Only draft horses and brood mares. This one's got blood and spirit.

The girl bent over the card writer's table, oblivious of Pride's gaze.

"Write this," she said, and gave the old man a slip of paper.

Swiftly the penman began his work, the letters flowing from under the point of the pen. *Dressmaking,* Pride read, *and Millinery Work. The Latest Modes. Ladies' Hats Made to Order. Miss Sharon O'Neil, Prop.*

The penman finished his task and the girl searched in her purse for a coin. Then she took the small showcard and straightened up. As she did so, her eyes met Pride's.

He raised his derby.

"Mighty proud to make your acquaintance, Miss Sharon," he said. "I trust business is good?"

Sharon O'Neil measured him with level brown eyes.

"The state of my business," she said evenly, "is none of your concern." Then with great dignity, she turned and walked away. For the first time, Pride noticed that her small head was crowned with a mass of soft, dark brown hair. In two long strides he overtook her.

"Oh, but it is," he said. "Because if business ain't so

good, I'm fixing to buy you a nice dinner." He looked down at her and grinned. "Heck, even if it is good, I'm going to."

"I don't know where you come from, Mr.—"

"Dawson—Pride Dawson, at your service, ma'am."

"Mr. Dawson, in New York ladies don't accept invitations from strange men."

"Now look, Miss Sharon, we're not strangers any more. I know your name and you know mine. Where I come from, folks are more friendly. And if you have to know more about me, I'd be mighty pleased to tell you my life story over some fried chicken. I'm a Southerner. Come from the Red River Valley—near Colfax, Louisiana."

"Mr. Dawson," she said, "I haven't the slightest interest in where you're from or where you're going. All I ask of you is to stand aside and cease blocking the way."

"Now, Miss Sharon," Pride began, but Tim was pulling at his sleeve.

"For the love of Mike, Pride," he growled, "will you stop pestering the young lady and come along?"

"Nicest young lady I've pestered in a long time," Pride grinned. "But just because you've got a wife and kid waiting for you in New Orleans ain't no reason for you to spoil my fun. Have a heart, Miss Sharon. I've been out West. I haven't seen a nice girl in so long that—"

Sharon O'Neil's head turned swiftly in the direction of the policeman who was directing traffic. He was the same big man Pride had seen untangle the teams a short time ago.

"Must I call the officer?" she asked calmly.

Pride smiled. He was a good bit bigger than even the big policeman.

"I reckon I could handle him," he said. "I haven't seen the Yankee yet I couldn't whip."

"Don't be a fool," Tim snapped. "He'd blow that whistle and you'd have twenty of them on your neck in half a minute." He turned to Sharon.

"Please, ma'am," he said, "excuse my friend. He's kind of impulsive."

"So I see," Sharon said and, in spite of herself, she smiled. Her teeth were even and white; when she smiled her whole face underwent a transformation. If it did not quite become beautiful, her face certainly became fascinating, as an alert sensitivity combed all its planes and angles into an enchanting revelation of the intelligence and spirit that lay behind it. I will never, Pride suddenly realized, forget this face.

"Good day," Sharon said to Tim, "and try to teach him better manners."

"That," Tim said drily, "is impossible."

Pride was looking at the girl with intense concentration. I've got to see her again, he thought, I've just got to! Then his eyes, moving, fell upon a curious feature of her dress. It had pockets, wide flaring ones, deliberately sewn in to hold the instruments of her trade. This in itself would have been sufficiently unusual to attract his attention, but at the moment he was thinking of something else—he was exulting over them as a godsend.

"Good-bye, Miss Sharon," he said. "I'll be seeing you." As he spoke, he leaned forward and his hand moved faster than the eye could follow. When he straightened, his hand was empty, and the gold nugget reposed in Sharon's wide flaring pocket.

The two men stood there, watching her walk away, until Tim, turning, saw that Pride was carefully noting the direction in which she had gone.

"You," he said, "leave that one be."

"Why?" Pride growled.

"She's a nice girl—a real nice girl, Pride. What have you ever brought any woman besides trouble? This one's different—she's something kind of special."

"Something kind of special," Pride echoed. "Reckon you're right. Don't worry, I'm not going to do her any harm. A gal like that could come close to making me change my ways—yessir, mightly close."

On the corner Sharon had stopped, and stood now with her face averted, waiting for the horse-car.

"Come on," Tim said, "I'm thirsty."

"Wait a while," Pride said, "we ain't seen anything yet."

They moved down the street, with Pride looking back every few moments at Sharon, past rows of tobacco shops, each with its wooden Indian before the door. Actually few of the elaborately carved polychrome statues, mounted on casters so that they could be rolled inside out of the rain, represented Indians. That vogue had passed almost ten years ago. Now Punchinello rubbed elbows with Lord

13

Dundreary, and a queued Chinese stood near a lady of high fashion. The only Indian in front of a tobacco store was not an Indian at all, but a carving of Edwin Forrest in the title role of the tragedy *Metamore*. Pride examined them all carefully, but Tim was growing more and more tired of the aimless walk.

"Pride—" he began.

"I know, you're thirsty. So'm I. Come on—we'll have a drink."

They turned toward the doors of one of the concert saloons from which shrill, tinny music issued. From the corner Sharon O'Neil saw them enter, and frowned. . . .

It was almost two hours later when Sharon O'Neil reached the lower end of Broadway once more. She had spent most of the time with her father in the shanty settlement north of Fifty-ninth Street. She glanced idly at the rows of awnings above the store fronts that extended all the way up Broadway to Grace Church, but she scarcely knew they were there. The clopping of the two horses that drew the Broadway Stage set up answering rhythms in her mind, but her thoughts moved in oblique tangents without any governing pattern.

Daddo's sick, she thought. He's too old for that sort of life. He's worked himself almost into his grave, to give me an education. And for what? So I can die of slow starvation in that miserable little shop. He's so proud of me, too . . . tells everybody I'm in business. Business, indeed! I don't remember when I've eaten a really decent meal.

That big man now—I wonder what it would have been like to have had dinner with him? He seemed kind. And he wasn't really handsome—just big and healthy-looking. . . . Mercy, what on earth am I doing thinking of him?

She looked up now at the driver's legs, which could be seen through an opening at the front of the stage. A stout leather strap was fastened to one of his legs. To stop the stage, one jerked the cord attached to the strap and pulled the driver's leg. The miserable thief, Sharon thought bitterly; he's short-changed me again. Doesn't he know that some people can't afford to be short-changed? Now I'll have to have my tea without a roll, thanks to him.

She put her hand into one of the wide flaring pockets where, among other things, she kept some loose change.

She'd have to count it carefully now—stretch it to the limit to make it do. Then the motion was abruptly halted, her face frozen into blank incredulity—her fingers had closed over an object that had no business being there, something round and smooth, unlike anything that she owned. She drew it out and looked at it. It lay in her palm, glowing softly, and as she turned it the words leaped up at her: *Pride Dawson—His Luck!*

"How on earth!" she gasped; then, even as she said the words, she knew: Pride Dawson had put it there. And he had done so because he wanted to see her again. It was much too forward of him, but in her heart Sharon was not displeased. I'll have to give it back, she thought, as she reached for the cord to pull the driver's leg; if he gets fresh I'll . . .

But just what would she do? She suspected that handling Pride Dawson would be no easy task. Still, she could not keep so valuable a gift from the hand of a stranger. . . . The stage jolted to a stop and she got down.

Now, she thought, I'll have blocks to walk and through the Whiskey Wards, too. But it was just about here that he went into that saloon—only a few streets over. If he's gone the barkeep might know where he went.

She was walking now, straight down the side street toward the Bowery block where she had seen Pride earlier in the day. The street down which she was walking clung grimly to its respectability. It was unpaved, and every other house showed a broad expanse of dusty street in front of it where the frugal residents had refused to pay the fee for the watering cart. Sharon did not even glance at the houses or the street. Instead, she continued to walk, unconsciously increasing her pace, until, to her chagrin, she noticed she was almost running. By an effort of will, she slowed to a more sedate stride; but as she rounded the corner of the Bowery she was surprised by the beating of her heart.

Through the Bowery the crowds still moved, but nowhere was there a big man who towered by more than a head above them. Sharon felt like crying.

"Now," she said aloud in exasperation, "I'll have to go into that saloon!" Nothing could have been a greater ordeal for her. Slowly, reluctantly, she started to walk toward it. She stopped, looking at the swinging doors. All her fears of drunkards and drunkenness returned. But she could not stand there; the gold nugget must be returned. She lifted her chin and started out, but she had not gone ten steps when a saloon door across the street burst open, and a knot of struggling men boiled out into the street. In the midst of them, she recognized Pride. He was roaring like an angry bull and using his big fists with devastating effect; but the strongest arm in the world is of little help against a crowd of determined men, armed with brass knuckles and black-jacks.

She saw him go down and fall in the street, while his opponents proceeded to work upon his inert form with their boots. Tim was beside him, doing what he could to ward off their attack; but a smart clip to the side of the head sent him down beside his friend.

Sharon did not hesitate. She dashed across the street so quickly that both her slim ankles were plainly visible above her high-buttoned shoes, a fact which ordinarily would have caused her almost to die of shame. She sailed into the crowd of toughs, using her frilled umbrella as a weapon. Startled by this new rain of blows, Pride's attackers whirled, their brass knuckles ready. But when they saw their small, modishly dressed assailant, they broke into roars of cheerful laughter.

"All right, lady," they grinned, "you kin have your gentlemen friends. They ain't so pretty now, but a hunk of beefsteak'll fix that."

"Cowards!" Sharon shouted. "Twenty of you against two! And look how you've hurt him! He's all bloody!"

"He should of knowed better than to start a ruckus in Joe's," the leader of the gang said mildly. "Well, so long, ma'am. Treat him good tonight and he'll fergit all about it!"

They turned then and trooped back into the saloon. Sharon knelt in the street, forgetful of the dirt, and tried to lift Pride's big head into her arms. After a moment, she succeeded. Beside her, Tim groaned and sat up, shaking his head. Already a bluish semicircle was beginning to show below one of his eyes. He stared at Sharon with a look of open-mouthed wonder that slowly changed to admiration. His gray eyes traveled from her slim form to the broken umbrella that lay beside her on the street.

"Thank you, ma'am," he said. "You sure came just in time."

"I'm afraid that your friend is badly hurt," Sharon whispered. "Help me get him up. Where are you staying?"

"Nowhere, ma'am. We hadn't found lodgings yet. Now —we can't. Damn Pride's stupid hide!"

"You—can't? I don't understand."

"No money! They must have doped Pride's drink in there, and when he came to, he started a fight. You saw what happened after that. The money's gone now. . . ."

"They took all your money?"

"Every cent—over three hundred dollars."

Sharon frowned thoughtfully. Then her face cleared and a decisive line showed about the corners of her mouth.

"Let's get him up," she said. "We'll take him to my father's place. Daddo will take care of him. Afterwards you two will have to find work."

"Ma'am," Tim said gratefully, "you're a mighty fine lady."

Between them, they got Pride Dawson to his feet and set out toward Broadway. Pride managed to mumble a word or two as they went, but what he said made little sense. They reached Broadway at the height of the rush hour, when most of the workers had completed their twelve to fourteen hours of daily labor. Sharon turned a despairing face toward Tim.

"We'll never get one now!" she said.

One glance showed Tim exactly what she meant. The stages had all gotten fresh horses and were racing uptown in a wild stampede. The drivers were fighting for fares, some of the more daring cutting in ahead of the others. The losing driver had to haul back on the reins with such force that his team reared, their forelegs beating the air in a frenzy, while the driver shrieked curses and lashed out with his whip at the man who had robbed him. Nearly all of them permitted small boys to ride on top of the stages— boys who had labored since long before daylight in the dusty shops and mills and who fought for the chance to remain in the open air. The drivers, Sharon knew, encouraged the boys—not because of any love for youth, but because they could pocket the fares, since the boys did not have to pass the coin box on the inside.

The boys were nimbly dodging the lashes of the enraged drivers. Tim looked at the spectacle in wonderment, but Sharon was almost weeping. Then one stage came along more slowly than the rest—an older, dirtier and more dilapidated stage than any of the others, drawn by horses which must have escaped the abattoirs and glue factories by a minor miracle. Wildly, Sharon signaled it, and it drew to a stop. At once she saw the reason for their good fortune. With the exception of one or two soddenly drunken Germans and Poles, the stage was filled with Negroes. She and Tim dragged Pride into it, Tim supporting him while she dug into her purse for the fares. A sign over the entrance read: *Colored People Allowed to Ride in this Car*.

"Pride'd have a fit," Tim said, "if he knew this."

"Why?" Sharon snapped. "They're just as human as you or I."

"Yes'm," Tim said mildly, "I reckon they are. Pride's a bit peculiar, but you'll get used to him."

Sharon did not answer. In fact, there was no answer she could give. Obviously, Tim took it as a matter of course that some sort of relationship would continue between herself and Pride Dawson. Yet, even during their brief acquaintanceship, Tim had revealed himself as being less than enthusiastic over Pride's qualities.

The stage rattled steadily uptown, easily outdistanced by the faster vehicles. Above Forty-second Street the buildings became fewer, and by the time they had passed Fifty-ninth Street they were in open country. Somewhere in the vicinity of Sixty-eighth Street the stage stopped, while teamsters set about harnessing the "hill horses," the extra teams necessary to drag the stage up the steep approaches to the village of Harlem.

Sharon turned to Tim.

"We'd better get off here," she said. "This is about as close as we can get."

Tim looked at Pride and saw that his eyes were open. Quickly, Tim glanced about the stage. All of the Negroes had gotten off somewhere between Thirty-fourth and Fifty-second streets, to walk to the area along Sixth Avenue, where they lived. Tim heaved a sigh of relief. Pride would have raised a ruckus about those Negroes.

Sharon smiled gently at Pride.

"So you're back with us," she said. "Can you walk?"

"Reckon so," Pride mumbled. Then: "Glory be! It's you!"

18

"Please," Sharon said, "You've been hurt. You'd better be quiet."

Tim and Sharon got down then, holding Pride between them. Pride was able to walk, though somewhat unsteadily. He was acutely conscious of Sharon's shoulder beneath his arm, so that although his strength rapidly returned, he still pretended to be shaken and leaned heavily upon her.

They came to a path that ran upward among the rocks. Looking up, Pride could see the whiskered face of a goat staring solemnly down at them. There were chickens along the path, and pigs, to say nothing of numerous filthy urchins, their rags scarcely covering their nakedness, who ran like wild things at the approach of Sharon and the two men.

But the houses, once they had reached them, were stranger still: they were built of old packing cases or scrap lumber. From every fence and clothesline, bright festoons of colored rags fluttered, managing somehow to mitigate the grim impression created by the squalor.

Pride looked at Sharon.

"You live—here?" he demanded.

"Not any more. I did once, though."

Pride passed a big hand over his brow, feeling the ridges of dried blood.

"Who would have thought it!" he said with genuine amazement.

Sharon turned on him, her brown eyes alight with sudden fire.

"Do you expect me to be ashamed, Mr. Dawson? My father still lives here. That's where I'm taking you. And I'd better tell you one thing: there's no prouder man on earth than Stan O'Neil. He can't write his name, but he's honest —and so are all these folk. They're ragpickers—right enough. But digging in dumps and garbage scows for bottles and rags and old shoes hasn't taken the heart out of them, or the decency. My father gave me an education— and starved himself to do it. So don't expect me to apologize for these surroundings, Mr. Dawson!"

Pride shook his head heavily, as if to clear it.

"I'm sorry, Miss Sharon," he said quietly. "It came as a surprise. . . . But any place that produced you doesn't need an apology. . . . Wish I could say the same for myself."

He was now, though Sharon did not know it, in one of those dark, sullen moods that were the reverse side of his usually buoyant temperament. She's sweet, he was thinking, sweet and good as a spray of Queen Anne's Lace. Too good for me. Besides, she's poor. Nothing plus nothing, Ma used to say, adds up to nothing—and "nothing" don't chew like bread. I'm going up this time. I can't be saddled with a woman who'll take my mind off business. A gal like this would take your mind off most anything. . . .

Still thinking, he turned his face toward Tim.

Lost the money. Getting bushwhacked and rolled like a greenhorn. Tim's money, too—half of it. I've got to make it up to him. I've got to get rich. Rich, damn it, rich! No little stakes this time. We've been poor too damned long. They say money don't make you happy. But you sure can't be happy without it. Ma died of hunger. Pa, too—hunger and likker and cussed meanness. I got that from him—and the laughing and the singing from Ma. And the sadness that was down deep inside of her, even though she sang like a mockingbird. I've got Red River clay in my belly and a mixed-up mind like a snake-bit hound dog, so that sometimes I don't know myself whether I'm going to bite or wag. . . .

He stopped short, feeling Sharon's hand resting lightly on his arm.

"You're worried," she said gently. "Don't be. Daddo'll help you find work."

Pride smiled—a slow, quiet smile.

"You're sweet," he said. "You make a man want to grab hold of you and still feel too weak to do it, at the same time."

"I hope," Sharon said quickly, "that I'll always keep you that weak, Mr. Dawson." Then she stepped ahead of him lightly and almost ran up the path.

The O'Neil house was the largest in the shanty settlement. It had been built of scrap lumber and, despite the fact that it had never been painted, had an imposing air about it. For one thing, it had four separate rooms, which in Shantytown virtually made it a mansion. On both sides and in back of it were mountains of old iron, bales of paper, piles of bottles and rags. Near its little stoop stood a rusty scale which was used to weigh the junk brought in by the ragpickers. Clearly, Stan O'Neil was an entrepreneur.

As they approached the house, he came out to greet them—a small man with iron-gray hair and something of Sharon's sensitivity of line about his face. He was stooped, and his hands trembled. There was, Pride saw, something else in his face. And, after a moment, Pride recognized it for what it was. Death peered out of Stan O'Neil's tired eyes. He isn't here for long, Pride thought. Then he heard the music of Sharon's voice making the introductions, and put out his big hand.

"My father," Sharon was saying, "Stanton O'Neil."

"I have a wee dram in the house," Stan O'Neil said. "You look as if you could use it."

"I could," Pride said. "Your town don't take kindly to strangers."

"Oh, it's good enough to them as keeps their wits about 'em. I don't think anything like this is going to happen to you again."

"No," Pride said, "it isn't."

Afterwards they sat on the tiny stoop and sipped the fiery Irish whiskey. Pride could feel the slow warmth it brought, curling down to the tips of his toes. Sharon sat there with a cup of tea and looked at him with her soft brown eyes, as though she were studying an unusual problem.

"Daddo," she said at last, "do you think you could find work for my friends?"

Stan O'Neil considered the question.

"Well," he said, "they can take a poker and go out with the others. 'Tis dirty work for sich fine lads, and sure they will find it unpleasing. But 'twill keep them eating."

Pride's big head jerked upright.

"You mean," he got out, "I should pick rags?"

Tim looked at Pride, his gray eyes hard.

"You've done dirtier things," he said.

Pride turned to him, anger mottling his cheeks.

"When have I ever—" he began.

"I wasn't talking about your hands," Tim said calmly, "though, if I remember right, digging bayou canals wasn't exactly clean work. And we did that. . . ."

Sharon leaned forward, something close to understanding in her eyes.

"What about his hands," she asked. "What were you talking about?"

Tim stood up and spat, very deliberately, upon the ground.

"He," Tim said evenly, "got dirt on his soul." Then he walked away from the house.

Pride got up at once, the great vein on his forehead beating visibly. But Sharon was before him, both her hands gripping his wrists.

"No," she said, "I won't have it, Pride!"

Slowly the dark color ebbed from his face.

"Come," Sharon continued, "take a walk with me. You don't mind, do you, Daddo?"

"No," Stan O'Neil said, "I don't mind."

She slipped her hand through Pride's elbow and they went down the path together.

Pride walked along silently, while a little breeze caught his heavy black hair and lifted it back from his forehead.

She was conscious that Pride was gazing down at her with wonder in his eyes.

"You," he smiled—"you called me 'Pride'!"

"Did I? I didn't mean to. I guess I got excited because you looked so angry. Do you mind?"

"Mind? I never heard it sound so fine before."

"Then I'll go on calling you Pride. I like that name. It's odd, yet it fits you, I think. How in the world did you ever get such a name?"

Pride looked away from her, back toward the dim lights of Shantytown.

"My ma," he said, gruffly. "She named me Pride—so's I wouldn't forget to have it."

"Oh, Pride—"

"Yes, Sharon?"

"Here's your luck piece back. You shouldn't have done that, you know."

"Keep it. I want you to have it," Pride grinned.

"No, Pride," Sharon said. "It's your luck—not mine. Besides, I really couldn't take gifts from you."

Pride held the nugget in his hand and looked at it.

"It's not good enough for you, anyhow," he said. "One day I'm going to give you diamonds!"

"Thank you," Sharon laughed. Then she sobered abruptly.

"Pride," she asked, "why were you so angry with Tim?"

Pride frowned, looking down into her small face. He opened his mouth then closed it again, grimly.

"I'm sorry," Sharon said. "I shouldn't have asked that, should I?"

"Yes," Pride said, "you had every reason to ask it. I just shut up because I was about to lie. But somehow or another I can't lie to you. You're the first woman I ever knew I couldn't lie to—outside my ma. It's funny—your face is pure goodness, so I'm going to turn you around right now and march you back to your pa."

"Why? I'm enjoying myself, Pride."

"Because Tim told the truth. I've got a black devil inside me—and any woman that smiles at me lives to cry over it later. Come on!"

"No," Sharon said, "I don't want to go back."

"I said come on!"

Sharon's brown eyes were filled with mischief.

"No," she laughed, "let's walk—let's walk for hours!"

Instead of answering her, Pride stepped up to her in one long stride. His arm moved out and drew her to him. She saw his face above her, blotting out the sky. Then his mouth caught hers and twisted it cruelly, his arms tightening, bending her backward. Her own lips were tight, and cold with surprise and fear; her hands came up to strike him, to push him away, when suddenly his mouth on hers was soft again, warm with tenderness, then as abruptly demanding, the tenderness still there, strangely poignant, inexplicably mixed with desire, so that even the sensation of pain, of being hurt was exquisite. Something was being born in her, full-blown and mature, and her blood beat upward from the pit of her loins in scalding waves. She felt her own mouth slacken and part, burning with surrender. Then there was more than mere acquiescence, all her taut and singing nerves crying out their own demands, and her own body surged upward suddenly, trembling against his giant's frame—but it was then that he released her, stepping back so that their parting was as sharp and sudden as a whipcrack.

He stood looking at her. Then he took out a cigar and lit it, his lips curling about its end in a smile that was the cruelest she had ever seen. Sharon could feel the tears start, hot upon her cold face. And for the life of her, she could not stop trembling.

"Now," Pride said, "now, will you go back?"

"Yes," she whispered. "Yes, oh, yes!"

He took her arm then, and led her back toward the house where Stan O'Neil waited, rocking on the little stoop.

CHAPTER TWO—1870

DIGGING HIS LONG POKER into the rubbish, Pride Dawson could see the others from where he worked. They moved over the garbage scows like a line of ants, each with his bag slung over his shoulder and his poker prodding endlessly through the refuse, bending eagerly at the sight of a choice bit of rag or an unbroken bottle. The older ones could recognize a fine bit of linen—which, because it was the stuff out of which paper was made, commanded the highest prices, no matter how encrusted it was with dirt.

But Pride was a novice. As a result, much of what he collected was worthless, adding only to the already burdensome weight of the canvas sack. He looked down at the rags fluttering at his knees and elbows and ran a hand over the bristles sprouting on his massive jaw.

I look the part, he thought, damned if I don't! Still it was kind of Sharon's pa to lend me these clothes. Mine were in bad enough shape from that fight. Sharon said she'd bring 'em back tonight, all clean and mended. She will, too. Tim's right: I shouldn't lay a finger on her.

He glanced at Tim, who was working at his side. Tim's face was red and grave. He drove his poker savagely. Finally he turned and faced Pride.

"Look, Pride," he said. "I'm sorry—damned sorry."

Pride's big head came up slowly.

"Why?" he said. "You told the truth."

"I know. But it's not good to tell the truth sometimes. Better to keep your mouth shut. That girl now—she's falling for you. I hated to see that. You know what happens to your women. . . . Besides, I was mad about the money."

"You'll get yours back," Pride growled. He looked at Tim, a puzzled frown on his dark face. "I don't understand you," he said. "You don't trust me, yet you let me carry the money. You don't think too much of me, but you stick with me. Why? Why don't you just pack up and leave?"

Tim considered the questions in silence, bending and gathering up the bottles he had uncovered.

"I don't rightly know," he said. "Been with you so long, I guess—since we were kids. You're my friend. You saved my neck a dozen times and you'd do it again. I reckon it's because I know you're going somewhere and I kind of hanker to see it—as if by sticking with you I know I'll get somewhere, too. But that ain't it. Even when I was little I hung on to a hound dog that was crazy mean 'cause I just liked the cuss. That's the way it is with you. That hound, now—for me he worked wonders . . . best 'coon and 'possum dog in the parish. You're like that. With me, you work out all right. We get down, but we always come up again. And next time I'm going to stay up and not let you drag us down again with your crazy ideas. Anyhow, when I've been with a critter long enough and take a liking to him, I can go on liking him even if he's meaner'n a wolf from Bitter Creek."

"Thanks," Pride said drily.

"Besides," Tim went on, "you're not all mean. I think you've got good in you, even if you do keep it hidden. Trouble is, you aren't really smart. If you was, you'd know you can't get up on the back of folks' necks. No matter how high you get, somebody you've hurt will drag you back down again. A man can get up—really up—by making friends who'll give him a boost. It's slower that way, maybe, but a heck of a lot more lasting."

"You do it your way," Pride said, "and I'll do it mine. By now you ought to know which way works."

Tim looked at Pride, a long, slow look.

"I want things," he said. "I want them bad. I want Lucy with me and I want to see little Lance. But not enough to do *anything* to get them. I don't want any dirty money—or any stolen happiness. I couldn't enjoy 'em, if I got 'em that way."

"You're a fool," Pride said evenly. "Every time it rains

25

you feel that minnie ball you got at Shiloh Church. And you'll carry that saber cut that Yankee cavalryman give you to your grave. But for what? Did you ever own a slave? How come you fought to help them keep theirs? They used to spit on us—called us white trash and sent us around to the back door with the bumboes—and that made me not good enough to have a glass and a cigar with the same men who bought 'em and worked 'em. How come you and I had to dig those damned, stinking canals when we were no more'n boys? I'll tell you why—'cause a black man costs too much money to risk in the fever-stink and the landslides. That what you fought for? I got mad one time and slapped one of them pretty little frenchified New Orleans boys. Did he meet me like a man? No sir. He sent five big bumboes to hold me, then he beat me with a cane."

"So," Tim said, "that was why the Laveau plantation burned."

"I had nothing to do with that," Pride said, quietly. "But I laughed like hell when it happened. I got drunk and celebrated. But you fought for them. What chance did we have as long as they had their slaves? It was cheaper to buy and work a black than to hire a white man—so we starved."

"You didn't fight for the Yankees either," Tim said pointedly.

"No. I fought for Pride Dawson. I ran the blockades. I ran cotton to the Yankees and got paid for it. I ran Yankee guns and quinine to the Johnny Rebs—all right, to the honorable Confederate Army—and got paid for that in gold. None of Jeff Davis' shin plasters. Reckon you'd call me a coward. Only I fought like hell. I fought anybody who got in my way—no matter whether he had on blue or butternut brown. There were times when both of 'em were shooting at me, but I come back without a scratch—and with ten thousand dollars to boot."

"Which," Tim said softly, "the gambling houses and the women on Gallantine Street took every penny of."

Pride nodded.

"That's true," he admitted. "I've got a crazy streak in me. No more, though. I'm going to keep what I make. You watch."

"I'll be watching," Tim said.

They came back to Stan O'Neil's shanty that night,

stumbling with weariness, straggling in a long line of human scarecrows, the rags they wore fluttering at knee and elbow, their bodies bent over sideways from the weight of the bottles and the iron in their great canvas bags. Up on the hill Stan O'Neil waited with his scales and his mounds of copper pennies, as they quietly lined up before him. He sorted and weighed the junk, paying each man carefully according to the weight and value. He was, Pride noticed, a little generous, if anything. But when Pride and Tim came up to him, he discarded much of what they had brought, explaining what to select in the future.

Pride shook his head ruefully. Even ragpicking, he reflected, has to be studied. I never thought there was so much to it. There's a hell of a lot more to most things than folks ever think. I'm going to do some real studying: going to learn how folks get their hands on real money. First I'm going to pay Tim off, and then—

He did not finish the thought. Sharon had come flying up the hill, her fine, intense face working with excitement. Before she reached them, she cried out:

"Daddo, I've got it!"

O'Neil smiled at her, his brown eyes—which matched hers exactly—soft with tenderness.

"Yes, lass?" he said. "And what is it you've got now?"

"An idea. A wonderful idea! You know old Mr. Stillworth you used to work for?"

Stanton O'Neil's face darkened.

"Black Tom Stillworth? Sure and 'tis much too well I know the likes of him."

"Now, Daddo—you said yourself that Mr. Stillworth wasn't the worst—"

" 'Tis the truth you're speaking. But Sharon, lass, you've no idea how bad the worst is."

"But don't you think he might give Pride and Tim jobs, if you asked him?"

Stan O'Neil rubbed his chin and looked at the two men.

"He might," he said at last, "if I asked him."

"Well, aren't you going to?"

Slowly, sadly, he shook his head.

"No, lass," he said. "I'm not. For years I worked for the man. Clean work it was, too. You remember, lass, I was a gardener—all day in the open with the smell of the good earth in my nostrils, and the green things growing under

27

my thumb. But one day an agent of his fell sick—the man, mind you, who used to collect his rents for him. None of the others was about, and for a time it looked like Stillworth would have to collect his own dirty money. Then his eyes lit upon me.

" 'Stan,' he says, 'you're my man. Terence will drive you about, and you collect my rents.'

" 'But,' says I, 'I have no proper clothes for such a task.'

" 'Don't let it fret you,' says he, 'I'll provide them.' "

"And did he?" Pride asked.

"Aye, Pride, and fine duds they were, too. Then I set about my task. Within the hour I wished I hadn't. Never in the old country have these eyes looked upon such misery. Women keening and weeping at the sight of his carriage. Men hiding themselves. And Terence—the nerve of him!—telling me I should order the poor devils out into the streets. Though, bless me, the streets were not much worse than the filthy, broken-down hovels they lived in." He turned to Pride again.

"You may think that I have my nerve about me to be saying such of other men's houses when I don't live so well myself. But, Pride, I pay no rent for the privilege of starving, and this place of mine is clean. I went back to Black Tom Stillworth without a cent, and before he could raise his voice to me I told him, I did, that I could no longer work for the likes of him."

"Wasn't he angry?" Pride asked.

"No. He asked me to reconsider, saying I was the best gardener he'd ever had. But I told him that I would always remember where the money that paid my wages was coming from, and we parted without more words."

"I reckon," Pride drawled, "that you couldn't do us much good there."

"No," Stan O'Neil said, "I fear I could not, lad."

Sharon's face relaxed slowly into an expression of disappointment.

"I'm sorry," she said to Pride. "I guess my idea wasn't so good after all." Then she turned to her father. "But 'Black Tom,' Daddo—why do you call him that?"

O'Neil took out a short pipe of white clay.

" 'Tis the color of his evil heart," he said.

Sharon looked up at Pride.

"Well, anyhow, I brought your things," she said.

"Thank you kindly," Pride said. "Feel like taking another little walk with me?"

He saw her mouth tighten; an expression of fear was reflected briefly in the little pool of lamplight her pupils had caught. Pride bent close to her ear.

"I'll be good," he whispered. "I promise!"

"Well . . ." she began, her eyes searching his face, moving in queer little starts as though they looked for something hoped for. "All right, Pride, I'll walk with you for a little while."

"Good," he said. "You wait right here while I go and change."

"You don't have to change," Sharon smiled. "I don't mind those clothes at all."

"But I do," Pride answered sharply, almost savagely, and turning, went behind the little house.

"Sharon, lass," Stan O'Neil said quietly, "be careful of that young man."

"I can take care of myself, Daddo," Sharon said.

O'Neil shook his head. Looking up, he saw that Tim's head was moving also, in exactly the same gesture of half-expressed doubt.

"You don't understand him, neither of you!" Sharon flared. "He's got his faults; but who hasn't? He's got greatness in him, Daddo—"

"Great evil," Stan O'Neil said.

"Oh, you!" Sharon said and fled around the corner of the house. She stopped short, in a paralysis of confusion, for Pride stood there, his back turned toward her, washing himself at the rain barrel. He had stripped to the waist, and his enormous trunk rippled with muscle, moving smoothly under the coppery skin that the lamplight somehow made golden. He doused himself vigorously, the water penciling silver streaks on his broad back. She shivered as with sudden cold, knowing the feeling that here was something primitive yet splendid, reminding her somehow of the beast-gods of ancient mythology, Centaur-trunked and lean-fleshed, despite all his immense size.

She half-turned to go, but his face, seen in profile, held her. It was weather-beaten, rough-hewn of ancient rock, as old as time, yet somehow ageless, the nose hooking down to his mustache, the strong jaw blue-shadowed in the lamplight. With an effort she freed herself from her reverie, and turned to go to the front of the shanty; but the rustle of her skirts caught Pride's ears.

"Is that you, Sharon, honey?" he called, walking toward her, looming up as he approached like a creature of darkness, so that her trembling started all over again and she felt powerless to utter a word.

He put out his great hand and lifted her chin, seeing her small face ghost-white in the moonlight, shadow-sharpened into an angular mask of fear. Throwing back his head he laughed aloud.

"I didn't mean to scare you," he said, not unkindly. "Run along now like a good girl while I get dressed. I won't be a minute."

Sharon's cheeks, as she fled around the corner of the house, were hot to the touch. Why did he have to hear me? she thought. Oh, what will he think of me now?

But when Pride finally did join her, his manner was calm, almost preoccupied. They walked without haste along the steep, rocky paths, until they came to a place where the ground leveled off before sloping down toward the city which slept below.

"Sit down," Pride said roughly.

Sharon's brown eyes darted from stone to tree to barren hillside, the pupils dilating with fear. Then her gaze swung back to Pride himself. He had sunk down upon an outcropping of rock and his big hands were searching in his jacket pocket for a cigar. He was not looking at her at all. His face was turned toward the broad, blue-silver expanse of the Hudson, and every line of his big frame expressed indifference to her very existence.

Slowly, Sharon sat down beside him, wondering what feeling had replaced her fear of a moment ago. Pride lit a brimstone match, shaking it furiously to rid it of the flaring sparks and the smell of sulfur. Then he bent down to it, cupping it between his hands so that his face was caught in the flickering pool of yellow. Watching him, Sharon knew what it was she had felt. It was, she realized with a stab of horrified recognition, disappointment.

What's happening to me? she asked herself. This was real wickedness. She shook her head to clear it of the confusion of her thoughts, and resolved to go the next night to Confession, though what she would confess or how she would phrase it, she scarcely knew.

30

Pride turned to her suddenly.

"You know where this Stillworth lives?" he demanded.

"Yes," Sharon faltered, "why yes, of course."

"Tell me how to get there."

"You—you're going to apply for a job?"

Pride grinned and drew in on the cigar, its end glowing red in the darkness.

"Well," he drawled, "not exactly. But old Stillworth's going to give me one just the same. I've got some plans."

"What are they?" Sharon asked.

"I'll tell you after they work. But they call for money— have you got any?"

"I—I have fifty dollars at the house. I was saving it up to pay back to Daddo for opening my shop for me. Will that be enough?"

"Plenty," Pride said. "I'll pay you back the first of next month—double. I always pay my debts. Ask Tim."

"Oh," Sharon said, "I believe you. I'll give it to you when we go back to the house."

"Good! Now tell me how I get to Stillworth's place."

"It's on Fifth Avenue," Sharon told him, "just below Thirty-eighth Street. You get off the stage at Forty-second and walk east. . . ."

Pride listened carefully. When she had finished, his face was grave and thoughtful. Then he got up.

"Come on," he said, "let's go back."

"No," Sharon said, surprised at her own boldness, "sit and talk to me a while. It's early yet."

Slowly, Pride sank down again. He looked at her calmly, waiting for her to speak. "What'll we talk about?" he said at last.

"I—I don't know. You, maybe. I don't know anything about you, Pride."

"Do you want to?" he asked suddenly.

"Very much. For instance: how old are you? I can't tell by looking at you. You might be twenty-five—or forty. Your face keeps secrets."

"I trained it that way. I'm thirty-seven, and I'm not married."

Sharon stiffened.

"I didn't ask you that!" she snapped.

"I know. But you wanted to know just the same. Didn't you?"

Sharon hung her head.

"Yes," she whispered miserably. "I did want to know."

Pride patted her hand with his great paw.

"Don't worry," he said gruffly. "If I ever marry anybody, it'll be you."

Sharon sat bolt upright, staring at him.

"And what," she demanded, "makes you think I'd have you?"

"You would, though," Pride said calmly. "You'd marry me tonight if I asked you."

Sharon was on her feet now, trembling with real fury.

"Why, you . . ." she began.

"Don't even know the words, do you? That's good. A sweet little thing like you hadn't ought to know the words that fit me. Sit back down. I was only plaguing you. Your cheeks get like peonies when you're mad."

"I think," Sharon said, "that we'd better go back now."

"Why? I haven't even kissed you yet."

Sharon stared at him, her eyes burnt-copper moons in her pale face.

"Don't!" she said. "Don't you dare!"

"Scared of me?" he murmured, moving closer. "Or are you scared of yourself?"

Sharon stood up again, her eyelids scalding with her tears.

"You—" she got out, "you take too much for granted. And you're a brute. You hurt me—that time . . ."

"And you," Pride grinned, "liked it. Now, say you didn't!"

Sharon swung her open hand hard at his face, but he caught her wrist deftly and dragged her into his embrace.

"No, no, no!" she wept. "Let me go! Let me go, Pride! Please, Pride, please . . ."

But she felt herself being drawn forward, as his big hand came up and imprisoned her face. Then he bent down and kissed her—lightly, his lips brushing hers as though she were something infinitely rare and precious, something so fragile it would be destroyed by a breath. A moment later he released her and stepped back.

"Better?" he said.

Sharon swayed before him, her eyes tear-shattered, her wide, warm mouth trembling uncontrollably; then wordlessly she stepped forward again into his embrace. Her arm stole up and lay about his neck, and her face was pillowed against his chest.

"Yes," she whispered, "oh, yes, Pride—much better!"

"I love you," Pride said then, his voice spring thunder, far off and tender. "I don't know why. You've got a funny little face, all freckles and a turned-up nose and wide mouth—but I love you. I love the way you walk—like you've got fire inside. I love your voice that sounds like angels singing. I love your eyes like big pennies, and your hair that's so brown that it's a comfort to a man's eyes to see it. I love you so much that I ache inside from wanting you and yet I can't touch you, because the goodness in your face gets in between us like a stone wall."

"I'm glad," Sharon wept. "Oh, Pride, I'm so glad."

"I never loved a woman before. I wanted 'em, yes. Had 'em, too. But I don't want you like that. I want you in a veil in the church. I want to carry you across the doorsill. I want you in my house with the gray getting into your hair, and our kids whooping and hollering and stomping the place down all around us. Like the idea?"

"Yes," Sharon whispered, "yes, oh, yes! But when, Pride? When?"

Pride's big face darkened.

"I don't know," he said gruffly. "I've got to get some money first. Lots of money. I've been poor too long. I don't want to be any more, and I don't want you to be."

"Pride—" Sharon murmured.

"Yes, Sharon, honey?"

"I don't care about the money. You're all I want. I could be so good to you, even if we were poor. I could work for you and mend your things and make suppers that would cost so little. . . ."

Pride stood away from her and glared down at her, his whole face suddenly fierce.

"That's plain damn foolishness!" he growled. "You ever been hungry?"

"Yes," Sharon said truthfully, "many times."

"Really hungry, I mean? Starving hungry? Well, I have. I've lain in a haystack with my belly sticking to my backbone, too weak to move. I saw my ma die of it—of being hungry all the time, of being beaten too much by a man who was a good man turned poison-mean by too much want. Ma was good, too—all good. She took a piece of

33

stove wood and whipped my hide every time I tried to stay away from the McDonogh School. I'm grateful to her for that now, even if I did hate it at the time. At least I learned to read and write and figure. I didn't know how important that was—especially the figuring."

"Daddo's like that," Sharon said. "So are most of the ragpickers. A newspaper journalist came up to Shantytown once and talked to Daddo. Then he went back and wrote a little piece about him and the others. He called it 'The Aristocracy of the Lowly.' You see, Pride, those people could steal, or beg or get into trouble. But they don't. They do the hardest, dirtiest kind of work; and they stay honest. And nearly every one of them sends his children to school. The journalist listed dozens of distinguished New Yorkers who have come from just such surroundings."

"They aren't too bad," Pride growled. "Not like the hunger and misery we had. You've never seen anything like that. Did you ever eat frogs and bayou muskrats—they're full of oil and taste rotten the minute you kill 'em. Ever eat dirt—plain red clay—to stay alive? I have. Ever steal food from a slave cabin and take it to your dying ma? Corn pone and side meat and red beans that the blacks had and we didn't. It wasn't any good, though—she was too weak to eat it. . . ."

He looked above Sharon's dark head, his face bleak as granite.

"You never had blacks call you white trash, and big folks show you the door, saying, 'Come around back where you belong, you dirty scum!' You never had to dig canals where one man out of every four dropped dead of Yellowjack, and one of the others got buried alive in the stinking yellow mud? That's what happened to me, Sharon. And when I pulled myself up and made money by slave-running, I still wasn't good enough for them. There wasn't a decent house I could go to. I never got to know a girl like you. I knew high-yellow girls in New Orleans. I knew whatever women were for sale. I knew the dance-hall girls out West—but a girl like you, never. I drove rail spikes clear across the country. And I almost died of thirst in the desert country looking for gold. I took squaws from the Indians and lay behind a dead horse all day fighting off the braves. I'm telling you all of it. I want you to know what I am. There's no good in me—except that part of me that loves you, Sharon. Except that part that looks at you and remembers my ma, the only other good woman I ever knew."

"I'll make it up to you, Pride," Sharon told him. "I'll make you forget it all."

"I don't want to forget. I want to remember. I want to remember and think and plan and learn so it can't happen any more. I've got to make a queen out of you. I'm going to give you a big house so you can send *them* around back! I've got to hold my head up and remember what my ma said while she was dying: 'Pride's your name, son. Don't never forget to have it!' "

Sharon's hand came up and rested lightly over his mouth.

"Don't talk," she whispered. "Don't tell me any more. It —it kills me inside hearing it. Just hold me, Pride. Just hold me and kiss me until I feel warm again."

Slowly the stiffness went out of his giant's frame. He bent down and found her mouth. But the memory was there in his kiss—the bitterness, the terror and the hurt. Sharon stood on tiptoe, kissing him back, her warm mouth clinging to his, her pale hands working gently against his cheeks, until she felt the darkness go out of him, and the slow joy, too, and she could feel the pounding of his blood. It was then that she should have ceased her caresses, she knew, but the alchemy between them was too strong, and with incredible swiftness her own body set up its own wild clamor. She could feel her blood rolling out to meet his, leaving a weakness in her, a tropical languor, a warmth, a melting, a fainting, a dying, a flame. . . .

Then his hands were upon her shoulders, thrusting her roughly from him, his fingers iron-hard, hurting her, so that the pain brought its own awakening.

"No!" he growled, "no—not like this!"

She stood there looking up at him with her eyes brimming over, but the smile upon her lips was pure gratitude.

"Thank you, Pride," she whispered.

Pride drew out a kerchief and mopped his brow.

"That," he said, "was a near thing. Come, we'd better be getting back now. . . ."

That same night, Pride paid a visit to Harry Hill's Concert Saloon on Houston Street. Strangely enough, he did not even buy a glass of beer. Instead, he leaned over the bar and spoke to Harry.

"Do you know a couple of strong boys who don't care how they make an honest dollar?" Pride asked.

Harry glared at him, suspicion written all over his long face.

"Who's got that honest dollar?" he demanded, looking at Pride's clothes, which not all Sharon's mending and cleaning had been able to make entirely presentable again.

"Me," Pride grinned, and showed him the fifty he had borrowed from Sharon.

"That's different," Harry said. "I know two dozen."

On the third day after he had borrowed the money from Sharon, Pride was loitering outside the great Stillworth brownstone mansion on Fifth Avenue. He was not directly in front of it, but lingered idly some two houses up the street, on the opposite side.

"Why don't you just go in," Tim demanded, "and ask him for a job?"

Pride grinned.

"He'll be out. He always goes out about this time."

"Then what are you going to do?"

Pride pushed the battered derby further back on his head and took out his gold nugget. He tossed it up and caught it, over and over again. Tim, who had seen this gesture many times, found it maddening today.

"I asked you," Tim snapped, "what you're going to do."

"Wait," Pride said.

Tim gave a grimace of disgust and started to move away. But the door of the brownstone opened and an old man came out with a girl on his arm. Tim saw Pride stiffen. Clearly there was an unexpected factor in the matter now, for Pride's face was troubled. . . .

Damn it all! Pride was thinking. I didn't expect him to have a woman with him! I wonder if I can head them off. . . . He straightened up and was on the point of setting out when he looked again at the girl on Thomas Stillworth's arm.

He saw at once that she was lovely. Her blond hair was of a shade so light as to be almost silver, yet her lips were not the shell-pink usually found in pale blondes, but deep rose, and her eyes were sea-blue, soft and velvety. She was

36

slender rather than thin, high of bosom, soft-curving, and she swept along in her exquisitely tailored walking-suit like a princess.

Pride waited. Let them come! he thought. It's all the better, if they do come now. A girl like that. . . . He had, for the moment, forgotten Sharon completely.

Tim was watching also. He saw Stillworth and the girl come down the stairs and start off on what must have been a regular afternoon promenade. Then, suddenly, he seized Pride's arm and pointed. Down the street, behind Stillworth and the girl, dashed two villainous-looking thugs.

Pride calmly put the nugget back into his pocket. Then he started off, at first walking slowly, carefully, as though he, too, were going for a stroll. Breathlessly, Tim followed him.

But Pride was running now, his long legs eating up the distance, and as Tim struggled to keep up, he could see that the thugs had seized both Stillworth and the girl, and were forcing them toward a carriage that had just driven up. The timing was perfect. Too much so. A dark suspicion began forming in Tim's mind as he ran, but it was time now for action, not for thinking.

Then he saw Pride, who had drawn a full ten yards ahead of him, fall upon the two kidnapers like an avenging Jove. The great fists pumped out, delivering hammer blows. The men staggered back, releasing their victims. Pride squared off at one of the men, pivoting on his left foot, leaning forward with the blow, putting his weight behind it, hooking the thug's jaw so hard that Tim expected to see the man's head leave his body. Instead, he crumpled like a suddenly emptied sack. His confederate measured Pride briefly with his eye, then made a dash for the carriage. He swung himself up into it and the driver brought his whip down on the horse's flanks. The carriage careened away through the empty street, and Pride turned toward the young woman, ignoring the fallen man who lay almost at his feet.

Then, to Tim's astonishment, the man whom Pride had downed, jumped to his feet and scurried away. Pride made not the slightest attempt to stop him. Suspicion crystallized into certainty in Tim's mind. He had seen Pride fight before; no man whom Pride had hit solidly had ever gotten off the ground in under a half-hour. He came up to where Pride was standing, his battered derby in his hand, gazing like one mesmerized into the face of the blond girl. Tim took off his own hat and stood beside him, but could not resist the temptation to whisper out of the side of his mouth:

"How much did it cost you?"

Pride pretended not to hear him.

Thomas Stillworth's face was gradually returning from a pasty gray to its own natural purplish red.

"Young man," he squeaked in a high-pitched voice, "I don't know how to thank you."

The girl cast him a sidelong glance filled with amused contempt.

"Tangibly, Father," she said. "That would be the best way."

"That's so, Esther," Thomas Stillworth said, and his thin hand crawled into his coat pocket. But Pride put out a hand and stopped him.

"No, thank you, sir," he said. "I can't take money for a little thing like that."

Tim's eyes were round with astonishment. It was the first time he had ever seen Pride refuse money for any reason whatever.

But the girl was studying Pride, her eyes soft and innocent.

Too innocent, Tim realized suddenly. This one knows men, he thought. She's been around her old pirate of a father too long. She'll take Pride Dawson like he never was taken before.

"No money?" Esther Stillworth said. "Then some other reward, perhaps. What would you like?"

Pride glanced quickly at Thomas Stillworth. The old man was momentarily busy, flicking bits of invisible lint from his frock coat, so that Pride with a sudden motion was able to bend over close to Esther's ear.

"You," he whispered, and straightened up at once. Esther's blue eyes widened, then her chin came up and she loosed her laughter.

Thomas Stillworth jumped at the sound.

"What ails you, girl," he squeaked. "Are you daft?"

"No, Father," Esther smiled. "This gentleman just said something terribly amusing, that's all."

Pride turned brick-red.

"Foolishness," Stillworth snapped. "All you think about. Now look here, young man—there must be something I can do. . . ."

"There is," Pride said coolly. "Me'n' my pal here have been out of work for a long time. Now, if you had some kind of work for us . . ."

He had, he saw at once, struck the right note. Black Tom Stillworth hated to loosen his hold on even one battered coin. But he worshiped industry and ambition. He himself had come over from England in steerage long ago —many years and forty million dollars ago. But he still remembered it.

His little watery gray eyes moved quickly, and took in Pride's immense frame. My God! The man could knock down a carriage horse!

"Yes, Father," Esther whispered sweetly, "he's big enough."

"Come into the house," Thomas Stillworth said incisively. "I think I may be able to do something about this."

Obediently, Pride and Tim followed the Stillworths up the steps to the front door of the mansion. Tim was looking at the leaded glasswork of the door, but Pride's mind was on more mundane matters. He was fascinated by the graceful sway of Esther's bustle as she walked. Sharon, he was quite sure, never wore one. But the thing did have its advantages—if only of generous exaggeration.

They went into a hallway with a tile floor, and Stillworth hung his stovepipe hat on an iron hatrack made in the shape of deer antlers. Then he put his hand on the knob of still another door; a butler forestalled him and threw it open with a flourish. They all went in.

The room in which Pride Dawson found himself was like no other he had ever seen in his life. A soft blue glow spread itself over everything. After a moment, Pride saw the reason. All the windows were blue.

Seeing the expression of wonder on his face, Esther said:

"Father has rheumatism, you know." That statement was supposed to explain everything. But seeing that Pride still did not understand, she added quickly: "Didn't you know that blue glass is good for aches and pains?"

"It's good for many things," Thomas Stillworth said expansively. "Yes, sir, it's very healthy."

Pride nodded as though he were in perfect agreement, and continued to look around the room. It was incredibly crowded. All the woodwork was carved in tortuous Moorish patterns. Scarves of every conceivable size and color lay over everything. Huge bows of blue satin ribbon were tied about the legs of the piano; in every corner stood tall whatnots, their three-cornered shelves covered with mountains of varicolored china bric-a-brac, tiny figurines and small vases, every one of which held its poorly dusted and fading wax flowers. The coal scuttle, painted with fanciful scenes, stood before the fireplace, which was covered with a fire-board bearing a Currier and Ives lithograph of the wooden swans in Central Park. Even the brass pokers and fire-tongs had blue bows of ribbon around their handles, as did the whisk broom which hung above them. On the marble mantelpiece stood a piece of statuary by the famous John Rogers, without which any parlor of the 'seventies would have seemed bare; this one was the immortal "Speak for yourself, John," depicting John Alden and his Priscilla in a gently amorous pose.

On the walls were pictures dwarfed by their massive frames, and framed wreaths of hair. What little space was left in the room was taken up by small tables, footstools, and the huge, overstuffed, horsehair furniture. On the table, before the formidable sofa rested that prime aid to courtship: a stereopticon, complete with its case of double views to which the instrument lent the illusion of depth. Fringed chenille curtains framed each archway, and the stains on the antimacassars of handworked linen testified mutely that Esther's suitors were addicted to the use of pomade to slick down their unruly locks. The ribald peasantry north of Fifty-ninth Street called it "bear grease" and would have none of it, but among the fashionable, it was very popular.

Pride was properly awed by so much magnificence; but, for the life of him, he could not repress the feeling that a man would have to go outside in order to breathe.

"The rewards of hard work," Stillworth said smugly. "Some day you, too, may have a home like this."

I'll have a better one, Pride was thinking. A hell of a lot better one, but he smiled and nodded his agreement.

"Now to business," Tom Stillworth went on. "A man in my position, unfortunately—and undeservedly—acquires enemies. Envy, you know, and the hatred of those who through their own—shall I say—incapacity, put themselves in positions where, through no fault of my own—of that you may be certain—their interests run counter to mine. My interests, of course, prevail; and they find themselves faced with certain losses—for which they blame me."

He lowered his voice to a tense conspiratorial whisper, all the time tugging gently at his mutton chop whiskers.

"I don't mind telling you that there have been several attempts upon my life. You, fortunately for me, witnessed one such attempt today. I would wager that I could put my hand on the man responsible for that outrage if I cared to."

Tim, seeing Pride's slight start, thought mockingly: Stretch out your hand, Stillworth! Just stretch out your hand!

"I was impressed," Stillworth went on, "with the speed and capability with which you handled the situation. Besides, you seem quite strong. . . . As for your friend here, I'm afraid there's nothing I can do."

Tim shrugged.

"It's all right," he said. "I'll find something."

"Briefly, sir," Stillworth went on, looking at Pride, "my offer is this: I should like to engage you as a bodyguard for myself and my daughter."

Pride's black eyes sparkled. He had tried for a minnow and landed a whale. But when he spoke, his voice was calm.

"And the salary?" he said.

"One hundred fifty dollars a month!" Stillworth said grandly.

Pride was about to open his mouth to accept the offer, when Esther spoke.

"Don't be so stingy, Father," she said, calmly. "He's worth at least two hundred."

Stillworth's face purpled at this unexpected blow, but after a moment he recovered.

"All right," he quavered, "it's far too much, but I'll pay it."

Tim was not sure he had heard correctly. He looked at Pride, but the big man's expression had not changed.

"You'll stay here at my house. A room will be provided for you on the top floor. Whenever I, or my daughter, go out, you will accompany us. And, of course, there may be other matters in which you can be of service." He turned to his daughter. "Esther," he said, "ring for Malcolm—tell him to show this gentleman to his room."

"Yes, Father," Esther said. "But don't you think you'd better ask him his name first?"

"That's so." Stillworth took out a small notebook and wrote in it briefly. "Now, sir?"

"Pride Dawson," Pride said.

"Pride?" Esther echoed. "That's odd. But it fits you."

Pride suddenly felt a little stir of uneasiness. Then he knew why. Sharon had said the same thing before—in almost the same words: "It's an odd name; but it fits you, I think." He frowned. Not once during that long day had he given a thought to Sharon. He felt guilty in some obscure way. Sweet, lovely little Sharon, he mused, and me letting this palomino filly turn my head.

He turned to Tim and put out his hand.

" 'Bye, Tim," he said. "I'll see you tomorrow."

"Good-bye," Tim said, and bowed slightly to Esther and her father. Then he walked to the door and waited for someone to let him out.

"Come with me," Esther said. Old Stillworth's head came up with a jerk, his mutton chop whiskers bristling.

"Esther!" he began.

Esther laughed, ignored her father. "Come, Pride."

Pride went up the long stairs behind her. He held back a bit and Tim, still standing by the door, looked up at him questioningly. Then he followed Pride's gaze and saw the reason. Each time Esther Stillworth climbed another step, an exquisitely formed ankle was plainly revealed.

On the top floor, Esther turned. "This way, Pride," she said. "Come with me."

Something in the way she said his name disturbed Pride. Slowly, as he walked behind her, he turned the matter over in his mind, trying to discover what the false note was. It came to him at last with devastating completeness; a girl of her class should never have called him by his given name at all, unless . . .

"Miss Esther," he growled. "You called me 'Pride.' Why?"

Esther turned to face him, the pale oval of her face filled with maddening serenity.

"Why not?" she said, coolly. "I call Malcolm, 'Malcolm.'

And I call Terence by his first name. Why shouldn't I call you 'Pride'?"

Malcolm, Pride remembered, was the butler. And Terence was the coachman! He straightened, looming up before her so tall that his head almost touched the crystal chandelier.

"I don't think you need to show me that room," he said quietly. "And you can tell your father I've changed my mind."

Esther stood quite still before him, her blue eyes widening in her white face. Then, very softly, she began to laugh.

"You *are* proud," she said. "Don't be so silly. It's a very good job, you know. Here's the room." Then, without taking her eyes off him, she thrust out her arm and opened the door.

Pride bowed slightly, and she entered before him. Pride stood looking about him, his dark eyes bleak and forbidding.

Esther glanced up at him. When she spoke the laughter bubbled up through her voice.

"Like it?" she said. "Pride?"

Pride put his derby down upon a table.

"Come here," he said.

Calmly, Esther approached him. When she was close he put out his arms and drew her to him.

Esther found herself thinking, my God, he's strong! Then Pride bent down and found her mouth. He kissed her slowly, expertly, lingering upon the caress. Against the solid strength of his arms, she was powerless. He tried deliberately to hurt her, watching the lines of pain forming about her closed eyes, then he changed at once to gentleness, until at last the response he sought was there, the lovely face pivoting upon the slim column of her throat, the warm lips moving upon his, giving, giving until they parted.

Her hands jerked convulsively, the fingers digging into the shaggy brush on the back of his neck until suddenly, contemptuously, he drew away his mouth.

"Pride," she whispered, "oh, Pride!"

"That's better," he growled. "Say it like that. 'Oh, Pride!' Not 'Come here, Pride! Do this, Pride!' " He grinned down at her wickedly, seeing her face drained of color, her lips bruised, and her eyes filling slowly.

"Now get out of here," he said. "Tell Malcolm to bring

me up a razor and a shaving mug. Tell your pa to advance me some money. I need some clothes."

"How much?" Esther faltered.

"Two hundred dollars."

Esther's hands worked tremblingly at the catch of her purse, but Pride's face darkened.

"Not your money, damn it! Get it from your pa."

"All right," she whispered. "And, Pride . . ."

"Yes, Esther?"

"Don't do that again. Please don't."

"I won't," Pride grinned. "Not until you ask me kindly."

Esther turned and fled down the long hall. Pride watched her go, the laughter rumbling in his throat. Then he went back into the room, closing the door behind him.

CHAPTER THREE—1870

SHARON SAID GENTLY, "You needn't have paid me back so quickly, Pride. And this extra fifty dollars—I can't take that. Really, I can't."

Pride smiled at her.

"Tell you what. You put it in the bank—for us. A start on the furniture, maybe."

"Oh!" Sharon said, and her brown eyes filled with so much joy that Pride turned his face away from her.

Sharon saw the gesture. She got up from the chair on which she had been sitting, pausing to stick her needle carefully into the top part of the fine silk dress she was making, and came over to him.

"What is it, Pride?" she said. "You're troubled. Do you want to tell me about it?"

"No!"

"I see. Pride—is it a girl? Another girl, I mean?"

"Dammit all, Sharon!" Pride burst out. "You aren't going to be that kind of wife, are you?"

Sharon put up both her hands and let them rest along the line of his jaw.

"No, darling," she said. "I'm going to be exactly the kind of wife you want me to be. I won't be jealous—no, that's not true. I will be jealous. I am jealous now. But I promise I won't say anything or show it in any way—as long as you come back to me. You'll do that, won't you, darling?"

"Do what?" Pride asked gruffly.

"Come back to me." Her arms went up about his neck and tightened, and her body moved suddenly, convulsively. "Don't ever leave me, Pride," she whispered. "Not for anything. Not for anybody. Don't you know I'd die?"

Pride brought one hand up and stroked her brown hair. How soft it is, he thought, how soft and easy to look at. Not like . . . Oh, damn!

"You haven't a thing to worry about," he said. "Not a thing. There ain't another girl in the world like you—not another one."

"There are lots of much prettier girls. . . ." Sharon whispered.

"That's just it. Sure there are. So pretty you get tired looking at 'em. So pretty that you've got to tell 'em about it every day or they think you don't care about them. Girls so used to flattery that they've got to have it like a drunk has to have whiskey. Get so they need more and more of it until finally the amount I could dish out without gagging wouldn't be enough—and every time I left the house I'd have to loose a pack of mastiffs in the yard to keep other men out. No sir, not for Pride Dawson!"

Sharon swung back at arm's length and looked up at him, her eyes filled with light and love and mischief.

"So, Mr. Pride Dawson," she teased, "you want to marry me because you're quite sure that nobody else would have me? I like that!"

"You know better than that," Pride grinned. "You're a good-looking woman and you know it. Only your prettiness is kind of different so that a man's got to study you to realize it. But the main reason I'm marrying you, Sharon, is because you're good. Good all the way through. Just plain filled up and overflowing with goodness. I could trust you any time, anywhere with anybody. You'd never change

45

—unless I was to start being mean to you. Unless I was to beat you . . ."

"Would you?" Sharon said merrily. "Would you beat me, Pride?"

"You," Pride said earnestly, "are much too good. If I was ever to lay a hand on you while I was mad, I'd go right out and cut my throat!"

He uttered the threat so seriously and with so much force that Sharon was startled.

"Pride!" she said, "don't talk like that! It—it's wicked!"

"I'm wicked," Pride growled. "That's why I need somebody good."

Sharon frowned thoughtfully.

"Am I good, Pride?" she asked. "Really good? Once or twice when you kissed me, I felt . . . I felt like saying . . . no, like doing . . . Oh, Pride . . ."

"What a good girl shouldn't do," Pride finished for her. "So now you think you're wicked—because when I want you, you want me, too—that's it?"

Sharon bowed her head, and nodded miserably.

"That's it," she whispered.

"Thank God, I'm not quality," Pride said, "or I might have grown up without understanding about real things, too. Look, honey, that's natural. You love me and you're going to give me kids. Would you rather get the cold shivers and the horrors when I touched you? You've got to live with me, remember? Besides, there's not a bit of difference between good girls and bad, except the ones we call good have sense enough to wait till it's lawful."

"Oh, Pride!" Sharon laughed, "you say the most terrible things!"

"I'm a terrible man," Pride said complacently. "Only good thing about me is loving you. You're so little and gentle and sweet, not like—"

Sharon's eyes were very large and dark, suddenly.

"Not like whom, Pride?" she whispered.

"Damn me for a clapper-tongued fool!" Pride said. "Nobody, honey, don't fret yourself at all."

"Pride—?"

"Yes, honey?"

"You said you wouldn't lie to me—that you couldn't. Tell me, Pride—who is she?"

"Esther Stillworth," Pride said. "Black Tom's daughter."

"Is she—pretty?"

"Very. Pretty as a picture. But she ought to be spanked!"

"Do you like her, Pride? I mean are you fond of her—really fond?"

"You mean am I in love with that blond filly?" He put down his big hands and cradled her little face between them. Then he bent down and kissed her quietly.

"Now," he said, "you be the judge of that."

Sharon put down her face and sighed against his shirt front.

"Forgive me," she said. "I'm just so afraid of losing you, darling. I—I looked into the mirror this morning and saw my pitiful little face with all these freckles, and my wide mouth and . . ."

". . . And a turned-up little nose that's cute as the dickens, and hair that's soft as thistle-down and the prettiest, quietest color in the world, and a heart inside of you that's big and generous, and just filled up to the brim with love."

Sharon's face came up and the tears spilled over the upturned corners of her mouth where her lips were smiling.

"You know just how to handle me, don't you?" she said.

"Sure—sure, I do. . . . Look, Sharon, talking about Esther gives me an idea! She's got more money than she knows what to do with—and she's always complaining about her clothes. Suppose I send her to you! You can sew better than most anybody . . . and all her friends are rich, too. What do you say?"

"I think that would be wonderful, Pride. Besides," Sharon's voice dropped even lower, "I'd like to meet her—very much."

"Why? She's just a high-toned filly with no brains—or manners either. Arrogant as the devil."

"And pretty as an angel, Pride?"

"Still thinking about that?"

"Thinking, yes. But not worrying, Pride. Not any more. I'd fight her if she tried to take you away from me. A person has a right to fight for her life. Even the law says that. And you are my life, darling—all my life."

Pride bent down and kissed her gently. He had learned now always to be gentle with Sharon.

"I've got to go back, now," he said. "I probably have to

take the old man somewheres." He kissed her once more, lightly, and went out into the street. When Sharon picked up her needle again she realized, to her surprise, that she was humming.

Through the door of Stillworth's study, Pride could hear voices. One was old Tom's, while the other, Pride recognized after a moment as that of Warren, Stillworth's broker.

"So," Stillworth cackled, "they're selling short! When have they promised to deliver the stock?"

"Next Monday," Warren said.

"How much of it do we hold?"

"Not enough. But I've already given orders to my boys to buy. They're taking their time. They know damned well that nobody wants Tuckahoe & Ravensville shares. Why, that road has had ten accidents in the last three months, and its rolling stock is so depreciated that—"

"But we are not taking our time, are we?" Stillworth chuckled.

Warren laughed.

"By Friday night, we'll hold every bit of their paper that's outstanding."

"Good, Mr. Warren, very good. So they feel bearish! We'll have them over a barrel Monday afternoon!"

Pride's face was furrowed with frowning when Warren came out. Of this conversation he had understood exactly nothing, but he knew at once it was important. This was how money was made—real money. If he was ever to get his hands on his share, he'd have to know such things. Quietly, he walked into Stillworth's study.

"Ready for your afternoon constitutional, Mr. Stillworth?" he asked.

One of his duties was to accompany Stillworth on the long walks the old financier's doctor had ordered. Pride doubted that Stillworth really needed a bodyguard, but the idea seemed to please the old man. Got a guilty conscience, Pride decided. Figures if he got his just deserts, everybody'd be out to kill him. But it's mostly his imagination, I reckon.

"Yes," Stillworth said. "A walk would do me good! Fresh air is invigorating—yes, very!"

Pride held up the old man's frock coat, which, because it was a warm day, he had taken off.

"Mr. Stillworth," he asked, "what do you mean by 'selling short'?"

The thin mouth made a cavernous *O* in the purplish face.

"Why do you want to know that, Pride?"

"Might like to take a stab at the market myself one day. I don't mean to be a poor man all my life."

"Good boy!" Stillworth cackled, "that's the spirit! Now, I'll tell you: Suppose I was to come to you and say, 'Pride, I want some Westcreek & Briartown Railroad stock.' You'd say, 'All right, sir, how much do you want to pay?' 'One hundred,' I'd say. 'Very well, sir,' you'd say, 'I'll deliver you five thousand shares on Monday.'"

"But, Mr. Stillworth . . ."

"I know. I know. I haven't explained the important part yet. You don't own one scrap of Briartown paper. Not one scrap. But you know that people don't think much of that line—because of, say, too many accidents. So you figure you can get Westcreek & Briartown at much cheaper than one hundred. You go to a broker and get it for fifty. Even if I find out before Monday that the stock has dropped from the hundred and five dollars it was when I asked you to get it, down to, say, seventy-five dollars, I'd still have to pay you the hundred. That twenty-five dollars per share is your profit."

Pride nodded with grim joy. This, he thought, is really something.

"But, my boy," Stillworth continued gleefully, "it's a risky business. Suppose somebody finds out you want that stock to deliver to me. You're under bond to deliver it to me, remember. Just as I have to pay you what I promised, you have to deliver the stocks you promised—no matter what it costs you to get them. Now say that Jones—fictitious name, of course—knowing you had to deliver those stocks to me, bought them all up at fifty before you got there. So you go to him. 'Jones,' you say, 'I've got to have those five thousand shares!' 'All right,' he says, 'you can have them—at two hundred dollars a share!' Or five hundred, if he doesn't like you too well. Or a thousand, if he really feels mean. You'd have to pay it, even if it ruined you. You'd have to let me have for one hundred, stock

49

you'd paid five hundred for. That's why stupid people who try the market blow their brains out. . . . Are you sure you can make the grade?"

"No," Pride said truthfully, "I'm not sure." But his mind was busy. So this was how Stillworth had put a group of his rivals over a barrel. They had sold short and now had to deliver. The old pirate was clearly out to ruin them. They had gambled on the stocks falling in price between the time their clients had placed the order with them and the date of delivery—and they had won. But Stillworth was out to do them out of their winnings and ruin them to boot, by making them pay out of pocket much more than the stocks ever possibly could be worth.

He thought the whole thing over, carefully, slowly. There was one thing it seemed to him that Black Tom had not figured on: the possibility of still another trader robbing him in turn. And that, Pride decided almost at once, was precisely what was going to happen. But how—how?

He would have to have money to buy the stocks and, so far, he had scarcely a dime. If, he mused, there were some way I could get my hands on, say, five thousand dollars . . .

He had had that much and more in the past, but he had gambled and wenched it all away. But now, at thirty-seven, his mind had grown more serious.

Will Bleeker, now, he thought. If there were a way I could take his place for a day, I might be able to slip a blank check among Stillworth's papers and get him to sign a draft without knowing it. I could fill in the figures later. . . . Or if I were Stillworth's clerk instead of Will, he'd send me to the bank to cash checks. I could raise one or two. Not much—just a figure or two changed here or there and "borrow" the difference myself. . . .

But even as he laboriously plotted these devices, he knew that they would not work. In the first place, Will Bleeker, Stillworth's confidential clerk and secretary, had never missed a day since he had come to work for Stillworth three years before. Of course, there were means by which a man could be kept at home . . . a few drops in his drink perhaps, or—

Actually, even that would make no difference. Thomas Stillworth distrusted his fellow man so completely that he would probably detect these clumsy ruses of Pride's at once.

I'll bet, Pride thought, looking at his employer, that he reads every line that Will writes, and puts some kind of secret marks on his checks. No, I've got to think of something else.

If only he weren't so suspicious! I don't believe there's a soul on earth. . . . He stopped short, inspiration blinding his eyes. "Esther!" he said aloud.

"Eh?" Stillworth said, tugging with one gloved hand at his whiskers. "What did you say, Pride?"

"Nothing," Pride answered quickly, "nothing at all, sir."

He could scarcely wait for the walk to end. That was the perfect solution. Crabbed and distrustful as he was toward everyone else, to his daughter Stillworth was fatuously indulgent. I'll bet, Pride decided, that she spends more than that in a week!

When Esther came into the drawing room later, she found Pride awaiting her. He came forward at once and faced her.

"Look, Esther," he whispered, "I've got to talk to you. Right away—it's important."

Esther looked up at him coolly.

"What's the matter," she demanded, "are you in trouble?"

"No. Only I have an opportunity to do something— something big. Can anybody hear us here?"

"No," Esther said.

"I need some money. An awful lot of money."

"How much?"

"Five thousand dollars."

"That's not an awful lot of money. But what made you think you could get it from me?"

"Look, Esther—it's something I can't ask your father for. It's a business deal—stocks that I've got an inside track on. Why, I can make a killing! It's only a loan I'm asking for. I'll pay you back with interest—and in two weeks, too!"

"I don't think you're a good risk," Esther said, mockery in her blue eyes.

"Esther, for the love of God!"

Esther smiled at him quietly, coolly.

"Remember that time you kissed me?" she murmured.

"Yes," Pride growled. "Why?"

"I think I ought to have some revenge for that. Aren't you sorry you did that?"

"Hell, no!" Pride exploded. "It was fun!"

Esther threw back her head and laughed merrily.

"I agree," she said. "It was—wasn't it? Very well, Pride, I'll let you have the money—to be paid back in two weeks. I'll think about the interest later." She went into the study and picked up a pen. Then she swiftly wrote a draft for the five thousand dollars and passed it over to Pride. The funny part about it, she thought, is that I believe he'll make his killing—and pay me. He's the type. He might even be richer than father some day. I wonder how it would be to . . .

Then she smiled at him softly.

"Good luck, Pride," she said.

"Thank you," Pride said. "This is mighty nice of you, Esther."

Esther laughed a little.

"Perhaps," she murmured. "And then perhaps it's merely a little investment in the future. My future, Pride."

Pride's big face was puzzled.

"Your future? I don't understand you, Esther."

"Ah, but you will," Esther said. "You will." Then she turned quickly and left the room.

Pride stood for a moment staring after her. I wonder what the devil she meant? he thought. Then he remembered how little time he had. When he passed through the front door, he was actually running.

It took him several minutes to catch a cab. When he sat down he was surprised to find that he was trembling.

"Merchants and Seamen's Bank," he ordered, "and make it fast!"

It was dangerously close to closing time when he entered the bank and there was a line before the teller's window. Pride took his place, eying the big clock nervously. But in a surprisingly short time the teller was looking up at him and saying:

"Yes?"

Pride pushed the check under the bars.

The clerk studied it, then looked up calmly.

"Any identification?" he asked.

Pride fished out a card bearing his name and under it the words, "Associate to Thomas Stillworth, Esquire." He had

had these cards printed himself, with the address of the Stillworth mansion upon them. They had already been of use to him on several occasions. The clerk studied it.

"Anybody can have cards printed, mister," he snapped. "You've got to do better than that. Got any letters addressed to you—with the postmarks on 'em?"

Pride dug feverishly into his pockets. Then his hand closed over an envelope. The moment he touched it, he knew what it was. Since his departure from Shantytown, Sharon had formed the habit of writing him daily, despite the fact that Pride usually found time to stroll by her little dressmaking shop almost every night. The letters were full of a shy tenderness and an almost grateful love. But Pride was not thinking of that now. His mind was entirely upon the business at hand. Bless her! he thought, and dragging out the letter, gave it to the clerk.

"All right, sir," the clerk said, and brought his stamp down on the back of the check. Pride was fascinated by the quantity of bills that were pushed downward by the clerk's counting thumb. Then the man gathered them up into a neat sheaf and passed them over, saying, "Here you are."

Pride managed a dignified exit from the bank, but once outside he ran into the street and hailed a hansom cab.

"Morrisons, Brokers!" he ordered. "And go like the devil!"

The cab driver brought his whip down on the horse, and the little two-wheeled vehicle sped through the streets.

He paid the driver and dismissed him. Then he strode into the brokerage office. Morrison looked up curiously.

"I want you to get me some Tuckahoe & Ravensville shares," Pride ordered. "All that this will buy!" Then he laid the sheaf of bills down on the man's desk.

"That will buy damn near all there is," the broker declared. "They aren't worth much."

"Get them!" Pride demanded. "Get them right away!"

"I'll have them for you, eleven o'clock tomorrow," the broker declared. "Your name, sir?"

"Pride Dawson," Pride said.

Morrison bent down and wrote out a receipt for the money in an expert Spencerian hand.

"You'll pick them up?" he asked, and handed Pride the receipt.

"Yes," Pride said. "I'll pick them up in the morning."

At eleven o'clock the following day he was waiting at the brokerage office. Seeing him, Morrison came forward with a smile.

"I got you a thousand shares common at five dollars the share," he said. "There's something funny about that stock. Last week, it wasn't worth a dime. This week somebody— somebody big, I think—is trying to buy it all. So it went up. Take a tip from me, son, and hold these a while before you sell. Next week you can get twenty-five per share maybe." He leaned forward confidentially. "I hear Thomas Stillworth's buying them. If that's so, they may go any-where—maybe even up to a hundred."

"Up to a hundred from five dollars?" Pride laughed. "Poppycock!"

But they will go to a hundred, he thought, and more if I can get it. Speaking of barrels, Black Tom—who's over one now?

When he got back to the house, he found a neat little road wagon of the type used by flashy drivers for racing, drawn up before the door. In it sat Esther and a young man whom Pride had never seen before. And never want to again, he told himself immediately.

The young man was slim and blond, with hair not two shades darker than Esther's own. He straightened up as Pride approached, with a motion like a ballet dancer's. Then he sat very still studying Pride through golden lashes that were even longer than Esther's.

Now, Pride mused with ribald contempt, if he only had some lace on his drawers . . .

"So," Esther said, impatiently, "there you are—at last!"

"Waiting for me?" Pride said.

"Yes. Father got some threatening letters yesterday, so now he insists that I can't go riding with Mr. Fairhill un-less you go along! Have you ever heard of anything so sil-ly?"

"Sorry to trouble you, Mr. Dawson," young Fairhill said. "The whims of our elders, you know."

His voice was unexpectedly rich and deep. Pride looked at him, a little startled. He glanced downward at the young man's hands. They were clean, long-fingered, manicured. But they were strong hands, firm upon the reins and entire-ly capable. Against his will, Pride was forced to revise the impression of effeminacy he had gained at first glance.

True, Fairhill was all grace and beauty, but it was the grace and beauty of a spirited male of a line whose breeding seemed to have been carefully planned for generations. He reminded Pride of a picture he had once seen of a gentleman of the Renaissance, but Pride, who had no head for such things, could not remember its title. In spite of himself, Pride could not help looking at his own hands, seeing how gnarled, rough and thick-fingered they were. Peasant's hands compared with the hands of a prince. Prize fighter's hands against the hands of a swordsman.

"Come along, will you!" Esther said, and her voice was genuinely angry.

So, Pride said to himself, she's in love with Fairhill. He found the idea oddly displeasing. He did not want Esther himself—except perhaps casually; but neither did he want Joseph Fairhill to have her. I've been like that all my life—wanted to have my cake and eat it at the same time, he mused. I want to marry my Sharon, but I'd like to tumble Esther all night, too, on the side. Damn! I can't have both —I can't . . .

"Tell you what," he said gravely. "I'll see if I can't rent a riding hoss. Then I'll keep behind and let you young folks have your peace. No fun having a chaperon—even a big ugly chaperon in pants."

"I say," Joseph Fairhill laughed, "you're all right, Mr. Dawson. Rather a good sport, aren't you."

For the first time, Esther smiled.

"I told you he was," she said to her escort. Then to Pride: "You don't have to rent a horse. Father has a stable-full. Go around back and get one."

They were still waiting when Pride came back, leading a huge black gelding. Esther watched him as he mounted, which, before her eyes, he did with an extra flourish. At least, she mused, he rides like a gentleman. If only he weren't so sure of himself. I'd like to bring him to heel. Only, he's not the groveling type. He's the kind that founds dynasties that end up with men like Joseph.

"You were thinking of something," Joseph Fairhill whispered. "Something unpleasant. What is it?"

"You're quite right," Esther snapped. "I was thinking of Pride."

"Dawson? Monstrous chap, isn't he? I should hate to make an enemy of him!"

"That," Esther said mockingly, "would be most unwise."

"I'd say. He looks like a primordial brute from before the dawn of history."

"He *is* a brute," Esther said wickedly.

"I say, how do you know that?"

"He kissed me once."

Joseph Fairhill's blue eyes widened, then a slow flush of anger stole over his handsome face.

"Damned presumptuous of him, I'd say," he muttered grimly. "Did you tell your father?"

"No."

"You *didn't* tell your father?"

"I said no."

"Why not?"

Esther smiled—a slow enigmatic smile. Troy was sacked, Joseph thought, because of such a smile.

"I said, why not?" he repeated, his voice hoarse and unnatural.

"Because—" Esther whispered, looking straight ahead, "because I liked it."

Joseph Fairhill's hand jerked on the reins so that the horses half-reared.

"You—you love that—that—"

"No. I love you, Joe. Love's a different thing. Love is very gentle and sweet. I don't even like Pride. I hate him. Yet—he fascinates me. He makes me feel so—so delightfully wicked."

"Esther!"

"Sorry. You've a lot to learn, Joe. Women, I'm afraid, aren't at all like they're supposed to be. You expect me to be a fragile little thing with no brains and no emotions—entirely passive. Well, I'm not passive, Joseph, darling; I could even be aggressive. And if you think I'm going to be a dutiful little wife, faithfully submitting to a repugnant ordeal, you're going to be shocked. I'm afraid I'm going to be as much fun as one of those girls at those—those places you men go to. And as for you, you'd better be lots of fun, too!"

"Esther!"

"Oh, stop saying 'Esther!' and looking so shocked. One of these days women are going to get the vote. One of these days, we're going to run industries, and get elected to office, and pick and choose our husbands as we ought to.

No more children working in factories. Decent wages and hours for the laboring class, and . . ."

"Esther," Joseph said, "truly you amaze me. Is Dawson responsible for all this?"

"Partly." She turned to Joseph, and her eyes were suddenly warmer. "Forgive me," she said, "I didn't mean to upset you. I—I just felt like being honest for a change. Wouldn't you rather know what kind of woman you're going to marry?"

"I know," Joseph said. "The best and the loveliest, and the sweetest in all the world."

Esther turned to him and kissed him lightly on the cheek. But Joseph glanced uneasily over his shoulder at Pride. Damn him to hell, anyway, he thought.

When Pride returned from visiting Sharon that night, he found Esther seated at the piano, playing softly to herself. He paused, listening. Esther played well, her fingers moving expertly over the keys. She was playing a Mozart andante, but when he entered the room she changed abruptly to the Beethoven *Sonata Apassionata*. She did so quite unconsciously, and it was not until she came to the great chords that she realized what she was playing. At once she stopped, her hands making a crashing discord on the keys.

"Go on," Pride said calmly. "I liked that—that last piece, I mean. It's like you. What's it called?"

"That, Mr. Dawson," Esther said tartly, "is none of your business!"

"Play some more of it," Pride said. "It's your kind of music—like you really are—not like you try to be."

"You know an awful lot about me," Esther declared.

"I do. . . . For instance, you're not in love with that pretty boy you rode with today."

"I'm going to marry him!"

"Want to bet on it?"

"Pride Dawson," Esther snapped, "you're positively outrageous!"

"I know. It's restful, eh?"

Despite herself, Esther could not keep from laughing.

"You're right," she said at last, "it is. Everybody I know is so stiff and formal and correct that you are a relief. That's what I like about you."

"Then you do like something about me. I was beginning

to wonder. Lately, you been keeping away from me like I was the plague."

"You know why."

"Because I kissed you? Heck, a kiss is nothing. You just needed bringing down a peg. That was a favor."

"I'd thank you for no more of that kind of favor, Pride."

"Why?" Pride grinned. "Afraid you might kick over the traces? You look like the kind who would."

"I think," Esther said coldly, "that you're disgustingly vulgar."

"I am. So's life. Or it's pretty damned beautiful, depending on the way you look at it. When you figure out a way of bringing a Joseph Fairhill the Third into a world that hasn't a mite of vulgarity attached to it, you let me know. I'd sure find it interesting."

"You get out of here!" Esther snapped.

"Why? Afraid I'll kiss you again?"

"I'm not afraid of anything!"

"Oh, yes you are. You're scared to death of a girl named Esther Stillworth, who's got white-gold hair and sea-blue eyes and a mouth made for kissing. You're living in mortal fear of a girl with skin like snow and boiling springs underneath. You're afraid all right, frightened sick! You won't let me kiss you again, because you don't dare!"

Esther stood up from the piano, her blue eyes suddenly soft. She walked very slowly to where he stood and put up her arms.

"Kiss me, Pride," she said.

CHAPTER FOUR—1870

ESTHER'S FACE WAS very white after that kiss. Wordlessly, she backed away from him, the pupils of her eyes dilated until only a thin rim of blue showed around them. Pride did not follow her, but stood still watching her until she reached the piano. There she stopped, still gazing at him.

Then she brought up her left hand and began tugging at it with her right. Pride saw the flash of fire as the enormous diamond engagement ring came free. Slowly, carefully, she placed it on top of the piano. It lay there, throwing back the light in a hard, blue-white blaze.

Good-bye, Joe! Pride exulted.

Esther leaned back against the piano, studying him. Then she came forward again, and put up her arms once more.

"Why?" Pride growled. "Why did you do that?"

"I can't marry him. Not now I can't."

"Because you love me?"

Wildly, Esther shook her head.

"I don't love you, Pride! I don't . . . I don't, I don't."

"I see," Pride said drily, "you're not going to marry Joseph, because you don't love me. Fine. Only it don't make sense."

Esther went up on tiptoe, her mouth so close to Pride's that her breath rustled against his lips.

"Must you talk?" she whispered.

As Pride bent down to her, he saw that her lips had parted even before he touched them. He was aware, after a time, of feeling a sharp pain. Esther, he realized suddenly, was digging her long nails into the back of his neck. He attempted to draw his mouth away, but her lips fought for possession, clinging fiercely.

There was, Pride decided, only one thing to do about this. He bent down and picked her up, looking around him.

Esther searched his face, her lips swollen and trembling. Then she raised her hand and pointed to one of the doors.

"That's the spare bedroom off Father's library," she said clearly. "He's at the club tonight. In it is," she paused, lending bitter emphasis to the word, "—a bed. And the door can be locked from the inside."

Pride stood still. The words were clear, but their tone was wrong—all wrong.

"I'll go in there with you," she added. "I'll do what you want—what I want, too. I'll probably enjoy it. But afterwards I'll go straight to my father and tell him what I— what we—have done. And he'll either hire someone to kill you, or—" her voice was petal-soft now, rich and vibrant, "he'll force you to marry me. Is it worth it?"

Carefully, Pride put her down again.

"No," he growled, "it's not."

Esther stood there, looking up at him.

"So," she whispered, "it's true."

"What's true?"

"That you're in love with that—that common little dressmaker you tried to send me to this morning."

"She's not common!" Pride flared. Then suddenly he grinned wickedly. "What difference does it make to you? You told me a couple of minutes ago that you don't love me. 'I don't love you!'" he mimicked. "'I don't . . . I don't, I don't!'"

"Pride Dawson," Esther said, "you're a fool!"

"Don't doubt it. Hell, I'm getting tired of this. I think I'll go upstairs to bed."

"Wait. When I said that about Father's having you killed, it didn't bother you, did it? No, I can see it didn't. You're not afraid of being killed. You're too big and too strong to be afraid that way. But you were afraid of having to marry me, weren't you? Yet I think you will marry me. . . ."

Pride's jaw dropped. He stood there staring at her in astonishment as she continued.

"Because my father is worth forty million dollars. Because I have twelve million in trust for me which I'll receive when I'm twenty-one—two years from now. Because you can be bought much cheaper than that. Oh, yes, Pride, you'll marry me all right."

Pride frowned.

"But I didn't know you wanted to marry me!" he said.

"Oh, yes," Esther said simply, "I do—very much."

"You—you'd have a man who married you for your money?"

Esther shook her head.

"Not just a man," she murmured. "You!"

Then she turned and ran up the long stairs.

Pride stood still, looking up after her. The crash of her door, slamming, awakened him from his reverie.

"Well, I'll be damned!" he said. "I'll be double damned!"

He climbed the stairs slowly, pausing outside her door. He put his hand forward to try the knob, but jerked his fingers away before they had touched it. Then he went on up to his own room on the top floor. He took off his collar and his tie and his shoes and lay down upon the bed with his hands under his head. He stared at the ceiling.

Twelve million dollars in two years, he thought. And she's pretty. Hell, she's beautiful. How'd she know me like that —know just where to hit me? Black Tom's getting old and he's got no other children. Twelve plus forty equals fifty-two million dollars! No, there isn't that much money in the world. But there is. And not one drop of ice in her veins, but—but Sharon's so sweet and good and I love her little freckled face more'n I love Esther's whole body. I'd never know a miserable minute with Sharon. She's good and sweet and gentle and loves me so much I feel ashamed. No, I haven't got a right to so much love—no right to a girl like her. But fifty-two million dollars . . . Oh, dear God! I'd better go see Sharon right now. I'd better kiss her and hold her close. I can't hurt her like this—can't. . . . But fifty-two mil—God!

He had turned out the gas jet before he lay down. Now something disturbed him. Turning, he saw what it was. The ray of light that stole under his door from the chandelier in the hall had been cut off abruptly.

"Esther!" he breathed, and swung his long legs over the side of the bed. But as he reached the door he heard the swift scurry of her slippered feet down the hall. He put out his hand to jerk open the door, then his fingers rested, nerveless and cold, on the knob. At his feet lay a little square of white, glowing in the light that once more came under the door.

He bent down slowly, and picked it up. Then he held it in his big hand a long time before he turned up the gaslight once more. He was, he realized, afraid to open it. He, Pride Dawson, who had never been afraid of anything in his life.

Swiftly, he tore open the envelope and read:

"I love you, I love you, I love you! If you had taken me into the bedroom I would have been the happiest woman alive—and I would have hated you. Oh, Pride, how can you keep me so confused? I don't know right from wrong any more. I love you. I always have. I always will. Only, Pride, I didn't want the kind of love you've brought me. I wanted moonlight and romance and gentleness. I still do. I don't want to lie all night upon my bed with my skin screaming—so that I cannot bear for even a gown to touch it. I hate you for making my bones melt to water—not water merely, but scalding water, so that when I closed the door I could not stand. I hate you, Pride, for making me love you like that, because it's wickedness. I hate you so much I'd like to see you dead. But if you were dead and I saw you lying there, I'd fall upon your body and kiss your mouth and then my heart would stop too. Yes, I'm insane —and you have made me so! I'm crazy with love of you. Crazy from wanting you so. I hate you and I love you, and now the two feelings are the same thing. Oh, Pride, my dearest . . ."

The letter ended abruptly. There was no signature.

Pride sat down at the edge of the bed holding the letter in his hand. It was a very cool night, but when he touched his shirt, he found that he was sweating so that it had stuck to him.

"God," he groaned. "Oh, dear God!"

When he came down the stairs the next morning, the first person he saw was Esther. She was dressed for the street. Her face was very pale.

"Wait," Pride called, "wait, Esther."

She turned and faced him.

"Look," he said. "I got that letter. I—"

"I know," she whispered. "You don't know what to say. Neither do I. I'm horribly ashamed, Pride. I lay awake all night, thinking."

"And what did you think?" Pride asked.

"That I'd ask you for a favor. A real favor." She looked at him, her eyes véry blue and grave. "It's this: I want you to have mercy, Pride. You're strong. I'm not. Don't kiss me any more or hold me close—not even if I ask you to. Not now—not until we're married. . . ."

"You're damned sure we're going to be married," Pride growled.

"Yes," Esther said simply, "I am." Then she turned coolly and walked through the opened door.

Pride stood there a long moment before he turned and went toward Stillworth's study. Before he reached it, the uproar burst upon his ears.

"You fool!" Stillworth was screeching. "You utter incompetent idiot!"

"It wasn't my fault," Pride heard Warren answer. "How

did I know somebody was going to buy up that stock? You know as well as I do that Tuckahoe & Ravensville wasn't worth the paper it was printed on. So I didn't hurry the boys."

"You didn't hurry!" Stillworth groaned. "But somebody else did! Now instead of my having Watkins and Bolley over a barrel, somebody's got both of us!"

"I don't see that," Warren said. "It just means you can't catch Watkins and Bolley. You don't lose a dime."

"Oh, don't I, though! Since I talked to you, I had lunch with Vanderbilt. *He* wants that damned little railroad. Wants it to piece out his lines near Chicago. And I sold him those shares short! I wasn't going to sell them to Watkins and Bolley at all! From Vanderbilt I could get twice as much. Now I haven't got them—thanks to you, Henry Warren!"

"Oh, my God!" Warren whispered.

"You know who bought them?" Stillworth demanded.

"Yes. Some operator I never heard of. A man named Dawson."

"Dawson!" Stillworth shrieked. "Don't tell me his first name's Pride!"

"It is. I remembered it because it's so odd."

The rest of Warren's words were lost in the clatter of Stillworth's racing feet.

"Pride!" he called, his weak voice failing him as he threw open the door. "You come here, you ungrateful bastard!"

Pride smiled quietly and approached the old man. Tom Stillworth was trembling all over as though he had the ague.

"Come in, come in!" Stillworth whispered, holding open the door. Pride entered the study.

"You bought a thousand shares of Tuckahoe & Ravensville," Stillworth said. "Where are they? Give them to me this instant. I'll give you what you paid for them."

Slowly Pride shook his head, a grim smile lighting his eyes.

"I think I'm entitled to a profit on the transaction, Mr. Stillworth," he said.

Stillworth's voice again rose to a frenzied shriek.

"Not a dime!" he cried. "Not a dirty dime!"

"All right," Pride grinned. "I'll go see whether Watkins and Bolley feel that way about it. Or Mr. Vanderbilt."

Stillworth buried his fingers in his mutton chop whiskers and yanked until wisps of gray hair came out in his hands.

"Look, Tom," Warren said, "be reasonable, Mr. Dawson's got you."

"Reasonable! I took the beggar off the streets! I fed him, gave him clothes! I pay him twice what he's worth! And you say be reasonable!"

"If he can figure out a transaction this slick," declared Henry Warren, "he's worth twice whatever you pay him. I say, Mr. Dawson, how would you like a job in my office?"

"No, you don't, Henry Warren! Dawson works for me and I aim to keep him. All right, Pride, I'll give you twice what you paid for that trash. Fair enough?"

Pride shook his head.

"You'll pay me twenty-five dollars per share," he said quietly.

"That's twenty-five thousand dollars!" Stillworth groaned. "You robber! You thief! You blackguard!"

"I wonder," Pride grinned, "what Watkins and Bolley are going to call you, Mr. Stillworth?"

Stillworth sat down abruptly and drew out his checkbook. Finally, a glint of amusement appeared in his shrewd old eyes.

"All right," he said, "all right. Twenty-five thousand it is."

Henry Warren leaned back against the marble mantelpiece. His head went back slowly. Then the laughter came out in peal after peal.

Thomas Stillworth sat before the desk with the pen in his hand. Then, suddenly, he too began to laugh—a thin, high-pitched cackle, vibrating through the room.

"Damn my soul, Pride!" he gasped, "but you're a shrewd cuss! Took me, didn't you! Clear over the jumps! Well, I'll be damned!" He bent over his desk and wrote swiftly. Then he blotted the check and handed it to Pride. "Now give me those shares and get out of here," he said.

Pride handed over the stock, which he had been carrying in his pocket, and left the room, but he lingered for a moment outside.

"That man," Henry Warren said, "is going far."

"I don't doubt it," Stillworth said slyly. "Only, Henry—

if you've finished laughing your fool head off—I'll tell you something. Vanderbilt is paying me one hundred dollars per share for this stock!"

Rage mounted up and beat about Pride's ears. He had been outsmarted after all. He could have held out for ninety-five dollars the share—hell, for the whole hundred—and instead of twenty-five thousand dollars, he'd have had a hundred thousand! Then, slowly, his anger subsided. After all, twenty-five thousand dollars was twenty-five thousand dollars. A slow grin spread over his face. He took his hat from the rack and started for the door. On the way out, he thoughtfully purloined a checkbook from Will Bleeker's desk. He'd use the Merchants and Seamen's himself. After all, any bank good enough for Thomas Stillworth was good enough for him.

He went up the stairs toward Esther's room and knocked on the door. Esther opened it and stood there, looking at him a little fearfully. She still wore her walking-suit and her hat. Apparently, she had returned almost immediately after he had seen her an hour earlier.

She saw his glance.

"I didn't feel like going out after all," she said. "What is it, Pride?"

"You have a pen in here?" Pride demanded.

"Yes—why?"

"I want to write you a check," Pride said. "I owe you five thousand dollars—remember?"

"Oh," Esther said; then: "Come in, Pride."

Pride entered her boudoir and crossed to an ivory desk. He picked up the pen, dipped it into the inkwell and hesitated.

"How much interest, Esther?" he asked.

"You—you really have the money?" Esther said. "I could wait, you know."

Pride drew out her father's check and showed it to her.

"You'll have to wait until day after tomorrow to cash my check," he said, "while I have a chance to deposit this one. How much interest, Esther?"

"You got that from Father! But how, Pride? How?"

"I sold him some stocks I bought with your money. It seems that he happened to need them. . . . I'd still like to know about that interest."

"Oh, that," Esther said. "None, Pride."

"Why not?"

"You've paid it already. Last night, Pride."

Pride shrugged and wrote swiftly. Then he turned over to a fresh check and wrote a draft for Tim for twenty-five hundred dollars—many times the amount of Tim's share of the money he had lost their first day in New York. Tim could stop picking rags now. That was a good thing. Tim might not have known it, but he seemed to Pride to be growing much too fond of Sharon. He was seeing her every day, while Pride could not. I'll get him away from there, Pride thought grimly, and remind him that he has a wife and child. Then he straightened up and looked at Esther.

"I'll be seeing you," he said. "I've got things to do."

Down to seventeen thousand five hundred already, Pride mused as he stood on the sidewalk. I won't have it long at this rate. I'll drive down to the scows and find Tim and give him this check. Then I'll go to see Sharon and tell her all about it. We can get married now, all right. Dear Sharon. I wonder . . . he began, and raised his hand to a passing cab. But the cab had stopped and he was inside before he completed his thought. I wonder what Esther's going to do?

Esther, a short time later, was doing the very last thing on earth that Pride would have wanted. She was sitting very quietly in Sharon's little shop, fingering a fine piece of goods.

"Your dresses are beautiful!" she said to Sharon. "Pride Dawson told me about you, and I intended to come here before now. But I kept putting it off. You know how we women are."

Sharon nodded, trying to keep the mute misery out of her face. She is so beautiful, she thought. How could Pride help loving her? And her manners are exquisite, while I—

Esther put out her hand.

"What's the matter, my dear? You seem sad."

"I am sad," Sharon said. "Forgive me. I shouldn't have shown it. Now about the frocks, Miss Stillworth?"

"I'll have five. The blue silk first. Then the brown taffeta, then—but you know what they are. How much will they be?"

Sharon hardened her heart.

"They'll be one hundred dollars apiece," she said coldly.

"I say, you are expensive, aren't you?"

Sharon said calmly, "I do very fine work."

"That's true," Esther admitted. "Here's a hundred dollars on account. You'll get the rest when the dresses are delivered. You can send them to me—by Pride."

"Oh!" Sharon said.

"I know all about it, my dear. Do you love him very much?"

Sharon's brown eyes flashed sudden fire.

"What concern is it of yours?" she demanded.

Esther smiled.

"It's of great concern, Miss O'Neil," she said quietly. "You see, I love him, too." Then she turned and walked from the shop. Sharon stood up and ran out behind her.

"Please!" she said. "Please, Miss Stillworth. You could have any man. Don't take him from me."

Esther's eyes hardened. Then her gaze swept over Sharon's thin face, seeing the wide lips trembling, the cheeks gone dead-white except for their spray of golden freckles, and the first tear-mist rising in the soft brown eyes. She was conscious of a swift upsurge of pity for Sharon O'Neil, whose life lay in the palm of her hand. She could give her happiness back to Sharon. Or she could close her hand and in an instant Sharon's future would be so many fragments. Then she remembered Pride, and the choice was no choice at all, her slim hand closing. . . .

"I wish I could," she said gently. "I didn't want to fall in love with him. I fought against it. But—you know Pride."

"Yes," Sharon said wretchedly, "yes, I know Pride."

"Don't hate me," Esther said, "whatever happens. I shan't—if you win."

"No, I shan't hate you," she answered. She turned and went back into the shop. She laid her cheek upon the table and wept for a long time, until she had no tears left. Then she straightened up, thinking:

"No, I shan't hate you. For when it happens I'll be dead!"

CHAPTER FIVE—1870

THE SUMMER was gone now. Outside Pride's window the air was crisp. Here and there among the leaves of the oak that shaded the room, could be seen a spray of brown and gold.

Pride studied himself in the full-length mirror. He had bought it and all the other furnishings when he had moved out of the Stillworth mansion and taken this modish bachelor suite. Now the image that stared back at him from the mirror pleased him immensely. His pomade coarse black hair swept over his left eye in a majestic curve. His mustache, clipped to the fashionable handle-bar shape, was scented, and his clean-shaven face glowed from the steaming and massage it had received from his barber. His evening dress was flawless. Pride toyed with the golden studs that held his stiff-bosom shirt in place, and pulled down his snowy cuffs still further, so that the diamond chips in his cuff links would be more plainly visible. Over the chair lay an opera cape of midnight-blue lined with white silk, while on the rack, along with many other hats of various styles and shapes, rested a high silk hat.

It's a hell of a lot different than five months ago, Pride mused complacently. I didn't have a dime then. Now I have over fifty thousand dollars in the bank and I'll have more. Black Tom's all right. Every tip he's given me has paid off—plenty. He even wants to know why I don't come around much now. That's simple, Black Tom. It's because I can't keep my hands off your daughter—and hers off me. If she really wanted to play the game, I'd be around every night. But she doesn't. She wants to get married. I don't think you'd like that, would you, you old pirate? You want her to marry that pretty Joe Fairhill—a real blueblood. Sorry, but I think she prefers it red.

He paused, grinning at himself in the mirror. That's

true, but she also wants things legal and permanent, and that's not so good. It would be if I loved her—but I don't. I can't figure out this brain of mine. I can have the richest girl in New York—and she's damned near the prettiest too —and I don't want her. I want a little gal named Sharon. That soft mouth of hers and those brown eyes with no meanness in 'em anywhere can make me so weak I can't think of doing her any harm. Funny, about the two. They're the first two girls I ever knew longer than a week whose skirt tails I didn't have over their heads.

Both of 'em more'n half-willing, too. Esther won't unless she sees both our John Hancocks on a license. And Sharon, damn it, because *I* don't want to. Because I look down into her little face and see the goodness in it, and I haven't got the heart.

I'll have to marry her sometime soon. She's getting thinner and paler from the waiting. I ought to have done it before now. Only, every time I open my mouth to ask her I see fifty-two million dollars blowing away in the wind. Kind of a high price to pay for any woman. Oh, damn!

He picked up the opera cape and swung it over his wide shoulders. Then he took his hat, his white gloves and his cane, and went down the stairs.

The policeman on the beat greeted him as he came out into the street.

" 'Evening, Mr. Dawson," he said.

" 'Evening," Pride said, "how's the missus and the kids?"

"Oh, the old woman ain't doing so well. Too many babies, I think. Still, what's a man to do?"

"Get yourself a little dilly on the side," Pride grinned, "and give the little woman a rest."

The policeman broke into a roar of laughter. Afterwards, Pride knew, he would repeat the conversation, much expanded and larded with a dozen or so "and he says to me's" as a reflection of his familiarity with the great Pride Dawson. The great Pride Dawson! Pride liked the sound of it. He blandly countenanced the gossip that was already calling him a millionaire; he even permitted the rumor to spread that he was Thomas Stillworth's partner. At the Stock Exchange he was on terms of easy comradeship with Commodore Vanderbilt, with the rotund Jim Fisk and spidery little Jay Gould. They, too, he realized, had no idea of how little money he actually had. Fifty thousand dollars

—hell, that wasn't even chicken-feed to such men. Their plunges started at five million and went on up. And all he would need to do was to say, "All right, Esther, get your things and let's go down to City Hall."

"Oh, damn!" he groaned again and raised his hand in a signal to a hansom cab.

He had not seen Sharon in two months. He had, however, answered her letters faithfully, explaining that he was "all tied up" with business deals, or giving other excuses that she had cried over, seeing Esther's lovely face between her and the page. But tonight he was going to see her. Tonight the uncertainty was going to be ended. One way or the other, it was going to be ended and Pride himself did not know what his own decision would be. He loved Sharon and he hated to leave her. He did not love Esther, though he did want her physically; but Esther Stillworth was fifty-two million dollars.

When the cab drew up before Sharon's shop, he got his first surprise. It was empty, and a card read: "Moved—across the street." He turned and looked across to the other side. There was another shop with wide windows, through which he could see five young women busily sewing. Sharon was standing near the benches, dressed for the evening. She was talking to the other girls. Wonderingly, Pride crossed the street. As he approached he saw the sign: *La Mode Dressmaking & Millinery Shop. Miss Sharon O'Neil, Prop.*

He broke into a wide grin as he entered.

"Gosh, Sharon," he said, " this is great! You didn't write me business was so good!"

"Yes, Pride," Sharon said gently, "I'm doing well. I've had to hire seamstresses—thanks to you."

"Thanks to me? I didn't do anything!"

"You sent—your Esther to me," Sharon said. "She's been very kind. She brought all her friends. I may even have to hire more girls."

"So Esther did come! Funny she never said anything to me. But then I don't see her much."

"You don't, Pride?" Sharon said, and Pride could hear the half-suppressed note of joy in her voice.

"No," Pride said grimly, "I don't."

Sharon turned to the girls, and said:

"You may go home now—take the rest of the evening off."

Joyfully, they rushed for their hats, for it still lacked two hours of the completion of the usual twelve-hour day.

Pride took Sharon's arm and led her to the waiting cab.

"Booth's Theater," he said. "Sixth Avenue and Twenty-third Street."

"Oh, that's the new one!" Sharon said. "It just opened last year. What will we see?"

Pride consulted a small playbill he had in his pocket.

"*Romeo and Juliet*," he said. "Booth's playing Romeo. And Miss Mary McVicker is Juliet. Think you'll like that?"

"I'll love it," Sharon murmured and nestled closer to his big arm.

Pride sat miserably in the theater and listened to Sharon's low sobbing. On the stage Miss McVicker was trying to obtain a drop of poison by kissing Romeo's dead mouth. Then when she raised the dagger, Sharon buried her face against Pride's coat.

"Hush, honey," Pride whispered, "it's only a play."

Afterwards, over their oysters at Delmonico's, Pride said:

"It's all so silly. People don't die for love."

Sharon put down her fork, and her heart was in her eyes.

"Don't they, Pride?" she whispered.

Going home from the boarding house where Sharon lived, Pride sat morosely, his big head sunk upon his chest. He still had not asked Sharon to marry him. Instead, he had merely kissed her twice, quick, preoccupied kisses, and said good night. Sharon had stood there a moment, staring at him, and he was afraid she was going to start crying. Instead, she had said very simply, "Good-bye, Pride," and gone up the stairs.

Pride jerked upright on the leather seat. That *was* what she had said: "Good-bye"—not "Good night!" She had stood there with her face full of longing and said, "Good-bye, Pride," and in her voice was all the finality in the world. All the way the thought had been nagging at the edges of his consciousness that there had been something wrong with their parting and now, finally, he had pinned it down. One word: Good-bye. Not "Good night, darling, when will I see you again?" Just good-bye.

Well, he told himself angrily, if she wants it that way . . . but he could not delude himself. Sharon did not want it that way. She was simply, with her haunting sweetness, bowing to the inevitable. Good-bye, Pride—good-bye, my lost love, good-bye. . . .

Through most of that night and all the next day Pride wrestled with his problem. When evening came, he could stand the suspense no longer.

"Oh, damn!" he muttered. "I'll fix this. I'll go to Esther and tell her it's no go. Then I'll go back to Sharon and . . ." He dressed with care, left the house and hailed a cab. As he got in he directed the driver:

"The Stillworth mansion! Fifth and Thirty-eighth!"

Malcolm bowed grandly as he opened the door for Pride. Carelessly, as though it were a lifelong habit, Pride passed him his hat, his cane and his gloves.

"Your cape, sir?" Malcolm inquired.

"No," Pride said gruffly, "I won't be long."

Then he walked into the parlor. Esther got up from the piano and came toward him, her blue eyes softening and widening.

"Oh, Pride!" she said clearly, "how handsome you are!" The next instant she was in his arms.

How long old Thomas Stillworth must have stood there, his face purpling into near-apoplexy, neither of them knew; but finally they heard the choking gurgle of his breath.

Esther drew away her mouth and looked at her father. She smiled softly.

"Pride and I are going to be married, Father," she said, sweetly. "I hope you don't mind."

"Mind!" Thomas Stillworth shrieked. "Mind! I'll see you dead and in hell first!"

"Father!"

"I mean it! Don't you know he's no good?"

Esther made an impish face.

"Yes, Father," she laughed, "I do. And he's also a seducer of innocent young girls, but I love him."

Thomas Stillworth collapsed weakly into a chair.

"Esther!" he gasped. "You didn't—you haven't . . . Esther!"

"No, Father," Esther said gently. "I didn't and I haven't. But I might—if you don't give your consent."

"Never! And if you persist in this folly, I'll cut you off without a cent! Then see how devoted he'll be!"

"Pride doesn't care about the money," Esther said confidently. "Do you, darling?"

Pride did not answer. Instead, he stared down at her, his face wintery and bleak. And through his mind ran the one word: *trapped!* Caught by wanting money too much—outsmarted by a slip of a girl, roped and hog-tied and the money gone too!

"Pride!" Esther said, shaking him by the lapels of his tailcoat, "answer me, Pride!"

"I think," Pride muttered, "I'd better be going now."

"You—you beast!" Esther's voice was hoarse with fury. "You vile, unspeakable beast!" Then she slapped him hard across the face, swinging with all of her quite considerable force, left and right and left again, her hand making a sound like a small fusillade of pistol shots, as red splotches began to appear on his cheeks.

Pride caught her by the wrist and held her hard.

"Don't do that again," he said, quietly.

"You could have lied!" Esther wept. "You know I don't care what you want me for—as long as you do want me. You shouldn't have shamed me so. I don't care about the money—I'll give you every cent I have! If I have to pay you to hear you say 'I love you,' then I'll pay! Only you should have lied for me, my darling—you should have lied. . . ."

Then she collapsed against him in a shuddering heap, her whole body racked with sobbing.

"Hush," Pride murmured. "Hush, honey—please."

"You," Thomas Stillworth shrieked, "get out of here—and don't come back!"

"Don't worry," Pride said grimly, "I won't!"

He did not go directly home when he left the Stillworths'. Instead, he wandered through the streets, his mind aching with confusion.

Lord, he thought, what a mess! I've made an enemy of Black Tom and made Esther furious with me and hurt Sharon all in two days! There won't be any more hot tips from Stillworth now. And that fifty-two million—a fine chance I have of getting it! I might as well go back to Sharon now—might as well make somebody happy out of the whole damned mess.

But he did not really feel like going. He was in no mood for tender words or caresses this night. Tomorrow would do as well. The lights of a saloon caught his eye. He entered and put his foot on the brass rail.

"Whiskey," he called to the barkeep.

"Coming up, sir!" the barkeep said.

Two hours later, he gave it up. The whiskey might as well have been so much ice water for all the effect it had on him. In his present savage mood, he could have drunk a gallon. He paid for his drinks and, walking out into the street, hailed a cab. Then he sat brooding until the horse clopped up to the house where he lived.

As he got out of the cab he looked up. The lights were on! Someone had turned on the gaslights in his room! He went up the stairs very quickly and tried the door. It was unlocked. He pushed it open and walked in.

Esther sat in his great chair looking up at him. He stared at her, his face flushed and angry.

Esther stood up.

"Your landlady let me in," she said. "I told her I was your fiancée. I—I came to say I'm sorry. I behaved abominably. Please forgive me, Pride—please."

"All right," Pride said, "I forgive you. Now get out!"

He saw the tears gathering about her blond lashes. Damn it all, why must women always cry?

"I love you, Pride," she whispered. "Must you always hurt me so?"

"Oh, damn!" Pride said.

"I—I talked to Father after you left. He was much more reasonable. He said he was only trying to protect me. Only —I don't want to be protected from you, dearest. Not ever. I told him that. I told him I'd go on loving you no matter what happened—that I'd never marry anybody else even if I died an old maid. I think that that's what got him. So he said to tell you that he would consent—when you showed him one million dollars you had made."

"Good God!"

She came up to him and put her arms around his neck.

"You can do it, Pride! I know you can! You've made an awful lot of money since you've been here. I'll help you.

74

I'll find out things and. . . . Will you, Pride? Please say you will."

Pride heard his own voice, far off and deep, saying:

"All right, Esther, I'll do it." And he groaned inside his heart, knowing he was really caught—caught in the net of his own greed, beyond any chance of escaping.

"Darling!" Esther cried, and rising on tiptoe, kissed his mouth. Then, drawing back, she said very simply and plaintively, like a child:

"Do you—want me to stay here tonight, Pride? I can if you want me to—Father wouldn't know. . . ."

"No!" Pride growled, though for the life of him he did not know why.

Esther sighed.

"You're right," she said reluctantly. "It would only make me want you more. Now most of the time I can keep a grip on myself. But once I—I found out what it's like, I'd drive you insane." She looked up at him, smiling through her tears. "I'm bad," she whispered. "I'm very bad. . . . Know what, Pride?"

"I don't—not with you."

"Once we're married, you'll never want anyone else. You won't have the time—or the energy." Then, kissing him lightly, she said good night and left the room.

Pride stood very still in the middle of the room. He was not thinking. His mind was far too stunned. Tomorrow, then, he would have to begin.

His hands came up slowly and fumbled at his cravat. He drew it off and tossed it over the back of a chair. Then he started to take off his stiffly starched collar, but he had only succeeded in loosening it from the neckband of his shirt, when he heard a knock. He whirled, his face flushed and angry, and threw open the door.

"Damn it all," he began, "I told you—"

"Yes," Joseph Fairhill whispered, "just what did you tell her, Dawson? I'd like very much to know."

Pride stared at the younger man, the feeling of clumsiness he had experienced previously in the presence of Fairhill's grace, returning with full force.

"Come in," he growled. "A hallway's no place to talk."

Joseph Fairhill strode into the room, his gaze searching every corner, lingering upon the curtains, probing into the shadows.

Pride saw the look.

"She's not here," he said grimly.

"I know," Joseph said. "I saw her leave."

"Then speak your piece," Pride said, "and be done with it!"

Joseph put his slim fingers into his waistcoat pocket. When he brought them out again Esther's engagement ring rested lightly between them, glittering in the light of the gas jets.

"You're responsible for this," he said softly.

"So?" Pride drawled. "Do you want me to give her back to you?"

Slowly Fairhill shook his head, his heavy blond ringlets moving with the gesture.

"You don't understand Esther," he declared. "No one could give her back or take her away or do anything with her that she didn't want done. I want one thing only, Dawson—let her alone and give her time to come to her senses!"

Pride growled. "You're saying that it's not sensible for her to be in love with me—that marrying me is downright foolish. Well, I want to know one thing, Joe—why? You think I'm not good enough?"

Joseph Fairhill made a quick, expressive gesture with his hands.

"I *know* you're not good enough," he said.

Pride walked toward him, stepping lightly as a cat for all his bulk. And the hatred in his black eyes was absolutely bottomless.

"Because I was poor, eh?" he said. "Because I haven't any 'family'? Because there's no 'the Second' or 'the Third' tacked on to my name?"

Fairhill looked at the big man and there was no fear in his glance.

"My grandfather," he said coolly, "died without being able to write his name. He trapped animals and traded with the Indians. He sold them whiskey and muskets and steel tomahawks with which to scalp other whites. He was a thief and a scoundrel. He stole the Indians' lands and came back East with a small fortune. Then he went on to bigger things—all crooked, all heartless—and died worth more millions than I can count. So my father was reared as a gentleman on Grandfather's dirty money. He was gentle

76

and good and managed to lose half Grandfather's fortune. But I'm a little like Grandfather—I haven't lost a dime."

"You said all that to say what?" Pride demanded.

"That family has nothing to do with it. I knew my grandfather—he lived to be ninety. If I couldn't have her, I could see Esther marry a ragpicker and be somewhat contented. But you're too much like my grandfather. I don't want to see the woman I love hurt and broken by the type of man you are."

Pride stood there, staring at him, then a wicked grin lighted up his big face.

"Noble, aren't you?" he chuckled.

"No. I'm selfish. I think that if Esther has time to consider the matter, she'll come back to me—the only way I want her back—of her own free will."

Pride crossed to a cabinet and drew out a decanter of whiskey and two glasses. He poured a drink for Joseph Fairhill and one for himself.

"Suppose I don't give her time to think," he said. "Suppose I marry her right away, then what?"

"I'll ruin you," Joseph Fairhill said. Then, he sipped the whiskey and looked up, smiling. "Excellent stuff."

"I always keep the best. . . . But a minute ago you were about to ruin me. I'd be obliged if you'd make yourself a little clearer."

"Oh, it's clear enough. I know Esther. She couldn't stand poverty—not for an instant. She'd leave you flat and come to me. I assure you, my dear Dawson, that if you marry Esther Stillworth, your affairs will not prosper—your investments, for instance, will always be, from that moment on . . . unfortunate. Your holdings will decrease steadily in value. Inside of a year, you'll be crowing on the same dungheap from which you came. I can do it. I have both the connections and the money. I can squander more money than you'll acquire in a lifetime, just to see you get yours." He put out his empty glass. "May I have another?" he said.

Pride filled his glass with a steady hand.

"I never ran from a fight in all my life," he said flatly. "You'll have yourself a fight, little Joe."

Fairhill downed his glass without a grimace and he did not waver when he stood up. Pride, who knew the potency of the whiskey he had served, could not repress a feeling of real admiration. You're all right, he thought. But aloud, he said:

"Since you've come here to threaten me, what makes you so sure I won't break your neck now and head off any trouble you may start?"

Joseph smiled.

"You mean to be rich," he said. "I don't think that even you could manage that from behind bars—not to mention how fatal the gallows is to all ambitions." He smiled again and shook his head. "The great Pride Dawson," he said. "They call you that now—to your face. Behind your back they call you other things: thief and blackguard and scoundrel. But one thing they never call you—not one of your many enemies, Pride; not one of them calls you a fool." He bowed then and walked to the door. Then, he turned again and said quietly, "I didn't even bring a weapon." Then he was gone, his footsteps echoing down the long hall.

You're all right, little Joe, Pride thought again. Too bad we're on opposite sides of the fence. Yes, it's too bad. . . .

CHAPTER SIX—1870

ONE MILLION DOLLARS. That was the round sum. Ten hundred thousand dollars. That was Black Tom Stillworth's asking price for the sale of his daughter.

Hell, Pride thought, for that much money, she should be stripped and stood up on the block so I could see what I was getting. But it isn't Esther alone—it's the gamble. Twelve million first—in two short years. Forty million more when the old man dies. More than that, with twelve million dollars, I can plunge—big. A million a throw. Run it up. Fix it so that I can match the old miser dollar for dollar long before he cashes in his chips. A fine lot of good sitting here thinking about it'll do me. I've got to get busy —now.

He put on his tall hat at a jaunty angle and went down

the stairs. Outside he stopped, as was his custom, to talk to the policeman on the beat. Today that custom cost him dearly, for by precisely the number of minutes that he spent chatting idly, he missed seeing Henry Warren, Thomas Stillworth's agent, leaving the offices of Morrison's, Brokers, just before his own arrival.

"Mr. Dawson!" Morrison greeted him. "Good to see you! You came at just the right time."

Pride looked at the broker keenly. Morrison was seldom so effusive. In this, as in all other forms of gambling, it paid to know your man.

"Well," Pride drawled, "glad to see you so cheerful. Makes a body think that the old Commodore had sold you the Hudson and Albany for ten thousand dollars."

"Not that," Morrison laughed, "but something almost as good."

He's nervous, Pride thought, damned nervous. . . . I wonder what the devil's up?

Morrison leaned forward confidentially.

"Ever hear of Millville & Western Pennsylvania?"

"No. Never did. What is it?"

"A railroad. Runs from a little town called Millville, which is fifty miles northwest of Pittsburgh. The M. & W. P. started out to build a line to St. Pierre on Lake Erie. They got ten miles of track down and ran out of money. But they operate one train every other day. The line is solidly in the red. That's why I can buy most of the stock for you—enough to control the whole damned railroad."

"That's great," Pride said, his voice heavy with sarcasm. "Move over, Commodore, and make room for another railroad baron—ten miles of him!"

"Now, wait a minute!" Morrison said. "You can get control for almost nothing."

"Which," Pride said, "is just about what it's worth."

"Agreed. But it's going to be worth plenty—and soon. Look, Mr. Dawson, this is a bull market. Let me tell you about Millville. It's a little place, not more than a hamlet. But three years ago some mining engineer stumbled onto the fact that the iron deposits there are richer than those around Pittsburgh itself. To top it off, they found coal there, too. Mountains of it. Ever know Ed Bolley and Rad Waters to go off the deep end? Well, they've built a steel mill there. And Thomas Stillworth, whom you know even better, is dickering for the coal mines right now! Do you know what that means? They'll have to buy that line—and extend it to Lake Erie. And if *you* controlled the line . . ."

"I could hold it and get my price for it," Pride said.

"Exactly. Shall I buy it for you? I can pick up thirty thousand shares for fifty thousand dollars."

Pride frowned thoughtfully.

"Why," he asked quietly, "haven't they bought that line before now?"

Morrison smiled.

"You know how they operate. Penny-pinchers, every one of them. Why would they buy the line and lose money on it before they could use it? Once the steel mill is finished the railroad instantly becomes profitable. And when the coal mines open up . . ."

"I see," Pride mused. "But what's to stop Bolley and the others from by-passing that line and leaving it there to die rather than pay me my price?"

Morrison smiled. Stillworth's man, Warren, had anticipated everything. He turned and opened his desk. From a drawer he took a large map.

"See this?" he pointed. "Those are hills. They call them the Iron Mountains. Here's your line. See where it runs? Through the only decent valley in miles. How else could they get to Lake Erie?"

"What do they want to get to Lake Erie for? It seems to me that the East and England buy damned near all of their stuff."

"True. But, Mr. Dawson, consider what they ship. Coal by the thousands of tons, and pigs of iron. What railroad could compete in point of economy with the Lake barges? Railroad to Lake Erie, barges to Buffalo and along the Canal and then down the Hudson for the East Coast. Barges down the St. Lawrence for the European trade. . . . It's perfect. They'll have to buy your line!"

Pride studied Morrison in silence.

"I'll let you know tomorrow," he said.

"Tomorrow may be too late."

"I'll chance it," Pride said, and left the office.

The rest of the day he was very busy. He called at office after office and asked questions. It checked: every word that Morrison had told him was true. Bolley and Waters' mill was already in partial operation, the great blast furnaces spewing flame into the night. Thomas Stillworth had already sunk his first shaft. And the Millville & Western Pennsylvania was there waiting to be taken.

He went back home at last, his head aching. The situation was so pat as to be almost unbelievable. It was obvious that Stillworth and the others had to have the M. & W. P. Then why in God's name hadn't they bought it already? He did not believe Morrison's explanation; surely those men were too smart to get themselves into a knothole to save a few paltry thousands. . . . Yet, apparently, that was just what they had done. Even the smartest men have their blind spots.

He was saved from the tangle of his thoughts at last by a knock on his door. It was Tim. With him was a woman, a slim dark creature who was decidedly pretty. But it was not the woman who caught Pride's attention, but the boy whom she held by the hand. He was perhaps twelve years old, and his dark beauty was magnetic. Young as he was, his bearing was manly; yet there was in it that same curious grace that Pride envied in Joseph Fairhill. People like this boy made him uneasy; they made him feel like a draft horse beside a racing thoroughbred. This lad was a changeling, a prince born in a peasant's hut. His dark eyes measured Pride with a look that had already found, Pride knew instinctively, few men his equal and none his better.

"This," Tim said with simple pride, "is Lucy—and Lance."

"Glory be!" Pride rumbled. "I'm mighty proud, ma'am. I've heard Tim talk about you for years. And you, son— glad to make your acquaintance. Look, Tim, this calls for a celebration. Had dinner yet?"

"No," Tim smiled, "they just got in two hours ago. Brought them by here first."

"Then you're having dinner with me at Delmonico's."

"Is that anything like Antoine's, Papa?" Lance demanded suddenly.

Pride threw back his head and laughed aloud.

"No, son," he chuckled. "Delmonico's is the best restaurant in New York, but it's not like Antoine's. These Northern cooks just don't have the gift."

"I was never in Antoine's," Lance said gravely. "We never had that much money."

"Lance!" Lucy said.

Lance turned his great dark eyes upon his mother

"Papa said I was always to tell the truth," he said.

"That's right," Pride agreed, "always tell the truth. And your papa's going to have enough money soon to take you anywhere you want to go."

He was busy with his collar, repressing the desire to swear as it put up its usual resistance. Lucy McCarthy crossed over to him and put up her slim hands. Pride saw that they were rough and reddened from hard work. But her fingers were deft, and in half a moment she had the collar fastened and was busy with his cravat.

Then they all went out into the street. Pride hailed a cab and took them to the famous restaurant. He was greeted with marked respect by the headwaiter and led to a large table. Tim noted this fact with some surprise, but after a moment he reconsidered the matter.

Pride's going up, he thought. Why wouldn't he eat in this tony place with all the swells? He's been hating and envying them all his life; now he's set to join them. Join them and show them up. He'll do it, too, unless . . .

The waiter passed them the menu and Pride frowned. It was in French and the only thing he could read on it was *Canvasback duck*. But he made a brave attempt, mangling the French words until young Lance could no longer repress a grin. Pride glared fiercely at the boy, but Lance's answering gaze was calm.

"Hell," Pride growled, "bring us the works! I never could twist my tongue around that lingo. Half the time you don't know what you're getting anyhow."

Tim, who had been only half-listening to Pride, looked at his wife tenderly as he spoke to Pride.

" 'Twas quite a comedown for Lucy to marry me," he said. "She was Brad O'Donnell's daughter, Pride. One of the richest families in Louisiana. She was kind of headstrong—married me even though I was a nobody. Her folks disowned her for it, and I don't blame them a mite. She's been working and starving ever since." His glance fell on his wife. "I'll make it up to you, my dear—before God I will!"

Lucy looked at Tim's rugged, weather-beaten face, with the little lines puckering the corners of his gray eyes. It was a strong face beneath the reddish hair that was graying now, as strong as his short-square, great-thewed body; yet his mouth was as gentle as a woman's and his whole expression radiated kindness. She stretched out her hand across the table.

"Marrying you, Tim," she whispered, "was the wisest and best thing I ever did."

Pride talked little during the rest of the evening. His thoughts were troubled. Tim's better off than I am, he thought bitterly. God, how Lucy loves him! So gentle and sweet and pretty, too—like. . . . His mind was about to form the mental image of Sharon, but he choked off the thought before it was half begun. It was no good to think of that now. He must never think of Sharon again—no, never. Through his own greed he had lost Sharon O'Neil with her spray of golden freckles and her soft brown eyes and the wide sweet mouth atremble with tenderness.

I've sold myself now—right down the river—for round pieces of metal and printed green paper. My God! I must be going crazy to think about money like that.

He shook his big head to clear it and glared down at the creamy dessert that the menu call *Glacé: Pouding Nesselrode*. Not for the life of him could he eat it now, so he downed his black coffee with a gulp and stood up.

"Come on," he said gruffly. "I've got to be getting back now—business. . . ."

Lucy stared at him with a strange expression on her face. If he had divined her feelings, he would have been sick with rage. For the expression in Lucy McCarthy's eyes when she looked at Pride Dawson was—pity.

They got up and left Delmonico's. Pride's voice, as he asked Tim for the address of the rooms he had rented, was actually curt. But Tim knew Pride's moods almost better than did Pride himself, and his friendship for the big man had survived much greater trials. So as soon as they had reached the McCarthys' address on Thirtieth Street, Tim bade Pride a calm good night and gazed quietly after the hansom cab as it drove away.

"What ails him?" Lucy demanded.

"Women or money," Tim said sadly. Then more gently, "Come in, my dear. It's been a long, long time. . . ."

As Lucy entered the doorway on her husband's arm, her cheeks, despite the tall son beside her, were as pink as any bride's.

The next morning, Pride did not go at once to the office of Morrisons, Brokers. Instead, he went first to his barber and went through the ritual of being shaved, steamed and massaged. But he was so preoccupied that he did not even smile as Pierre took down his own china shaving mug with his name blazoned upon its side in golden Gothic letters—though this simple act usually brought him the keenest kind of pleasure. A gilt-lettered shaving mug at Pierre's was perhaps a small thing; but it was almost the equivalent of the Garter in America's new heraldry. With half a glance Pride Dawson could see beside it others bearing the names *Drew, Gould, Fisk, Vanderbilt;* but this morning he had no time for such glances. A fortune lay at his finger tips. The turn of one card and it would be his.

Yet, try as he would, Pride could not shake the feeling that something was wrong. In none of his previous dealings had the outlines of the whole transaction been so clear. Before, there had been ramifications which had to be explored, complications which required ironing out; but here there were none. It was all very simple—much too simple. Damn it all, it should be more troublesome! He had the feeling that the jaws of the trap were there, inches below the bait; but sniff at it and paw at it as much as he would, he could not find them.

He got up slowly from the barber's chair, paid Pierre, and walked out into the sunlight. Then, making one of his characteristically swift decisions, he hailed a cab and drove to the Stillworth mansion.

Malcolm hesitated when Pride asked to see Esther, but he was relieved of the necessity of deciding between the quite contradictory orders given him by his young mistress and her father; for Esther appeared in the hallway before the butler had a chance to make up his mind. Now, thank God, he was out of it and could tell Stillworth, truthfully, that Esther had admitted Pride Dawson herself.

Esther's blue eyes were alight wih pleasure.

"Pride—" she began; but he interrupted her harshly.

"I've got to talk to you," he growled. "Now."

Wonderingly, Esther led him to the blue-glass parlor and sank into a chair, gazing half-fearfully into his face. Pride's expression was bleak, his tone had an edge of controlled ferocity about it. This was not the first time that Esther doubted the wisdom of loving such a man. Then suddenly, with terrible clarity, she knew that she would doubt it again and again; that the price she must pay for her passion was exorbitant: black years of pain and shoreless seas of tears. But, being what she was, she knew also that she would not turn back.

"Your pa," Pride said flatly, "owns most of Millville, doesn't he?"

"Yes," Esther said. "Why?"

"I'll tell you later. What I want to know now is how's he going to get his stuff out of that danged little town?"

Esther thought earnestly. Her knowledge of her father's operations was exceedingly vague.

"There's a railroad," she said at last. "Though, to tell the truth, I don't know much about it."

"The Millville & Western Pennsylvania?" Pride demanded.

Esther's lovely brow knitted with frowning. She made a helpless little gesture with her hands.

"The Millville & Western Pennsylvania? I don't really remember if that's the name of the railroad father's interested in," she hesitated. "I don't know for certain, Pride—but it's something like that."

"Is this railroad finished?" Pride demanded impatiently. "Did your pa say he planned to work on it?"

Esther's face brightened.

"Yes," she said, "he did say that! No, Pride, I'm quite sure it's not finished."

Pride's face split into an enormous grin.

"All right," he chuckled. "Now I've got to go!"

"But, Pride—" Esther protested. She got no further. Pride bent and stopped her protests with his mouth. Then he was gone, shaking the hallway with his heavy stride.

At Morrisons a few minutes later he signed away half his fortune and was given a receipt for the margin he had put up.

"Look," the broker said, "don't be alarmed if this stock declines a bit before it begins to rise. It'll take a while before things hit the upgrade."

"You'll require additional margin, is that it?" Pride demanded.

Morrison frowned.

"Yes," he said, finally. "I'd like to make an exception in this case, Mr. Dawson, because I have every confidence . . ."

"Rot," Pride said. "Any one of these deals can blow up and you know it."

"That's true. And you know how business is; my partners would never understand if I didn't ask for margin in case of a decline."

"Don't fret yourself," Pride said. "You'll get your margin if you need it." Then he turned and left the office, holding the receipt tenderly in his big hands.

A month later Pride Dawson had slightly more than twenty-five hundred dollars left; and he had no intention of touching this last reserve, no matter how much Morrison cried for additional margin. Now, standing in the broker's office, his face mottled with rage, he swore that he was completely insolvent.

"Yesterday," he roared, "I put up my last red cent for margin and still the damned thing drops! And now you're asking for more! Why, you dirty, bloodsucking little leech, I've a good mind to . . ."

Morrison's round face was ashen with fear. He spread his hands wide.

"Mr. Dawson, Mr. Dawson!" he implored, "control yourself! I told you the truth about this stock as far as I knew it. *I* have nothing to gain by tricking you. Why, you've earned this office some of its biggest commissions! Why should I lose one of my best customers?"

Pride's big hands came down slowly to his sides. What Morrison had just said was true. Then what *was* the answer?

Morrison saw his advantage and pressed it.

"Look, Mr. Dawson, somebody's been dumping large blocks of this stock. And not for business reasons, either. Don't you see that nobody stands to gain by forcing a decline? Somebody, Mr. Dawson, is taking a deliberate loss himself in order to get you!"

Pride's face cleared, but a nagging doubt clung like a burr in his mind.

"Suppose," he said, "that Tom Stillworth wants to force it down so's he can get it for nothing?"

Morrison did what he had to do: he covered up for Stillworth. "There're limits even to that. It was low enough in the beginning. Low as it is now, Black Tom would have difficulty financing its rebuilding, unless he wanted to do it out of his own pocket. Nobody would take the risk of putting up funds. And you know Stillworth—he's always cash-poor. He couldn't finance it himself without liquidating some other holdings."

Morrison hoped he had been convincing.

The nagging doubt was gone in Pride's mind now. He had wanted to be sure. If Thomas Stillworth did not stand to gain by the M. & W. P. debacle, that ruled him out and left one other person: Joseph Fairhill. Little Joe had announced that he was out to get Pride, that he would spend more money than Pride could earn in a lifetime, just to see Pride ruined. Well, little Joe had won. But, Pride decided grimly, he was going to pay for his victory, though how and at what price he hadn't at the moment the faintest idea.

"I'm cleaned," he said. "What do I do now?"

"*You* don't have to do anything," Morrison groaned. "But *I* have to try to sell that worthless stock."

"The devil you do! Isn't it mine?"

"Technically, no. All you have is a receipt for your margin. You failed to put up the required additional margin, so the stock reverts to my hands. I have it in my safe. Under the law, I should sell it and return to you whatever I cleared above the margin. But frankly, Mr. Dawson, I hate to try it. I could never unload that stuff now. Yet, I have to sell it—the owners need the money, and I have to recover at least a part of their investment."

Pride looked at the broker. His mind worked slowly. I should buy it now, he thought. Morrison would sell it for two thousand and be glad to get it. Only—it's no good. Who says so? Stillworth? Since when has his mouth been a prayer book? Or little Joe's either? All right, it's no good—for them. Black Tom's got some other way of getting his stuff out of that town; but that doesn't mean somebody else wouldn't want to ship over the M. & W. P. . . . I've got a hunch about this thing. I've always been lucky with things that other people threw away. Like that mine; folks out there said that whole section was played out; but Tim and I made it pay. . . .

"If I could get anything for that stock," Morrison said, "anything at all, I could get the owners off my neck; but as it is . . ."

It's a gamble, Pride thought. If I buy this stock, I'll be

really cleaned—down to five hundred dollars or so. And all I'll have is some pretty gilt-edged paper that's not worth what it cost to print it. But I've been cleaned before—and with that paper I'll control a real railroad. A dead one, but I'll stake my neck that I can bring it back to life!

He said suddenly, "If I were to make you an offer, would you deliver me the stock right now?"

Morrison looked at him in amazement.

"But you just said . . ." he spluttered.

"Never mind what I said. I haven't any money to go on paying margin on a stock that's going to keep on dropping as long as I hold it on the cuff. But I've got two thousand dollars for all the loose stock on that line—providing I get it outright, free and clear! What do you say?"

"That you're crazy, but I'll let you have the whole damned lot if you want it."

"I want it," Pride said and, bringing out his checkbook, wrote a draft for two thousand dollars.

Morrison took the check and, unlocking his safe, drew out the heavy, gilt-encrusted stock certificates. He passed them over to Pride.

"Here you are," he said, "but I'd give my right arm to know why you're buying stock that you know is absolutely no good."

"Call it a hunch," Pride said. "Things don't have to stay no good, do they? That dinky little line just might show a profit—with me running it."

"It might at that," Morrison mused.

"Now," Pride declared grimly, "I've got a job to do. I'm going to call on little Joe Fairhill and show him it's not smart to go after Pride Dawson!"

He turned then and stalked from the office. Morrison sat down thinking: Joseph Fairhill! What on earth makes Dawson think it's Fairhill who manhandled that stock, instead of Black Tom? . . . Oh, well—all I'm praying for is five minutes of uninterrupted peace before my nerves give way!

But the broker was not to be spared further disturbance, for a few minutes later, Esther Stillworth ran in. This in itself was enough to give the little broker acute palpitations. But Esther Stillworth *running!* And she was unmistakably agitated and quite out of breath!

"Pride—Mr. Dawson," she gasped, "where is he?"

"He—he just left, Miss Stillworth," Morrison faltered. "Is there anything I can do for you?"

"Tell me where he went?" Esther panted.

"He said something about seeing Joseph Fairhill," the broker got out.

"Pride—going to see Joe?" Esther demanded. "Why, Mr. Morrison—why?"

"I think he means to kill Mr. Fairhill," he said.

"Oh, my God!" Esther groaned. "But Joseph hardly knows Pride. What reason on earth could Pride have . . ."

"Perhaps you're the reason, Miss Stillworth."

"I?"

"Yes. Mr. Dawson took an awful beating in the market —due, I think, to someone's manipulating some railroad stock. And not for financial gain, either. No one stood to gain by that damned railroad's decline. No, Miss Stillworth, the reasons were personal—and, until this minute, I didn't realize what they were. Mr. Dawson stated quite positively that Mr. Fairhill was responsible. So he must have a reason. Perhaps Mr. Fairhill threatened him . . ."

"Joseph," Esther whispered. "So it was Joseph! And all the time I thought—"

"Yes?" Morrison urged gently.

"That it was my father!"

And you were right, Morrison thought grimly. But what's to be gained by telling you? Black Tom would ruin me, so fast that . . . but this is good. Fairhill's a perfect scapegoat. Particularly with you here to save his neck . . .

"I helped ruin Pride," Esther said miserably. "He asked me about that railroad—the Millville & Western Pennsylvania, wasn't it?"

Morrison nodded.

"Pride asked me about it and I told him that Father was rebuilding the line. It was only this morning that I found out that Father isn't interested in that little road at all—the one Pride mentioned—that the line he's rebuilding is the Millville Valley branch leading south to connect with the Pennsylvania itself. Oh, what a fool I've been!"

"Scarcely that," Morrison murmured. "One doesn't expect a young and lovely woman to have a first-hand knowledge of business. But you can make up a thousandfold in Dawson's behalf for any slight error you may have made."

"How?"

"By saving him from the gallows. That's just where he was walking when he left here. Now, if I were to get you a cab and you were to hurry over to Mr. Fairhill's . . ."

He had no need to complete the sentence, for almost as soon as the words were spoken, Esther was up and hurrying to the door.

That she was able to reach the Fairhill residence long before Pride was due entirely to the confusion in Pride's mind. He was in no hurry. He preferred to stalk along slowly and savor his anticipated vengeance. He walked the entire distance, which took him more than an hour.

Joseph himself opened the door to Esther's insistent knocking. When he saw her his eyes lighted with sardonic joy.

"I'm honored," he said. "And delighted. And—"

"A fool," Esther finished for him. "Didn't you know you couldn't get away with it?"

"You're lovely," Joseph Fairhill said, "and mystifying. But then you always were. Come in, my dearest, and tell me what I can't get away with. Abducting you? Under the circumstances, you could scarcely expect me not to try."

Esther walked through the doorway. Inside the sitting room, she turned, ignoring the graceful gesture that Joseph made toward a large chair.

"Didn't you know that Pride would kill you if you ruined him? Didn't you realize that I would marry him, even if he were blind and crippled as well as poor? Oh, Joe, why did you do it? Now everything's in such a mess! I've got to keep Pride from killing you. And I'll have to wait until he makes some more money before he'll marry me. . . . I shouldn't save you! I should let him—"

"Softly, my dear. In the first place, I didn't ruin Pride Dawson—though I am heartily glad he's done. I had no need to. Your own beloved father accomplished that without my lifting a finger. I sounded out Warren a month ago on the possibility of seeing that Dawson got his—you know, Warren acts for me too. But he only smiled and told me not to worry—that Dawson was already well taken care of. I asked him who was behind it, but he refused to talk. Then, thinking out loud, I said, 'Only one man has as much reason as I to hate Dawson: Black Tom Stillworth.' His answer was, 'Remember that *you* said it—not I.'"

"So," Esther whispered, "it *was* Father."

"Who else? Who had the essential information? A month ago nobody knew about the mills at Millville—or the mines—except your father and his faithful enemies Bolley and Waters. It was only yesterday, when your father relieved Bolley and Waters of their holdings, that the story came out. How could Dawson find out about the M. & W. P. unless Tom Stillworth wanted him to find out? Or conversely, why didn't Dawson find out that Thompson offered your father so large a rebate to ship via the Pennsylvania that it actually became cheaper to ship by road than by barge? If Dawson knew so much about Millville a month ago, he should have known that too. He should have known that the Millville & Western Pennsylvania was going to lie there and rust because nobody was going to need it to ship anything—ever."

"You needn't go on," Esther said quietly. "I'm convinced."

"And now that you are, what shall it be? Port? Sherry? Claret?"

"Nothing, thank you."

"That's right—you don't approve of drinking, I'd forgotten. You used to be frightfully straight-laced—before Dawson. You were something out of Molière—*Les Précieuses Ridicules,* perhaps. A real blue-stocking feminist. It's a pity it took Dawson to teach you to be a woman. I never could. It's quite a change."

"Oh, blazes!" exclaimed Esther. "If we have to spend time in such silly talk, let's go somewhere else. I'm in no mood for witnessing a murder. Besides, Joseph Fairhill, I like you. Just because I'm no longer in love with you, doesn't mean I want you killed. I intend us to go on being friends."

"Friends!" Joseph exploded. "Good God!"

"We'll argue the point later. Come on."

"You expect me to run away from Pride Dawson?"

"If you aren't an idiot—yes."

"Then I'm an idiot. . . . Besides, since you walked into my parlor, I'd like to explore some of those new-found emotions Dawson has uncovered in you—the more animalistic ones. Should be fascinating, don't you think?"

Esther backed away from him.

"Don't you dare!" she snapped.

"Oh, come now," Joseph laughed. "I can be as primitive as Dawson—and I'm a damned sight better-looking."

Then swiftly, deftly, he stepped forward and took her in his arms.

Esther started to struggle, but thought better of it. She knew Joseph. To fight with him would only increase his sense of ironical triumph. So she resorted to the one thing that he could not bear. She allowed him to kiss her, but made no response at all. She was like a statue of wood, her lips cold, unmoving, until at last he drew away his face.

"Finished?" she asked calmly. "Or do you want to play some more games? I have nothing but time."

"Damn you!" Joseph got out. "You aren't human. You've an icicle for a heart, and . . ."

Esther smiled at him.

"Pride doesn't think so," she whispered.

"You—you've given him reason not to?" Joseph's voice was hoarse and unnatural, his usually handsome face distorted with passion. "How much reason, Esther? Tell me, how much?"

"You figure that out for yourself," Esther said mockingly. "Now, if you still feel romantically inclined, let's go for a walk, or a ride—anyway, let's get out of here. Pride'll be here any minute now."

"No!" Joseph snapped. "No! I'll show you. . . ."

Then he dragged her once more into his arms. He tightened his grip about her waist and kissed her hard, trying deliberately to hurt her. It was a long time before she was able to free herself. When he finally released her he stepped back, his eyes widening in his pale face, staring over her shoulder, so that Esther knew at once that the comedy had played on too long, sinking into farce, and now, cruelly, into tragedy itself.

"Pride," she whispered, as she turned. "Pride . . ."

"A scoundrel," Pride said evenly, "and his tart. You two make a mighty pretty pair."

"Pride!" Esther gasped. "You don't understand! Listen, Pride . . ."

"Reckon I don't. I never met a woman like you before. Never knew one who could play a part so well. You had me going. But I made it easy for you, didn't I? I ate up that bill of goods you sold me about that railroad your pa isn't

92

building. I lost my shirt believing you. Hell, I feel sick." He turned upon Joseph, smiling grimly.

"Well, little Joe, you've won. And you can thank her for saving your miserable life. I was going to kill you, but I have a better idea now. I'm going to let you live—live and have her—with her pretty white face and pink mouth that can't tell anything but lies. Birds of a feather—I hope you enjoy yourselves."

He turned and strode away from them, closing the door very softly behind him.

It was still in the room after he had gone. So still that Joseph could hear the half-strangled note of Esther's breathing. He could see her lips trembling uncontrollably as they shaped the name. And when it came out, it was pain-shattered, its fragments cascading down the bright glissando of her sobs.

"Pride!" she wept. "Oh, Pride!"

He stood there woodenly, listening to her cry. There was something familiar about it, as though he had heard it before. Then suddenly, he realized he had—as a drummer boy at Shiloh Church. There had been a raw young recruit there, gut-shot and dying. A man newly wed, with all of his life before him. He hadn't wanted to die and he had cried like that. Out of rage, out of frustration, out of terrible physical agony. Joseph remembered that he had been able to distinguish the different notes of the weeping: the rage and the disappointment had been bearable—but the agony, no. That was not bearable. Listening to it, he had felt sick, death-sick with the green taste of bile in his mouth. And it went on and on until an officer had taken out his Navy Colt and silenced it, butt forward toward the young recruit's hand. The quiet, afterwards, was like a benediction.

But he couldn't do that now. There was nothing he could do—absolutely nothing but stand there and listen to Esther's dreadful weeping, until even standing became impossible, so that he knelt beside her and whispered clumsily:

"Hush, Esther . . . hush, darling, hush. . . ."

CHAPTER SEVEN—1870

BY NINE O'CLOCK the next morning Pride Dawson had covered a good portion of lower New York in his wanderings. It was Sunday. Pride stood looking with uncomprehending gaze at a sign that read: *Largest Schooner of Lager Beer in the City—Five Cents.* It showed an immense stein of foaming beer with a five-cents sign on its sides surrounded by human figures so tiny that the stein dwarfed them completely. But, if anyone, a moment later, had asked Pride Dawson what it said, he would have been unable to answer, for though his eyes were fixed upon it, he did not see the sign at all.

He moved on slowly until he reached Catherine Slip between Cherry and South streets, and there he paused once more. The noise and confusion broke in on his reverie and he looked toward the open-air market on the east side of the Slip. The Canarsie fishing boats were in, and the broad board counters resting on the heads of two barrels were alive with a mass of writhing eels.

"Come an' get 'em!" the eel vendors were crying. "You sees 'em alive. You sees 'em skun and you knows what you're agettin'!"

The crowds about the counters consisted of people from all walks of life. Pride saw several men whom he knew— millionaires, by all accounts—examining the slippery eels shoulder to shoulder with housewives from the Whiskey Wards.

The market was incredibly noisy. The people in the crowd chattered and laughed as they made their purchases or watched the street musicians and the dancing Negroes. A dance contest was in progress and the Negro who won was rewarded with a live eel. The dancers had a uniquely native grace and a pronounced African sense of rhythm. Pride moved closer, mingling with the jostling, laughing

94

crowd. But unlike the other bystanders, he did not laugh at the wild abandon of the dancers.

I would have laughed yesterday, he thought grimly, but today's different. It's strange how seeing Esther with Joe hurt. I don't love that palomino filly. Guess it sort of hurt my pride. First time I've ever really been whipped. Before, I always left women when I was tired of 'em, and threw money away for the hell of it. But that little Joe really is something. I'll get him one day, though. Him and her both.

Sharon, now. I could go to her. She'd marry me tonight without a dime. Only I can't crawl in like a whipped hound dog with my tail between my legs. I've got to come riding with my saddle bags ajingle. I've got to come back high and fine. Oh Ma, when you gave me this name, you never told me how much I'd have to pay for pride. . . . Sometimes I think it's not worth it.

He turned his head in another direction, to where an eel vendor was selling dried and smoked eels. The crowd before his stall was smaller, consisting mostly of robed and queued Chinese to whom the dried eels were a great delicacy. As Pride watched, one of them made his purchase and started homeward, only to be set upon by a crowd of toughs who brandished knives. Their object, Pride knew, was not to do the ancient and dignified Chinese gentleman bodily harm, but merely to cut off his pigtail. The old man fled with a speed amazing in one of his years, and as he disappeared around the corner with the hoodlums hot on his heels, Pride felt a surge of fellow feeling for the old man.

It's not right for them to do that, he mused. Just because the old Chink looks funny to us. A man can't help being a stranger somewhere. Me, I'm always a stranger. I've been chased and kicked enough. I've got to be the top dog somehow. Just like Sharon used to say about the colored people. They got a right to live, too, same as me.

He moved away from the noise and turned into South Street. It was quieter than the Slip, for the markets were mostly vegetable stalls and second-hand clothing stores. As Pride passed an odds and ends store, the dealer cried out to him:

"Genuine Japanese lacquers, right from Japan—six cents apiece, two for ten, mister. They're genuine!" And as

Pride moved the man switched to: "Here you are, mister! Jumbo for only three cents!" Pride did not even glance at the tiny brass elephants, intended for watch charms, which the storekeeper held out. He walked on, his face morose, past the man exhibiting tapeworms preserved in alcohol and offering Doctor Tom's Guaranteed Worm Medicine, and the peripatetic dentist before his board counter, as ready to sell spectacles as to extract teeth. He brushed out of his way an alleged sailor who offered him smuggled lace, and moved toward the end of the street where the cunning oyster men were offering "Real Coney Island clams up from Coney Island this morning," or genuine Rockaway oysters. Pride heard them laughing scornfully at one of their more effete fellow vendors who had the temerity to offer such "foreign" delicacies as Blue Points or Little Necks or Saddle Rocks.

It was after nine o'clock now, and the police were arriving to clear the streets of the merchants to make way for the churchgoers.

There was nothing for Pride to do now but go home. His few hundred dollars would pay for his rent and food for months if he were careful, but Pride had no intention of remaining in the city that long. He would head again for California, where money could still be made quickly, and afterwards he would return. He would make no more mistakes. The next time he would be ready to play the game on even terms—and when he won he would show no mercy.

He was conscious suddenly of being intensely hungry, so he selected a cheap restaurant and entered. A burly waiter in a remarkably filthy apron passed him a flyspecked menu. On the tablecloth were the mute reminders of every repast eaten on it in the last two weeks. Pride suspected that the tablecloths had once been white, but it was merely a suspicion.

Finally, he ordered roast pork and boiled potatoes and black coffee.

After an interval long enough for the cook to have prepared a nine-course dinner for twenty stevedores, the waiter brought back a greasy vile-smelling mess. To his surprise, Pride found that he could not eat it. He had eaten worse food in the past—hardtack and rancid bacon and meat covered with green mold. But that was long ago. . . .

What's happened to me? he thought angrily. I've become

a swell—really high-toned and no mistake. I've got to have it printed in French and cooked just the right number of minutes. I've got to have everything like that: silk and broadcloth shirts, and tailored suits. I've got to wear diamonds down my front and have the waiters bow and call me Mr. Dawson. I found the kind of life I was born to live and got used to things I didn't know existed. I let Sharon and Esther teach me ways I used to laugh at and call womanish—and now I can't get along with less! I need soft living now—silk pillows and silken women that smell of imported perfume. . . . There ought to be some way to get back fast. I'm thirty-seven years old now, and it's time to steady down and climb to the top and stay, dammit! Stay . . .

He tossed a bill to the table and walked out. Half an hour later he was back at his lodgings.

But when he entered his rooms he found that a visitor was awaiting him. It was not, as he had half-expected, Esther; it was Thomas Stillworth himself.

Pride frowned. Whatever had brought Stillworth here, it almost certainly meant more trouble.

"Come in! Come in!" the old man cackled. "Esther told me of your misfortune." She had told him, too, that Pride blamed Joseph Fairhill for his ruin, and this had pleased the old financier almost as much as it astonished him.

"Got a job for you, son. I want to give you another chance. You've good qualities—and everybody goes broke once or twice before he succeeds. I did myself. Don't let it fret you. Yessir, I've just the job for you, and you're just the man for the job."

"What's the catch?" Pride growled.

"There isn't any. Let's put our cards on the table, Pride. I haven't a thing against you, except that I don't think you're the right man for Esther. Well, I understand that she and Joseph have made up, so there's no basis for any further quarrel between us."

Pride waited quietly for him to go on.

"Didn't I always give you the right tips before? Did that sound like the act of a man who hated you? I'll do it again, because you're the kind of man I need in my organization. Can't we shake on it and be friends again? There are plenty of other girls around besides that daughter of mine. Anyway, she'd be as bad for you as you'd be for her. . . . This is business, son. Let's let bygones be bygones, shall we?"

Pride hesitated a moment longer, then slowly put out his hand. He needed a job, and this might be his big chance to recoup all he had lost.

"All right," he said. "We're friends. Now what about this job?"

"It's in Millville," Stillworth said. "You know that I have—ah—acquired certain properties there?"

"A steel mill," Pride said, "from Bolley and Waters. And coal mines."

"So you do know. All right. Now when I—ah—purchased the Bolley Mill, I found its financing in a shocking state. Those gentlemen had overextended themselves. Why, the wages they were paying were fantastic! And you should see the company houses they provided for the workers! Palaces, virtual palaces!"

"So," Pride said, "you cut the wages. What did you do about the houses?"

"Nothing. There was nothing I could do. But I took over a mess. That tomfool idea that Ed Bolley has of coddling the laboring classes just won't work. The minute I cut the wages down to a reasonable figure, the bloody beggars struck!"

A man, Pride thought, could starve to death on your reasonable figure; but what business is that of mine?

Aloud he said: "You want me to break the strike?"

"Exactly! I'll pay you five hundred dollars a month—and give you a bonus of a thousand dollars if you succeed."

"And if I fail?"

"You still get your five hundred. But you won't fail. I'll give you an open account for expenses. Hire anyone you need. Buy anyone who needs to be bought. Spend money—but break that strike!"

This, Pride mused, must be mighty important to him.

"I've got to think about it. When do I have to let you know?"

"Right now. Today. It's important, Pride. I can't afford to wait."

"Then let me think a minute. Can I hire the Pinkertons?"

"Of course. And I'm sending McCarthy with you. I hired him two weeks ago."

Pride stared at Stillworth, his jaw dropping.

"You hired Tim? Why? I didn't think—"

"That he'd come to work for me? Why? Because he has principles, that friend of yours? Well, he did come and he asked me most politely. There's something about working on garbage scows that blunts a man's principles. Tim wants to go up, like any sensible man. He said to tell you that he'd try it your way for a while. Now, you go ahead and think. Take ten minutes: that's enough!"

He sat there, gazing first at Pride's frowning face and then out of the window. He was small and spiderlike and acutely watchful.

Think! He laughed inside his mind, what thinking do you need, Pride Dawson? *I* do the thinking. *I* have thought. Nobody else in my position would hire you now. But I will. And why? Beacuse you're strong as an ox and a scoundrel, to boot. I like that. A man always knows where he stands with a blackguard. Ethical people are unpredictable. Besides, damn your hide, I like you. I need just such an assistant as you to do what I want done, now and later. And, it takes you away from Esther—how easily you swallowed that story about her reconciliation with Joseph! If I didn't have her locked in her room, she'd be here now. . . . Perhaps you'll actually break the strike—which would be good. And one of those mill workers might blow your head off, which would be better; then I wouldn't have to worry about you any more. Any way it works out, I win. If you come back this time, I'll send you out to Pittsburgh, and then to Chicago. . . . Why don't you stop wasting my time? You know you're going to accept.

"I'll do it," Pride growled. "When do I leave?"

"Now. I took the liberty of having Terence come upstairs to pack a bag for you. Here's your ticket and Tim McCarthy will meet you at the station."

"You were damned sure of me, weren't you?" Pride said.

"Of course. You've tasted soft living, Pride. You've got to make your start again. I knew you'd jump at the chance."

Outside the train window, a dirty, cold drizzle was falling. The clouds were slate-gray and ugly, and the gusts that blew through the end of the car were bitter cold.

Pride sprawled in his seat, his big frame loose-muscled and relaxed, but his face was frowning.

"I don't like it," Tim said.

"You said that before. It's a job, isn't it?"

"I took this job because I need the money, but now I don't know. . . . Some jobs are just too dirty, Pride," Tim said quietly. "We were workers ourselves once. Have you forgotten how it was? Do you think you'd like to come home at night with your whole body one long ache, and see your kids hungry—and not enough pay to buy 'em food? A man can be just so mean. I can't picture myself beating down a man who's fighting for his life. I haven't got that kind of meanness in me. Nobody—nobody at all, Pride—has got the right to live high and fine when the house he lives in, the food he eats, the carriage he rides in, and the clothes on his back are bought with human blood. Nobody, Pride—not Stillworth, not Ed Bolley—not even you."

Pride looked at him.

"Who said anything about beating?" Pride asked. "Black Tom give me a drawing account. Money talks, Tim. I'm going to see the ringleaders and slip 'em a fast dollar. Get 'em to call it off. I'm not anxious to break anybody's skull. It's not necessary. Just put a little cash here and there where it'll do the most good."

"You think that everybody's got his price, don't you?" Tim said.

"Think? I know it!"

Tim looked out of the dirt-filmed window pane, at the rain that was changing to sleet, the trees trailing fantastic icicles.

"I reckon you're right," he said. "Only, sometimes it isn't money."

Pride grunted. The short sound held all the contempt in the world.

They passed through Pittsburgh and transferred to the Millville Valley Branch line, which Thomas Stillworth owned. Its cars were older, dirtier and more dilapidated than any Pride had ever seen. It ran northward among the hills through country of depressing bleakness, wind-whipped under a murky sky. Here and there shanties clung to the hillside, black against the patches of snow, and the smoke plume lay back over the train and shadowed them.

About two miles out of Millville itself, a crude bridge spanned a high gorge. It was made of rough-hewn timbers, and the engineer brought the bell-funneled locomotive to a pace slower than a man could walk, and crept across. Even so, the bridge creaked and swayed dangerously.

They puffed and groaned into the shanty shed of a station, and Tim and Pride got down, looking about them. The first thing Pride looked for was the other tracks, running northward toward Lake Erie. He put his hand to his breast pocket, and felt the stiff, gilt-edged stocks; then he looked back at the other tracks—the Millville & Western Pennsylvania tracks. His line! He owned a railroad! Even if the line were dead, it was something tangible. Perhaps, some day, he would revive it.

Millville was a pattern of blacks and grays. Even the snow was sooted into dirty grayness, and the single main street was an unrelieved sea of black mud. The houses, Stillworth's "palaces," were new; but aside from the fact that under the film of smoke and grime the remains of one thin coat of watery paint could be seen, they were like company houses everywhere, not to be compared in actual comfort to even the packing-box hovels of Shantytown.

There was no one at the station to meet them, so they picked up their valises and plodded up the street, ankle-deep in the icy mud. Now and again, the bearded face of a man, red-eyed and gaunt, would be pressed briefly against a window pane, or sometimes Pride and Tim could see a hollow-cheeked woman with brooding fear tugging at her mouth. But there was nobody in the street. From the skies there still poured a mixture of sleet, snow and rain—and soot, from the fires of the blast furnaces that Stillworth's foremen were desperately keeping banked against the day when the strike would end.

They could see the mill now, rows of tall, double-roofed sheds, with great stacks pointing black skeletal fingers into the lowering sky. Wisps of inky smoke which had clung to their tops were borne downward by the searching wind. The piles of coal to feed the maws of the furnaces were half-covered with snow, and the slag dump was ash-gray and cold, while the little slag train waited beside it, its great bell-shaped dump-cars filling up with the drifting snow.

Outside the mill, Pride could see a little knot of men, black pigmies against the dirty whiteness, their breaths

101

steaming from their nostrils in streamers that rose about their heads like clouds. But Pride paid them no attention. He looked about until he found what he sought: the manager's house, an ugly gray two-storied structure, tortured into fabulous cupolas, wings, buttresses, and ornamented with that peculiar scroll-sawed fretwork that was later to be called American Gothic. It was a house of fantastic ugliness, but to Pride it was beautiful.

He and Tim waded through the slush and mud up to its doors, and pounded the brass knocker with half-frozen fingers. They were admitted by a tall, thin man with a worried expression.

"I'm Dawson," Pride growled, "this is McCarthy. You're John Bently?"

"Right," Bently said. "And am I glad to see you! Come in, won't you, and warm yourselves."

Pride strode forward at once, but Tim gazed down ruefully at his mudcaked trousers. John Bently saw the glance.

"Come in," he repeated. "We're quite used to mud."

He led them through the hallway and paused at the stairway.

"Tabby," he called, "the gentlemen have come!" Then, turning to them, he explained, "My wife—Tabitha."

Mrs. Bently came down the stairway at once. She was a plump, ugly woman whom her husband obviously adored.

"My!" she gasped, "you're all wet! Bring your bags upstairs and get into something dry."

They followed her up the long stairway and waited while she opened a door.

"This will be your room while you're here," she said. "As soon as you've finished changing, come right down so we can talk!"

The room was comfortably furnished, with a bed and chairs and a highboy, as tasteless and ugly as the house itself. There was a washstand in the corner, but the room was so cold that neither Pride nor Tim was tempted to use it.

Changed into dry clothing, they rejoined the Bentlys in the parlor and took their seats in a wilderness of frostbitten rubber plants, gilt-framed pictures of the entire Bently family, massive horsehair furniture, faded drapes, and sprays of brittle wax flowers.

Pride looked at John Bently wonderingly. How had this

gentle, quiet man ever become boss of a steel mill? He had anticipated meeting a burly, cigar-smoking individual, heavy of fist and tread, but John Bently was quite different.

Bently saw the look.

"I was hired by Mr. Waters, Mr. Dawson," he said. "Mr. Stillworth kept me on, though he doesn't know me . . . I doubt that he would hire a man of my type."

"I didn't—" Pride began.

"I know. But I could see you were puzzled. You're right. I'm not the man for the job. My resignation will be on Mr. Stillworth's desk in the morning. . . . Oh, I could do well enough if given a free hand. I could make the mill pay and produce."

"How?" Pride said.

"By paying the workers even more than Bolley and Waters paid them. By adding to their pay when they produced more than a set quota. You see, gentlemen, I quite agree with the strikers—which is the reason I must resign."

"I see," Pride said heavily.

"They're good people," Tabitha Bently put in, "and that mill is so dangerous! Why, in less than a month, three men have been killed and five more crippled for life, not to mention minor injuries."

Bently looked at Pride.

"Might I ask what you propose to do, Mr. Dawson?"

"I'll see the ringleader," Pride said, "and talk to him man to man. I'll get him to call it off—pay him, if necessary."

John Bently smiled a slow, quiet smile.

"Stepan Henkja is your man," he said. "But paying him off won't work."

"Why not? Doesn't he need the money?"

"Terribly. But not that much. Not enough to take your thirty pieces of silver, Mr. Dawson."

"No harm in trying, is there?"

"None."

"Then where'll I find Henkja?"

"Third house from the end. You'll like him. He's a wonderful man. He's a university graduate—educated abroad, of course. But I'm sure you'll find him a capital sort."

Pride stood up.

"That remains to be seen," he said evenly. "Coming, Tim?"

"Yes," Tim said wearily, "I'm coming."

"I have some boots," John Bently said, "that Mr. Mc-Carthy could use. I'm afraid I have nothing to fit you, Mr. Dawson."

"It doesn't matter," Pride said. "A little more mud won't hurt me."

Outside, however, it had grown much colder, so that Pride did not need the boots after all. By skirting the edge of the street, he was able to find spots where the mud had frozen into stonelike hardness and he arrived at Henkja's house with his feet almost dry.

Stepan Henkja opened the door and motioned to them to enter. He was a short, powerfully built man, so broad across the chest and shoulders that he seemed almost square.

"Yes?" he said quietly. "What is it that you want?"

"Look, Mr. Henkja—" Pride began, but he was interrupted by the sound of coughing from the other room. It was an ugly sound, racking and convulsive. It went on for several minutes before it subsided into a low, pitiful moaning.

"My wife," Henkja explained simply. "She's dying. Lung sickness and hunger. The one is never without the other."

"Then you should see my point," Pride said. "End this strike. Go back to work. Then she can have food and medicines."

"So?" Stepan Henkja spread wide his hands. "Even when we work we are hungry. It's better to go more hungry for a while and afterwards have enough. Medicine, you say? She is so sick now, because working I could not get her food enough or a coat to keep her warm. She will die, my poor Magda, if I work or if I do not. Better then to try for what a man should have, is it not so?"

Pride frowned heavily. Ma died like this, he thought bitterly. Tim's right. Some jobs are just too dirty.

"You want to save your wife, Mr. Henkja?" he said.

Stepan Henkja nodded.

"That you know. But how?"

"By calling off this strike. I can pay you enough so that you can send her away—to a good hospital, with doctors and medicines and good food."

Henkja studied Pride curiously.

"You say this thing," he said. "I should take your money

104

and go and say to the others: 'Go back. Go back and die as you died before. Blind your eyes with the steel splashes. Go back and work all day in the heat and come out into the cold and die. Remain hungry because you cannot buy food. Watch the babies grow up with a softness in the bones—or with big bellies and legs like broomstraws.' Is it this you are asking me?"

"I'm asking you to save your wife's life!"

"My wife. While other men's wives die. I know my Magda. She could not live a life bought at such a price. The shame would break her heart. No, Mr.—"

"Dawson. Pride Dawson."

"Mr. Dawson. What you ask of me is a thing I cannot do."

"Then there's no use talking any more," Pride growled. "Come on, Tim."

"Wait," Tim said shortly. Then his hand went into his pocket and came out with some bills. "For your wife," he said to Henkja. "No strings. Take it and keep fighting and I hope to God you win!"

Outside in the snow, the anger and the shame inside Pride Dawson were bitter as wormwood. And because his own part in the matter was something he dared not face, he turned savagely upon Tim.

"That was a damnfool thing to do!" he snarled. "S'posing Stillworth finds out?"

"I'm damned if I care!" Tim said quietly. "Looking at you right now makes me sick to my stomach."

"Then be sick and be damned!" Pride said, and strode away, leaving Tim behind him.

That night he took a bottle of whiskey from Bently's cabinet and got drunk. When Tim came in, he found Pride sprawled out in a chair, his eyes glazed, his lips sagging.

"I'm quitting," Tim said. "I've been in the houses. All the houses. Down South, we take better care of a hound dog! Have you ever seen a nine-year-old child that can't stand up because her bones are rotten—hunger-rotten? I saw that tonight, Pride. I heard the women cry. I listened to men tell me about it—no goggles while they're working around the casting molds! Always hungry, always too tired, always driven—even Bently can't do anything with his straw bosses because Black Tom Stillworth sent 'em here!

Oh, God damn his black soul to bitter hell and may he burn forever! I'm quitting, you hear me? Quitting!"

"I hear you. You're quitting. You said that before."

Tim was almost weeping now.

"How can you do it! They're our kind of folks, Pride! Foreigners or not, they're poor folks—like we were. How, Pride! Tell me: how?"

Pride looked at the flames flickering in the grate.

"I've been poor too long, Timmy boy," he said. "I'm sorry for these poor devils, but I've got a job to do. I've got a chance to come up once more. I'm taking that chance, Tim. These hunkies are cold and overworked and starving —but better them than me. I'd rather their kids go hungry than a son of mine. He's got to have the best. He's going to have the best, no matter what I have to do."

Tim looked at Pride. He was trying to think of something to say, words to express a disgust that was bottomless. But there were none.

"I'm not leaving, Pride," he said slowly. "I'm staying here. But I'm against you now. I'm on their side. And I'm going to fight you to the last ditch. I'm warning you!"

"I heard you," Pride said.

The next morning Pride took the train to Pittsburgh. When he returned, he brought with him two carloads of the filthiest, most nondescript specimens of humanity that Tim had ever seen. He also had fifty Pinkerton detectives, every one of them armed with a shotgun, sling-shot or revolver.

He marched his motley crew up to the knot of men before the mill.

"We're starting up again," he said. "Those of you who want to, can join us. Those who don't, had better go home peacefully. We don't want any trouble. We just aim to make steel!"

The men before the gate huddled together under the leaden sky. The wind whipped down in gusts, driving the snow before it. One man left the others and sped away toward the houses. Then, as Pride's strikebreakers moved forward, other workers began to gather. He could see them coming, looking like black ants against the surface of the snow.

But he moved forward steadily at the head of his line toward the men who stood in the driving snow-gusts before the gate. The wind came down crying. It sounded to Tim's ears like a woman keening for her dead.

They were very close when someone threw a lump of coal. It struck a Pinkerton agent on the head, felling him. Immediately the air was filled with flying coal.

"Don't shoot!" Pride roared to the Pinkertons, but he might as well have addressed the wind. He heard the deep, dull, slow crack of revolver fire, and the boom of the shotguns. Then there were black objects in the snow, sprawled out limply, and from under them thick pools of blood started spreading, steaming in the frosty air.

Tim started running toward the struggling knot of men, but before he could reach it, the issue was decided. There was one brief surge forward. A tall youth reached Pride and tried to bring a length of pipe against the side of his head, but Pride ducked quickly aside. The Pinks fired once more. There were other black mounds in the snow, and the men of Millville ran off, zigzagging through the snow while the Pinks knelt and fired. So strong was the wind and snow swirl, that most of their shots missed.

Tim could see Pride, roaring like an angry bull, running after the young man who had struck at him. Tim raced after them, gaining steadily, so that he was close by when the youth disappeared into one of the company-built hovels with Pride hard upon his heels.

Inside the house it was dark, but Pride put out his hands and caught the young man. They swayed back and forth, splintering the flimsy furniture until Pride was aware suddenly of other hands tugging feebly at his coat. He released the boy, and turned his attention to his new opponent. Pride's big hands encircled a thin throat and squeezed hard, but a woman's voice shrieked:

"He's blind! Don't kill him, he's blind!"

Pride turned the man loose, and at that moment Tim entered the room. They heard the scrape of a brimstone match, and a lamp spread its smoky glow about the room.

The man Pride had been choking was very old; he wore a dirty bandage around his head and over his eyes. Wordlessly, the young man walked over to where he lay whimpering on the floor, and took the bandage off.

Pride felt the slow sickness spreading through his middle, as he saw that the old man had no eyes. There was a

cavernous hole that ran from socket to socket without a
break—the bridge of the nose gone, where the molten steel
had burnt through.

Pride took a step backward, glancing warily at the thin
youth who panted from exhaustion in the corner, then
again his eyes, against his will, shifted to the shattered face
of the old man.

It was then that Tim stepped forward. He drew his right
fist back and smashed it with all his force into Pride's
mouth. Pride's lips broke under the impact, the blood running down over his chin, but his hands hung heavily at his
sides.

Again Tim hit him, pivoting off his forward foot and
putting his weight behind the blow. Pride crashed against
the wall, then came upright slowly, but he did not raise his
hands.

"Fight, damn you!" Tim wept, his red face tear-streaked
and working, "you lousy bastard, fight!"

Slowly, Pride shook his head.

"No, Tim," he said huskily, "I've got no fight left in me.
Go on now—leave me be."

"Leave you be!" Tim muttered. "I'll leave you be all
right!" Then he swung again, hooking his left to the side of
Pride's head, then following it with his right so that the big
man's head rolled on his neck as he hung there, taking his
punishment and making no effort to defend himself. It was
finished after a moment by the Pinkertons, who broke in
and seized both of Tim's arms.

He struggled furiously in their grip, his eyes blinded with
tears. The Pinks looked into Pride's badly battered face:

"What'll we do with him, Mr. Dawson? You want us to
rough him up a bit?"

Wearily, Pride shook his head.

"No," he muttered. "Just put him on a train for New
York—and see that he doesn't get off before it's out of the
state. He used to be my best friend."

Then he turned and left the house. Outside in the darkness the torches flared as Millville gathered up her dead.
Pride walked through the snow toward the Bentlys' house,
his head bowed, his footsteps dragging.

John Bently stood on the porch with Pride's suitcase in
his hand.

"There's an empty house at the end of the row," he said,

quietly. "I'll send over some coal for the grate and some bedding."

"I—I don't get you," Pride mumbled through his swollen lips.

"I think you do. This house is still mine for a day or two. And while it is, it'll shelter no murderers under its roof."

Then he turned on his heel and strode back into the house. Pride stood there for a long time with the snowflakes whitening his hair. Then he put out his hand and picked up the bag.

Some jobs, he thought slowly, bitterly, are just too dirty. . . . And once more he started walking through the darkness that filled the world.

CHAPTER EIGHT—1870

IN THE IRON GRATE the fire burned feebly, and the room was cold. Pride stood by the window looking out into the night through the thick snow-swirl. There was nothing anywhere to be seen. His bag lay unopened beside the low bed, and his face was still unwashed. Small red streaks extended from the corners of his mouth where Tim's hard fists had smashed his lips. His head ached dully, both from fatigue and from his efforts to keep from thinking. It would not do to think of black mounds lying like piles of old rags in the snow—and under them the thick, spreading flow. . . . He must lie down and get some rest; he must sleep. Sleep? The bitter laughter rumbled in his throat, but his broken mouth would not open wide enough to let it out. Sleep—yes, sleep —and be haunted by a raw, red hole where a man's eyes had been, and hear again Tim's voice weeping: "Fight, you lousy bastard, fight!" . . . "Ever see a nine-year-old child that couldn't stand because her bones are rotten—hunger-rotten?" And other voices: "Save my wife while other men's wives die? I know my Magda. She would not have her life at such a price. . . ." "This house is still mine for a day or two. And while it is, it'll shelter no murderers under its roof. . . ."

No murderers. No murderers like big Pride Dawson—a black devil with bitter hell gnawing at his entrails and the blood of innocent men gagging in his throat. If he could give way like Tim, it would be better. If he could cry and rave and let it out, it would be some relief. But there were bands of iron wrapped around his heart, welded there by thirty-seven years of struggle, and though he burst asunder, he could not weep.

He was aware, after a time, that someone was knocking at his door. The pounding had been going on for some time before it penetrated into his consciousness. Slowly, stiffly, he turned and went to the door and opened it. Stepan Henkja stood before him in the snow.

"Come in," Pride growled.

"Thank you," Henkja said. He strode into the room and stood there looking at Pride.

"I came to tell you that you win," he said. "We cannot fight guns. Tomorrow the men will come back to work. But it is only this time you have won. Perhaps the next time also—and the next. But you cannot win forever, Dawson; nothing that is evil ever can."

Pride did not answer.

"I also want to thank you," Henkja continued. "I heard you order those—those devils not to shoot. I don't think you meant it to be like—it was."

"I didn't," Pride mumbled through his swollen lips.

"I feel sorry for you," Stepan Henkja said. "You mean to rise in life and your methods are not pretty. You will rise, I think. All alone you will rise and maybe reach the top while you still have your youth and strength. But one day you will be old and tired, and the packs will gather. And you will lie there in your den, listening to them howl in the darkness waiting to pull you down. It will be a lonely life, for the mountain-top is always lonely. And every man's death is lonely, too, for it is a thing that a man can do just once and always by himself. But I hate to think of yours, Dawson, because you will be more alone than any man can bear to be, with no one there to stretch out a comforting hand. Yes, it will be like that. . . ."

Then he turned and went out. The fire leaped and flared as the door opened and closed behind him.

After he was gone, Pride took off his coat and stretched out upon the bed. It groaned under his weight. He lay there a long time in the darkness watching the fire-shadows flicker against the ceiling. How long it was he never knew, but it was more than an hour—perhaps even two after Henkja's departure—when the knocking sounded once more.

He got up groaning, feeling the weariness in his limbs like a weight of lead. His whole body was one big ache and the pain inside of him was slow-smoldering like the fire in the grate.

He pushed open the door. His thickened lips came apart, but he said nothing. At that moment there was nothing to be said!

"Well," Esther Stillworth whispered, "aren't you going to ask me in?"

He stood there a moment longer, looking from her slim form in its greatcoat of Russian sable to the Cossack fur hat that crowned her silver-blonde hair, and finally to the horses that stood reined to the sleigh, their breaths pluming under the night sky.

Esther saw the glance.

"I almost had to buy that thing to get here," she said. "The train stalled just across the bridge."

Wordlessly, Pride stood aside and held open the door. Esther came in and sat down before the fire. The snowflakes clung to the rich fur, making her seem a little unreal, like a princess out of a Northern fairy tale, and the fireglow flickered across her face and filled her eyes with somber lights.

Pride poked up the fire and added more coal. It leaped and crackled derisively.

"Pride . . ." Esther said at last.

"Yes, Esther?"

"I—I've come to you. I'm not going back. Not alive."

Don't say that, Pride was thinking. Don't talk about living. There are men dead, Esther, gun-shot and stiff, lying in the little houses. Don't talk, Esther. This is no time for talking. Don't chatter about love or life or tomorrow. It's not decent. Be still and bow your head. . . .

"There's an explanation for what you saw," Esther continued. "I could tell you about it, but you wouldn't believe me."

Pride heard her words, but they only half-penetrated.

Explain? Explain what? Oh—about you and little Joe. But that was a thousand years ago. I forgot it. You kissed him; maybe you bedded with him. I don't know. I don't know and I don't give a damn. I don't want to hear it. All I can hear is the women crying in those little houses over the bodies of their dead. . . .

"But you must believe me, Pride—you must! Morrison told me you were out to kill Joseph. I couldn't let that happen. Oh, my darling, do you think I could bear to stand by and let you be hanged?"

But I should be hanged, Pride thought. There's blood on the snow, Esther. Blood that I spilled. I killed before and it didn't bother me, because that was against armed men who could shoot back—not against men with empty hands hanging down . . . not men with nothing but lumps of coal with which to fight. . . .

"Besides, Joseph was innocent! It was Father who ruined you, Pride! I have proof; he admitted it to me himself!"

She had his attention now. He looked at her, his eyes widening in his battered face.

"Your—your pa! Why?"

"Because he didn't want me to marry you. I went to Joe to try to get him out of your way, but he wouldn't leave. Instead he grabbed me and kissed me and then you came in. It was nothing, Pride. Can't you see it was nothing? Don't you know how much I love you?"

"I see," he muttered thickly and turned his face toward the fire. Esther gave a little gasp and sprang up at once.

"You're hurt! Your face! Oh, Pride, my poor darling!"

"Don't talk about my face," Pride said. "Men have been killed here tonight, Esther. Poor men, hungry men. And I killed them!"

"I know. I heard about it. One of the detectives told me. But you didn't kill them, Pride. The man admitted that you tried to stop them from firing."

"I killed them. I brought those bastards here."

"But you didn't know, Pride—you didn't know."

"Will that give those women back their husbands? Will that put food in those orphan kids' bellies? Just because I didn't know?"

112

She stood up then and came toward him, her face tender in the firelight.

"Pride," she whispered, "don't think about it now. Not any more tonight. Afterward you can make amends. But tonight is mine—no, ours. Yours and mine. Don't take it away from me because of this. Not over this or for any other reason."

"No!" Pride said hoarsely, "no!"

"We can be married in the morning, if you want. What does the ceremony matter—it won't make us belong to each other any more than we do tonight."

"No!" Pride got out, the word strangling in his throat. He was filled with rage; he was a man of huge appetites, of gigantic lusts; but tonight he wanted no woman. Tonight it would be a kind of blasphemy to make love in the presence of those dead.

"Pride," Esther whispered. "Please, Pride."

"Afterwards," he said, "not before. I don't want you like this." It was a makeshift reason, and not what he meant at all. It was an excuse, a means toward escape, and even it failed him.

Esther bent and picked up his coat.

"Then we'll go and find a minister. Do you love me now, Pride? Tell me, do you?"

"Yes," he muttered. And in a curious way he did. He loved her as he had loved many women: happily, thoughtlessly, with his body's splendid vigor. Not as he loved Sharon. He loved Sharon with his heart, perhaps even with his soul.

"There isn't any preacher in this town who would marry us," he told Esther flatly. "Not after what happened."

"Then we'll go to another town. There's one about ten miles farther north. Come, Pride."

He allowed her to take his hand and lead him out into the snow. He helped her up and took the reins himself. The horses moved off through a dead world, even their hoofbeats muffled into soundlessness.

They found a minister in the next town, who heard their vows in dressing gown and slippers and a red flannel nightshirt, while his wife stood by and held the lamp. A twenty-dollar bill stilled the preacher's look of wonder at the contrast between the fabulous richness of Esther's attire and Pride's battered face.

"Yes," the minister said in answer to Pride's query, "Mrs. Tompkins takes roomers—she's down to the end of the street."

Mrs. Tompkins was a lean iron-jawed female of such acute suspicions that she had to be thawed by Pride's showing her the marriage certificate the minister had signed. She sent her son out to stable the horses and she made supper for them, late as it was. The supper was good, but Pride could not eat. He sat brooding miserably over the hot rolls, coffee, sausages and cake. Esther saw the look, but said nothing.

When they were leaving the dining room, Mrs. Tompkins and her son showered them with rice. Then they climbed the stairs to their room. Inside, a fire had been started. It was crackling merrily, throwing a glow of warmth through the chamber. A great four-poster bed had been made, but Pride looked at it with a gaze as bleak as the winter night.

Esther, who was standing before the fire, looked over her shoulder.

"Help me off with my things," she said.

Pride's hands upon the lacings of her boots were clumsy and cold. He drew them off finally and she stood up in her stockinged feet. Then she opened her bag and drew out a gossamer nightdress.

"Turn your back," she said to Pride.

When he looked again she was propped up among the pillows, her hair spread out over her shoulders like a white-gold veil. Still Pride stood there, making no move to undress.

"Come here," she whispered.

He went over to her and when he was close she put up her arms and began to kiss him—soft, clinging kisses, light enough not to hurt his broken mouth; soft kisses that had their own quiet insistence.

Suddenly, convulsively, Pride brought up his big hands and broke her grip.

"I can't!" he said hoarsely. "Tonight I just can't!"

Then he turned his back and walked away from her. At the door he did not even pause, but went on down the stairs and out into the icy night.

Esther sat there, propped up among the pillows, and stared at the door that Pride had closed behind him.

My wedding night, she thought, my wedding night! How long have I dreamed of—this? I chased Pride across the country. I let him have the money with which he got started. I thought he could be bought—but he can't really; he'll die free. . . . Then suddenly, softly, she began to laugh. She laughed very quietly, but her slim body was shaking. It went on and on and she could not stop. It was not until she lifted her hand to her face and found it wet that she discovered that the sounds she was making were no longer laughter. No—not laughter. They were wild, bitter sobs. . . .

In the morning Mrs. Tompkins joined them at breakfast; but though she was sorely puzzled at Pride's moroseness and the quiet hurt in Esther's face, she chattered away at a great rate. And one thing she said caused Pride to lift his head and stare at her eagerly.

"Yes sir, we're better off than them mining folks. This here is farmland—all this part is broad valley land. Don't know what we're going to do now. The Millville & Western Pennsylvania Railroad used to take our produce down to Millville. It connected with the Millville Valley Branch line so we could sell in Pittsburgh and even farther east. But since this new man—Stillton? Stillway? . . ."

"Stillworth," Esther supplied gently. "Thomas Stillworth."

"That's right. Since this Stillworth took over, the Millville Valley Branch won't take nothing but iron, steel and coal. Reckon we're going to have a bad year, come summer . . ."

Esther could see the excitement in Pride's face, but she did not guess its cause. Whatever it was, she was glad of it, because much of the look of sullen self-torment had dissipated before it.

He bent forward, looking at Mrs. Tompkins as though she were the most beautiful woman in the world.

"If," he demanded, "somebody were to start the M. & W. P. up again and build it right up to St. Pierre on Lake Erie, what then, Mrs. Tompkins?"

"Why—I don't know. There's nobody much on that section of lake shore to eat our produce. Not much of a market there, Mr. Dawson."

"No—there isn't. But there's such a thing as a lake barge. Barges can hold more produce than you can grow—

and they can be towed up the lake to Buffalo and then eastward to New York City, and westward to Chicago, and north to Canada, and down the St. Lawrence to the Atlantic coast and . . ."

Mrs. Tompkins was looking at him with wide-eyed admiration.

"You are one smart man!"

Pride was almost smiling as he helped Esther into the sleigh. It was no longer snowing on their return trip to Millville and they made good time over the road that paralleled the M. & W. P. tracks. Every time Pride glanced at the tracks, his excitement mounted. This was his railroad—his. . . . By the time they had reached Millville he was actually grinning.

When they pulled into Millville's single street, John Bently came out and waved them to a stop. He had a bunch of keys in his hand.

"My wife and I are leaving this morning," he said. "You're welcome to the house, Mr. Dawson."

"Thank you," Pride said gruffly. "Meet my wife. Esther, this is Mr. Bently, your father's manager."

"Esther?" John Bently said. "You're not . . . ?"

"Yes, I'm Thomas Stillworth's daughter," Esther said quietly. "But I'm not proud of it—not after what happened here yesterday."

"Thank you for saying that," Bently said. "And, Mr. Dawson, I owe you an apology. Henkja told me that you tried to keep the Pinkertons from shooting."

"I shouldn't have brought them here," Pride said savagely. "I wanted to avoid trouble. But they're leaving today—now. I'm going to pay 'em off and kick 'em out!"

"That might be dangerous," Bently said. "The people are in an ugly mood."

"I'll chance it," Pride answered, and turned the team toward the house. As soon as he had taken their baggage inside, he started out again.

"Pride," Esther said, a note of anger creeping into her voice.

"Sorry, honey," Pride grinned, "but this is business. I've got people to see."

"Then I'm going with you."

"All right," Pride said, "come along!"

He spent the next hour paying off and dismissing the de-

116

tectives. Then he sought out the men who had run the now completely defunct M. & W. P. He found most of them working in the mill and realized at once that he would have to overcome their hostility.

Without hesitation, presuming upon an authority he did not actually possess, he ordered the foreman to let them off for the day with pay. Then he asked them to meet him and Henkja at his new home. In the parlor he stood up and faced them.

"Men," he said, "what happened here yesterday will cause me sorrow all my life. I didn't want anybody hurt. I brought those light-fingered bastards in to see that there wouldn't be any fighting. And I told them before they came they were not to shoot. I told them again yesterday when the trouble started—ask Stepan here!"

Henkja nodded.

"Mr. Dawson speaks the truth," he said quietly. "I heard him order the Pinks not to fire."

"So did I," an older man put in, "but he shouldn't ought to of brought them devils in! Can't nobody control them when they smell blood!"

"That's true," Pride admitted. "I was wrong and I'm sorry."

"Sorry don't bring dead men back to life!" one of the men cried.

"Hush," Stepan Henkja counseled. "Let Mr. Dawson have his say."

"All right," Pride went on, "it won't bring 'em back, but it can make things better for the living. Why are things bad in Millville and in Martintown, where I went last night, and all around this section? I'll tell you. It's because one man's got this place sewed up. I aim to get it loose. Look here. See these? These are the stock certificates of the M. & W. P. I own that railroad now—lock, stock and barrel. Most of you were farmer folks before the mills and mines came. I want to ask you one question: What would happen if the Millville & Western Pennsylvania were to keep going north till it reached St. Pierre?"

The men looked puzzled, but, to Esther's great relief, much less hostile.

It was Henkja who answered the question finally.

"We could ship our produce by lake barge. Is that what you're getting at, Mr. Dawson?"

"Exactly! You know what would happen then? Markets in Buffalo, in Albany, in New York City! More money than you've ever seen before—and you can ship cheaper by barge!"

He had them now. These were facts and they knew it. Esther sat there hugging her knees with joy. This man she had married had more to him than she had suspected.

"But," the young man who had challenged Pride before put in, "that line don't go nowhere near Lake Erie."

"It's going to. With your help it's going right to St. Pierre. I want you men to get out and scour the country-side—talk to the farmers. Tell them the truth. Tell them I can't pay them one red cent now because I'm broke. But tell them that every man who volunteers his labor will get his share in the line, and I promise you the M. & W. P. is going to be the richest line in the state! Tell them I won't be in an office giving orders. Tell them to meet me Monday and see where I'll be—right out there on the rails with a pick and shovel breaking ground with the rest of you! . . . Right now you can't ship your produce. Men, before the living God, I swear to you that come next fall you'll ship more than ever, farther than ever and cheaper than ever! . . . Are you with me?"

The little parlor shook with their cheers.

After they had gone, Esther came up to her husband, her blue eyes bright with happy tears.

"You were magnificent, darling," she cried. "And I'll help. I can, you know. Because I'm known in every bank in Pittsburgh. Through me you ought to be able to borrow enough money to get all the supplies you need! We'll fix Father! We'll make the worthless stock he dumped on you the richest on the market!"

"I knew you'd help," Pride smiled. "I'd counted on your being able to help me raise the money—but I'm glad you made the offer yourself. Thanks, Esther. Come on, get your things! We're going down to Pittsburgh now!"

But Esther shook her head, her cheeks a deep scarlet.

"Not tonight," she whispered. "Tonight I'd—I'd like to find out if I really have a husband. Do I, darling?"

Pride looked down at her, seeing her slim, lovely, desirable.

He bent down suddenly, and found her mouth.

"Now," he grinned, "what do you think?"

"I think," Esther whispered, "that being married to you is going to be—enchanting." Then, breaking his rather loose grip, she turned and fled up the stairs.

Pride hesitated. It was still hours until nightfall and there were many things to be done. In a moment his big face broke into a grin. Hell, he thought, a man can work any time! He turned and went up the stairs after Esther.

CHAPTER NINE—1870

"Don't worry," Lucy McCarthy said to her husband, "you'll find another job."

Tim put his coffee cup down and looked at her.

"I want you to get this thing straight, Lucy," he said. "I wasn't fired. I quit. I quit a good-paying job. And we haven't got but a few dollars to fall back on."

Lance sat across the table studying his parents with his grave, dark eyes. He had turned thirteen the day before, and felt himself quite grown up.

"Be Christmas soon, too," Tim went on. "I don't know. . ."

"Now, Timothy McCarthy," Lucy said, "don't fret yourself! I know why you quit that job. And I say praise unto all the saints that you did!"

"You—know?" Tim said wonderingly. "But I never said a word. . . ."

Lucy picked up a newspaper from a small table and opened it to the last page. Then she placed it beside Tim's plate.

Tim looked down and a small item caught his eye.

"Disturbance in Millville," it read. And under that heading: "Agents in the employ of Thomas Stillworth, Esq., were forced to fire upon a mob of strikers led by foreign agitators, who were attacking Mr. Stillworth's steel plant in the town of Millville. It is said that the mob, whose grievances Mr. Stillworth yesterday characterized as 'largely imaginary,' attempted to break into the plant with the intention of destroying valuable machinery. Six men were killed before the riot was put down. Mr. Pride Dawson, who commanded Mr. Stillworth's agents, was wounded in the fighting. He was ably assisted by Mr. Timothy McCarthy. Mr. Stillworth had high praise for the courage and devotion of both men."

Tim put down the paper.

"Of all the black-hearted dirty liars!" he exploded. Then he saw Lance's face. He passed the paper across the table to his son.

"Read this, boy," he said. "Read it and afterward I'll tell you how it really was. You're growing up now. Time you were learning about things—how some men lie and steal and murder for money and power, and how they lie to cover the evil truth about their lives."

Lance read the account swiftly—then looked up, his eyes fastened upon his father's face.

"Sit down, Lucy," Tim said, "and let me tell you how it was." Timothy McCarthy had had little education, but there was a rough poetry in him. As he talked, Lance could picture the scene: the starving mill people standing in the mud and snow before the gate, the arrival of Pride Dawson with his mercenaries, the swift, bitter slaughter.

"They died there," Tim said quietly, "in the snow and it was so cold their blood made a steaming. It wasn't a fight. It was murder, pure and simple—murder of men who had tried to get their simple rights the only way they knew how. I wasn't in on it—I quit the day before—but I saw it. And these eyes will carry that sight to their grave. Don't you forget it either, Lance. Don't you ever forget it!"

"I won't," Lance said, and looked over to where his mother sat, her head bent over the table, cradled on her arm, crying aloud. And neither son nor father tried to stop her weeping, because it was a thing to cry about.

"Afterwards, Pride chased the man who'd hit him into one of them dirty little shacks. I caught him there and I beat him. With these two hands I beat Pride's face to a pulp. Only it was no good, because he wouldn't fight back. He wouldn't even raise his arms. . . . He was ashamed, I think. Ashamed and sorry almost as much as I was."

"There's good in the man," Lucy said. "I always said so from the things you told me about him. Only Pride doesn't

120

seem to give it much of a chance. Maybe this will change him."

"No," Tim said, "he won't stay sorry long enough. He'll go plunging along into something else, and before you know it, he'll do some more harm. . . . Well, that's how it was. Now I got to go out and find another job." He looked once more at the paper. "Say, Lucy," he said, "this is yesterday's paper. It won't do me much good to look for a job in that. Hasn't today's come?"

"I'll go see, Papa," Lance said, and went to the door. He came back after a moment, the paper spread out between his hands.

"Look, Papa," he cried, "here's some more about the Stillworths."

Tim took the paper, while Lucy stood up and looked curiously over his shoulder.

"Elopement of Heiress!" the headline read. "Daughter of Financier Marries Employee of Father." And in slightly smaller type: "Thomas Stillworth prostrate at news!" To the left there was a very bad pen sketch of Esther's face, giving only the faintest idea of her beauty. Tim read on: "News reached this city yesterday of the elopement of Esther Stillworth, daughter of the celebrated financier, and Pride Dawson, one of Mr. Stillworth's employees. Mr. Dawson figured prominently in quelling the recent disturbances at Millville and was warmly praised by Mr. Stillworth for his part in the affair. Yet, this paper was reliably informed, the financier has long bitterly opposed a match between his daughter and Dawson, though he was aware of their growing romantic attachment. The ceremony was performed by the Reverend Huntly Drake of Martintown, Pennsylvania, and the young couple are said to be honeymooning in the vicinity of Pittsburgh, though their actual whereabouts are unknown. Mr. Stillworth, suffering from nervous shock, is under the care of his physician, Doctor Charles Wurtburger, and could not be reached for a statement."

Tim looked up, meeting Lucy's eyes, and they both said it at the same time: "Sharon!"

He had introduced Lucy to Sharon shortly after his wife's arrival in New York, and a warm affection had sprung up between them, one of those friendships so rare among women.

Lucy was already racing for Tim's hat and coat.

"You go to her, Tim," she said. "Bring her here if she'll come. I talked to her a couple of days ago, and she was despondent, much too despondent. I hope she hasn't read this yet."

"What did I tell you?" Tim said grimly. "Didn't I say it? He'll go plunging along into something else and do some more harm! Pride didn't give a damn about Esther Stillworth. He was in love with Sharon. I'll bet you my last dollar that he still is. I never saw him in love before; he always was kind of carefree as far as women were concerned. But Sharon was different. He worshiped the ground she walked on. Only it's the money. Pride would do anything for money—like killing people and breaking Sharon's heart."

"I know, I know," Lucy said impatiently. "Now, get along with you—and take a cab!"

When the cab drew up before the door of Sharon's establishment, Tim got down quickly and went in. His worst fears were instantly realized: Sharon was not there.

"She said," one of the girls told him, "that she was going to see Father Shannon. She was terribly upset over something she read in the paper. I didn't see what it was because she took the paper with her."

Hearing the name of Father Shannon, Tim was momentarily relieved. He knew the old priest, who added to an almost saintly devoutness a native kindliness of heart and a wise and tolerant compassion for the follies and sins of men. If Sharon had gone there, she was in good hands. But had she? He had better make sure, for if she hadn't, Lucy would have his head!

He made his way as quickly as he could to the rectory and sought out the old priest. Father Shannon received him gravely, but with a merry twinkle in his eyes.

"Ah, Timothy, lad," he said, " 'tis strange indeed to see your face. These many Sundays I've looked for it among the worshipers. And one would think that you had beaten your old mother the way you stay away from the confessional."

"I'm sorry, Father," Tim said quickly, "but I've no time to talk of my sins, today. Sharon—Miss O'Neil. . . . Was she here? Have you seen her?"

"Ah, there's a good lass! Such goodness of heart. . . . But no, I haven't seen her. Not since early mass last Sunday. You look troubled, Tim—is there something wrong?"

"Yes," Tim said grimly. "Have you read this?" He thrust the newspaper into Father Shannon's hands.

The old priest fumbled in the folds of his robe and brought out a pair of spectacles. He adjusted them and began to read, mumbling the words through half closed lips as he did so. Then he straightened up, frowning.

"She was in love with this man, wasn't she? Yes, that's the name—Pride Dawson. A heathenish and wicked name for a man of the same nature. I counseled her against him often, for everything she told me about him led me to know he was wrong for her. It was not only that he was not of our faith, for love has made some real and beautiful conversations. No, it was something else. . . ."

"Pride Dawson," Tim said bitterly, "is a murderer and a blackguard and a scoundrel. But you like him, Father—that's the trouble. He can do almost anything and you still like him. That's what's got me worried. Sharon loved him. You know her, Father: she's not one of those light-minded girls who fall in love every week with a different man. No —with her it would be just once, and for good. The day we met her I told Pride to leave her alone—that she was something kind of special. . . . But that's not what I'm worried about. Sharon left her shop this morning to come to you. She should have been here hours ago . . . and it's snowing again, Father."

"I see," Father Shannon said slowly. Then he stood up. "Come, Tim," he said, "we've got to find her."

When Sharon O'Neil left her shop that morning she went straight to the rectory. But at the door she paused. The Cathedral stood a little way off, soaring up into the steel-gray sky. The wind came down through the branches of the naked trees and made a noise like a woman crying. Sharon stood there listening to it, hearing the echo of the sound within her heart. She moved off toward the Cathedral, and the wind tugged at her skirts and ankles, blowing up the snow in dry, powdery gusts that stung when they struck her face.

Sharon's hands, inside her muff, were cold. She was cold all over though she was warmly dressed. The Cathedral loomed up now, its stately spires piercing the gray sky, and the figures of the Saints looked down at her, benign under their mantles of winter white.

The doors were of heavy oak, hung with strap-iron hinges, and it took all Sharon's strength to get them open. Inside it was warmer, and the scent of incense and burning candles came to her nostrils. She dipped her right hand into the font, made the sign of the cross on her forehead and genuflected toward the altar. Then going up to the image of the Holy Mother, she lit a candle before it and murmured a prayer:

"Dear Mother of God," she whispered, "give me strength."

She stole into her pew and, kneeling down, took out her rosary. As the beads moved under her stiffened fingers she could hear the murmur of her whispering: "Hail Mary, full of Grace, The Lord is with Thee. . . ." (But not with me, and I haven't the grace or the strength to bear this thing.) "Blessed art Thou among women, Blessed is the fruit of Thy Womb, Jesus. Holy Mary, Mother of God, pray for us, now and at the hour of our death, Amen." (Oh, pray for me, pray for me now. . . .) She lifted another bead and began again, but to her surprise it was the last of the Ave Maria that she began: "At the hour of our death, at the hour of our death, now at the hour of my death, Holy Mother, pray for me!"

She got up slowly. (This is wrong, terribly wrong; this is mortal sin: Now at the hour of my death. . . . What God has given you, Father Shannon always said, you have no right to take away. . . . But did God send this anguish at the core of the heart, and not the strength to bear up under it? Did He?)

Now at the hour . . . But those were not the words. The "Hail Mary" did not go that way . . . She tried again: "Holy Mary, Mother of God, pray for . . . me . . . (the lost, the forsaken. Pray for me, for by this thing am I slain!) . . . now . . . at the hour of my death. . . ."

She fled wildly down the aisle of the Cathedral, but just inside the door she paused once more, for there stood the statue of the Magdalene. She would understand. She even more than the Mother of God, for she had been a reckless, passionate woman—a woman of many sins. . . .

Then she pushed open the door and went out into the snow.

It was colder now, and the snow came down so fast that she could not see five yards before her. She walked northward, moving without conscious thought toward Shantytown and the house of her father.

He was not there now . . . he had died weeks ago, going out while the trees were still bright with fall. He had loved the red and rust-brown and vivid gold of autumn. "Kind of a glory," he had called it, and he had gone forward to meet the fall, gone in a glory. But for her, Sharon, there was no glory. There was only winter, white-robed and cruel, with the winds pitifully crying (Oh, pray for me . . .). There were only the snow gusts stinging her eyelids, only the frost-ache in her fingers and the death-ache in her heart. . . .

She heard dimly the muffled voices of the stage drivers swearing at their teams, and the whipcracks, pistol-shot clear in the frosty air. But she walked on, looking neither to the right nor the left, while the snow clung to her hat and whitened her brows and hair. She walked very slowly, and as she walked her lips moved, praying, a strange, rhapsodic prayer of her own invention:

"It is finished now—Oh, God—the life You gave me. I ask You to take it back again. Merciful God, do not require of me a service greater than I can render, or put upon me a task I cannot bear. Consider how I met him; You could have prevented that. You might have made me go to another place, for there were penmen in many streets —only *he* was there at that hour, in that street, in the one place in all the world where I must meet him. . . . Or You could even then have sent him away before I came to love him fully—there were a thousand times and places where it could have been ended before it had begun. . . .

"But no, You let me come to love him, knowing that I had the kind of spirit that could love only once, and then with all my heart and mind and soul and body, so that I would be consumed with loving and would live from then on only for him—that I would live and breathe and have my being only for his delight. And now he is gone, forever gone, and there is nothing left for me. Oh, God, men call You merciful. You would not ask me then to live when living itself is anguish, and every breath a new torture, remembering him?"

She bent her head and walked faster, the tears stinging and freezing upon her cheeks. She did not see the streets she passed. She was unaware of people. She plunged on through the driving snow, her head bent, hearing old words in her heart: "Don't ever leave me, Pride. Not for anything. Not for anybody. Don't you know I'd die?" And Pride's bass rumble: "Don't worry, if I ever marry anybody, it'll be you. . . ." And: "I never loved a woman before. I wanted 'em, yes. Had 'em, too. But I don't want you like that. I want you in a veil in the church. I want to carry you across the doorsill. I want you in my house with the gray getting into your hair, and our kids whooping and hollering and stomping the place down all around us. Like the idea?" (I liked it so much, Pride—it was all I ever dreamed of.) Then finally at Delmonico's, after the play: "It's all so silly. People don't die for love." And her own voice answering: "Don't they, Pride?"

She had passed Fifty-ninth Street now and was out in open country. Here there were no buildings to break the force of the wind. It tore at her savagely, worrying her clothing; it picked up needles of ice and flung them blindingly into her face. It caught her breath and snatched it away so that her head reeled dizzily and she was aware that her perceptions were becoming disordered.

There were moments when Pride seemed to be striding along beside her, talking gaily in his deep, rich voice. But that could not be, for Pride was far away and married. . . .

At other times it was her father who walked beside her, talking wisely, kindly, though she could not comprehend a word he said or remember it after he had spoken. Still, it was conforting to have him, only he could not stay, fading off abruptly into the wilderness of snow.

The cold was creeping upward now, along her limbs. They were stiffening but the pain was going, everything was going, the world blurring before her. She went down, quite suddenly, into a drift. Then she was up again, stumbling blindly ahead. She fell again and got up . . . how many times? There was no reason for it except the blind instinct for survival, the overpowering desire to reach once more the house of her father.

"Daddo'll be glad to see me," she said, "he'll take me

in." Then all her breath left her at once and she lay on her face in the snow. She felt strangely warm and comfortable and at peace. She was more than a little sleepy; she burrowed even deeper into the drift and lay there calmly watching her life go out on the ebb of the storm. . . .

Then suddenly, annoyingly, her sleep was broken, strong arms were lifting her, and she could see Tim's red face, sick with fear, looking into hers, and beside him, the kindly old eyes of Father Shannon. They were filled with tears.

"Don't cry, Father," she said clearly. "I was going home. . . ."

"Yes," the old priest whispered, "yes, daughter, I know." Then: "Come, Tim, we'd better get her back—fast!"

CHAPTER TEN—1870

FOR TWO DAYS, in Pittsburgh, Pride savored the heady feeling of what it meant to be married to a princess. They had gone to three banks and in each of them Esther had been instantly recognized, for she had spent much of her childhood in the industrial city and had visited these banks before. She had been greeted by the highest officials, the presidents and their staffs. No mere tellers or third vice-presidents for Esther Stillworth. And Pride observed once more that characteristic common to bank presidents everywhere: that fawning servility before the holders of the enormous accounts. He grinned at it, for he knew, from his own experience, how quickly it could freeze into icy formality once the accounts had slipped below a certain figure.

There had been need for haste, for, as Pride said to Esther: "Your pa is sure to cut you off without a cent when he finds out you've married me."

"He might," Esther said, "or he might not. The point is we can use my trust fund for security against almost any size loan. I brought the papers with me. It'll take Father some time to draw up new ones revoking these. How much will we need?"

"A hundred thousand dollars," Pride told her. "I'll have to pay wages, and get the rails and ties for the building. The road's got the right of way to St. Pierre—providing it hasn't lapsed."

The right of way had not lapsed—due largely to official inertia. And the banks had almost fallen over one another in their eagerness to grant the loans. It was a wise move to split the money among the three banks, though any one of them would have let them have the entire sum. The bankers had all found it amusing when Pride had asked for exactly thirty-three thousand three hundred thirty-three dollars and thirty-four cents.

"Why the thirty-four cents?" they had all demanded.

"For luck," Pride had answered. Then he had reached into his pocket where the nugget luck piece still lay and had given Esther the two pennies above the hundred thousand dollars that the three loans totaled.

"Keep it," he grinned, "to give our kids a start in life."

Yes, it had been a wise move, for the bankers were much less likely to worry over thirty-odd thousand than over a hundred thousand.

The next day Pride had been very busy ordering supplies and insisting flatly that they be shipped immediately. He knew well that he had to get his rails and ties and picks and spikes and roadbed rock into Millville before Black Tom found out about his plans. It would be only too easy for Stillworth to stop their shipment by forbidding the Millville Valley Branch to load them, or even by influencing Thompson not to take them out of Pittsburgh on the Pennsylvania. By the end of the day, he was very tired, but he had won. By arguing, threatening, pleading—and by the judicious placing of bribes—he had seen his supplies leave Pittsburgh even before he returned to the hotel.

It was his intention to go back to Millville that same night, but Esther would not hear of it. The hotel was very warm and comfortable, which the house in Millville was not.

"Besides," she said demurely, "people always go off on honeymoons, don't they?"

Pride frowned as he nodded agreement. The truth of the matter was that Pride Dawson was shocked. It is paradoxically true that rakes make the most conventional of husbands. All his life Pride had taken his pleasures where he found them, lightly and without thought. It was also true, as he had told Sharon, that he had never known a woman of decent morals and strict upbringing. And Esther Stillworth, despite her talk, was both. She was still virginal, Pride discovered, in body; but certainly not in mind. And it was this that shocked him. For he had held all his life the roué's dream of marrying a paragon of purity. He had expected shyness, timidity, tears. He had even looked forward to these things as an added fillip which would lend zest to the whole proceeding; and instead he had found—ardor.

He was, at first, puzzled and confused. Esther was as playful as a kitten, and full of a youthful passion that was practically inexhaustible.

"Children!" Esther laughed, when he mentioned the possibility of such an outcome. "We'll have children later. Right now I want to keep my figure and enjoy myself. Besides, I want to keep you so occupied that you won't have time or energy for anyone else. I'm a jealous woman, Pride!"

Early the next morning Pride sat up in bed and gazed at the sleeping figure of his wife. It was long before daylight, but one gas jet was still lighted. ("Why turn off the lights?" Esther had asked. "There's no one here but us.") Looking at her, long-cool in the semi-darkness, sweet-sleeping, her gossamer nightdress still hanging in the closet, Pride muttered to himself:

"I must be crazy. I ought to be happier'n a lark, and I'm not. I have one of the prettiest women who ever drew breath, and I'm sitting here thinking like this. I've got a chance to make all the money in the world, and I'm actually miserable. I've got more loving than I rightly take care of and I'm mooning like a snake-bit hound dog baying a frosty moon. . . . Don't know what's wrong with me. . . ." He brought his thick, heavily-muscled arms up and cradled his face between his hands, resting his elbows on his knees.

"I wonder," he murmured, "how it would have been—with Sharon. . . ."

The moment he voiced the thought, he was sorry. It was out now, the thing that had been nagging in the back part of his mind since the night of his marriage—that strange wedding night that had not been a wedding night at all. Not even then, while he had trudged through the snow and the darkness, had he dared think of Sharon.

But he had said it now and she was there in the room with them. She was between him and Esther. He could see her thin little face, her freckles, her wide, soft mouth. It was moving, talking to him, gently, tenderly; but he could not hear the words. She was telling him something—something that he badly needed to know. But strain his ears as he would, he could not hear it. Then, abruptly, in a blinding flash of clairvoyance, he knew that something was wrong—horribly, hideously wrong, for he could no longer see her face. He was suddenly aware that he was cold, his whole massive body bedewed with icy sweat.

He sprang from the bed and paced the floor. And though he could not see her she was everywhere about him, his outstretched fingers missing contact with her body by inches. He realized suddenly, with a misery that was bottomless, that she would always be there between him and Esther, and that never again in this life would he draw a completely happy breath. But there was nothing new about that. He had known that before. What baffled him, what he could not explain, was this icy terror that beat about his head like invisible wings. Something was wrong, he knew, wrong, wrong, wrong . . .

"I'm out of my mind," he groaned. "I'm crazy. Better lie down—better try to sleep."

And he did sleep after a while. But even his sleep was troubled, filled with wild, formless dreams that escaped him completely the moment they had passed. He was awakened finally by Esther's slim hands shaking him furiously by the shoulder. He sat up, blinking, and stared into Esther's face, twisted by rage.

"If ever again," she whispered, "you call me 'Sharon' in your sleep, I'll kill you, Pride Dawson!"

Then she sprang from the bed and ran to the closet, her long, beautiful legs making a white blur of movement.

The next afternoon, when they reached Millville, the supplies were there ahead of them. Without waiting to eat, Pride stripped off his clothing and put on work clothes and high boots. Then he went out to the tracks and directed the

130

transfer of the rails to one of his own flatcars. He waited impatiently while Pat O'Malley, the engineer, got up steam on the undersized locomotive of the M. & W. P. and then he rode with his crew past Martintown to the place where the rails ended.

Stepan Henkja handed him a pick and all the men looked on wonderingly as Pride lifted it and sent it whistling downward to bury itself to the haft in the frozen ground. Then one by one they climbed down from the cars and joined him. Pride was much better at the work than any of them, for only a year ago he had worked his way across the entire country laying rails. Besides, he was bigger and stronger than they, and he had eaten well all the while they had starved. By nightfall he was still working tirelessly, performing prodigies of labor that were to become a legend in the history of American railroading. The others were strung out behind him, only Stepan Henkja being able to maintain anything like his pace.

Going home at night on the open flatcars, huddled together for warmth, the men talked about it among themselves, casting furtive glances toward Pride, who was talking earnestly to Henkja.

"Look, Stepan," Pride was saying. "I got off on the wrong foot here, but I mean to set it right. I'm going to take over. I'm going to relieve Stillworth of this town just like he relieved Bolley and Waters. And when I do, things are going to be better. I'm going to pay better wages, put up a hospital and bring in doctors. It's not smart to do it any other way. Men don't work well for a boss they hate. If these people were well-fed they could produce twice as much."

It was not humanity that moved Pride, but hardheaded common sense. Therefore Stepan Henkja believed him. If Pride had put the matter on the basis of humanitarianism, Stepan would have profoundly doubted his words, for he suspected how shallow the vein of love for his fellow man ran in Pride's nature.

That night, as he eased his aching frame into bed, Pride realized how badly out of condition he was. It was a long time since he had done such hard work. And when Esther turned to him and sought his mouth, he repulsed her:

"Go 'way and let me sleep!"

But the next day he was out with the gang again, working harder than before. And before nine o'clock, more than two hundred young farmers had joined him. Pride and Stepan's visits to the country people had borne fruit. The farmers were tall men, rock-hard, thin-lipped and sparse of speech. Pride noted one in particular, a blond youth of middle height who was called Ernie, and who could almost maintain Pride's own pace. By mid-afternoon, Pride made him section boss in charge of one crew, and put Stepan Henkja in charge of the other.

After that the work went better, the pickaxes rising in perfect rhythm, pausing on the top of the arc then crashing downward, and afterward the shovel crews throwing the earth aside. The line moved on like a black gash through the wilderness, a long wound that bled dark earth, and cut through the valley's heart. And behind them, the other crews shoveled small stones to make a roadbed that would not sink, and then they all laid the ties across and hammered the rails home with the great spikes. Along the roadway, the fires cast palls of smoke into the steel-gray heavens where the creosote boiled, and the crude winches lowered in the wooden ties, so that they might be protected from insects and the weather. Men huddled about the fires drinking gallons of scalding coffee, and then came back to work some more. The rails unwound like twin ribbons, while the little engine puffed over them, waiting to take the crews home and to bring in more and more supplies.

Pride went home that second night with a singing in his heart. It was good to work like this, to do a man's work against all odds and to wrest his future from the wilderness. Some of the ache had gone out of him, his muscles unkinking, roping loose and smooth-moving under his dark skin. Yes, it was good to work again after the scheming and plotting of the city. It made him forget his longing for Sharon O'Neil for many minutes, it eased his mind of the worry about what Thomas Stillworth would do.

He came into the house, snow-powdered, happily tired, feeling clean again, feeling almost healed inside of the dark, half-realized hurts that drove him. But, to his surprise, Esther did not come forward to meet him. She always met him when he came home—met him and kissed him warmly and led him to the table to eat the food that she had proudly prepared with her own hands. She was quite skilled at it, having an instinct for cooking, inherited

132

no doubt from her lowly ancestors; and Pride, all of whose appetites were huge, found this good. But now, tonight, there were no savory smells from the kitchen. The house was silent and almost cold, with a brooding air about it that pricked the small hairs at the back of his neck. Pride dropped his short, heavy workingman's coat and went in search of her. He found her in the bedroom, face down upon the great bed. When she looked up he saw that she had been crying.

She straightened up and looked at him with her heart in her eyes.

"Pride," she whispered, "oh, Pride . . ."

"Yes, Esther," Pride rumbled, the note of questioning deep in his voice. "What is it, hon?"

"There's a telegram on the table," she said slowly. "It came this morning, just after you left. I've—I've been trying to bring myself to destroy it all day . . . but I couldn't, Pride, I couldn't!" Her voice trailed off into the smallest of whispers. "For if I did, I'd never know—I'd never know . . ."

Wordlessly, Pride crossed the room and picked up the telegram. He stood there a long while gazing at his wife across the little square of paper and then he bent down his head and read:

Sharon is dying. Asking for you. It was signed: *Tim.*

He looked up again from the telegram to his wife, seeing the color draining abruptly from her face, the lips moving, shaping the question, and the pain in her eyes as though she knew the answer before the words were said.

"You—you're not going?"

"Yes," Pride said, his voice endlessly deep. "Yes, I'm going." Then, without glancing at her again, he turned to his closet and took out his clothes.

Esther sat very still and watched him as he dressed. (There must be something a woman can say at a time like this; but what is it? What are the words? Say: "Don't go, my darling—it's a trick, a ruse to get you back!"? But Tim would not be a party to deception and Pride would know that well. It *is* a trick, though; it *is!* She's done something to herself—stabbed herself or taken poison, so that in dying she does what she could not do in life . . . She defeats me utterly, destroys a life I hadn't yet begun. Oh, Pride, Pride, why couldn't you have said what I most wanted to hear: "Let her die! I've got you!" I would have been generous then and sent you to her, knowing she could not win. But you didn't say it, and I've got to live out my life knowing I love a man who doesn't love me. . . .)

He was finished dressing now, and he stood there before her, terrible and grand, even his rough-hewn features adding to his grandeur.

"Well, Esther," he said, "I'm sorry."

She stood up then and faced him.

"I love you, Pride," she said quietly. "I've always known I was wrong to love you. I've hated myself for it, and hated you for making me want you so. I can't help it. I'll go on loving and wanting you all my life, but the hatred will go on too, until it destroys you—destroys us both. . . ."

"You've finished?" Pride said, his big voice filled with contempt.

"Yes," she said, and walked down the stairs with him to the door. "Suppose," she whispered, as his big hand closed over the knob, "suppose I'm not here when you come back?"

"I'll chance it . . ." Pride said, *"if* I come back." Then he was gone out into the echoing dark.

The next afternoon when Tim opened the door to his apartment, Pride said one word only:

"Where?"

"St. Joseph's Hospital."

"She—she's not . . . ?"

"No, she's not dead. Not yet. Want a spot of coffee before we go?"

"No. For the love of God, man, come on!"

Tim got his hat and greatcoat and went down to the cab that Pride had left waiting in front of the building. Tim gave the address of the hospital and they moved off. Tim sat tight-lipped and grim, looking neither to the right nor the left. Pride touched his arm.

"What happened, Tim?" he demanded. "I've got to know!"

Tim looked at him distastefully.

"She read in the paper that you'd married your forty million dollars. So she took a walk—in one of the worst blizzards in fifteen years. Father Shannon happened to remember the habit she'd gotten into of going up to that shanty to look at the place where her pa used to live—he died a couple of months ago—so we were able to find her. Too late. Pneumonia. The docs at St. Joseph's don't give her a Chinaman's chance. So you can add her to the list of the people who got in the way of the great Pride Dawson —on his way up."

"That's not fair!" Pride growled. "You know it's not!"

"Do I?" Tim said and shut his jaw hard.

At the hospital an orderly led them to the door of the room, but there one of the Sisters motioned to them to wait.

Looking up at Pride, Tim saw the icy sweat appearing on his brow, saw the slight, almost unnoticeable tremor run through his massive frame, heard the swift tattoo of his fingers against the brim of his tall hat. Suddenly Tim felt a surge of pity for Pride Dawson.

The door opened and Father Shannon came out. Seeing the priest clad in full robes, Pride's big face turned gray as death, and the trembling in his limbs increased so violently that Tim put out a steadying hand.

Father Shannon studied Pride curiously, noting the palsied effort of Pride's lips, out of control now, to shape the question.

"No, son," the old priest said gently, "she's not dead. In fact, she's going to recover. She took a turn for the better about an hour ago."

Pride's knees buckled suddenly, so that he might have fallen if the Sister had not pushed forward a chair. As it was, he sat there a long time, wiping his face with a large handkerchief.

"I'd go in to see her now," Father Shannon said. Then nodding to Tim and the Sister, he left the waiting room.

Pride got to his feet and walked into Sharon's room. She lay there upon her narrow bed, so small and pale that she was half lost among the pillows and coverlet. When she saw him, she let out a glad cry, and Pride went down on his knees beside her and buried his big face against the hollow of her throat.

"Don't, darling," she whispered, "please don't . . ."

Then as he raised his head she kissed him, covering his face with light, brushing kisses, filled with such an agony of tenderness that the pain inside his chest was like brine and fire.

135

"I shouldn't kiss you," she murmured. "You aren't mine any more. But it was so good of you to come—so good. You know I tried to die? I won't again, Pride—not any more. It wasn't very brave of me. Only, I didn't know how I could bear living without you . . . I still don't. But I'll try, my dearest, for your sake. I wouldn't want to give you any cause for regret."

"I'm not going back!" Pride said suddenly, fiercely. "I was a fool. I love you, Sharon, and nobody else on earth is going to."

But her thin fingers, blue-white and almost transparent, came up and rested across his mouth.

"No, Pride," she said gently. "Marriage is a sacrament, blessed in the sight of God. And no power on earth can dissolve it. Go back to Esther—and I shall pray for your happiness . . ."

"But your happiness?" Pride muttered. "What about that?"

"Oh, I shall find it. In a different way, perhaps. Maybe by doing good and helping other people and living the best way I know how here upon earth. It won't be the glorious happiness I would have known with you, darling; but it will be very real, nevertheless, very quiet and full of peace."

"You'll find somebody else," Pride said. "Some nice young fellow, who—"

But Sharon's dark head shook fiercely.

"After having known you, Pride?" she whispered. "Never!"

The Sister tiptoed into the room and touched Pride on the shoulder.

"I'll come back tomorrow," he said, but again Sharon shook her head.

"No," she said weakly, "don't. Please don't. Go home to your—wife. . . . Tomorrow, I might not be so brave."

And Pride Dawson, coming out of the hospital under a sky turned black, suddenly wondered where all the light had gone—all the light in the whole world.

Still there was work to be done—in Millville, where Esther waited. There was a life to be lived, sons to be conceived, and a fortune to be built.

So thinking, he took his seat in the cab beside Tim and pushed up the little door in the roof so that he could see the driver.

"Pennsylvania Railroad ferry," he ordered.

And then he was back in Millville again after a train ride that had seemed endless. He was striding up the now familiar street once more in the darkness and the cold. At last his hand was on the knob of his own door, hesitating there before pushing it open. The hand moved convulsively and it was done; he was inside the hall, hearing the tangled rush of Esther's breathing.

She stood there in the lamplight, paler than he had ever seen her before—and infinitely more beautiful.

"Pride," she whispered, "you came back! Oh, my darling, you did come back!" Then she was running wildly into the shelter of his arms. . . .

CHAPTER ELEVEN—1870

IF PRIDE had performed wonders before, he now proceeded to miracles. He and his crews were laying a mile and a half of track every day, working like demons despite the December cold. The farmers in the neighborhood, who had already contributed their sons and some of their hired hands, did more: they cut down the timber on the heavily wooded sections of their lands and dragged it to Pride's right of way in sleighs. For Pride was a man to capture the imagination, and one and all they were hypnotized by him: his giant's frame, his bull-bellow of a voice, his prodigious feats of strength, even his rough-hewn ugliness were things to conjure with.

"Yep," they agreed, taking the corncob pipes from between their teeth, "he's a man all right. Nothing folderol about Pride Dawson!"

"Wouldn't trust no citified man what sits in his office all day and watches people work. But Pride don't do that. See him any time, at the head of the crew, doing more work

137

hisself than any of 'em. My boy Hiram sez to me, 'Why, Mr. Dawson kin pick up a cross-tie out of a sleigh by hisself and set it across without a soul helping him!' "

And the women without exception adored him. Esther found herself invited to farmhouses along the right of way, with the express admonition to "bring yore husband!" Tired as he was, Pride went. He knew only too well how much he needed these people. The Dawsons' presence at a gathering was a treat to the farm wives. It provided a double thrill: Pride's powerful, masculine charm, and Esther's exquisite clothes and beautiful manners. The younger, unmarried women hated her, for Pride troubled the dreams of all those who remained maidens. "He's so handsome!" they sighed. To which the Widow Tompkins, at whose house Pride had spent his wedding night, replied tartly:

"Fiddlesticks! He's as homely as a hawg in a gate. The truth of the matter is that big cuss gives a body ideas that no decent woman ain't supposed to have—leastways not until after she's married!"

Mrs. Tompkins was permitted such liberty of speech, because it was generally agreed that her husband's death had left her a little "queer."

The work went on. Then, shortly more than a month after Pride had begun operations, disaster struck.

Pride heard the thin squeak of Thomas Stillworth's voice the moment he opened the door, and the blood rose and beat about his ears.

"So you won't go home with me?" Stillworth was screeching at Esther. "You want to stay here with that scoundrel you married! Suppose I take you anyhow? Suppose I say to Rad and Walter, here: 'Pick her up and—' "

For all his bulk, Pride, moving, made less noise than a cat.

"Get out," he said. His voice was very quiet, but so deep that Stillworth could feel it. It reverberated through the room like an organ chord held hard.

It was a moment before Stillworth recovered.

" 'Get out,' he says! You forget where you are, Dawson! This is my house! My land! My mill! Mine!"

"I said, get out!"

Thomas Stillworth nodded to the men he had brought with him. They were big men, almost as tall as Pride himself, and they stepped forward together.

138

Pride watched them come, pure joy lighting up his black eyes. He kept his hands down at his sides, until one of the men lunged forward, the gleaming circlets of brass upon his knuckles glinting in the light of the gas jets. At the last possible instant, Pride moved his head aside a little, the motion graceful, exactly timed, so that he scarcely seemed to move at all. The brass knuckles whistled over his shoulder inches from his ear, and the man who had aimed the blow, thrown off balance by the effort, fell against him heavily.

Then, though it was apparent that Pride had not raised his hands, the man doubled in terrible agony. If they had watched closely, they would have seen Pride's knee come up, catching Stillworth's henchman squarely between the thighs.

Pride chopped him behind an ear as he went down, using the edge of his open palm like the blade of an ax. The man lay upon his face and did not move. The second man circled him warily. Then, apparently having thought the matter over, he brought out an owl's-eye pistol—a short heavy weapon with two barrels. He drew the hammers back one at a time, and Esther knew that she had never in all her life heard a sound more dreadful.

Then, a slow grin lighting his eyes, Pride started forward, step by slow step toward the muzzle of the pistol.

"Thought you might miss over there," he said cheerfully. "I want to be sporting about it—give you a better chance."

Esther could see the beads of sweat on the man's forehead, his finger tightening on the trigger; but still Pride came forward. Then she hurled herself upon the man, catching his arm and falling across it with all her weight, so that it was deflected downward; the two heavy balls, fired at the same time, plowed into the floor. She heard the impact of Pride's big fist as it landed full in the man's face, the small bones splintering, making a sound like the crumpling of stiff cardboard, the knees going rubbery, bending under him, the whole of him bending forward, and it was then that Pride hit him again.

The second blow lifted the man from his feet and sent him crashing into the sofa. It gave way under his weight and broke raggedly in the middle, the two ends bowing inward.

Pride grinned at her.

"Thanks, hon," he said. Then he turned to Stillworth.

"If you had your choice," he said softly, "would you rather walk out that door—or be thrown out?"

Thomas Stillworth's face was a battleground for his emotions. Fear struggled with rage. Fear won.

He clamped his tall hat on his bald head and stalked to the door. But then he turned, quivering with fury.

"I'll have the law on you, Dawson!" he got out. "I'll have an order dispossessing you in the morning. . . . I'll have this marriage annulled."

"How, Father?" Esther inquired sweetly. "I have witnesses that I came of my own free will, and I'm twenty years old—two years over the age of consent. Just how would you go about it?"

"I'll revoke your trust," Stillworth screamed. "I'll find out what banks gave you the money to start that damned little railroad and I'll force them to call. Then where will you be?"

Pride knew only too well where they would be, so he started forward again. Thomas Stillworth, before whom half of Wall Street bowed in reverence, turned and scurried through the door like an ancient rat.

Pride bent and picked up one of the unconscious men, lifting him easily. Then he walked out on to the porch and tossed him into a snow drift.

"Wait!" he called after Stillworth, "don't forget your playmates!" Then he repeated the performance with his other assailant. He remained long enough to see Stillworth get back into his hired sleigh and order the driver to get down and drag the two victims on to the vehicle. He grinned once more. He had enjoyed himself hugely.

But when he got back into the house, he found Esther in tears.

"Oh, Pride," she wept, "what'll we do now? Those bankers will jump through a hoop for Father. They'll call our notes so fast that—"

Pride patted her shoulder with a clumsy hand.

"Hush, hon," he said. "I'll think of something, never you mind. Just don't fret about it—don't fret at all."

Esther turned to go up the stairs, but Pride did not move.

"Esther," he called after her, "get your things packed."

Esther turned toward him wonderingly.

"It's a fact that your pa owns this house and can get us dispossessed," Pride said. "Only, we won't be here so he can have the satisfaction of doing it. I'll get Stepan to drive us up to Mrs. Tompkins' in Martintown. Your old man won't be able to find us there."

"All right," Esther said, "but that still won't help as far as the notes are concerned."

Pride knew that it wouldn't, and hadn't the slightest idea, at the moment, how to deal with this much greater threat.

Stepan Henkja was stopping his sleigh in front of the Widow Tompkins' house before Pride did get an idea.

Pride leaned forward suddenly and caught Esther's arm in a grip that hurt even through the thick fur of her greatcoat.

"Tell me," he said, "haven't Ed Bolley and Rad Waters an office in Pittsburgh?"

"Their main office is there. Most of their holdings are between here and Chicago. Their New York office is mostly for show. Why, Father always said—" She stopped suddenly, for she had finally caught the import of the question. "Oh, Pride, do you think they would?"

"I *know* they would! Your pa has beaten them five or six times now—and cost 'em a fortune each time. Besides, I could cut them in a little bit. If there were only some way I could get to Pittsburgh tonight!"

"There is," Stepan Henkja said. "A train passes through Valley Junction at midnight."

Pride looked at his watch.

"Two hours from now," he groaned, "and we're forty miles away from Valley Junction!"

Stepan smiled and pointed toward the station with his whip. Pride followed the gesture with his eyes. The little bell-funneled engine stood there. A wisp of smoke was stealing up from the huge stack, for the engineer had left the fires banked so that it could be started easily for the next day's work on the line.

"That little engine," Stepan said, "has pulled three cars, loaded with men and supplies, at forty miles an hour. How much faster could she go if there were no cars?"

"Stepan," Pride roared, "I could kiss you—only you wouldn't appreciate it."

"Then I will," Esther said, and gently kissed Henkja's swarthy cheek.

"Now I'm rewarded," Stepan smiled. "Go and awaken O'Malley while I get up steam."

As it was, Pride had to wait for the Pennsylvania Line's night train for almost an hour. But he was in Pittsburgh before daylight, and proceeded at once to Edward Bolley's residence.

Bolley was anything but pleased at being awakened at such an hour, but ten minutes later he was grinning broadly.

"So you own the M. & W. P., Dawson," he said, "and you've pushed it almost to St. Pierre. Good. Now, if there were only some way to force Stillworth to ship the billets from the mill and the coal from the mines over your road . . ."

Pride smiled quietly.

"Suppose something happened to that dinky little bridge the Millville Valley Branch has to cross?" he said. "Suppose something happened to it and kept on happening?"

"By God, he'd have to ship over your line!" Bolley roared. "You'd have him over a barrel. You could charge him whatever you wanted to!"

Slowly Pride shook his head.

"Suppose I were to tell him that the M. & W. P. was built with the help of the farmers for shipping farm produce—exclusively? No billets, no coal. Just eggs and butter and corn and lard and wheat and . . ."

Bolley's eyes were round in his fat face. His lips puckered in a whistle of admiration.

Pride continued calmly: "Get the picture, Ed. Black Tom's sitting there in Millville on his bony rear end. His bridge is down so he can't ship over the Pennsylvania. So he's got to ship over my line, and I won't let him. . . . You finish it."

"He'll either have to sell or dump his stock on the market. Either way you take over all of Millville."

"Except your steel mill. You get that back—for lending me the two hundred thousand dollars I need to get out of the hole I'm in. . . . And I'll pay the money back, too—later. What do you say? Is it a deal?"

Ed Bolley did not hesitate a half-minute. He thrust out his beefy, red hand.

"It's a deal," he chuckled.

Late the next morning Thomas Stillworth appeared at the first of the three banks that held Pride's notes. He was in no hurry. His son-in-law could be ruined at leisure. In fact, he spent the first ten minutes in the banker's office pleasantly chatting about business conditions in the country at large. After they had agreed between them that all signs were promising, Stillworth revealed the actual purpose of his visit.

"I understand that you let my son-in-law have a hundred thousand dollars," he began with a reproving shake of his head. "That was foolish of you, Morris—very foolish."

But the banker's expression did not change.

"I don't think so, Mr. Stillworth," he replied. "In the first place, I only let him have thirty-three or -four thousand—and besides he was in earlier this morning and paid off the loan in full. He deposited fifty thousand on top of it."

"But he couldn't have!" Stillworth gasped. "He doesn't have a dime!"

The banker smiled pityingly, as one smiles at a man in his dotage.

"I'm afraid you've been misinformed," he said gently. "Dawson brought the money in cash—peeled it off a roll that could choke a horse. He said that you'd be in later, that you rather disapproved of him as a son-in-law. You know, Mr. Stillworth, I think you should reconsider. Dawson seems to be quite a chap. Good head on his shoulders, I'd say."

Thomas Stillworth, at that moment, was beyond speech. He clamped his top hat on his head and went out without even saying good-bye.

He made the rounds of the other banks before he was convinced that he was beaten. Still, he was not a man to give up. When he got back to his hotel he sent for the two toughs whom Pride had so soundly beaten.

"Go down to Pipetown," he commanded. "You know the district, near Colwell and Stevenson streets—the Hardscrabble district—and get me some lads. Boys who don't care how they make a dollar. Try Suke's Run, too—and Riceville. Go into that beer tavern, Hatfield Garden. And sign them up and send them on to Millville. I'll tell them what to do when they get there."

He sat back after they had gone, rubbing his thin fingers together.

"Ah, Pride Dawson," he grinned, "you asked for it! Ah, how you asked for it!"

Above Martintown Pride's new railroad curved gently toward a break in the towering hills. The tiny locomotive puffed up the rails to their very end, and there Pride and his crew got down and went to work. Pride had lost the last ounce of city fat: he could now work all day long and not be aware of his fatigue until he started home at night. What worried him most was that his supplies were diminishing much too rapidly. He could get all the cross-ties and roadbed rock and cinders he wanted. But once the rails were gone, what then? Rails had to be brought from Pittsburgh, and the only way they could reach Millville was over the Pennsylvania and the Millville Valley Branch, and Thomas Stillworth could stop them from being shipped over either line.

He was thinking about it while he swung his pick. But neither the thought, nor the nagging worry it caused him, reduced his speed in the least. He was, as usual, well ahead of Ernie and the others when something sang over his head, making a high-pitched whistling sound. It was only after it had plowed into the earth a few yards beyond, kicking up a small puff of snow, that he heard the crack.

He had heard that sound before—too many ' times, as a gunrunner during the War, in the mining camps of the West, even in his native Louisiana.

"Rifle shot!" he bellowed. "What the devil!"

It came again, much closer this time. Pride straightened and put one big hand alongside his mouth.

"Hey, up there!" he roared. "What do you think you're doing?"

"Target practice!" a mocking voice floated down from the hillside. "Any objections?"

"You damn near blew my head off!" Pride called. "Shoot somewhere else!"

"I like it here," the answer came. "We all like it here! Besides, live targets are more fun. They look right peculiar when they jumps!"

Black rage mounted in Pride's face. He threw down his pick and started up the hillside. Then a whole volley crashed down, and spurts of snow leaped up all around him. Pride Dawson had more than his share of physical courage, but he was no fool. Slowly, he turned back to his crew.

"That's all for today, boys," he said. "I don't aim to get any of you killed. Tomorrow, we'll be better prepared."

"Stillworth?" Stepan Henkja demanded.

"Who else?" Pride growled, and climbed aboard the flat-car. The engine backed away. And from the hill there came a roar of derisive laughter.

Back in Martintown Pride turned to his crew.

"Any of you boys good shots?": he demanded.

Most of the men stepped forward. Hill people, farmers all, they had hunted since childhood.

"Go get your guns," Pride commanded, "and meet me here!"

By the time most of them had returned, much of the day was gone; but Pride took the crews out again and succeeded in laying a few more yards of track. Stillworth's gunmen apparently had not expected them to return, for there was no more shooting that day.

"Leave your firearms on the flatcar," Pride told them when they started out the next morning. "Stepan, get some canvas and cover 'em up. The minute those bastards start shooting, make a break for the guns. Shoot for the smoke —and *we* aren't going to any target practice. We're going to hit what we aim at!"

The little engine rolled out of Martintown bearing a grim crew. Pride had a revolver buckled around his waist and a Sharps rifle under the canvas. Most of the others had Enfields, brought home from the Civil War; but there was a new Winchester or two among the weapons.

They had been working less than an hour when the first rifle shot echoed from the hill. Pride's big hand flashed down and his revolver lifted and barked, smacking against his palm. Six shots followed one another, straight for the smoke wisp, while the crew ran for a flatcar. Before they reached it, they heard a rifleman scream.

Then a heavy volley crashed down from the hill and Pride threw himself flat upon his face while the bullets sang inches over his prone form. Stillworth's gunmen were shooting to kill.

But Pride's crew had their guns now, and they squatted

behind the cars and in the cab and tender of the locomotive, well protected, sending a hail of shot pouring into the smoke cloud from the hill. The Suke's Run boys fired back raggedly, and the Sharps and Winchester rifles among Pride's crew answered in unison, shooting for the gun flashes. There were more screams from the hill. The train crew fired another volley, and now there was a great scurrying on the hill. Dark figures darted out from the rocks and ran farther upward, some of them throwing away their guns in their haste.

"Try not to kill any of them," Pride called to his men. "We don't want trouble with the law if we can help it."

Pride and his crew crouched there, waiting for more fire, but there was none. Pride reloaded his Colt.

"Keep me covered, boys," he called. "I'm going up." Then he bent forward and started to run, darting from outcropping to jagged ledge, as he ascended the hill.

"He sure got his nerve!" Ernie said admiringly.

Pride had almost reached the ledge from which Stillworth's gunmen had fired when he saw a glint of sunlight on a rifle barrel. It was moving, following his path as he ran. He stood still, looking for cover, but there was none. The rifleman raised, sighting, and Pride could see the blood on his face. Then the rifle jumped, spitting a tongue of orange flame, and Pride felt a sledgehammer blow hit him in the left side, spinning him completely around before he hit the earth. He lay there, face downward, his revolver hand outstretched. The rifleman waited. Pride could feel a hot burning in his side, then a sticky wetness. But the rifleman still kept his cover. Pride played dead, waiting. Below him, the crew had seen their leader go down, and Stepan Henkja, ashen-faced and grim, was leading five men up toward him. Slowly, Pride began to move, inching himself around until he faced the cleft in the rock. Sooner or later, he knew, the gunman would have to raise himself, to see if his shot had gone home.

He was right. The man's head appeared, but withdrew instantly while Pride held his breath. Reassured, the gunman looked up once more, then raised himself half erect and sighted carefully at Stepan and the men toiling up the hillside.

Pride waited until the man had set himself, then the Colt jumped and bucked in his hand, as he fanned the hammer,

Western style, sending out four shots so fast that the rifleman jerked four times, still standing, before he went down, sprawling grotesquely over the face of the rock.

Clumsily, Pride got to his feet. There were no further shots. Stepan and the others came up to him.

"Thought you were done for," Ernie gasped.

"Not me," Pride grunted. "Take a look around, boys, and see if there are any more of them."

"You were hit," Stepan said, concern in his voice. "Let me have a look." He stretched out his hand but Pride pulled away from him.

"It's nothing," he growled. "Only a scratch. Besides, there's work to be done. . . . Go and help the others."

They found three badly wounded men on the hillside. The man Pride had shot was dead. They brought the three wounded men down the hill and bandaged them as best they could. Pride sent them back to Martintown on a flatcar, but he remained on the job. Stepan and the others buried the dead man where he lay, and erected a crude wooden cross over him on which Ernie carved the single word "Hardscrabble" after the district from which most of the gunmen came. Afterwards the spot was woven into the legend of big Pride Dawson, and as trains passed the spot, the conductor would point out to the passengers the Hardscrabble Grave.

As the day wore on, Stepan noticed that Pride was working much more slowly. Ernie had passed him, and now others of the crew were ahead. Like so many others, Stepan had developed a real liking for Pride, and his expression grew more and more worried as the hours passed. It was dusk before Pride collapsed, bending forward with his pick and following the blow on down.

They gathered about him and opened his clothing. They turned pale when they saw where the bullet had gone in— the round, bluish hole still bled sullenly. And that, too, became a part of the legend of Pride Dawson: how he paced his work crew all day long, with half an ounce of lead in his guts.

They lifted him carefully and carried him to the flatcar, but they had to wait until the engine returned from Martintown before they could take him in. Pride regained consciousness after an hour and saw them standing around him, their faces pale and awed.

147

"Get back to work!" he roared. That day, the crew laid two full miles of track—an all-time record.

Esther had been watching the clock for a long time before they brought Pride home. They were more than two hours late. She was standing at the window when four men came up the road bearing his heavy bulk. She came flying out into the snow, coatless, her arms bare, her lovely face whiter than the drifts.

"Pride," she whispered, "oh, Pride . . ."

"He's been shot, Mrs. Dawson," Ernie explained. "Your pa sent some men—"

Esther swayed dizzily, and for a moment Stepan thought she was going to fall. But she straightened up proudly, and when she spoke, her voice was very quiet.

"Bring him in, boys," she said.

So, Stepan mused, this is what it is to be a lady. Magda—dead now, since the last snowfall—would have been screaming by now. But not this one.

Muddy, wet and bloodstained as he was, they laid Pride down upon the great bed, while Ernie raced for the doctor. Esther turned to Stepan.

"Help me undress him, Stepan," she said.

Together they pulled off his clothes and dropped them in a sodden heap on the floor. Mrs. Tompkins had the water boiling and tore up her best sheet for bandages. After they had made Pride as comfortable as possible, Esther knelt beside his bed.

Pride's eyes opened.

"It's nothing, Es," he muttered. "Just a scratch. Somebody got careless with a shooting iron."

"One of Father's hired gunmen," Esther said grimly. "Well, there's no Esther Stillworth any more. Just Esther Dawson." Then at last, and with great dignity, she began to cry. Stepan held her hand and patted it with his huge bear's paw.

"Don't cry," he murmured. "Pride wouldn't like it. He worked all day with that bullet inside of him. It was foolish —but it was also magnificent. He didn't say a word to let us know how bad it was. I don't think he'd want you to cry."

Esther came erect slowly, dabbing at her eyes.

"You're right, Stepan," she said gently, "he wouldn't want it."

The doctor came at last, and examined the wound.

"It's bad," he muttered, "very bad. He's lost too much blood. Any other man would be dead by now, but I think I can pull him through. He's got the vitality of six ordinary men." He turned and looked at Esther.

"Mrs. Dawson," he said, "I think you'd better leave the room. I'll have to probe for the bullet—otherwise gangrene might set in. It won't be pretty. . . . Mr. Henkja, would you get another man to help hold him?"

Stepan nodded and left the room in search of Ernie. But Esther stood her ground.

"I'd rather be here with him," she said firmly.

"All right, all right," the doctor said testily; "but I won't have time to attend you when you faint."

"I won't faint," Esther said.

And she didn't, all through that terrible time that the doctor's instruments probed and twisted in the wound, and Pride's thick blood dyed the sheets scarlet. Finally, the doctor straightened up triumphantly, the flattened slug of lead held in his forceps.

"Here it is!" he said. "Now I'll dress the wound."

He did so expertly and with dispatch. When he had finished he looked at the Widow Tompkins.

"Put some hot broth on the stove," he said. "When he comes to, Mrs. Dawson, you feed him. He's lost an awful lot of blood, and he's going to need nourishment. If he takes a turn for the worse, call me. If not, I'll be back in the morning—early."

He crushed his shapeless hat upon his head and left. Esther sat down weakly, taking Pride's inert hand and rubbing it gently along her icy cheeks.

"I've got to fix that broth," Mrs. Tompkins muttered. She looked into Esther's face and added: "Mrs. Dawson, you're all right. Never thought you had it in you!" Then she fled toward the kitchen.

When Pride regained consciousness, Esther succeeded in feeding him. Gently, tenderly, she forced his mouth open with one hand and poured the hot broth with the other. After that Pride drifted off into sleep, but toward morning he woke up and started talking. He was delirious.

"Sharon," he whispered. "Poor dear Sharon . . . Why are you lying here like this. You're thinner than ever—half-starved . . . and it's all my fault. You believed in me, didn't you? . . . You know I loved you . . . only I was bought. I never loved anybody before you—never will again . . ."

Esther placed her fingers across his mouth.

"Hush, Pride!" she wept. "Oh, my darling, please hush!"

"I don't want to hush. I've got to tell you about it, Sharon. . . . I'm married now; never meant to . . . never meant to marry anybody but you . . . all that money, Sharon, all that money—all that damned money . . . and I've been too poor—so long. . . . Married Esther—she isn't like I thought—she's good too. One of the best women there is, I guess. . . . She's good and sweet and I could be happy with her if it weren't for loving you so damned much! . . ."

Esther was on her feet now, backing away from the bed. But Pride could not distinguish her face, or the anguish in her eyes.

"Don't go," he muttered, "I want to talk to you some more. . . . I want to think and plan—how to get you back. . . . I want to . . ."

But Esther was gone, fleeing down the long hall. On the porch she stopped, feeling the icy air blowing across her face.

"Give me strength," she prayed. "No—not strength—give me grace and gentleness and a heart big enough for two. Help me to teach him to love me, oh, God—so that one day he will really be mine." Then she grasped one of the carved posts, shaking all over with weeping.

Mrs. Tompkins found her there and put a thin arm around her.

"He ain't—Oh, Mrs. Dawson, he ain't—Oh, no!"

Esther turned to her quietly.

"No," she whispered, "he isn't dead. I—I guess my nerves gave way. . . . I—I'll go back now." Then she turned very slowly and went back into the room. To her relief, Pride was sleeping quietly.

She sat down beside him in the darkness, thinking:

I love you so, my great clumsy darling. I'd do anything for you—anything at all, except give you up. I'd do that too, only I haven't the strength. . . . Don't ask that of me. Ask anything else—ask for my life; but don't ask me to leave you. That I cannot do.

She bent her head and gave way to a storm of weeping.

It passed and she straightened up thinking:

We must have a child, a son—and soon, God, soon. . . .

CHAPTER TWELVE—1871

PRIDE SPENT his Christmas in bed, and most of the month of January, 1871, as well. Stepan Henkja directed the crews, driving them even harder than Pride had done. Nightly he reported progress to Pride, while the big man lay in bed, a broken hulk, and bemoaned his weakness. He lost forty pounds during his illness, his weight returning to the trim two hundred that it had been when he was nineteen. On his great frame two hundred pounds was virtual emaciation, and those who saw him now were shocked at the change in him.

He fretted and swore and was a very bad patient, continually trying Esther's patience. Yet, as she well knew, he had reason to fret, for her father attacked ceaselessly and with consummate ingenuity. No longer did he make a direct show of force. Instead, he resorted to more devious methods: a section of track torn up during the night and replaced without being nailed down, so that the locomotive was derailed; landslides caused by heavy charges of dynamite; explosives placed under the tracks themselves. Despite all Stepan Henkja's efforts, Pride's crews were building a scant half mile of track a day, and often having to build the same sections over again the next morning.

Pride countered as best he could. Armed guards patrolled the tracks at night. Empty flatcars were pushed, uncoupled, ahead of the locomotive, so that the engine could be braked to a stop if the track had been tampered with. The older men wandered through the hills, seeking the saboteurs. Soon the accidents were reduced to almost nothing, and again the mileage soared.

But Stillworth still held the trump card. Pride was rapidly running out of rails, and although he had the money to buy more, he had no way of getting them into Millville. During the last week that he lay confined, Pride's brain was busy. The first day of February, when he was at last on his feet, he wired for Tim McCarthy.

Tim came—out of necessity, for he had worked only sporadically during the early part of the winter, and with a family to support, he was badly in need of money.

Upon his arrival at Martintown, he went to see Pride. He stood back, his jaw sagging, seeing Pride thin, bent, his cheeks hollow, great dark rings around his eyes.

"Stillworth had me shot," Pride explained. "Damn near killed me, too. But that's not why I wanted you here. I've got a job for you, Tim—if you'll take it."

"I'll take it," Tim said sullenly, "providing it's clean."

"It's clean as the palm of your hand. Look, Tim, I need some rails to finish the M. & W. P. Not many—and I've got the money to pay for them. The trouble is, Stillworth won't let me ship 'em over his line. Now, his men in Millville know me, but they don't know you."

"Yes, they do—I was there before, remember?"

"The workingmen might remember you; but they won't talk, because they're on my side. None of his straw bosses have ever seen you. I want you to go to the plant, order those rails, and pay cash for 'em. Then have them sent to Stillworth's freight depot for shipment to Ohio."

Tim looked at him wonderingly.

"You can't take 'em to mine," Pride explained. "They'd smell a rat and not let you have them. Use a different name. Whatever day they say they can ship, order 'em held over till the next. That'll give me a chance to lift them."

"I told you no dirty—" Tim began. "Hell, it isn't dirty, is it? You'll have paid for the rails. Rightfully they're yours. The dirty work is on Black Tom's side because he ought to let you have 'em in free and honest trade. I'll do it!"

Pride put out his hand.

"Folks around here have sort of forgiven me for that shooting scrape. They know I didn't want anybody killed. How about you, Tim? Let's be friends again. What do you say?"

Slowly, Tim put out his hand and Pride crushed it in his big paw.

"Never could get around you," Tim said gruffly. "Reckon we were meant to stick together."

Ordering the rails, Tim found, was surprisingly simple. The new mill was still looking for orders, since most of the roads and heavy industries were too accustomed to saying "Pittsburgh" for everything connected with steel. Stillworth's plant carried almost enough rails on hand to fill the order. It took them less than a week to pour, cast, roll, shape and temper the others.

Then the carts moved out from the steel mill loaded with the heavy metal sections. They took them to a siding of the Millville Valley Branch and unloaded them there.

Anyone watching that next night would have witnessed a strange scene: Sleighs, farm carts, Conestoga wagons, farm vehicles of every sort arrived by the score at the depot. It was very late and no train was expected until morning. When the watchman wonderingly came out to investigate, a masked man stuck a revolver in his ribs and warned him against crying out. In two minutes he was bound, gagged and deposited in a corner of his office. With strange concern for his victim's welfare, the brigand threw more coal in the potbellied stove, for the old man might otherwise have frozen.

Then there was the clear clang of steel striking steel in the frosty night, endlessly repeated as time wore on, and the groan of heavily loaded carts. When the day agent came to relieve the night man, there was not a single bar of steel left. Two weeks later, the M. & W. P. reached St. Pierre.

Another week was spent in building a great terminal and in informing the offices of the lake steamers and barges that they had another port of call. But Pride had no produce for them as yet—and the line had to show a profit at once.

So he paid a call on Stillworth in New York.

"Let's let bygones be bygones," he pleaded. "Those lake steamers need coal like crazy. You've got the coal—I've got the line to ship it to 'em. It'll be profitable for us both."

But Stillworth, though he loved even the smallest profit, was firm.

"I'll be damned and in hell, first!" he roared.

"All right, Mr. Stillworth," Pride said quietly, "but you're going to be sorry!"

Though his business was urgent, Pride lingered another day in New York. He spent the day with Sharon, as Esther had known he would.

Sharon was overjoyed at the sight of him, but she concealed it well.

"You shouldn't, you know," she said. "Your wife won't like it. I wouldn't if I were your wife."

"I had to see you, Sharon," he whispered. "I had to rest my tired eyes on you. It does me good to see the goodness shining out of your face."

"Really?" Sharon snapped. "'It does me good,' but it wasn't enough, Pride Dawson—not when measured against all that money. Or was it the money? Your—wife is the loveliest creature I've ever seen."

"I know," Pride said sadly. "But I love you, Sharon. I always have—and always will. I can no more help it than I can help breathing. I thought I needed money for happiness—now I'm not sure. I can't be happy without you. Esther's as good as gold—so good it makes me ashamed that I can't love her as she deserves. But it's you, Sharon—you're always there getting in between before I can—"

Sharon's hands flew up suddenly and covered her ears.

"I won't listen to you!" she said. "You've no right to say such things—and I've none to hear them. You're married, Pride: married. Remember that. Why you did it doesn't matter in the long run. For whatever we do—even when we think we're being smart and managing our affairs to our best advantage—in the end turns out to be the will of God. If it weren't," she went on gravely, "He would prevent it. When He lets us do what we want, it's because what we want to do just happens to be what He wants done. You understand what I mean, Pride? I know it sounds frightfully confused."

"I understand," Pride said grimly. "But what about happiness, Sharon? Haven't we a right to be happy, you and I?"

Sharon looked at him, her dark eyes soft and tender, her mouth smiling a little; but Pride did not like that smile. It isn't natural, he thought; she looks like one of those old pictures of the saints she used to keep hung up in her pa's house—or like one of those black-robed Sisters, happy to be giving up everything.

"A right to be happy? No, Pride—not selfishly. When I —was sick, Father Shannon explained that to me. God

154

does not guarantee anybody happiness in this life. Some of His greatest saints led miserable lives. They were poor, hungry, even tortured. You see, Pride, God has a plan—a kind of universal order that keeps things working. And all of us, even you and I, have a part in that plan. We don't always understand it. We may never know what it means. And when the things we want get in the way of that plan—well, the things we want have to go. It's so much bigger than we are, Pride—so much bigger, and more important, and more beautiful. When we realize that, we can be happy to be doing our share, even if—it does hurt—sometimes. . . ."

"That's a hell of a thing to believe!" Pride said fiercely.

Sharon got up quietly.

"But I believe it," she said.

Pride stood up too and looked down at her, seeing her—tiny, fragile, thin, hollow-cheeked, wide of mouth, freckled; and there was pain at the pit of his heart. Her dark brown hair was clubbed on top of her small head, and her eyes looked out on hidden mysteries. He groaned inside himself, thinking: What's it she's got that makes every other woman on earth seem like nothing beside her? Why can I look at her and melt, when Esther, who looks like a princess out of a story book, can't make me feel this way?

And then, suddenly, he had his answer. It poured illumination into his face, and he stared at Sharon as though he were seeing her for the first time.

Sharon put out a small hand and let it rest on his arm.

"What is it, Pride?" she whispered. "What's happening to you?"

"I just found out something," he muttered, his voice far off and deep. "I just now found out, after all this time, why I love you. You know, Sharon, I've seen lots prettier girls than you, but I've never been in love with them. Loved them, yes, but been in love—never! Know why? Because no woman before now has been a person to me. They've been bodies—smooth long legs and pretty faces that I enjoyed looking at. But not you. I cared about you, Shay. It mattered to me what you thought. The way you feel about things is important to me—your goodness is, too. The way you look isn't—except as it reflects, like a mirror, what you are. And what you are is wonderful, Shay: goodness walking. Sweetness wrapped up in bones and flesh. An angel come down to earth to heal the sickness in a man's heart. And my heart, Shay, sure is in need of healing! It has bitterness in it, meaner than dirt; it's got a black devil ranting and raging inside. It's got pain and lonesomeness. And only you can drive them out, only you—not Esther, not forty million dollars, not anything else on God's green earth except you!"

Sharon looked up at him, her eyes tear-bright, her wide, soft mouth trembling.

"Please, Pride," she whispered, "don't talk like that! Please, Pride!"

He bent down swiftly, and took her in his arms. He kissed her until the stiffness went out of her, until the tenderness was there: the tenderness and the haunting sweetness, and the love that was not wanting in passion, but that went beyond passion; until he was filled up with it—with a warmth like spring sunlight, with a joy that was like many voices singing, with great and all-pervading peace.

He loosened his arms and stepped away from her. She collapsed in a shuddering little heap upon the sofa.

"That plan?" he said. "What becomes of it now?"

"Go, Pride," Sharon wept. "Please, go!"

And Pride went. It was a measure of his love for her.

In the after-midnight darkness, Pride waded among the ice floes of the little stream that ran through the gorge under Stillworth's bridge. He was all alone. In his pack he carried several bulky objects, but he splashed calmly through the cold water as though he were walking along a quiet street. When he came to the bridge, he tapped with his hammer on the stout timbers that supported it. It was strong, but not strong enough. In fact, it was dangerously weak to bear the weight of a loaded train.

Pride put the hammer back into his belt and began to climb. He went up the great timbers, catching perilous handholds on the ice-slickened piles, moving up inch by slow inch until at last he rested, panting just under the span of the bridge. He took out some lengths of rope and tied them to metal hooks in his broad belt. Then he fastened the rope ends to projecting timbers. Gingerly he tested. The ropes held, bearing his full weight and leaving both his hands free. He pulled out several of the long, bulky objects that were like great sticks tied together, and fastened them under the span, cutting the fuses long. Then he pulled himself up onto the bridge. He walked through the darkness until he came to the far end, and placed more sticks. He retraced his steps until he came to the end of the bridge on the Millville side. Again he fastened some sticks on the under side of the bridge, wiring them securely.

He walked back across the bridge and down the tracks for a half mile; then he drew out his short-handled pick and began to loosen the rocks that lay beside the roadbed. He piled them upon the track itself, and on them he placed three red lanterns which he lighted.

"Don't want people killed," he muttered. Again he came back to the first bunch of sticks. He kneeled and a brimstone match flared in his hand, as he cupped it, shaking it until it blazed and lit the first fuse. Then very calmly he walked to the next batch, and the next, lighting each fuse in its turn. He left the bridge, still walking slowly, calmly. He knew how long those fuses had been cut.

Sitting down on a pile of rocks on the Millville side, some five hundred yards from the bridge, he waited. He did not have long to wait. It happened very cleanly, just as he had planned. Both ends of the bridge lifted at the same time, and the hollow booming shook the hills. Then a second later the middle flashed fire and the bridge buckled with majestic slowness. It bent in the center like a live thing that had borne too much for too long; it bowed tiredly inch by inch, gathering momentum until it crashed down into the gorge, and the sound of its falling awoke echoes, hammering back and forth among the encircling hills.

Pride sat very still until the air was no longer filled with bits of iron and flying timbers.

Then he stood up, grinning.

"Well, Black Tom," he said. "Who's top dog now?"

It took Thomas Stillworth two days to reach Martintown. He had to be carried across the stream by one of his workmen. Then he stepped into the sleigh that had been sent from Millville to meet him.

By the time he reached Mrs. Tompkins' he was speechless.

Pride grinned at him, seeing his jaw working amid the forest of his mutton chop whiskers.

"Changed your mind, Black Tom?" he chuckled. "Come to talk business?"

"I'll have the law on you!" Stillworth screeched. "I'll put you in jail for so long that—"

"Which law, Black Tom? The law south of Millville? That's yours all right. But up here the law is mine. . . . And what are you so mad about?"

"The bridge!" Stillworth shrieked. "My bridge that you blew up!"

"Your bridge? Did something happen to your bridge?" Pride shook his head sympathetically. "Now, isn't that just too bad."

"You robber! You—"

"Wait a minute, Black Tom. Control yourself. You didn't come all the way from New York to scream at me—now, did you?"

"No, I didn't! I came to have you thrown in jail!"

"Now, look. While we're talking so peaceably about jail and such, suppose I go get the sheriff here, so you can tell him all about it. Only, Black Tom, remember that *I* had him appointed. And while you're telling him fairy tales about your bridge, I'm going to be telling him about the people who dynamited my tracks, derailed my engine, and put me in bed for two months with a bullet through my guts. He knows all about that, and he visited me while I was laid up, visited me often. Your engineers used to slow down and creep across that bridge, it was so weak. Everybody knows that. Maybe somebody sneezed on it. And assault with a deadly weapon with intent to murder is a serious charge. How about it, Black Tom?"

"I wish that damned fool had aimed better!" Stillworth got out. "I never would have hired him if I'd known he was such a poor shot!"

Esther, who had been standing quietly beside her husband, gave a gasp.

"So you *did* do it, Father!" she said. "You tried to have Pride killed!"

Mrs. Tompkins, whose ear, as usual, was pressed to the keyhole, pushed open the door.

"I heard him, too, Mr. Dawson," she said. "Now you got witnesses!"

Thomas Stillworth's face was a study in near-apoplexy.

"I'll build it back!" he screeched. "I won't ship a thing over your line, Dawson! Not a thing!"

"I'll wait," Pride said cheerfully.

A week later Stillworth was in a more reasonable f̲r̲
of mind. It would take him two months to build his brid͟
he discovered, and his inability to ship out of Millville was
costing him several thousand dollars a day. He could produce his steel and mine his coal, stockpiling his products to
the skies. But he could not get his finished materials to
market, and he had to pay wages all the time. Of course,
he could shut down the mill and the mines, but that would
be ruinous.

So, in the end, he came back to Pride and grudgingly
asked him to take the steel and coal to St. Pierre, where it
could be transshipped by barge and steamer. Pride agreed
gladly, but named a price that was just double what the old
financier had been paying before.

Stillworth screamed and tore at his whiskers, but he
paid.

The Millville & Western Pennsylvania was solidly in the
black now; it was even beginning to pay off its notes. And,
mysteriously, work on the bridge did not progress. Night
after night timbers were damaged, supply carts were overturned, and the workingmen received gifts of hard liquor
that left them totally incapable of work.

The job should have taken three months but it took five.
By that time Pride was hauling in seed and farm imple-
ments for the country people. In itself, it would not have
been enough to keep the M. & W. P. going, but Stillworth
found his trade in coal with the lake steamers so profitable
that he could not bring himself to discontinue it, even
though it benefited his hated son-in-law.

So the little engine puffed and snorted over the track,
throwing plumes of smoke from the big bell-shaped smoke-
stack which was so large that the engine looked topheavy.
When O'Malley the engineer gave the word, his fireman
opened the window that led out to the running board and
climbed out. Holding his tallow pot in one hand, he clung
to the hand-rail that ran along the boiler, while the train
stretched out along the track, running like wild, now and
again loosing the lonesome wail of its whistle. Slowly the
fireman dragged himself out to the steam-chest, and in an
instant the engineer closed the throttle. Then the fireman,
with beautiful timing, dumped oil into the vent of the
steam-chest, thus lubricating the valves. This was done several times during a run. In the whole of its first season the
159

.A. & W. P. lost only one fireman this way. Pride was lucky. Most of the other lines killed or maimed three in the same space of time.

Pride also got more business by making arrangements with the lake steamers to run excursions to Buffalo. This was very popular with the farm wives. That spring, several of them blossomed out in the very latest styles.

There was one thing Pride noted with great satisfaction. Stillworth had built another "beanpole" bridge of timber. When the summer had gone by without its being molested, Stillworth gradually relaxed and withdrew his guards. That was all Pride was waiting for. He struck again with terrible effectiveness. This time he dynamited the bridge itself and the shelf of rock that formed its approaches. When Stillworth, half mad with rage, came to view the wreckage, his experts told him that the bridge could not be rebuilt as an inexpensive wooden structure. The gap was too wide now—it called for steel. It might even be wiser, they suggested, to construct a suspension bridge, for otherwise, new stone or concrete pilings of tremendous height would have to be built.

This time Black Tom did not rush off at once to Martintown. Instead he remained in Millville and took stock of the situation. Even if he produced his own steel at the mill, it would still cost him a quarter of a million dollars to replace his bridge—and a year's time. Long enough to imperil his mines and his mill, or some of his other holdings.

Of course he could prosecute Pride. But Pride could bring effective countercharges against him. However, since God and the law were still on the side of the heavier battalions, it seemed likely that he would win. But what then? Pride would go to prison and he, Thomas Stillworth, would still have no bridge. Besides, he needed the Millville & Western Pennsylvania. Under ordinary circumstances, he would have railroaded Pride to jail and taken over the line. It would have been easy to do; all that was necessary was to buy up the notes outstanding against the line. But a routine check had revealed one salient fact: every note outstanding against the M. & W. P. was held either by Ed Bolley or Rad Waters, his sworn enemies. If he removed his son-in-law, he would be confronted with men even less disposed to be charitable toward him.

Pride, after all, wanted to do business with him. In fact,

160

Pride needed his shipping—so much so that he had destroyed the bridge to divert all the Stillworth traffic over his own road. Pride's rates were high, but barge fees were low, and he could make more profit by shipping via M. & W. P. than over the Pennsylvania, despite Thompson's rebates.

He decided to be conciliatory, while biding his time. Later, after Pride had redeemed his paper, he would strike. Pride Dawson would have to be brought to heel once and for all: he now realized, finally, that the man was dangerous.

So it was that the second interview was conducted in a vastly different manner than the first.

"Well, Pride," Stillworth cackled, "I have to admit you've got me. All right: I'll tell you what. Give me decent rates and I'll forget about the Millville Valley Branch. I'll ship over your road exclusively."

Esther leaned forward, her eyes bright and eager. This was capitulation. Her husband was on the way up.

But she had misjudged Pride; she had badly underestimated both his skill and the extent of his ambition.

"Sorry, Mr. Stillworth," he said quietly. "I'd like to oblige you, but I can't."

"You—you can't?" Stillworth gasped. "What the devil do you mean, Pride?"

Esther turned an amazed face toward her husband.

"Yes, Pride," she added, "just what do you mean?"

"Well, it's like this. All the minority stockholders are farmers round about here. I told them I was building for their benefit—and it's harvest time now. I need every inch of space to ship their stuff, and I gave my word." He looked at Stillworth and smiled gently. "You wouldn't want me to go back on my word, would you, Mr. Stillworth?"

"You thief!" Stillworth got out. "You robber!"

"Now you're repeating yourself," Pride grinned. "You said all that once before."

"But I'll be ruined!"

"I'm sorry, Mr. Stillworth," Pride murmured, "truly I am!"

"I'll fix you!" Stillworth spluttered. "I'll dump the stock on the open market—and I'll tip off Vanderbilt to buy it! Then let's see you buck him!"

"I hope you won't do that," Pride said evenly. "But I'll buck him, if I have to. I'll buck any man living."

Thomas Stillworth fingered the brim of his hat and glanced uneasily at the clock.

"What time does that damned little train of yours come back through here, Pride?" he demanded. "I came up here on it."

Pride stood up.

"Midnight," he said. "You're going back to New York?"

"No. I'm staying in Millville a couple of days to wind things up. But don't worry, I can do all the damage I want to do by wire."

Pride frowned. Then his face cleared.

"You're welcome to stay here and chat with Esther as long as you like," he said. "Me—I've got business to attend to. See you later. Sit." Then he went over to Esther and, bending down, kissed her cheek. He lingered over the caress, whispering: "Don't let on, but I may be gone for a week. It's important!" Then he strode through the door.

He ran back to the stables and harnessed the swift trotter to his little buckboard. Then he was off, racing down the road in the direction of Millville. He went directly to the station and roused the telegraph operator.

"You on till midnight, Harry?" he demanded.

"All night, Mr. Dawson," Harry grinned. Harry was one of the many local people Pride had won over.

Pride pulled out a roll of bills and peeled off two fifties.

"Here's a hundred dollars," he said. "Late tonight Mr. Stillworth is going to send a wire. Don't send that wire, Harry—hold it up for two days. If he waits, pretend to be sending—disconnect the key."

Harry's eyes were as round as moons in his thin face.

"It's a matter of life or death, Harry," Pride said. "Stillworth aims to ruin me—and I don't mean to be ruined."

"I get you, Mr. Dawson," Harry said happily. "And if he don't send it until tomorrow, I'll pass the word on to Jake."

"Good!" Pride grunted. Loyalty had its uses after all.

Then he went off in search of Tim. He found him at the M. & W. P. depot, supervising the loading of coal from Stillworth's mines.

"Come on!" he said. "You're going to do the biggest

162

thing for me that anybody's ever done. We've got to get across the gorge and down to the Pennsylvania. I'll explain on the way."

Later, as they waited for trains—one of which Pride was taking to Pittsburgh and the other of which was to bear Tim to New York—Pride did explain.

"Black Tom's going to dump his stocks—all the stocks he owns in his holdings here. I aim to buy 'em. The Millville Valley Branch, the mines, the mill and the town of Millville itself. You be waiting at the Merchants & Seamen's Bank tomorrow morning. A wire's going to come there giving you a million dollars worth of credit. Then light out for the Stock Exchange . . . no, get Bernstein and Goldblatter to act for you—they know better how to handle it. Get it?"

"I get it. But where are you going to get a million dollars?"

"Leave that to me!" Pride said.

The first thing in the morning he walked into the Industrial Bank of Pittsburgh, one of the banks where he had secured his former loan. He was greeted cordially, as a man who had firmly established his credit. But Pride did not waste time or mince words.

"I want to borrow one million dollars!" he announced.

The banker blinked at him. Pride gave him no chance to reply.

"Here," he added, "is the stock for the Millville & Western Pennsylvania Railroad. I own it. As you know, the line's completed now—and incorporated at two and a half million dollars. You can hold this as security."

"Any liens or encumbrances?" the banker asked.

"None," Pride said firmly. Fat chance you have of finding out about that money I owe Ed Bolley, he thought.

"It seems adequate," the banker muttered. "I've been hearing good things about that line."

"I've got a chance," Pride said, leaning forward confidentially, "to double and triple my holdings. I'll pay this back in one year at whatever rate you specify."

A gleam stole into the banker's eye.

"Seven per cent?" he suggested.

"All right," Pride agreed at once.

"Done," the banker said. "How do you want it?"

"In the form of a letter of credit, wired today to the

163

Merchants & Seamen's Bank of New York, in behalf of my agent, Timothy McCarthy," Pride said. "Can you do that?"

"Easily. Now, if you'll just sign these papers . . ."

Three days later, as he had threatened, Thomas Stillworth dumped his holdings in the state of Pennsylvania. That night Pride Dawson owned them all, mines, mill and railroads—if the fact could be disregarded that he owed Edward Bolley two hundred thousand dollars plus interest, and the Industrial Bank of Pittsburgh one million plus interest of seventy thousand dollars.

Back in Millville, Stepan Henkja found himself manager of the steel mill, with carte blanche to raise wages and institute any other reforms that would increase production. Tim McCarthy became boss of the mines. And Pride traveled all over the East, seeking markets. He cut his prices to beat the competition and he got the orders.

But he did not return the mill to Ed Bolley as he had promised. Instead, upon receipt of the first order for half a million dollars' worth of steel from a steamship builder, Pride paid off the loan and the interest. When Bolley demurred, demanding the return of the mill, Pride offered him forty-nine per cent of the stock of the Millville Valley Branch Railroad instead. Bolley flatly refused.

"All right," Pride said slyly, "I'll give you your damned mill, Ed. But remember: I own both lines out of town, and I just might be all filled up when you get ready to ship something."

Bolley sat back, looking at Pride with real admiration in his eyes.

"You win, Dawson," he said softly, "I'll take the stock."

"Good!" Pride said. "But you've got to help me out. Build me a suspension bridge over the gorge. I'll furnish the steel for nothing. You furnish the labor. Agreed?"

Bolley nodded grimly.

"I'm too smart to fight you, Pride," he said. "I know when I'm beaten. I'll build your bridge."

Pride consolidated the Millville Valley Branch and the M. & W. P. into one line, and enormously watered the stock in the process. By the simple use of the printing press, he increased the value of his railroads by five million dollars. Then, in less than six months, he paid off the Pittsburgh Bank.

For two years now, men had been calling Pride Dawson a millionaire. By the fall of 1872 they would be quite correct.

CHAPTER THIRTEEN—1871

PRIDE, HOWEVER, left Millville before he had achieved his ambition of becoming a millionaire. As soon as he had gained possession of Stillworth's holdings, he took Esther back to New York. He could do this with an easy mind, because he had left Tim McCarthy in charge of the mines, and Stepan Henkja managing the mill. And, best of all, he had lured tough, hard-driving Ben Stanley away from Vanderbilt's newly-acquired Michigan Central to take charge of his own growing lines.

Pride and Esther arrived in New York on October 9th, 1871, the very day that the old Commodore opened his magnificent Grand Central Station at the junction of Fourth Avenue and Forty-second Street. Pride had chosen to come home by way of the Central System for the express purpose of pulling into the new station. Besides, making connections with the Central was actually as easy as taking the Pennsylvania, now that his own line was in operation. It was considerably more convenient too, since getting into New York City over the Pennsylvania necessitated taking a barge across the Hudson.

Esther and Pride spent almost an hour inspecting the great train shed, and Pride filed away several ideas for future reference. Then he called a cab. The porter slung their bags up and with Pride's assistance Esther entered, while the driver stood waiting behind the passenger box, his reins flapping across the roof. Pride himself got in, and lifted the little trap door in the roof.

"Sixty-eighth and Fifth Avenue," he called to the driver, "right next to Central Park!"

Esther looked at him in wonderment. To the best of her

165

knowledge that region was pure jungle, except for a shanty settlement that encroached upon the Park itself.

"Sixty-eighth Street, Pride?" she gasped. "Why on earth are we going there?"

Pride patted her hand with his great paw.

"You'll see!" he chuckled.

The cab turned off Forty-second into Fifth Avenue and clopped steadily northward. Then Pride squeezed Esther's hand and pointed. Esther put her head out of the window and her blue eyes widened. What had been jungle before, was jungle no longer. Not a single packing box shanty marred the view. And there, towering above the trees, was a massive, block-shaped building.

Esther turned wonderingly to her husband. But Pride simply sat there, his mustache half-hiding a huge grin. The hansom cab drew to a stop, and a uniformed doorman ran forward to open the door. Carefully, he helped Esther down, then, stepping back, he made a quick bow.

"Mr. Dawson," he said. "Glad to see you, sir! This is Madame?"

"Yep," Pride grinned, "this is Mrs. Dawson. And, Louis," he added, giving the man a five-dollar bill, "pay off the hackie and send up our bags, will you?"

"This—is this a hotel?" Esther demanded.

"You'll see!" Pride said again and led her through a richly ornamented hall to a small brass-enclosed cage.

"An elevator!" Esther whispered. "Pride, what kind of a place is this?"

"You ask too many questions," Pride growled in mock wrath. "Come on."

The little brass box, with a handsome young Italian at the controls, ground and jerked upward for what seemed to Esther to be forever. Finally it halted, and Esther stepped out, almost falling in the process, for the elevator boy, as usual, had missed his floor by a good eight inches.

They stopped before a door of rich dark wood, and Pride took out a key. He unlocked the door and, turning suddenly, lifted Esther into his arms.

"Welcome home, Es," he said, and carried her into the room.

Esther looked about her at the huge room, as crowded as her father's parlor, filled with rubber plants and drapes and

166

what a later age would consider outrageously tasteless furnishings.

"Oh, Pride," she said, "it's beautiful!"

"They call these places 'French flats,'" Pride said expansively. "We have eight rooms, a bath and a kitchen—all on the same floor. Central heating, too." He crossed to the window and held back the curtains. "And just look at this view!"

Esther looked out over the autumn colors of the park, and southward toward where the city hummed in the dusk of evening. She turned back toward Pride, thinking: I can win, yet. If he doesn't love me, why did he do this? He's trying to make me happy. I—I'll make him forget her yet! Then going up on tiptoe she kissed him.

A polite cough sounded from the other side of the room. Esther whirled to find three strangers staring curiously at her. After a moment she saw that they were in uniform: a dark little girl in the black dress of a maid, a tall man beside her in the cutaway and morning trousers of a butler, and a fat red-faced woman in the white apron of a cook.

"This," Pride said, pointing them out, one by one, "is Simone. She's your maid, fresh off the boat from Paris. Pierre, her husband, is my valet and houseman. Bridget is the cook."

Simone curtsied, Pierre bowed, and Bridget stood staring at him in embarrassment.

"Excuse me, sor," she said at last, "but me name ain't Bridget. 'Tis Mary, begging your pardon, sor."

"I like Bridget better!" Pride growled.

The cook looked more and more confused.

"But, sor——" she protested.

"You can be Mary anywhere else," Pride said flatly, "but here you're Bridget. Understand?"

Bridget nodded.

"Very well, sor," she said. And Bridget it was for the rest of her life, until finally she herself forgot that her name had once been Mary.

Pride led Esther through the flat, pointing out the rich black walnut floors, the magnificent bathroom with its mahogany bathtub lined with porcelain, the spacious kitchen with its massive coal-burning range and upright hot-water heater. He opened a little door in the wall and pointed to a miniature elevator.

"They call these things dumbwaiters," he said. "At least, they'll keep the policemen out of my kitchen and Bridget can get some work done."

"Poor Bridget," Esther laughed. "How will she ever find a husband?"

"I hope she doesn't," Pride said. "Getting married is the ruination of good cooks."

That Bridget was a good cook she proved a half-hour later. Their first meal was perfect. Pride rocked back in the chair, his big face flushed with contentment.

"Bridget!" he roared.

Bridget came scurrying fearfully out of the kitchen.

"How much are you getting a month?" Pride demanded.

"T-ten dollars, sor," Bridget quavered.

"From now on," Pride said, "you're getting fifteen. Now off with you and bring the dessert and the coffee."

Bridget's red face, as she fled back into the kitchen, was a study in joy.

Esther looked at Pride, thinking: He wins them over—all his people, no matter how lowly. Even when they don't like his methods—like Tim or Stepan—they remain loyal to him personally.

"We won't be here too long," Pride told Esther over the coffee. "This is just temporary—till Millville and the railroad start to pay off. Then I'm going to build you a house that'll make Stewart's look sick. Out of the city—with parks and stables, like a castle. I'm going up—yes, hon, I'm going up. Millville's just the start. I'm going to be richer than your pa. Just wait and see!"

Esther put out a slim hand and caught his.

"I know you will, darling," she said. "But I don't care about that really. All I want is—" She stopped abruptly, her cheeks a bright scarlet.

"Is what?" Pride demanded. "Name it and it's yours."

"You," Esther whispered. "All to myself—not divided three ways between myself and your business and—and that girl."

Pride's face was suddenly black as a thundercloud.

"Don't talk like that!" he roared.

"I won't," Esther said quietly. "And, Pride . . ."

"Yes," Pride growled, "yes, Esther?"

"There's another thing I want. A child. A son who'll look like you and act like you and grow up to be—"

168

The thundercloud was gone now, and a happy grin took its place.

"Maybe we'd better work on it," he grinned, "starting right now!"

Esther shook her head.

"Later," she said gently. "I just want to sit here now and be happy. Besides I think it's your fault that it hasn't happened before now."

Pride stiffened.

"Don't be angry. It's just because you—you haven't cared enough. A great deal of love should go into the making of a son, Pride. I don't want ours to be the—the accidental result of a pleasure taken when you hadn't anything else to do. He's got to be intended, Pride. Wanted and loved and meant to be. I don't want you to ever look at him and think—" She stopped, glancing warily at her husband.

"Go on," Pride said ominously.

Esther's head came up. There was a flare about her fine nostrils.

"That he has the wrong woman for his mother!" she said.

Pride got up slowly. From where Esther sat he seemed to tower into the gathering gloom.

"Pierre!" he bawled.

The valet appeared as if by magic.

"My hat and gloves," Pride growled. "And my cane."

Esther looked up at him, her face taut and still.

"Where are you going?" she whispered.

"Out!" Pride said curtly and marched from the room.

Hearing the crash of the outer door as Pride slammed it, Esther thought: I've done it now. He was in such good humor. But I had to remind him. I had to harp on the subject —show my jealousy like a stupid chit of a girl. We could have had such a pleasant evening together. And now it's all spoiled. He'll go to some saloon and come back drunk and ugly. Or he may even . . .

She stopped, aghast at her own thought. For, even as she shaped it in the darkness of her mind, she knew it was precisely what Pride would do. He would go to Sharon O'Neil. And she, Esther, had sent him there.

Sitting rigidly in her chair she remembered the last time she had seen Sharon O'Neil. What would Sharon do, she

169

wondered—now that the situation was reversed? How could she expect mercy, who had granted none?

She bowed her head over the empty coffee cup, her eyes blinded with sudden tears. Bridget cleared her throat politely.

"Finished, ma'am?" she said.

"Yes," Esther whispered. "Yes, Bridget—quite."

When Pride reached Sharon's shop it was closing time. He told the driver to wait, and sat there in the cab while the girls came out in twos and threes until they were all gone. Then he paid the man and got down, crossing the street very slowly until he came to a halt before the door of the shop. It was open. Inside he could see Sharon, her back to him, busily putting away the partly finished dresses that the seamstresses had made.

He stepped inside the door and watched her. She turned, holding a frock up to the dying light so that she could inspect the seams. Her eyes widened until her cheeks were dominated by them. She took a step forward. Another. Then the dress she had been inspecting fell to the floor, a shapeless heap, and she was running toward him, her arms outstretched.

But when she had come halfway, she stopped abruptly, and the joy drained visibly from her face. She came forward once more, walking slowly, awkwardly; and when she was close she put out her hand.

"Hello, Pride," she said.

Pride did not answer her. He stood there, staring down at her hand. Then he put out his big hand and covered hers, holding it lightly for a long time, before he pulled Sharon forward into his arms.

"'Hello, Pride!'" he mimicked her. "That's a fine thing! You came running at first, didn't you? Came flying down that aisle to my arms, where you belong. Then you remembered what'd happened, and you thought about all the rules, and so you stopped. Hell, Shay, those rules don't apply to us."

Sharon rested her small face against his broad chest.

"Don't they, Pride?" she whispered.

"Why, hell no! The rules that were meant for us haven't been written yet. I was a fool. I made a mistake. A bad mistake, Sharon—the worst I ever made in all my life. But that doesn't mean I've got to go through the rest of my days being miserable from wanting you. I'm going to get a divorce."

"Pride . . ."

"Yes, Sharon?"

"A divorce wouldn't make any difference. I still couldn't marry you."

"Why in thunderation couldn't you? The law says—"

"The law," Sharon said slowly, patiently, as though she were talking to a child, "hasn't anything to do with marriage. Marriage is a sacrament, Pride—established by God. 'Until death do ye part.' Death, Pride—not divorce. If you went through every court in the land, if you got decrees from every state, I wouldn't marry you, because I couldn't. Men made those laws, Pride—men who strayed a long way from the sight of God and His church. And no matter if the whole world approved my marrying you like that, in my own heart I'd stand condemned. I'd be no better than a harlot. And I couldn't be a harlot, Pride—not even yours."

"Of all the damnable tomfoolery . . ."

"I'm sorry, Pride."

Pride glared down at her, his big face dark and angry.

"You're sorry!" he exploded. "There's only one answer to the whole thing. You don't love me! If you did, you couldn't talk like this. You don't even understand what love means. . . . I guess you don't know how it is to be sick inside, miserable as a poisoned hound dog in a black gum swamp, from wanting somebody you can't have."

Sharon looked up at him.

"Don't I, Pride?" she whispered. Then going up on tip-toe, she kissed his mouth, slowly, lingeringly, with so much tenderness that Pride could feel the pain inside his chest. When she drew away her face, her eyes were wet.

"You say I don't love you!" she whispered. "I who have been dying by slow inches since the day you went away. I who smother my head in my pillow every night so the people next door won't hear me crying. You say I don't understand! I walk the city streets every night from the Battery to Sixtieth Street so that I can make myself tired enough to sleep. I don't keep medicines in the house any more, Pride. I lock the scissors in the shop and stay away from bridges and high places—lest I be tempted beyond my strength. Have *you* ever prayed for death, Pride? Have *you* ever gotten down on your knees and beseeched the dear, kind God to relieve you of the burden of living? I have. I do still. For love of you—you great unthinking beast! For wanting you —whom I can never have!"

She collapsed against him. Pride held her close, stroking her dark hair with one great hand.

"There, there, Shay," he mumbled. "Don't you cry. I love you just the way you love me—maybe more. There're laws all right and there're sacraments. But there's nothing —absolutely nothing—that says we've got to be tormented like this. I'm going to get us a little place where we can be together, a nice little private house where we can lie all night in each other's arms."

He felt her stiffen, her whole body rigid suddenly, and when she looked up her face was blank with incredulity.

"Never!" she said.

"What are you scared of, Shay? Hellfire? Being without you is worse."

Slowly, she shook her head.

"It's—it's not fear, Pride," she said. "I don't believe in being good because of fear of punishment. Goodness ought to be a part of a person. It's like something Father Shannon used to say: 'You can't use a golden chalice as a spittoon, or the temple of the human spirit as a vehicle for senseless lust!' That's what we'd be doing, Pride. Do you understand that?"

"No. But it adds up to the same thing. You're saying no. . . . All right, Shay, but I want to ask you one favor. Let me come to see you once in a while. Go riding with me. Go walking. Talk to me sometimes, so I can kind of feast my eyes on you—so I can have the satisfaction of knowing you're still here, alive and in the same world with me. All right?"

"All right, Pride," Sharon said without hesitation; but the moment she had said it, she knew it was wrong. One should not lay banquets before the starving, or repeat temptations which one cannot possibly bear. . . . But Pride bent and kissed her quickly and was gone. Sharon stood looking after him in mute misery. As she went about her remaining tasks, she was not surprised to find that her fingers were stiff and awkward, cold with a nameless fear. . . .

CHAPTER FOURTEEN—1871

THOMAS STILLWORTH was tired. He had been tired before, but never like this. Always on other occasions he had, after a period of rest, come back from his defeats and turned them into victories. It was true that never before had he been beaten so soundly. Yet that was not what troubled him. Rather, it was something about the mood he found himself in: a lethargy, an unwillingness to rise and fight again.

He was not even angry with Pride Dawson any more. The marriage was an accomplished fact—and so was the matter of the mines, the mill and the railroad. The truth was that Thomas Stillworth felt a stir of admiration for Pride's financial generalship. And he was tired, much too tired. There was something else, too—a thought that had tugged all morning at his consciousness. He knew what it was, yet he did not like to express it. But his fatigue, finally, was too great.

"Why," he said, with mild surprise, "I'm going to die."

He was an old man, but he had never thought of death before. Life had been too good. From the time, some forty years before, when he had stepped off the boat from Liverpool, it had been good. Even groping and fumbling for the reins of power. Even the near-starvation, the days when he had lived on a half-roll and some weak tea had been good. There had been the beginnings of success and, among them, the miracle that still, so many years after her death, left him awed and humbled: his marriage to Esther Wallach—the slim golden woman who had given him more happiness than most men can bear, and left in his charge a lovely daughter.

He supposed, now that he had faced the issue, he had better do something about his sins. Not that he regretted them, really. They had been enjoyable sins: the rich wines

173

and richer foods and the bought, compliant women. He had enjoyed them most thoroughly. He supposed now that he should give a thought to the salvation of his soul.

He suspected that God would take a rather dismal view of his treatment of the poor. The rat- and roach-infested tenements with absolutely no provisions for sanitation would not help his case. The wages he had paid, which merely prolonged the agony of starvation over a period of years, might grease the skids into hell for him. And certainly his strike-breakers were the most grievous of his sins, for men had died at their hands. Six at Millville under the direction of Dawson. And before, at other places, at other times—how many? He didn't know. Wonderingly, he shook his tired old head.

"Why," he muttered, "there's blood on my hands!"

Well, he had to do something about that now. Esther was not a cause for worry any more. Pride had abundantly demonstrated his ability to take care of her. He's probably worth well over a million right now, Stillworth mused. Of course, a million dollars isn't much, but in Pride's hands it'll be a terrible weapon. He'll die richer than I am—he's got the gift. . . .

Still, it wouldn't do to leave Esther unprotected. He knew his daughter. If Pride were as careless and indiscreet as he had been in the past, Esther might leave him; she had her mother's fire and spirit. And if she ever found him insufferable, she must be protected.

I'll call in Bernstein and draw up a new will, he decided. Half to Esther, hedged about with every legal technicality so that Dawson can't get his paws on any of it. Half to designated charities, orphanages for the poor, hospitals in the mill towns—God knows, they need them!—and schools, too, for their ragged little brats. I'd better do it now, too; I haven't much time.

He rose and pulled the bell cord to summon Malcolm. Then he sat back and waited. Shrewd as he was, he did not realize that his belated philanthropy was a form of bargaining with God, differing only in degree from that of the men who left huge gifts to Trinity Church.

It took Bernstein, Stillworth's attorney, less than an hour to rough out the new will. Then he left, promising to bring back the finished draft the next day so that it would be signed in the presence of witnesses.

Thomas Stillworth had no sooner settled back in his chair when Malcolm reappeared with a bulky envelope. It had been delivered by messenger, Malcolm informed his employer, and the man waited below. He wanted, Malcolm added, the address of Mrs. Dawson and her husband.

"I was unable to give him the information," Malcolm said stiffly. "I do not know where Miss Esther lives."

Thomas Stillworth glanced up at his butler. Was there a note of reproach in Malcolm's voice? He couldn't tell. Malcolm was too well-trained for that.

"Send the man up," Stillworth squeaked.

After the butler had gone, he ripped open the envelope and looked at the heavily embossed card it enclosed. The card bore the emblem of a double-headed eagle. It was an invitation to a banquet honoring the Grand Duke Alexis, youngest son of Tsar Alexander II of Russia. The affair was to be given at Nillson Hall.

Stillworth chuckled, rubbing his thin, spidery hands together. He didn't ordinarily care about social functions, but a Grand Duke—ah, that was different. All the inherent snobbishness in his middle-class English soul came to the surface.

Malcolm came back into the room, followed by the messenger. The man stood respectfully before the tiny, frail old man.

Stillworth demanded: "Why do you want my daughter's address?"

"She and her husband," the man said, "are also invited."

Stillworth frowned. That rascal! Still, the messenger had said "She and her husband—" just as one said "The Princess and her consort . . ." It was, after all, the magic of the Stillworth name that did it.

The Stillworth name! But that had once been nothing, just as the name Dawson now was nothing. Did he dare doubt that in ten years men would use the same tone of reverence when they said "Dawson"? No, he did not doubt it. Age had made Thomas Stillworth wise. History was largely a long series of *faits accomplis*.

"All right," he said, "she lives at Sixty-eighth and Fifth, in the new French flats." Then a thought struck him. "Here," he said, "give it to me. I'm going there tonight. I'll save you the trip."

"Thank you, sir," the man said.

Stillworth saw the expression of surprise on Malcolm's face.

"Yes, Malcolm," he said gently, "I'm going. Time I buried the ax, don't you think?"

"Yes, sir," Malcolm said. "If I may be so bold, I do think so, sir. I'll tell Terence to get a carriage ready."

Pride was angry. With a muffled "damn!" he threw down the letter he had been reading and stood up, his face heavy with frowning.

"What is it, Pride?" Esther said.

"Tim. He's still writing me about those damned mines. He says they're unsafe. Hell, show me a mine that isn't. The minute you go poking around under the earth you take your life in your hands."

"Doesn't he have any suggestions?"

"Yep. That's the trouble. He's got half a million of 'em. Hoses on the face so the dust won't be set off by the blasting. Ventilation to take care of the fire-damp, whatever in blazes that is! Now he even wants canary birds!"

"Canaries?" Esther echoed blankly. "Why?"

"Seems that they keel over in five minutes if the air is bad—and that gives the men an extra twenty-five minutes to get out. One man carries a bird along in a cage. They watch the canary out of one eye while they work. How in hellfire does Tim expect them to dig any coal if all the time they're going to be watching a damn bird?"

"Human life is more important than coal, Pride," Esther said.

"Is it?" Pride said callously. "Seems to me it's about the cheapest commodity there is. Every minute another carload of brats comes into the world. And they all have to die sometime. What's the odds?"

"Pride!" Esther began.

"I know, I know. I don't mean it. . . . I'm going to put in all these things Tim wants—as soon as I get money to do it with. Right now it isn't profitable. It would cost more'n those mines are producing."

"So," Esther whispered, "until you make a profit, men will have to go on dying."

"They'll go on dying after I put 'em in. Look, Es, nobody rightly knows why mines catch fire and explode, or how poison gas gets in them. Even the things they understand don't always work out right. There were two men killed last week when a roof fell in. Tim says they timbered the roof right—put in enough big timbers to make the damned roof stay put. Only, the roof happened to be made of the wrong kind of stuff, something Tim calls 'draw slate' that softens up when air gets to it. So those timbers, instead of holding it up pushed right through it, and a couple of tons of coal and earth buried those poor devils. You see?"

"How horrible!"

"People have to have coal," Pride said patiently. "Would you rather those poor devils in the tenements freeze to death, so that a few miners escape getting killed? Life is like that. Men died hunting the seals for that coat I bought you. People were killed in the quarries blasting the rocks for this building. Trees fell on the men who cut the timbers for our houses. . . . Name me one thing that we use, Esther, that hasn't got blood on it?"

"I—I never thought about it like that," Esther said.

"The world's a jungle, Es. It has to be. That's how nature keeps things balanced. If there weren't any wolves, they'd be too many deer. No wars, no sickness, no starvation: too many people. And another thing—have you ever thought how there's always one big wolf leading the pack? Or one lion that makes the whole jungle shake when he roars? That's me! Head wolf—boss lion. If it weren't me, it would be somebody else. Your pa maybe—or old Commodore Vanderbilt . . ."

The jangle of the bell interrupted him.

"Now, who the devil can that be?" he muttered as he heard the butler open the door.

The butler returned, followed by Thomas Stillworth. Even Pride felt a swift surge of pity at the sight of the old man. Stillworth's gait was halting and feeble. He was bent over his great cane. Esther ran forward and caught him by the arm.

"Good day, daughter," he quavered, "you look lovely!"

"You look fine yourself, Father," Esther lied.

"Poppycock!" Stillworth snorted. "I don't have long to live and you know it. That's why I came to see you. You, too," he added, looking up at Pride.

"Sit down," Pride said quietly.

The old man sank, sighing, into the big chair that Pride pushed forward for him.

"I had to bring you this, anyway," Thomas Stillworth said. "The committee didn't know your address."

Esther took the envelope and opened it.

"The Grand Duke Alexis!" she gasped. "Oh, Pride, we're invited to meet the Grand Duke!"

"Naturally," Pride said, with a show of calm, but Stillworth could see his chest expanding. "He's got to meet all the best people, you know."

Stillworth hid a smile behind a parchment-thin hand. The best people! You—you great clumsy ox? But then why not? Every noble family in Europe could trace its descent from just such a burly fighting man who had built his castle athwart a pass, and collected tribute from the poor. There are no dynasties anywhere, he reminded himself, that do not ultimately go back to pillage, rapine and murder—either in the old world or the new. And what was the precise moral difference between the grandsons who clung to privilege with slim, aristocratic fingers—and the horny-handed, great-thewed "robber barons" who had amassed the blood-stained fortunes in the beginning? "God," he thought, "I'm old—old!"

"Buy yourself some new clothes, Es," Pride was saying. "You've got to be the best dressed woman there—as well as the prettiest!"

"Yes, darling," Esther said. "I'll do just that."

"Tomorrow," Stillworth said. "Tomorrow is time enough. I want to talk to you two, today."

"Why, of course, Father," Esther said.

"I'm going to die," Black Tom announced. "No, Esther —no denials. I am. I'm resigned to it. I've lived a long life and a full one. Just one thing bothers me, though. I want to make my peace with you and with Pride. I'm sorry I fought you, son. I should have known you couldn't be beaten. I should have welcomed you into the family from the beginning, but I wasn't smart enough. I had to take a beating before I came to my senses."

He put out a hand that was all bones under its purplish skin.

"Can you forgive a stiff-necked old fool?" he murmured.

"This isn't a trick?" Pride said warily. "You mean it?"

"Yes. I haven't the strength to fight any more. Bernstein has orders to liquidate all my holdings. I've provided well for Esther in my will, and I'm turning my seat on the Exchange over to you, Pride—as of now. Is that proof enough?"

Pride took his hand.

"Good enough for me. All right, Tom, we're partners. But you can't pass on right now. There's something you've got to do for me first."

"Yes?"

"I bought myself a couple of legislators in Michigan and Illinois. Now I got a right of way from Detroit to Chicago. Only, I'm not well enough fixed to build another railroad. That's where you come in."

"Pride, that's positively idiotic! What about the Michigan Central? What about the Pennsylvania? How much business can you expect to get away from men like Vanderbilt and Thompson?"

"Damn little," Pride said, "but I sure can make one hell of a nuisance of myself!"

"My God!" Stillworth gasped; his thin face lit up with respect. "That's right! Just like Vanderbilt bought that competing Canadian line and tied it into the Central. He'd have to—"

"Pay me my price to get my dinky little road off his neck."

"That's blackmail!" Esther said firmly.

"No, hon," Pride said fondly, "it's business."

"But," Stillworth pointed out, "I've retired. What good would any more profits do me now?"

"I'm not talking about you. I'm talking about me—and Esther. You and I'll split the profits two ways, and you can add your half on to what you're leaving Esther. Fair enough?"

"All right," Stillworth said wearily. And so it was done. Even before the new road reached Chicago, Commodore Vanderbilt bought it for four million dollars. With his share, Pride promptly purchased the controlling interest in the barge companies with which he did business. By the autumn of 1872 he would be dickering for a transatlantic steamship line.

On the nineteenth of November, 1871, New York City went crazy. In a poultry shop, the proprietor tied two turkey gobblers back to back to look like a two-headed Russian Eagle. You could get an Alexis cocktail in any bar on

Broadway, Pride discovered. The staid Astor House hung out blue bunting, on which white letters read: "Grand Duke Alexis, son of a noble father, representative of this nation's dearly cherished ally—this country most heartily welcomes you, from one extreme to another."

No one, apparently, saw the unconscious humor of those extremes. But, on the nineteenth of November, bootblacks were using Alexis polish to shine the shoes of their customers, Delmonico's entire menu consisted of Russian dishes, and all the tailors were making exact copies of the Grand Duke's clothes.

That there was a certain irony in all this exaltation of the twenty-two-year-old Romanov, son of the most absolute despot on earth, on the part of the nation making the loudest claim to democracy, bothered the citizens of New York not at all.

Sharon, Pride found, was as excited as the rest. As a result of the Ball in the Grand Duke's honor, she had more orders than she could possibly fill; yet she was ready to take the day off, just to see Alexis' ship arrive in New York harbor.

"Please, Pride," she begged, "take me down to the docks! I'd so like a holiday."

"All right," Pride said indulgently. "Be ready in two hours."

He returned to his flat, but when he got there he found Esther dressed for the street.

"Come along," she said gaily.

"Where?" Pride demanded.

"To see him land, of course! To meet the *Svetlana!*"

"No!" Pride said fiercely. "Hell, no!"

Esther's pink mouth opened a little behind the black netting of her veil.

"You don't want to see the Grand Duke come ashore?" she said.

"Why should I? That's for the mob. We'll see him tonight at the dance and the banquet. I don't feel like pushing through half a million people just to see a young squirt get off a boat."

Esther's head came up.

"Very well," she said, "you stay—I'm going!"

Pride's luck, that day, was miserable. Ten minutes after

his arrival at the pier with Sharon, he was seen by no less than three of Esther's friends, each of whom promptly forgot the Grand Duke in her haste to report the scandal to his wife.

By the time the third woman reached her, Esther was in tears. She knew that she could not afford to make a scene —that, indeed, she must appear utterly indifferent—but try as she would, she could not manage it. In the end, she allowed herself to be led close to the spot where Pride and Sharon stood, quietly watching young Alexis Romanov, as he stepped ashore.

Pride felt Sharon's fingers, fierce suddenly upon his arm.

"Oh, Pride," she whispered. "Oh, Pride—how terrible! Your—your wife . . ."

Pride turned and looked at Esther, seeing her face pale, her lips trembling visibly, though thirty feet of space separated them. Then he turned once more to Sharon, who was crying helplessly beside him.

"Come," he said gruffly, "we'd better go."

There was, perhaps, reason enough for the country's jubilant mood. When all of Europe had turned against the North, the Tsar alone had remained a friend of the Union, sending his fleet to the harbors of New York and San Francisco, with offers of aid. And now when the specter of revolution marched through the lands of Western Europe —when Karl Marx and Friedrich Engels were rallying the proletariat everywhere—Russia alone stood firm. There had been strikes and violence all over America—and in France, on March 8, the Communards had launched their bloody Commune.

In July, in New York City, Catholic and Protestant Irishmen had slaughtered one another to the extent of fifty-four dead. Moreover, the great fratricidal Civil War had not been forgotten entirely; and the city was just recovering from its discovery that Boss Tweed had stolen two hundred million dollars from its coffers.

Well, things could be worse! The spires of Brooklyn Bridge were rising; Boss Tweed was safely in jail; and the city had sent three million dollars to aid fire-gutted Chicago. Alexis, no doubt, was a good omen. He represented order and stability. A jittery land appreciated those qualities.

But all these considerations passed completely over

Pride's head. Sitting there, watching Esther sweeping through the graceful measures of a waltz in the Grand Duke's arms, he stared over the menus printed in gold upon satin, over the wreckage of the monumental banquet, past the spun-sugar statuettes representing Alexander II and Nicholas I facing a chocolate George Washington, and thought bitterly:

"I wonder what the hell *he's* looking so sad about?"

Alexis could have told him. In Moscow there was the beautiful young Zhukovskaya, a commoner, his mother's lady in waiting, from whom he was being exiled to suit the royal plans.

Esther's problem was simpler. She merely had a broken heart.

CHAPTER FIFTEEN—1871

"You MUST give her up," Esther said.

Pride ran a hand through his mustache, giving it a shaggy and unkempt look. It made his face much fiercer.

"I said," Esther began again, "you—"

"I heard you!" Pride snarled. "Now you're getting tiresome."

"I'll not stand for it, Pride!" Esther said flatly.

"Just what won't you stand for?"

"You and that—that—"

"Girl," Pride supplied. "That wasn't what you were going to call her. I know the words better than you do, because you aren't accustomed to saying them. Only—they don't fit Sharon. 'Lady' doesn't either, though she is one—"

" 'Lady'!" Esther spat.

"Yes," Pride went on calmly. " 'Lady'—in the sense people used to mean it, before they attached it to every high-priced tart who held out for a license before she'd sell herself to a man. A girl who's good and pure and honest is a lady—whether she's rich or not."

"Pure and honest and good!" Esther said. "You think I'm a fool?"

"No, but you've got a dirty mind. Look, Esther—did you ever hear me say 'I love you' to you?"

The tears were there in the blue eyes now. Miserably, Esther shook her head.

"Oh, you're right enough—about me. But not about Sharon. I asked her to marry me two weeks after I met her. She was willing, but I—dammit!—had to get rich first. You said I could be bought—cheap. Well, you bought me; but it turns out I'm not a bargain."

"Pride," Esther whispered, "oh, Pride . . ."

"Sure, what you're thinking would be true, if it were left to me. Only, it's not. It's up to a girl who says: 'Go back to your wife, Pride. She's a wonderful person. You married her, now stick by her . . .'"

"No," Esther wept. "No, no, no . . ."

"She says marriage is a sacrament. I told her I'd get a divorce and she looked at me like I was crazy. She's a Catholic and she believes in her religion. I could get a hundred divorces and she'd still feel I was married to you. So you're stuck with me, Esther."

Esther's hands covered her ears.

"I won't listen to this!" she cried. "I won't! I won't!"

"You asked for it," Pride said grimly. "So don't call Sharon names. She's not my mistress, though I wish to God she were. I don't get into bed with her, simply because she'd fight me, and end up by hating me—which is the one thing on earth I couldn't stand. Be grateful to her; it's her fault you still have a husband."

Esther put her face down upon the table and her body shook with sobbing. Some of the anger went out of Pride's big frame.

"Be patient with me, Es," he murmured. "I can't help this thing. I could love you. You're good as gold and so damn pretty it hurts. Give me a chance. This business about Sharon is going to die—of pure starvation if for no other reason. If you love me enough, you'll be there, waiting. It would be easy to love you, Esther."

Esther sat up suddenly.

"I don't want another woman's leavings!" she said angrily. "Go to Sharon, Pride. Go—and don't come back!"

Pride stood up, looking down at her.

"All right," he said quietly, "maybe I will."

It was very still after he had gone. Outside the window the late December snow came down in a silent tracery. There was no sound in the room except the hiss of the steam from the central heating and the thudding of Esther's heart.

Why did I say that? she thought. Why on earth do I always say what I don't mean? If he goes to her now, it will be my fault. I think he told me the truth about her scruples. But she can't keep it up—not if she loves him. No woman could. I'd never think about sin and sinning, if our positions were reversed.

She put her face back down upon her arm, but she did not weep. The matter now was past the help of tears.

Pride sat down on the edge of Beekman's Pond, between Fifty-ninth and Sixtieth streets, and strapped on his skates. Skating was the newest craze. Everyone skated: grandfathers, young lovers, children who had learned to walk only a little while before.

Gingerly, Pride moved out upon the ice. He was not very proficient at it. But it went better as he moved along. He managed to avoid falling and, as he gained confidence, began to increase his speed. He had learned to skate only the winter before, Esther having taught him during their stay in Pennsylvania.

He crossed the pond twice before he saw Sharon. She was skimming along, clad in a trim skating costume, her hands hidden in a white muff, a white fur turban upon her dark head. Pride stopped skating. She looked so lovely! She was moving swiftly, gracefully executing difficult figures, occasionally leaping into the air and dropping down in a swirl of petticoats and skirts.

He skated over to her, and when he was close by she saw him. Joy and sorrow mingled in her dark eyes.

"Pride," she whispered. "Oh, Pride, you promised!"

"Promised?" he said testily. "I reckon I did. I could promise to stop breathing too—but I couldn't do it."

"But, Pride," Sharon said with gentle insistence, "we can't any more. You and I know this is only friendship, but your wife doesn't. As long as we weren't hurting her, it wasn't so bad. But now—no, Pride. Please go. Some of these people here might know her."

184

The skaters swirled about them, silent and brisk. The white curving lines of the skates made arabesques on the ice. Pride still stood there, looking at Sharon.

The color slowly left her cheeks, so that the spray of golden freckles stood out vividly against her pale skin. At the corners of her mouth a little tremble started. She, too, stood still, looking up at him; then all at once she was against him, clutching at the fur lapels of his coat.

"Pride," she whispered. "Oh, my darling Pride . . ."

Pride bent down and sought her mouth, deep pink, soft-fleshed, wide and generous, but she turned her head so that his lips brushed her cold cheek. It was icy to the touch, cold as death.

"No, Pride," she said gently. "That was wicked of me. Come, let's skate."

They moved off among the skaters, the wind tugging at their ankles. He was acutely conscious of the slim hands lost in his great ones, warm and soft even through the thickness of her gloves. Each time he glanced at Sharon, an aching void formed in his middle and expanded and contracted with his breathing.

I want her, he told himself. Oh, my God, how I want her! But there was more to it than just wanting her. No, he corrected himself, I love her—that's the whole damned trouble! He had begun to comprehend, dimly, how vast a distance lay between the two words. He wanted Esther. He had wanted many women, and usually his desires had been satisfied. But with Sharon it was something far deeper.

"Pride," Sharon said suddenly, "you look so funny! What's the matter?"

"There used to be an old preacher down home who always called women 'the weaker vessel.' That's a hell of a thing to say!"

"Why, Pride?"

"You're nobody's vessel. You weren't meant to be used that way, and left and forgotten. You were meant to stand by a man and give him courage . . . meant to talk to a man and make him wise . . . meant to sing and be happy, so that watching you a man could have joy in his heart. I can't say it right—I haven't the words—but every time I look at you, there's love inside me. Every time I see you I'm weak all over from wanting you—in all ways, not just naked in my arms."

He was surprised, when he looked at her again, to see that she was crying.

"I should like very much," she said suddenly, fiercely, "to be naked in your arms!"

"Sharon! Oh, Sharon, honey . . ."

But she swung away from him wildly.

"No, Pride," she whispered. "I'm sorry. It's true, though. It's been true all along. But it's only since I—I lost you that I've had courage enough to admit it." She stood quite still, smiling up at him through her tears. "Come, Pride—you'd better take me home now."

Sharon no longer lived in the rooms above her shop. She had moved to a small, tastefully furnished old house that she had bought and redecorated. At the door she put out a slim, gloved hand to him.

"Good night, Pride," she said.

"Can I come up?" Pride pleaded.

"No, Pride."

"Not even for a minute?"

"No, Pride."

" 'No, Pride'!" he said bitterly. "Don't you ever say 'Yes'?"

"Yes, darling. My heart says it all the time. But it's a very wicked heart, Pride. That's why you can't come up. I could ask you to spare me, but you wouldn't. I might not even put up enough of a fight to ease my conscience with the thought that I truly tried. You see?"

"I don't see a thing! We were meant for each other, Shay. God meant us to be together. If there ever was a sin on this damned earth, it was when I married Esther! I got in God's way. I didn't do what He meant me to. So now . . ."

"No, Pride," Sharon said wildly, and fled through the door, slamming it behind her.

By midnight Pride Dawson was drunk—meanly, savagely drunk. He was very quiet about it, so that even the barkeep who repeatedly filled his glass was unaware of his condition. Whiskey, which usually put him into instant good humor, tonight curdled in him sourly. Even on those occasions when he had wrecked saloons, he had not felt like this. Then even the battle had been joyous—an excess of playful strength, a wanton desire to display his prowess.

186

But this silent, brooding drunkenness was another thing. He felt thwarted, frustrated, mocked. The desire inside him now was elemental and brutal, mingled with anger. He wanted to hurt Sharon now. He wanted to shame her.

She thinks herself so fine, he pondered drunkenly. She thinks she's too good to do what she knows she wants to do . . . Nobody's that good. It's not as though I didn't love her. I'd be good to her; I'd marry her, if she'd let me. Only, she won't do that either! God damn it to hell! What does she think I'm made of! This is flesh and blood—not iron!

He stood up suddenly, tossed a bill on the bar and marched out. There was only a slight sway in his walk. Outside, the snow came down cool and white. Somewhere along his route, Pride had lost his hat, and the flakes clung to his black hair, making him look like a grotesque snowman. He stumbled, then straightened up, swearing. But drunk as he was, he traveled straight as an arrow to Sharon's house.

Inside, Sharon stood by the old kitchen range, patiently waiting for a large tin tub of water to heat. She wore a flannel nightdress and slippers, but she had kept the house so warm that she felt no need of a robe.

After Pride's departure, she had gone to bed, only to lie awake for hours tormented by doubts and confusion until the tension had become unbearable. She had learned long ago how soothing, physically and mentally, a hot bath could be, and so she waited now before the huge range, occasionally poking up the coals in the firebox.

Pride stood on the sidewalk in the snow, looking at the door.

If I ring the bell, he mused, I wonder if she'll let me in? I'll have to try it, I guess. He went quietly to the little stoop and rang the bell, twisting the knob with great force. Then he stood back and waited. He heard, after a moment, the swift scurry of her slippered feet.

Sharon slid back the lock and opened the door a crack. Pride thrust a big foot forward, but she did not attempt to close it again.

"Oh, no!" she whispered. "No!"

Then he was inside, grinning at her, the melting snow making little streaks down his dark face.

"Sharon, honey—" he began.

She leaned forward suddenly, then drew back.

187

"You're drunk!" she said. "Please go."

"Yep. Drunk. Drunk as an owl. Drunker than a coot. All your fault. You freeze up a man's insides so that he has to warm them somehow . . ."

"Oh, Pride, Pride," she moaned, "how could you! This is dreadful! Oh, please, my darling, be good and go!"

"I'm not good," Pride declared, wagging his big head. "I'm terrible. I don't aim to go. I mean to stay here with you—where I belong."

Sharon backed away from him now, terror in her eyes. Her brown hair hung loose about her shoulders, soft-curling, and her eyes were big with fright.

"Kiss me," Pride murmured. "Come kiss me . . ."

Perhaps, Sharon reflected, if I humor him, if I talk to him gently . . .

"If I kiss you," she whispered, "will you go?"

"Sure," Pride said with drunken craftiness, "sure I will."

Sharon went up on tiptoe, her dark eyes closing. Her arms stole upward about his neck, and her lips caressed his, warm and tender. Pride made no threatening motion, but kissed her very gently. Sharon felt her fear leaving her. I can manage him, she thought. She brought her hands down and cradled his face between them, lingering over the caress.

It was then that she knew she had been wrong. The swift, backward motion of her head was almost anticipation—but Pride's mouth clung to hers fiercely, fighting for possession, and his big hands, about her waist, were hoops of steel.

The struggle went on in silence. Her hands came up, reaching for his eyes, but he twisted aside, and her nails dug long bloody furrows down his face. He merely tightened his grip. Vainly she hammered at his mouth with her fist. Slowly, inexorably, she was being bent backward. The air was crushed from her lungs, but she continued to fight, using her nails, her hands, even her teeth, until Pride muttered:

"You little wildcat! Claw away, honey—I like 'em wild!"

Then, suddenly, her strength was gone, and she was limp. He held her out at arm's length, and one hand closed over the collar of the flannel nightdress. She heard the sound of tearing cloth and felt the night air cool upon her skin. Then Pride lifted her up and walked up the stairs to the bedroom. He put her down gently; then his immense bulk was night descending, blotting out the lights . . .

"Hush, Shay," Pride mumbled. "Hush, please hush!"

But she continued her dreadful crying. Her entire body was racked with grief. Pride could see her throat quiver with the wild, unceasing sobbing, her head thrashing, her brown hair flying with the motion, the sides of her face striking the pillow alternately with audible force.

He could see the tears squeezing through her eyelids, held tightly closed, as though to shut out his face, and the sickness inside his own heart was the worst he had ever experienced—far, far worse than the night after the massacre at Millville: he knew instinctively that the ending of a life was a kinder thing than this.

He put a great hand gently over her mouth, but she twisted silently, her face purpling from lack of breath, so that he was forced to take away his hand. It was then that her eyes opened, and she sat up and stared at him, her lips bruised and swollen, moving in the effort to shape the word.

"Go," she said at last, the single syllable shuddering up from her throat. When he hesitated she screamed it at him:
"Go!"

There was nothing else to do. Slowly he got up and, arranging his clothing, went out of the room and down the echoing stairs.

Sharon cried for a long time after he had gone. Then she got up from the bed and dragged herself to a full-length mirror. She ached in every muscle but, compared to the grief in her heart, the physical pain was nothing. She stood before the mirror looking at her body, fragile, soft-curving, slender, and her eyes were Eve's eyes the moment after eating the fruit when she saw her nakedness for the first time. Sharon looked at herself a long time, as though trying to discover a visible stain upon her flesh. The face that stared back at her was haunted, the lips bruised and swollen, a dried trickle of blood at one corner of the mouth, the eyes blue-circled, sunken and swollen with weeping, the cheeks cavernously hollow, framed in a mass of wet, tangled hair.

She went into the bathroom and poured the almost scalding water into the tub. When she stepped into it, her skin reddened, and she had to bite her lips to keep from crying out. This was a rite—the ancient rite of purification, older than her religion—a thing purely pagan although she did not understand it all. Her hands were fierce, scrubbing at her skin. But after a time she gave it up and lay back in the hot water thinking: It's inside—that's where the stain is. It's on my soul.

Then she thought about Pride and, to her surprise, her thoughts did not follow the expected pattern. She had believed, in the split seconds of lucidity granted to her before, that she would hate him forever. But what came out of the echoing darkness of her mind was: "Poor Pride! He looked so dreadfully ashamed."

She knew that she had better get up and get dressed, for if she lay there in the water she would begin thinking and the core of her grief would be laid bare. But she could not move: the merciless thoughts tore at her, more cruel than flagellation, belaboring her heart.

No, no, she told herself, I did no wrong! I fought—oh, yes, I fought. But she was incapable of self-delusion. I fought, she told herself—but why did I put my arms about him? It would have been no sin if, being overwhelmed, I had afterwards taken no part in it. But participation is more than surrender, and she knew that well. An inert, ungiving body was one thing. She had tried to stay apart from what was happening to her; but in the end she had been dragged in and humiliated—not by Pride, for that he was powerless to do, but by her own body's criminal treachery against her spirit. There had been words—Oh, blessed God! —that she had whispered over and over into his ears. There had been caresses freely, joyfully given. She had capitulated to his lust, which was a shameful thing; but she had also surrendered to her own passion—and that was mortal sin.

She had of course known that men found in this act the keenest pleasure. Stanton O'Neil, for his times, had been amazingly frank with his daughter. But she had not been prepared for the unutterably intense bodily rapture that she had experienced at the last—that exquisite mingling of pain and ecstasy—and her frightened mind was capable of only one explanation for it: she, Sharon O'Neil, must be hopelessly depraved.

She had mortally sinned. There was no doubt about it. She was the woman taken in adultery, and in her own hand

190

was the stone. What now? Must she pity herself? Must she withhold her hand? Pity was for others. Charity was the thing that one extended to poor sinners—never to one's self. Self-pity was cowardice.

As she stepped from the tub, she remembered suddenly, blindingly, how it had been.

"Yes," she whispered, "oh, yes, I am damned!"

She would not flee God's wrath. She would go forward to seek it. Being damned, another sin, however mortal, could not increase the pangs of hell one iota. It was, besides, the easier choice. Living, she must face Pride again. Living, she might have to gaze at Esther whom she had wronged so terribly.

She fled naked through the rooms searching for a weapon, for poison. But there was nothing. She had feared too long her own grief at losing Pride; she had taken too many precautions. So, at last, she drew out another gown from the drawer, and put it on. Then she lay down upon her bed. Lacking food and water, she reasoned, she would die after a time. And there would be no marks upon her—nothing to betray her grief and shame to all the world.

She settled back peacefully on the narrow little bed and waited. The darkness was all around her like a living thing —around her and within, filling up the vast and echoing emptiness of her heart. . . .

CHAPTER SIXTEEN—1871

THAT SAME NIGHT, Thomas Stillworth died quietly in his sleep. Terence, his coachman, brought the news to Esther. He looked shocked that Esther did not cry.

Pride, Esther thought, has cost me so many tears that I have none left for my father. She went back upstairs and dressed, while Terence waited with the carriage. Then she came down again and got into the vehicle. She reached her father's house shortly after midnight.

So it was that when Pride reached home two hours later, he was spared the humiliation of another scene. He went at once to the Stillworth mansion, but Esther was not alone. Terence had summoned several of her father's associates, despite the hour. She noted with astonishment the scratches and the bruises on Pride's face, but she was in no position to question him in front of the other people.

She could see the lifted eyebrows, and the hands being raised to conceal the whispers.

Now, she thought, now of all times! Oh, Pride!

But he paid no attention to the looks or the whispers. His head ached dully, and his mind worked slowly, painfully, his unhappy thoughts groping through the lingering fog of liquor and the memory of his shameful assault on Sharon.

"Aah!" he snorted in self-disgust; and only when he saw the faces of the people around him did he realize that he had made the sound aloud.

I mustn't think about it, he told himself. Not here—not now. I owe Esther's father that much respect.

They gave Thomas Stillworth a funeral that would have done credit to a Roman Emperor. The whole block about Trinity Church was roped off, and policemen fought to keep back the crowds. There were fifty-seven coaches in the procession for this man who had never knowingly helped or befriended a fellow creature in his life. Of the ceremonies, Father Shannon was moved to say, in one of his rare descents into bitterness:

"Such a burial is never granted a saint. No—saints are crucified and their blessed remains thrown to the beasts . . . But barbarians like Thomas Stillworth—ah, *Sic Transit Gloria Mundi!*"

But Esther, dry-eyed behind her heavy black veil, found the quiet conducive to thinking. Forgive me, Father, she mused, but you had your life and it is finished. You did your best for me and I'm grateful. But now it's over. My life must go on; I have to think about myself now. I have to plan. You were beaten many times, but you always won in the end. And I'm your daughter. I'll win now . . . or if I fail, I'll take such revenge on Pride that he'll be destroyed by it.

She gazed quietly at her husband, sitting there beside her

. . . Sharon tried to fight you off, didn't she, Pride? How well did she fight, Pride? Enough to make you stop? Or were you successful? I suppose you were. God bless her for fighting. I shall not hate her. Oh, no—it's you I'll hate. And I am a Stillworth, Pride. We're wonderful haters: we can feed on hate for a lifetime.

She continued to gaze at him.

I shan't be foolish this time. I'll not make a scene. Oh, yes, I'll be very humble and submissive. I'll be patient. I may have to wait for years for the opportunity to strike, but when I do . . .

When, after the clean black earth had ceased thudding upon the bronze lid of Stillworth's coffin, and the procession had retraced its route, silent and slow, Pride knew that the time of reckoning had come. He kept his face averted from his wife, hoping against hope that she would not mention the matter. And, to his vast astonishment, she did not.

It was not until they were undressing for bed that Esther turned and faced him.

"Pride—" she began.

Pride ran his tongue over his lips before he could speak. "Yes, Esther?" he mumbled.

"You did it, didn't you? You—you forced that girl."

Lying was no good now.

"Yes."

"I thought so. And, Pride . . ."

"What?"

"You won't again, will you? Promise me that you won't."

There was, Tim had often said, a black devil inside Pride Dawson. It reared up now, brazen and angry.

"And if I don't?" he said defiantly.

"You'll regret it," Esther said quietly and, turning, got into bed.

That was all. It would have been better if there had been more. Tears and angry words would have been better, for he could have understood them. But this apparent acceptance was menacing. There was an implication here that he could not clearly define. It worried him. There was for a whole week a stillness in the house, a kind of funereal peace. Pride wandered about looking puzzled and depressed and angry. Not until the week was over did he get a chance to relieve the dark pressures within him.

It was then that the will was read. To his bitter disappointment Pride found that he was not one penny richer than he had been before Stillworth's death. The old man had left Esther only half of his fortune, and that half was so hedged about and fenced in with legalisms that, short of Esther's making an outright gift of her money to him, Pride could not lay a finger on it. And that, he realized, Esther would scarcely do—under the circumstances.

What made it worse was the fact that he could not protest. There was no way he could roar or bluster without sacrificing the quality that had given him his name; his pride. He went for long walks, he drank heavily—but he did not go near Sharon's house.

Not like this, he thought. Not bitter and ugly and smelling like a brewery cart. I'll wait until I'm sober—then I'll go.

He came home at last to find Esther waiting up for him, a telegram in her hand.

"You've been with her," she said accusingly.

Gloomily, Pride shook his head.

"No," he replied, "I haven't. What's that you've got?"

"You're lying," Esther said wearily, "but it's no matter. Here."

She gave him the wire. It was from Edward Bolley. The first thing Pride noticed was that it was written like a letter with no attempt at deletions or abbreviations to lessen its cost. Stillworth would have considered it criminally extravagant.

"Therefore," he read, "I don't think it necessary even to start building that nuisance line here in Colorado. The assayer assures me that the vein of silver is fantastically rich. Pride, you are a lucky devil. Who else ever had a laborer who discovered silver while digging a right of way? . . ."

Pride looked up.

". . . I've filed a claim here. You'd better do the same in Washington. Then join me in Denver. I put myself down as part owner—for a fourth—but I'm willing to discuss the matter. The land is, after all, yours."

Keep your fourth, Ed, Pride thought. If it hadn't been for you, I wouldn't even have known about this. Well, Black Tom, who's laughing now? You can beat everything but my luck! I'll die richer than you did!

He passed the telegram over to Esther. She read it rapidly and looked up at him.

"Congratulations," she said quietly.

"Can't beat me!" Pride laughed. "I have the best luck in
the world. Silver, Esther, silver! Just because I got Ed to
buy me that little strip of mountain pass in Colorado!"

"You're going out there?" Esther asked.

"Yes. But first I'm going to Washington. After that I'll
go west. I'll be there two months at least."

"When are you leaving?"

"First thing in the morning."

"I'll get your things ready," Esther said.

To his disgust, Pride found that he could not get a morning train to Washington. The first train left late in the afternoon. He sat morosely in the station.

I could go back home, but I'd have to face Esther again
and I don't want to do that. She keeps on watching me
quiet-like, as if she were waiting for something. I did
wrong; I know that. But there's no sense in keeping up this
suspicion forever. She treats me as though I were a stranger. I'm glad I'm going away; maybe she'll be over it when I
get back.

No, I can't go home . . . He stiffened suddenly. Sharon!
he thought. I can't go away and leave her hating me. I'll go
to her now and ask her to forgive me. I'll get down on my
knees if necessary! I can't leave her like this—I can't!

He was up then and running from the station. On the
sidewalk he lifted his hand in a quick signal to the driver
of a hansom cab. And then, once more, the luck of which
he so often boasted deserted him. As he was in the act of
climbing into his cab, another hansom pulled up a few
yards behind him. And in it sat Esther. She saw him get
into the little two-wheeled vehicle, and put her hand out of
the window to wave to him. But suddenly, savagely, she
jerked it in again.

He should be boarding a train—not engaging cabs. She
lifted the trap and spoke to the driver above her.

"Follow that cab," she said.

She had come to the station with the best of intentions. I
love him, she had thought. It's up to me to save him—and
our marriage. He's going to have enough to keep him busy
in the West. Why, then, shouldn't we live out there? Chica-

go—or San Francisco? Away from her, he'll never be tempted. He won't take up with another woman. In his own way, he loves me even now—and it's not merely beauty that turns his head. God knows Sharon's not even pretty!

She had looked at her watch. I can catch him! she had, decided. I'll discuss it with him and arrange to join him later! He'll see it my way. He must!

She had run down the stairs and found a passing cab, exulting in her good fortune in being able to obtain one so quickly—her good fortune that was now her misfortune, the worst upon the face of the earth . . .

Pride did not even look back during the drive to Sharon's shop. He was much too preoccupied. When he reached it, he told the driver to wait, for he intended to return to the station as soon as possible. Esther halted her cab half a block away and watched her husband as he got down and entered the shop. He came out in a surprisingly short time. He was, Esther saw, actually running.

"No," one of the girls had told him, "we haven't seen her. She hasn't been here in over a week. Oh, Mr. Dawson, we're so worried."

"Didn't you go to her house?" Pride growled.

"She's moved. She never got a chance to give us the new address. She's got a house somewhere and—"

The sentence was never finished. Already, Pride was racing for the waiting cab.

Behind him Esther spoke once more to her driver, and the two cabs moved off at almost the same instant.

Esther sat a long time before Sharon's residence, fighting for self-control.

At last she drew out a little memorandum pad from her purse and made a note of the address. Then she had the driver take her home.

At the door the janitor faced Pride.

"Miss O'Neil? Come to think of it, I ain't seen her in four days—no, in a whole week. She ain't been in or out to my knowing. What's that? Sure I have a key—but it's against th' rules to—"

"To hell with the rules!" Pride roared. "She's in there, man! Dead or dying!"

"Mercy on us!" the janitor whispered, and started up the stairs.

Pride was on his heels. The key grated noisily in the lock and the door swung open. It was warm in the house, for Sharon had not turned off the steam. Pride hurled himself past the janitor, almost knocking the man down, and raced up the stairs to the second floor. Then he was kneeling beside the bed, the frail little form cradled in his great arms.

"Is—is she . . . ?" the janitor began.

"No," Pride said. "Now get out of here and get some soup! Tell your missus to make it hot! Get going now!"

The janitor ran to the nearby basement where he lived.

Pride kneeled beside the bed, holding Sharon in his arms. For the first time in his life he felt something inside him loosen and give way; and, pressing his big face into the hollow of her neck, he cried like a child.

He felt her stir faintly. He glanced up, his face streaked with tears, and saw that she was looking at him, her eyes soft and clear. There was something else in them, too—something akin to tenderness. She made a pathetic gesture with her hands, as though to lift them to stroke his face.

He saw her mouth moving, shaping words, but they were so low that he had to bend his head to hear them.

"Don't, Pride," she whispered, "please don't cry."

Pride rubbed the knuckles of one hand into his eyes and wiped them angrily, but the tears kept coming each time he looked at her, and he could not stop them. He tried to talk to her, to tell her of his great shame and greater grief, but when the words would not come he bent his head and kissed her mouth.

After he drew his lips away, her eyes remained closed. His big hand flew out to her wrist, searching for a pulse-beat, but he could find none.

"Shay!" he whispered. "Oh, merciful God! Sharon—Sharon, darling—don't die! Please don't die!"

When the janitor's wife came into the room, Pride was sprawled half across the foot of Sharon's bed, his great bulk racked with frenzied grief.

"I did it!" he wept. "I killed her! I shamed her, and now she's dead!"

"Faith an' I'll take me own two hands and break your head if you don't move your great carcass!" the janitor's wife said. "The poor thing ain't dead—she's fainted, thanks to ye! Now move aside, while I see what I can do."

Pride stood there trembling, not even hearing the janitor's: "Now, now—don't you go an' excite yourself. Your lady friend is going to be all right." The plump, matronly woman lifted Sharon's head, and fed her spoon after spoon of the scalding soup.

He could see the color creeping back into the pale cheeks, thinner now than ever before. Sharon's breathing became more even, and when the janitor's wife lowered her head gently upon the pillow she went back to sleep.

"And me thinking the poor creature'd gone away for a while. Sure an' I should of known better than that!" The janitor's wife threw a glance that included both Pride and her husband in its withering contempt. "Men!" she spat, and started from the room.

Pride put out his hand and stopped her.

"I've got to stay here," he said, "to see that she gets well. I've got to talk to her and ask for her forgiveness or I'll never spend another peaceful day."

"I should worry me head about how you spends your days—" the woman began; but the janitor shook his head.

"Now, Mary," he cautioned, "let him stay—it might be all for the best."

The woman studied Pride briefly, seeing the richness of his clothes, the jeweled stickpin, the ring on his finger, the heavy gold watch chain across his broad chest.

"All right," she snapped. "There's a small room downstairs. You kin take that—but I promise you, mister, by God's Blessed Mother, if you bring any more harm to the poor child I'll have the law on you!"

Sharon had to be fed every two hours, and after the second feeding Pride relieved Mrs. O'Casey of the task. He dumped money into Mary O'Casey's lap—more money than she had ever seen before in her life—and told her to buy whatever Sharon needed, but to make sure it was the best.

Mrs. O'Casey softened.

"He ain't a bad sort, that fellow," she whispered to her husband. "Whatever he's done to the child he's sure sorry for. 'Tis thinking I am there'll be a wedding when she comes to herself!"

But it was two days before Sharon was in any condition to talk to Pride. He came into her bedroom that morning to find that Mrs. O'Casey had bathed her and combed out her long brown hair.

Sharon was sitting up in bed when he came in, and her

dark eyes were grave and tender as they searched his face.

"Shay," he began, "Sharon, honey—I don't know what to say . . ."

"Then don't say anything," she said gently. "There's nothing to be said."

"I was a fool," he went on doggedly. "Worse than that. I shamed you and you weren't meant for shaming. I was drunk—mean drunk and wild—but that's no excuse. I've been standing here trying to think of one, but there isn't any. What reason can a man give for being poison-mean? . . . You were dead-set against what I did—and you were right, as usual."

"No," Sharon said quietly, "I wasn't right—not entirely. I shouldn't have seen you any more after you were married. I knew how much I loved you. In a way I led you on, because it was such comfort to know you loved me, too. I was wrong, Pride, wrong."

"But I did it!" Pride insisted. "I came in this room and forced you. It wasn't your fault, Shay—it wasn't your fault at all!"

Sharon shook her head gravely.

"Pride," she whispered, "if it had been a strange man who did what you did, it wouldn't have been a sin, would it? Not for me, I mean. I would have been a victim, then, not what I was. I fought you, but not long enough, or hard enough, or—I realize now—not sincerely enough. It was a sham, darling; my heart wasn't in resisting you. I guess I was trying to fool myself. Only, I can't. I—your victim? Oh, darling, have you ever seen a more willing one?"

"That's not so. I was too strong."

"And I was too weak—too weak from loving you, Pride. Too beaten down with wanting you so long. Did I act like a conquered woman, Pride? Did I?"

"Well, not exactly . . ."

"That's why I don't want to live any longer. You saved me this time, but you can't always. I'll be quicker next time —and more certain."

"Don't talk like that! If you have to die that way because of something for which you aren't even guilty, then half the women on earth should be below ground right now."

"Pride, I'm not talking about other women; I'm talking about myself. Maybe other girls can stand looking in the

199

mirror every morning and seeing the face of—of an adulteress staring back at them. But I can't. Other people can make excuses and forgive themselves easily—but I'm not other people, darling. I'm Sharon O'Neil, and I can't live with such a sin upon my soul."

Pride sighed heavily.

"Reckon I can't convince you," he said. "Even if you were guilty of a sin—which you're not—you have to remember that Christ, Himself, forgave the woman they caught sinning . . ."

Sharon smiled sadly.

"And told her to go and sin no more. But—can we stop sinning, Pride? Can I? I thought I would hate you forever for what you did, but an hour later I had forgiven you completely. Love is a curious thing. I guess there isn't anything you could do that could change the way I feel about you."

"Sharon," Pride began, "I—"

"No, my darling—that's the way it is. I'm only human. I'm terribly afraid of dying, just like anyone else; but I'm more afraid of living now. Afraid that some day I'll have to look into Esther's face knowing how I wronged her. Afraid that you might come back once more and kiss me and hold me close . . . Oh, I couldn't bear that, Pride! I know myself now. I know I'm wicked enough to sin again and again, until—until I forget one day how wrong it is, until I turn my face away from God."

"Finished?" Pride growled.

"Yes, Pride, I'm finished."

"You've had your say. Now I'm going to have mine. You said a whole lot of things about sin and sinning that just don't make sense to me, but no matter. Just remember one thing. If you do yourself any harm, you'll make a murderer out of me. If there is a God, He's not going to allow my hands to be lifted up to Him covered with blood. You've been talking about your soul, your sin—but what about mine? You say you love me, but you don't care what happens to me, do you?"

"I guess," Sharon said softly, "I hadn't thought about your side at all."

"You're damned right you hadn't. Now, look at me, Shay. Look at my face. Have you ever known me to lie to you?"

Sharon shook her head.

"Well, I'm not fixing to lie now. I'm thirty-eight years old; I'm no lovesick kid. I'm a man, Shay, old enough to know what I'm saying. So you know I mean it when I tell you that if you lift a hand against yourself, I'm going to follow you the minute I find out, and I'm going to leave orders to be buried right alongside you. Even if you die you can't get away from me."

"Pride," Sharon whispered. "You wouldn't!"

"Oh, yes, I would! And you know it. I'm going now. I've got to go to Washington, then out to Colorado. I'll be gone two months. Mrs. O'Casey'll take care of you till you're well. And don't worry about the expense, because I'm paying her. When I come back I expect to find you alive and well. If not, you'll have my life on your hands."

Sharon straightened up in the little bed and put up her arms to him.

"Good-bye, darling," she whispered.

But Pride did not kiss her at once.

"Promise me?" he said gruffly.

"Yes," Sharon whispered. "Oh, yes—I promise!"

Esther sat very still in the horsehair chair. She had been thinking for hours, but her thoughts went round and round in endless circles. Pride told me he was leaving, but he had to go to her first. He'll always go to her. . . . I should leave him now, but I can't do it. I can't escape him. I can no more stop loving him than I can stop breathing. He's been gone five hours now—and it seems five years. December 1, 1871. I'll remember this day. I wonder how Christmas will be with just myself and the servants. Father is gone, Pride's gone; I haven't even a child I can make happy with toys and gifts. And New Year's Eve I'll be sitting here in this chair listening to the bells.

It was nice of father to leave us this house in which we're now living, but I'd rather be back in that cozy little flat. This place is too empty, too empty and echoing—just like my heart.

You had no right to treat me like this, Pride! You shouldn't have tormented me so. Right now I hate you worse than anything else on earth, and still I love you. I'd like to make you suffer the way you've made me—but how can I?

"How can I?" she whispered, her blue eyes narrowing. She stood up slowly, and walked toward the closet. "How can I?" she repeated as she drew out the sealskin coat and fur turban that Pride had bought her. She put them on slowly, like a sleepwalker, then turned and rang the bell for Simone.

When the maid came, Esther looked at her for some time before she spoke.

"I'm going away," she said quietly. "Pack some things for me. And tell Terence to get the carriage ready. I'm going down to Broad Acres—I'm sick of the winter . . ."

"Broad Acres, Madame?" Simone echoed blankly.

"It's an estate my father owned in South Carolina. He left it to me when he died."

"Yes, Madame," Simone curtsied. "Very well, Madame."

Malcolm came up later and took the traveling bags.

Outside, Terence waited beside the open door of the carriage.

"Grand Central Depot, Madame?" he asked.

"No," Esther said. "Not directly. Drive along, I'll tell you where later."

CHAPTER SEVENTEEN—1872

PRIDE SPENT a busy two months in the mountains of Colorado. The new mine was all Ed Bolley had said it was and more. If Pride were to make no further investments, this seemingly endless vein of silver would still insure his being a wealthy man for the rest of his life. But Pride saw in it only a tool toward greater goals.

By the time he came back all arrangements for the operation of the mine were settled, for Edward Bolley, whatever his faults, was an honest man. On his arrival in New York, Pride did precisely what Esther had feared: he went at once to Sharon's house. But to his intense surprise and annoyance, Sharon was no longer there.

"She moved two weeks ago," Mary O'Casey told him with grim satisfaction. "She didn't leave a new address."

Swearing under his breath, Pride went back down to his cab and drove to Sharon's shop. There he was greeted by a stern and matronly woman who looked him up and down and said coldly:

"Miss O'Neil? I'm sorry, sir, but I'm not at liberty to give information concerning her whereabouts."

"Did she sell this shop?" Pride demanded.

"No. She still owns it, but she's far too busy with office work to spend much time in the store. I'm manageress now."

Pride growled. "Well, when she comes in, tell her Mr. Dawson was here. Tell her I'd like to get in touch with her."

"Very well," the woman said, "I'll tell her."

Much good that'll do, Pride thought grimly.

Still he did not return to the Stillworth mansion, where he and Esther now lived. He drove first to the office of the Pinkerton Detective Agency, and gave the manager a detailed description of Sharon. A man stationed near the shop, he suggested, could follow her home the next time she came to the store and learn her new address. That, he told them, was all he wanted.

Then at last he gave the driver his address and drove up to the house that Black Tom Stillworth had left them. Again he met with a surprise. Esther, too, was not at home.

"She went down to Broad Acres, sir," Malcolm told him. "But she wrote, telling us to expect her any day now."

So it was that Pride Dawson spent his first night in New York alone. He did not like the idea at all. Colorado had been cold and lonely, lacking in comforts—almost unbelievably primitive. He had slept alone there for two whole months. I'm getting old, he mused. I don't want just any woman now. It has to be Sharon—or Esther. Esther can't understand that—how a man can love two women at the same time. I know that if I had Sharon all the time, I wouldn't want Esther. But if there weren't any Sharon I'd love Esther with all my heart. . . . God, it was a mess!

He stretched out on the bed and tried to sleep, but sleep wouldn't come. He didn't blame Esther: New York was too cold! Next year he'd arrange to go down to Carolina for the whole winter. She'd like that, if—if Shay didn't change her mind and all his plans.

He drifted off, finally, into deep slumber. Hours later he was aware dimly of someone kissing his mouth. He struggled up through layers of sleep, and forced his eyes open. Esther sat there on the side of the bed, smiling down at him.

She had taken off her greatcoat, and Pride saw that she wore a dress of blue velvet that marvelously matched the blue of her eyes. He saw, too, that she was lovelier than he had ever seen her before. Her cheeks were flushed and rosy, her eyes danced with happiness. Her lips were coral pink, warm and inviting, as once more she bent down towards him.

"Jehosaphat!" he exploded. "What happened to you!"

"None of your business, Pride Dawson! Aren't you glad to see me?"

"Middling," Pride grinned, "just middling. What did you have to run off for? I come home and—"

"You talk entirely too much. Shut up now, and kiss me!"

Pride did so, then lay back, grinning.

"All right," he said, "I kissed you. Now go away and let me sleep."

"No," Esther said, "I've been without a husband for two months. I don't intend to wait any longer."

She half-turned on the bedside, so that the velvet buttons down the back of her dress were toward him.

"Button me down," she said.

Pride worked at the buttons, but his big fingers were clumsy and slow.

"Hurry, Pride! Hurry!" Esther said.

The last of the buttons was free now, and the velvet gown dropped about her slim ankles. Then one by one she let her other garments fall, until she stood before him, slender-trunked, snowy-limbed, golden-downed . . . exquisite.

He put up his arms to her and she came to him.

Afterwards, it was a long time before he could go to sleep. A woman should be full of fire and spirit, but Esther had been positively wanton. He lay there, more tired than he could remember ever having been before, and stared at her face, so cool, remote and sweet-sleeping.

"Jehosaphat!" he murmured again. "I wonder what on earth's got into her?"

It took the detectives several weeks to locate Sharon. As soon as he had her address, however, Pride did not hesitate. He went at once to her house, one of the new apartment buildings that were springing up all over the city.

Sharon opened the door to his knocking and stood there looking at him for a long time before she whispered:

"Come in, Pride."

"Look, Shay," Pride said, "I know what you're thinking. But I won't lay a finger on you again unless you want me to. I had to see you. You don't know how it hurt when I came back and found you'd run out on me."

Sharon shook her dark head.

"Not from you, Pride," she said. "I was running from myself."

"I've a proposition to make to you, Shay," he said. "I won't come here any more. I don't trust myself that much. I'll meet you other places—out in the open, where we can be alone, yet not by ourselves. I'll take you sleigh-riding, skating, to the theater. In the spring, we'll go boating. I need you, Sharon, to talk to and to make me happy. I promise you I won't set a foot in this place unless you invite me up. Will you have it that way?"

"Yes," Sharon said. "I'll have it that way, Pride."

Pride did not own a sleigh, but he immediately purchased one. And being Pride Dawson, he could not be content with an ordinary sleigh. He bought an imported Russian droshky type, drawn by three horses rather than the customary one or two. The three thoroughbreds, whom he named "Prince," "King" and "Emperor," were adorned with great scarlet plumes and a high Russian yoke harness covered with little brass bells. To go with the sleigh, he bought a large bearskin robe, a fur greatcoat and Cossack hat. He could not have attracted more attention if he had hired a trumpeter to ride before him.

Sharon clapped her hands with delight at the sight of the beautiful sleigh, and hurried to don her ermine-trimmed coat and muff. They set out through Central Park toward the Harlem Kill. Pride waved his whip with easy familiarity to young William H. Vanderbilt, out behind his famous "Early Rose" and "Aldine." For a brief stretch they engaged in a furious race with two other drivers, but Pride's powerful trio, harnessed to the light sleigh, easily outdistanced them, and Sharon waved back gaily, her cheeks flushed scarlet by the icy air.

They stopped for dinner at Gabe Case's, where a banjo and a guitar made music. Pride gazed tenderly at Sharon, seeing her dark eyes bright with happiness, hearing the merry note of her laughter as Charley Johnson, despite his sixty-three years and two hundred pounds, gracefully executed the pigeon-wing and double-shuffle.

At other times they went to "Judge" Smith's, stabling the horses for the evening. They danced to the orchestra at John Harry's "Romantic," one of the most popular of the out of town roadhouses, but Sharon asked Pride quietly, after their second visit, not to bring her back again.

"It—it lives up to its name too well," she sighed. "We'd better avoid such places, Pride."

They skated on Beekman's Pond. They saw John Gilbert's impersonation at Wallach's Theater. They went to flower shows at the Opera House, for that august institution was, as usual, badly in the red, and was making up the deficit by renting its facilities for flower shows, horse shows and even boxing and wrestling matches. Pride squirmed through Shakespeare at Booth's Theater. It was a busy winter.

Such activities could not long escape being reported to Esther. The sleigh, of course, attracted wide attention, and there were many drivers who knew that Esther Stillworth did not have dark brown hair.

However, Esther held her peace with admirable fortitude. Only once during the entire period did she question Pride about Sharon.

"Yes," he admitted calmly, "I see her once in a while—but that's all, Esther. You haven't got a thing to worry about—not a blamed thing.

"I see," Esther said despondently. She did not mention the matter again.

Pride was busy with his affairs during the daytime, despite all his gadding about with Sharon. He had now brought the lake barge lines completely under his control. As a direct result of that transaction, he acquired a fleet of six old and leaky sailing vessels, which he promptly threw into the Australian grain trade. One thing always led to another. While investigating materials for the uniforms of his railroad conductors, he became aware of the possibilities in textiles: the next week he acquired three Massachusetts textile mills. Thereafter he was able to supply Sharon with materials at cost, for she would not accept them for nothing.

He equipped his steel mill with Bessemer converters. Despite the fact that Carnegie had been using them since 1868, few steel mills then employed this cheaper and better method of producing steel. He also built a combination rolling and booming mill alongside the steel mill, and gained both Vanderbilt and Thompson as customers for his rails.

He dickered endlessly with Thompson for a marshalling yard in Pittsburgh, coming to an agreement with him only after he had made the astonishing discovery that Thompson was an honest man. The agreement proved advantageous to both. the M. & W. P. and the Pennsylvania, for Thompson sold Pride a small section of the Pennsylvania's great Pittsburgh yards, and Pride in turn agreed to ship his loaded cars over the Pennsylvania lines up to the point of junction.

In the early spring Pride made a flying two-week visit to Colorado and witnessed the magnificent spectacle of the "long drive"—thousands of cattle being herded northward by cowpunchers to await shipment to the slaughter pens in Chicago. He was so impressed that he returned home by way of Texas, and brought with him the free and clear deeds to a 115,000-acre cattle ranch in that state.

It surprised no one when his picture appeared in *Harper's Magazine* under the caption: *Our Latter Day Midas —Everything He Touches Turns To Gold!*

With the coming of spring, the relationship between Sharon and Pride became increasingly awkward. After the rains, the smell of the wet earth was fresh and clean, and all along the Harlem Kill the fields were bright with blossoms. Gone were the heavy clothing and bearskin robes of the winter. They drove now in a light road wagon, drawn by a prancing pair, and Sharon's exquisitely cut summer garments were light and airy. Pride grew daily more conscious of her as a completely desirable woman. He was often ill-tempered and curt even when talking with her, and sometimes he did not speak to Esther for days on end.

By way of relief from the mounting tension, he plunged into a furious round of activity. He dragged Sharon from the rifle matches of the crack German-American teams to the archery shoots in Central Park. They sailed in a new catboat on Long Island Sound. They played croquet until it was too dark to see the wickets any longer. Pride even went so far as to take Sharon one night to a prize fight held secretly in the Jersey marshes; for prize fights, except as "exhibitions," were forbidden. There, under the flare of torchlight, Sharon saw "Beefsteak" John Ruggins belabor Timothy O'Hara. At first she paid scant attention to the fight. A few swift glances at the rough-looking crowd served to show that the few women present were prostitutes, and that they were all staring at her in open-mouthed wonderment.

So it was that she was grateful to O'Hara when he began to bleed profusely from the nose; for it gave her an excuse to retire under the pretext of delicate feminine sensibilities.

But riding along the Kill at night was far too much for their already tense emotions. The moon, coming out from behind a night-blue tracery of clouds, burnished the face of the Hudson with silvery mist. Below them, the boats were fairy lights on the surface of the water, and the Palisades stood up black and forbidding, crowned with a ragged fringe of trees.

The slow clopping of the horses drawing the road wagon made a rhythm like a double heartbeat and, looking at Pride, Sharon could see his profile tightening. He lit a cigar and it glowed redly in the dark, its fragrant smoke climbing upward about his head, visible in the darkness.

He sat hunched over, brooding over the view, and once more Sharon knew the feeling that he was something ancient and terrible and grand, something beyond the commonalty of ordinary men. She could feel the tightness beneath her eyelids, and she thought suddenly, I'm going to cry—and I mustn't! No, I mustn't!

Timidly she put out her hand and touched his sleeve.

"Take me home now, Pride," she whispered.

"Why?" he growled.

Why, she thought bitterly, must you ask "why"?

Then, without conscious volition, her arms flew up around his neck, and she dragged his face down, locking his mouth to hers in a savage kiss. She lay back in his arms,

208

her lips bruised and swollen, the unashamed tears making silver tracks upon the upturned oval of her face.

"Take me home!" she said.

Pride turned the pair in a wide circle and cracked the whip over their sleek flanks. The wheels of the little wagon blurred with the speed, and the trees sped backward like the ghosts of damned souls, dark and twisted. When they finally reached the apartment building, Pride lifted her down and held her gently in the circle of his arms. She looked up at him gravely, her eyes searching his face as though she would memorize his image. Then she said very quietly:

"Come up with me, Pride."

"You mean it?" Pride said. "You're sure?"

"I'm sure," Sharon answered. "Oh, yes, my darling, I'm very sure!"

The next morning, as Pride ate the bacon and eggs that Sharon had prepared for him, and drank the scalding coffee, he looked at her with awed tenderness. She sat across the table from him looking small and lost, wrapped in a soft pink robe. She did not say anything but simply sat there holding her cup and following his slightest motion with her great dark eyes.

"Shay," Pride said huskily, "you—you're not sorry?"

Slowly she shook her head.

"No, Pride," she said.

"And you won't—"

"Harm myself? No, Pride—not any more now. No more than I've already done."

Pride's sigh was gusty with relief.

Sharon sipped her coffee, her eyes, above the rim of the cup, never leaving his face. Then she put her cup down upon the table.

"I was a fool," she said. "I thought I could stay alive and in the same world with you—that I could see you daily and not have it come to—this. For months now I've been learning about myself. I loved goodness and I had faith. I still do. But now I know that *loving* goodness isn't enough. You have to *be* good. I'm not. To have faith is one thing, but to have the courage to practice it is quite another. I'm your mistress now. You—can come here whenever you like . . ."

She stared at him with dawning recognition in her eyes, as though she were hearing her own words from the lips of a stranger.

"I—your mistress!" she whispered. "I can sit here and say that word quite calmly. Oh, Pride, it's dreadful!"

"No," Pride said gruffly, "it's wonderful!"

"I—I guess it is, in a way," she said bitterly. "Now when you're old you can say: 'There was a woman once who loved me—past all believing, past all bearing—enough to damn her immortal soul into hell for my sake.' Oh, you must be very proud!"

"Sharon! Shay, honey, don't talk like that. It's not so; it's not the way you make it sound. Look at it this way: we're two people, you and I, who love each other so much that all the laws with which folks mess up their lives can't hold us back. We found everything that's real and true and beautiful in each other's arms. You can't make me feel like a sinner for loving you!"

"I don't blame you, Pride," Sharon said gently. "You're a different kind of person. I never believed that the rules applied to you. But I'm not different, and the sin is mine."

She gazed at him tenderly.

"Do me a favor, Pride," she said. "Go home now. I have to be by myself for a while."

"I'll see you tonight," Pride said.

"No—not tonight. Next week, maybe. We mustn't see each other too often now. You still have a wife, remember?"

Pride's big face was ugly, suddenly.

"I'll fix that!" he said.

"No, Pride," Sharon said sharply. "You mustn't. That's the one thing that would make me leave you now. I have enough to bear without having further sins upon my head. Esther must not know about this. She's your wife, Pride, whatever the reasons why you married her. I won't have her deserted because of me. I'll stay here—in the back of your life, but no more."

On the way home Pride turned the matter over in his mind. Sharon isn't the kind of girl a man can rightly keep, he thought angrily. If it was the other way around it would be better. She's my wife, really—not Esther. I never had this feeling before—of being all peaceful-like, of being where I belong. I'm going to talk to Esther. She's got money and I'll give her more—every cent I have if necessary. She'll see it my way. . . . I read in the paper yesterday that there were thousands of divorces last year. I don't want Shay for my mistress, I want her for my wife. If I hadn't been such a damned, greedy fool, she'd be that now.

When he reached the Stillworth mansion, Esther was up and waiting for him. She did not say a word about his night-long absence, but sat there over the breakfast table, where Pride joined her for another cup of coffee. An expression of quiet triumph glowed on her face. If she had spoken, it would have been easier for him to broach the subject of divorce. But she did not reproach him. Instead she sat there, daintily eating her breakfast, smiling softly and secretly to herself, as though she was finding life pleasantly amusing. Finally, Pride could stand it no longer.

"Esther," he said hoarsely, "I've got to talk to you."

"Is it important? I don't feel like talking this morning. I just want to sit here and be happy."

"Yes," Pride said grimly, "it's important."

"Oh," Esther said. "Well, since we must talk, I'd better tell you something first."

"What is it?" Pride snapped.

"I'm going to have a baby, Pride."

Pride sat there, his mouth dropping open foolishly, staring at the slim and lovely figure of his wife as though he were seeing her for the first time. A baby! A son—oh, it would be a son—to grow up tall and handsome at his side, to follow in his footsteps and to carry on the empire he was building.

"Oh, Esther," he exclaimed, "a baby! We're going to have a baby!"

"Yes," Esther laughed. "We are."

"A boy, Es—it's got to be a boy! I'll teach him to ride and shoot and you'll teach him good manners! We'll send him to all the best schools. He's got to have the best!"

"It may be a girl, Pride," Esther said. "Babies sometimes are, you know."

"No, it won't be! It's going to be a boy, sure as I live and breathe! Glory be! When did all this happen?"

"I think it started the night I came back from Carolina."

Pride remembered that night.

"Now I know it's going to be a boy!" he exulted. "Oh,

Esther!" Then he came around the table and took her in his arms.

Esther's eyes, looking up at him, were cool and remote. "You were going to tell me something," she said. "What was it, Pride?"

She saw his face darken.

"Nothing," he breathed, "nothing at all—now."

CHAPTER EIGHTEEN—1872

MEN TALKED of many things in 1872. They whispered bitterly of Ulysses Simpson Grant in the White House, accepting gifts of fine pacers, cigars, wine and stock in this and that. They dragged out the ancient word "nepotism" to describe the offices that he filled with near and distant relatives. From far below the public ("The public be damned!" . . . "canaille" . . . "a great beast") rumbled angrily when the Senate committees, intending both to press charges and whitewash James G. Blaine and James A. Garfield, revealed the fantastic scandal of the Crédit Mobilier—of railroads built entirely at government expense, which nevertheless were forced to yield $23,366,000 of profit to private speculators.

They laughed as Jay Gould continued to defraud the Erie stockholders; they went to P. T. Barnum's new circus to see the fabulous Jumbo. They stood on street corners in tight little groups and talked about Jubilee Jim Fisk—dead now with his boots on, shot down on the steps of the Broadway Central Hotel by Edward Stokes, a gilded youth who had defrauded him of much money, stolen from him his beloved Josie Mansfield, and now, crowning indignity, had taken his life. They discussed Jim's fabulous offices in Pike's Opera House, where, rumor had it, he had once kept thirteen members of the chorus as his mistresses at one time. They recalled the occasion when he and Jay Gould had rowed across the Hudson, with six million dollars of

Commodore Vanderbilt's money in a black bag, and barricaded themselves in Taylor's Hotel in Jersey City, surrounded by a hundred thugs armed with everything from shotguns to brass knuckles. They roared with laughter at the memory of the portly Jim, clad in his gorgeous self-designed uniform, as he fled with his broken Ninth Regiment, National Guards, before a howling mob of Irishmen the day of the Orange riots . . .

Yes, New York would miss Jim Fisk—he had added much color to its life. Got his just deserts, sober citizens said. It ought to be a lesson to others—like Pride Dawson, always riding around with that brown-haired little beauty, while his wife sits at home and waits for their child to be born. . . .

In Millville men went on dying in the mines and mills, and Tim wrote long, misspelled letters crying out to Pride against conditions there. Pride made a note to build a school and a hospital, then put the note aside and forgot it. He was much too busy with other things: piling up a mountain of gold, basking in the tender glow of Sharon's affection, and waiting for the birth of his child.

He lay, one cool night in September, by Esther's side and tried to fall asleep. But the bitter events of the day tugged at his mind. He had gone to Tiffany's and bought a magnificent diamond necklace for Sharon. It cost him a fortune; and feeling it heavy in its tooled leather, velvet-lined case as he drove toward her flat, made him savor in anticipation the way her eyes would light up at seeing it.

But Sharon had stood there holding the necklace in her hand without saying a word, and the slow tears had crept down from the corners of her eyelids. Then silently she had handed it back to him.

"What the devil—" he had begun.

"I am given, Pride," she said simply, "not bought. There's a name for women who take gifts and money in exchange for love."

Damn it all! he thought morosely. There's no understanding women! I wonder . . .

But just what it was he wondered he could never recall afterwards, for Esther's hand was tense and frightened upon his arm, shaking him furiously.

"Pride," she whispered, "wake up! It's coming! Oh, Pride!"

Pride rolled over and stared at her.

"It can't be!" he growled. "There was nothing wrong with you when I went to Colorado—and I came back in February, seven months ago!"

Esther stared back at him, her face white and frightened, bedewed with a fine tracery of sweat. He saw her twist painfully, and his jaw dropped open.

"Babies can't count," Esther whispered. "This one's coming! They do come early sometimes! Get Doctor Bergman, Pride! Do you want it to die?"

Pride was already diving into his clothes, all the old wives' tales running hideously through his mind. Babies did come in seven months, sometimes—Esther was right. But he recalled old wives' tales of how they usually were stillborn then, or terribly deformed—or, worse still, idiots.

"Oh, my God!" he groaned. "Oh, my God!"

He pulled the bell cord and the sleepy Malcolm met him in the hall.

"Get Terence up!" Pride roared. "I want the road wagon! Got to get the doctor, quick!"

"Madame?" Malcolm gasped.

"Yes! Don't stand there asking questions! Get moving, man!"

After what seemed an eternity to Pride, but what was actually only a space of minutes, Terence brought the little vehicle around to the front of the house.

"Better let me drive, sir," he said quietly. "I think you're upset!"

"All right, all right—but let's go!" Pride cried.

The horses raced down the deserted street, their hoofs striking fire from the paving stones. Pride hung on to the wildly careening wagon, his thoughts black and bitter.

A seven-months baby, he thought. He can't be perfect now. Maybe Shay's right about sinning. Maybe this is the hand of God catching up with me. If he dies . . . if he dies, I'll—I'll—

But he did not know exactly what he would do. It was characteristic of him that the thought that Esther also might die never entered his mind. He sat forward, squinting against the wind, his brow contracted in tight furrows of worry.

"My son!" he breathed. "He's got to live! He's got to!"

When they reached the house of Dr. Hans Bergman, the

maid admitted them with a sleepy calm that Pride found infuriating.

"Doesn't she know that somebody might be dying?" He raged inwardly. Doesn't she care?

"The doctor will be down directly," she yawned.

Doctor Bergman came down almost at once, and when he saw Pride a look of surprise crept into his eyes.

"Mr. Dawson," he said, "is something wrong? Has your wife had a fall? Or a miscarriage?"

"Neither," Pride growled. "The baby's coming—you've got to go back with me right now!"

Doctor Bergman turned to the maid.

"Put on a pot of coffee while I dress," he said calmly.

"Coffee!" Pride exploded. "You're going to stop for coffee?"

"My dear Mr. Dawson, I've practiced medicine for thirty years. Usually it is from eight to twelve hours after I'm summoned before the baby arrives. So calm yourself, please!"

"But this one's ahead of time!"

"A seven-months child," Doctor Bergman continued reassuringly, "can be entirely normal. In fact, they are more often than not. A little smaller and more delicate—and requiring greater care, of course. I've lost surprisingly few of them—among my better class patients."

"Why them?" Pride demanded.

"The poor," Hans Bergman sighed, "have neither the money nor the education to take care of a premature child. Among them such children always die. But among the wealthy, not so often . . . Your own wife, if I remember correctly, was also a short-term infant."

"Maybe that accounts for it," Pride said.

"It could be, though medical science has not definitely established that such things are hereditary. Well, I'm ready now. Shall we go?"

Doctor Bergman's examination of Esther was brief.

"Hmmm," he mused, "I guess I'd better stay here after all."

"Why?" Pride demanded. "Is anything—wrong?"

"No, but the labor is further along than I anticipated. She should give birth in another hour." He looked up into Simone's frightened eyes. "You," he said, "get out of here." Then he turned and saw Bridget's red matronly face, calm

215

and confidence in every line of it. "You stay," he said to her. "I'll be down in the kitchen having more coffee. Dawson, you come along. If there's anything on earth more useless than husbands at a time like this, I don't know what it is."

Pride, Terence afterwards told Malcolm, drank fifteen cups of coffee while they waited.

"Don't know where he put it all," he confided to his fellow servant.

Pride was filling the sixteenth cup when they heard Pierre's scurrying feet in the hall.

"Bridget says to come!" the valet gasped.

They raced up the stairs, but at the door of the bedroom Doctor Bergman put out his hand.

"You stay out of here," he said sternly to Pride. "I don't want you underfoot."

So Pride paced the hall floor as expectant fathers have done since mankind knew the meaning of fatherhood. He brushed the cold sweat from his forehead and tried to pray. But his words made no sense.

It went on forever, the soft scuffling sounds in the room, and Esther's intermittent moaning. Then there was another noise—the sharp clear sound of a slap, and a thin high wailing.

Pride burst open the door and hurled himself into the room. Doctor Bergman was laying the tiny, wrinkled little object in Bridget's thick arms. Pride inched forward and looked at it.

"A girl," Bergman said. "Congratulations."

It was small and mottled and as ugly as all new babies are. But it was not bald. Its tiny head was crowned with a mass of golden curls, as light as Esther's.

Pride bent down to Esther's white pain-ravaged face.

"Bless you, Es," he whispered. "She's the sweetest little thing."

Esther smiled—a soft delicate smile, with only the slightest hint of mockery in it.

"A girl," she whispered. "You wanted a boy."

"It's all right," Pride said with gruff tenderness, "she suits me just fine. She's just like you."

Esther's eyes clouded suddenly.

"A daughter," she said. "I knew it would be a girl, Pride.

I have a name for her, but none for a boy—I was that sure."

"What are you going to call her?" Pride said.

"Caprice," Esther whispered.

"Caprice?" Pride echoed. "Hmmmm . . . Caprice—Caprice Dawson . . . That's pretty. Hell, I like it!"

" 'All the world's a stage,' " Hans Bergman quoted suddenly, unexpectedly, in his deep, rich voice, " 'and all the men and women merely players. They have their exits and their entrances . . .' All right, Caprice Dawson, make your bow!" Then taking the child from Bridget, he placed her gently in the crook of Esther's arm.

CHAPTER NINETEEN—1873

LUCY MCCARTHY LOOKED across the table at the serious face of her son. Lance was frowning, his cleft chin resting on one hand, the other holding down the stiff pages of his book. The lamplight fell across the black deep-curling mass of his hair, giving it bluish highlights, and his full lips moved with the words on the page before him.

How beautiful he is, Lucy thought.

Lance looked up at his mother, the long lashes unveiling his eyes, and smiled. Lucy's heart melted within her.

My son, my son! she thought. My young prince out of the legends. Fifteen now. A man soon. With so much goodness in you and so much beauty. I pray God you keep the goodness—like your father before you. Don't let this place hurt you, Lance. Don't let the meanness and ugliness get you . . . And never learn to hate.

Lance put down his book.

"I'm going out to meet Ernie, Mother," he said.

Lucy sighed.

"But, Lance, it's so late . . ." she said.

"I know," Lance said, "but I won't be long."

He bent down and kissed her cheek.

My son, Lucy thought, my tall son.

Lance straightened up, towering above her. He was already taller than his father, and graceful almost to a fault. A trifle too slender now, but he would fill out, Lucy knew. Looking at him as he strode toward the door, she remembered, with a mixture of fear and anger, how the eyes of the miners' daughters lit up at the sight of him.

Bringing up Lance in Millville had laid heavy burdens upon Lucy. There was the matter of education. Millville boasted one tiny school, taught by a slovenly Irishman, who drank and forever smelled of whiskey, tobacco and sweat. He was but little better prepared for his tasks, Lucy had soon discovered, than the majority of his pupils. It was necessary, therefore, to supplement his teaching.

To Lucy's unending delight, Lance had turned out to have scholarly tastes. After an initial difficulty with the archaic language, he had devoured Shakespeare—especially the tragedies, many of which he read five or six times. He was, unfortunately, poor in mathematics; but in all of the languages, and in literature, he excelled. Soon he was aiding Sean Donaldson with the older classes—and many a Millville girl, who in former times would have chucked the whole thing, continued her education long past the customary time.

Lucy's second problem was that of religion. Most of Millville's population came from Eastern Europe, and the town's single church was Greek Orthodox. A devout Catholic herself, Lucy taught Lance his catechism and all of the common prayers. But it was not enough. There were tiny evidences that Lance was straying from the fold, and for this Lucy blamed Stepan Henkja.

Henkja had been a Lassallean Socialist in the old country, who had fled to America to escape the police. A highly educated man, he had become the natural leader of the Millville workers—a man of pronounced radical tendencies, whom Lucy thought exceedingly dangerous.

Yet Tim both liked and consulted Stepan; Lance worshiped him. He was, Lucy admitted ruefully, a likeable man. He came often to the house to study with Lance, and like most educated Europeans, proved to be well versed in Latin and Greek, which was, of course, a capital piece of

218

good fortune—else Lance would have lacked a tutor in the ancient tongues.

So it was that Lance McCarthy, growing up in the bleak mining town of Millville, developed a richly cultured, if somewhat undisciplined, mind.

When Lance came out of the house into the early January dark it was snowing. It was, he reflected, practically always snowing in Millville. There was a local superstition, not entirely unfounded in fact, that Millville had the worst weather of any town in America.

As he sniffed at the snow, Lance's fine brow contracted with worry. It was true, though the reasons for it were not entirely known, that most of the great mine disasters occurred in cold weather. One theory put it simply that the mines were drier in winter, and the fine coal dust, freely suspended in the air, mixed more easily with the deadly "fire damp," as the miners called methane gas. It needed only a poorly placed shot of black gunpowder on the face of the coal to set off an explosion of unbelievable force. Fine coal dust was nearly twice as explosive as grain, for instance, and it was everywhere in the mines—in the shafts, in the tunnels, even in the stables where the mules were quartered. Once ignited, it raced through the passages in an endless chain of fire, snuffing out the lives of everyone below ground.

Lance started toward the switching yard where Ernie now worked. The snow, smothering the world in white silence, muffled his footsteps. Lance moved on, wrapped in the swirling whiteness, thinking: I'd like to get away from here—go back to New York, where people are happy.

He crossed the first of the tracks and heard the sound of the engines. They were snorting and puffing as they moved down the tracks, coupling and uncoupling the freight cars. There was a shuddering crack as the cars slammed into each other. Lance's frown tightened.

Just then he heard the ground rumble beneath his feet and saw a tongue of flame, five hundred feet high, flaring up from the entrance shaft of the mine. He started to run blindly through the snow. Although it was night, it still lacked more than an hour to complete the fourteen that the miners worked. Before he reached the shaft, he saw the shawled women pouring out of the little shacks, hunched over against the wind as they ran toward the tongue of flame, speechless, black against the winter white.

There was another explosion, then another. Lance was thrown to the ground, hard. When his breath returned he looked up and saw that the mine shaft was black: the flame was gone, all light was gone, and he could no longer see the running women.

He got up heavily and lurched forward. When he got to the shaft, pushing his way through the wailing women, he saw that the entrance was closed by tons of rock and coal, except for a little opening scarcely as wide as a man's shoulders.

He was standing there looking at it when his father came up, panting, followed by Stepan and a group of men from the steel mill.

Tim McCarthy looked at the huddled little group of women and then at the opening.

"Bring me a rope," he said quietly.

A man ran off and came back with a rope. Lance watched wonderingly, as his father fastened it beneath his own armpits. Then he saw Tim send for a miner's lamp.

"No," Stepan said hoarsely. "No, Mr. McCarthy, let me!"

Tim looked at him, his red face silent and still.

"My job, Stepan," he said.

Then he started down, and Lance's heart was a hot ball, blocking his throat. Of such a man am I born, he thought, unconsciously imitating the rhythms of Stepan's speech, of such a man! Tim could have ordered another to go down. He was the manager of the mine; there was nothing that compelled him to take the risk. Nothing except that he was Tim McCarthy, who had never in all his life turned aside from what must be done.

Tim went down slowly, but after his feet were through the opening the rope slackened. He fought there silently, furiously, in the sight of the lantern, but try as he would he could not get through.

When they drew him up at last his face was black, except for the white streaks of his tears through the soot.

Lance measured the others with his eye. They were all great-thewed men, bulky of trunk and wide of shoulder, the result of the heavy work in the steel mill. There was not a one there who could squeeze through that opening.

"Get picks!" Tim shouted hoarsely, but Lance touched his arm.

"Me, Papa," he said. "I can make it—I'm thin enough."

"No!" Tim and Stepan both roared in unison.

But Lance shook his head.

"It's your job, Papa," he said, "and you can't do it—so now it's mine. There're men down there, dead and dying. Do you want to let them die, in order to save your son?"

"Hell, yes!" Tim exploded, but Stepan was looking at the boy fondly, his small eyes bright and proud.

"Let him go, Tim," he said.

"Are you crazy?" Tim roared.

"You were going down. Let him. He'll come back all right. Do you want your son to be any less a man than you are?"

"That's got nothing to do with it!" Tim said doggedly.

But Lance's hands were busy at the knots. Quickly he loosened them and passed the rope over to Stepan.

"Tie me," he said.

The silence about the mine shaft pounded upon their eardrums like the waves of an invisible sea. Inch by inch the men played out the line, and Lance saw the stars disappearing above him. He was suddenly, horribly afraid. He had known darkness before, but never like this. Never anything like this stinking, thick fume-filled darkness. A knot of ice formed in his belly and cold sweat broke out on his forehead. He felt his hand go up to the line to give the three jerks agreed upon as a signal to withdraw him, but fiercely he snatched it away. His feet swung pendulum-like, dancing upon nothingness, and the thick smoke swirled about his head so that he coughed wildly.

Down he went, down. There was no end to it: the shaft must be bottomless. Fear crawled agonizingly along his nerves. Tears stung at his eyelids, and the inside of his throat was burned raw with the harsh lung-stinging fumes.

Then his feet touched bottom. He fell over sideways, losing his grip on the lantern. It spluttered and almost went out. He groped for it in the darkness until his fingers closed over the handle. Then he pointed it toward where the tunnel had been. There was no tunnel any longer; tons of coal, earth and draw-slate blocked the opening completely. He went over it with his fingers, looking for openings, for crevices where explosives might be set. There were no openings but he found several places into which shots of black blasting powder could be inserted. His head ached dully, but the fear was gone now. He was aware that he was growing dizzy, that consciousness was leaving him slowly. But he did not stop looking until he had found every possible place for blasting.

Then, at long last, his hand crawled up slowly to the rope, suspended loosely above him. He tried to make it move quickly, but it would not. He felt the rope jerk three times as though it were someone else pulling upon it, then it tightened, and his feet swung free. . . .

He was almost unconscious when they drew him through the hole, but the icy air revived him at once.

"Powder!" he croaked. "Long fuses—we've got to blast!"

"Son," Tim whispered, "son . . ."

"I'm all right, Papa," Lance said clearly, surprised at the strength of his own voice. "I'll blow a hole through to them and then we can get them out."

"But," Stepan Henkja objected, "do you know how to blast?"

"Of course," Lance said stoutly. He was far less confident than he sounded, though he had had the process explained to him many a time by the miners, and had watched them do it on numerous occasions.

"And a bird, Papa," he said. "Get me a bird—the air is awful bad down there."

By the glow of the lanterns, Stepan could see Tim's face working. He opened his mouth to give the order, but for the life of him he could not speak.

However, the men understood, and one of them dashed off to the supply house without waiting for Tim's words. When he came back, he brought a tiny canary in a little wicker cage.

"Let the powder down first," Lance directed. The men lowered the bulky black powder with extreme care. When the rope slackened they turned to the boy.

One of the women rushed forward suddenly. In her hands she held an old world crucifix—a kind of ikon, actually. Wordlessly she thrust it into Lance's torn soot-grimed hands. Lance lifted his hands and hung the little cross about his neck. It clinked against his Saint Christopher medallion, making a pleasing sound. Then he picked up the short-handled pick, the canary and the safety lantern, and started down.

I won't be afraid this time, he thought. But he was. His nerves were a raw and quivering mass of terror. As he went on down, he accused himself of cowardice, never realizing that his was the highest form of courage. This time it did not seem to take so long to reach the bottom. Carefully he set down the lantern and the canary, placing the bird in a position where he could watch it. Then he raised the pick and began deepening the holes he had made. His head swam dizzily and, looking at the cage, he saw that the canary was already on its back, its pitiful little beak gasping for air.

He could not stop now. He picked up the powder and tamped it into the holes, blocking them tightly with coal dust as he had seen the miners do. Then he played out the fuses as long as he could. While he was doing this, quite abruptly, he fainted. He came to, after a time, and dragged himself upright. In the little cage, the canary now was quite dead. Lance lit a match; it went out instantly. He tried several more before he found one that would burn in the foul air. He applied it to the oily torch, which blazed smokily. Then one by one, moving despite himself with dangerous slowness, he lit the fuses. . . .

This time, when they drew him out, he did not regain consciousness.

Tim did not even wait to hear the blasts; he lifted his son in his arms and marched through the snow to his house, accompanied by Stepan. And never, as long as he lived, did Tim forget the look on Lucy's face when he walked into the house, with the inert soot-blackened form of their son in his arms.

Lance was in bed for three weeks. Three weeks of constant vomiting, high fever and headaches that were agony itself. "Black damp," the miners' widows murmured, and prayed nightly for his life to be spared.

In the end, being young and strong, he recovered. But when they told him what they had found after they had gone through the hole he had made through the fallen rock, he walked out bareheaded into the snow. They had found three hundred men piled up like cordwood at the entrance to the tunnel . . . three hundred men who had watched their lamps die for lack of oxygen, and who had died themselves, their faces twisted and blue with suffocation.

So Lance looked up into the night sky toward the high clear stars.

"God!" he cried. "God!"

There was no answer. The stars looked down as hard and cruel as death. Lance could feel himself shrinking to pigmy size under the gigantic sky. The wind went through it, crying. It stretched above him endless and black and utterly empty . . . and Lance was alone—alone in a vast universe become suddenly formless and without plan. . . .

CHAPTER TWENTY—1873

PRIDE HELD his four-months-old daughter in his arms, and bending down, kissed her pink cheek. As he did so, his mustache tickled her delicate skin, and she laughed aloud.

"Es," Pride roared, "she laughed! Did you hear her? Cappie actually laughed. I didn't know they could laugh so young!"

"They can't," Esther said calmly. "You're mistaken, Pride."

"The hell I am! . . . Oh, excuse me, Cappie. Your daddy's got to stop that. He can't cuss any more, can he? Not in front of you. He can't have you growing up hearing words like that."

"Pride," Esther said gaily, "I never would have believed you'd be such a fool over a child."

Pride grinned. "She's so little and sweet. I didn't deserve anything like this; I guess that's why I love her so. God, but she's pretty! Look at that hair, Esther—and those eyes! They're like yours, only prettier. You know, I can't half get my work done these days, thinking about her. So many things I've got to do for her. She's got to have the best of everything."

He poked at the baby playfully with his big thumb. Caprice lay in his arms and watched him with grave eyes. They were bright blue and enormous, and her mouth was as soft and pink as a tiny rosebud. Pride was right: she was indeed a lovely child.

He drew out his nugget luck piece and dangled it before the baby. Caprice made vague movements with her hands, but her coördination was not yet sufficiently developed for her to catch it. Pride gave it to her, his big face split in a huge grin.

Caprice took the nugget and at once plopped it into her mouth.

"Pride!" Esther shrieked. "Here, give her to me!"

Fearfully Pride surrendered the baby and watched Esther fish the nugget out of her mouth.

"You might have strangled her!" Esther snapped.

Pride's face was ashen with real fear.

"Damn my stupid hide!" he said. "I sure could have! Give her back to me now, Es. I'll be more careful."

"See that you are," Esther said sternly.

Pride continued to rock the baby until the big blue eyes closed. Seeing her there, sleeping in the circle of his great arms, his heart melted within him. Dear Lord, he prayed silently, don't ever let harm come to her—please. I'd want to die if anything happened to her . . .

"Pride," Esther said.

"Yes, Es?"

"Joseph was here yesterday. He asked to see you."

"Who? Oh. Joe Fairhill. What did he want—you to leave me and come back to him?"

"No," Esther smiled. "At least he didn't say so. Why don't you bury the hatchet, Pride? After all, Joe has never done you any real harm. I think he'd like to be friends."

"All right," Pride said indulgently. "Have him over to dinner some night. I always liked him anyhow, even if he did buck up against me. Plenty of nerve, that fellow. Did you show Cappie to him?"

"Yes," Esther said.

"How'd he like her?"

"Very much," Esther said quietly. "He said she's the most beautiful baby he's ever seen."

"Damned right she is! Joe's got sense—and taste too: he proved that by trying to marry you."

"I suppose that's a compliment?" Esther said.

"Yes," Pride laughed. "Cappie got her looks from you instead of me, thank God!"

Malcolm came into the room then and paused just inside the door. He had a letter in his hand. Pride gave the baby back to Esther and took the letter. Swiftly he tore it open and read it.

"Now," he said, when he had finished, his voice heavy with disgust, "I've got to get myself a new manager!"

Esther looked up in surprise.

"A manager?" she asked. "For what?"

"For the mines. Tim quit. He'll be back here tomorrow."

"Oh!" Esther said. "Why did he quit, Pride?"

"Some trouble in Millville. The main shaft blew up; it wrecked the winch and the lift, and blocked the main tunnel. Hell, I won't be able to get coal out of that place till spring!"

"And Tim quit over *that?*"

"Well," Pride said uneasily, "not exactly. Some of the men got killed—and you know how Tim is."

" 'Some of the men'—how many, Pride? How many were killed?"

"Well . . ."

"I asked you a question, Pride."

"Three hundred."

"Three hundred! No wonder Tim resigned! Tell me, Pride—those ventilators Tim was always asking for . . . Would they have helped?"

"Maybe," Pride said morosely. "Tim says it was fire damp and coal dust that did it. Ventilators are supposed to take care of that, but nobody knows. Mining is just dangerous—that's all there is to it."

"No, Pride," Esther said quietly, "that isn't all there is to it. I've been putting up with things like this all my life, and I don't intend to go on doing it. Father made his money any way he could. I didn't understand that until I was grown, but I do understand now. I don't want that kind of wealth. I don't want Caprice to have your sins fall upon her head."

"But, Esther," Pride protested, "those things cost a lot of money!"

"What does life cost, Pride?" Esther said. "What is the measure in dollars and cents of the grief of those men's widows?"

226

"Now you're talking foolishness!"

"Am I? I'm sorry. Only, Pride, you're going to do some of those things Tim asked you to do. You're going to put in the ventilators. You're going to build a hospital and a decent school. I'll do my share, too. I'll build an orphan-age for the Millville children and establish a relief fund for the widows."

"Esther, you're crazy! You sound downright radical, like those fellows who are always talking in Tompkins Square."

"Radical? No—I call it decency, that's all."

"You're daft!" Pride growled. "It's just like this fellow Darwin says: the survival of the fittest. The world's a jungle. The biggest and toughest win out. It's been that way ever since the beginning of time. You can't change things, Esther."

"Perhaps not altogether. But there are tall cities now where there was jungle before. A jungle doesn't have to stay a jungle, Pride. And this particular one isn't going to! Do you know why?"

"No—why?"

"Because I'll leave you, if you don't do something about those people. Oh, I know that doesn't bother you. You'd be sitting on Sharon's doorstep before my carriage was out of sight . . . Only, Pride, I'll take Caprice with me, and you'll never see her again as long as you live."

Esther could see the livid spots of rage appearing on Pride's cheeks. But she could see something else, too, the tiny glow of fear in his eyes; and she knew that she had won.

Pride crossed over to her and stood looking down at the baby. Then he put out one thick finger and Caprice caught it in her chubby fist, cooing with delight.

"You—you wouldn't," he said gruffly.

"Oh, yes, I would. Caprice is going to have a father she can be proud of—or none at all. Or," and Esther smiled wickedly, "perhaps another one."

"No!" Pride roared.

It's strange what a hold Caprice has on him, Esther thought. Thank God for that. Now I really have a weapon I can use against him. Next time I'll have to see what can be done about Sharon . . .

"You win," Pride croaked. "I'll have the papers drawn up first thing in the morning."

"See that you do," Esther said serenely.

Pride stood there looking at Caprice. She's so beautiful, he thought, the prettiest baby I ever saw . . . I don't even worry about her not being a boy any more. God's own gold on her head and eyes bluer than the sea. I never thought anything could grab hold of a man's heart so. . . . I never loved anyone in my whole damned life as much as I love Caprice—and she most likely doesn't even know me from Malcolm.

He bent down to the baby.

"Got to have the best, haven't you, Cappie?" he murmured. "Finest clothes, biggest carriage, best damn schooling in the land. The boy who comes to marry you is going to have a hard way to go."

"You do love her, don't you, Pride?" Esther said softly . . . "Oh, dear! Again! Now I've got to change her."

"Well, hurry up. I've got something I want to show you . . . I'll tell Terence to get the carriage ready."

Esther looked out of the window at the bleak sky.

"But, Pride," she protested, "it's so cold!"

"Wrap her up good, then. This is worth seeing. I wouldn't drag you out if it weren't."

"All right, Pride," Esther said.

It was warm in the carriage under the buffalo robe. Terence managed the well-trained four with expert skill. They went straight up Fifth Avenue, past the French flats they had formerly occupied.

They left the city behind them. Finally they reached an area that would be, Esther reckoned, in the neighborhood of Eighty-second Street, when the narrow footpaths became streets. Here Terence began to work the carriage westward.

He pulled at the reins and the horses drew to a stop. Looking out of the window, Esther could see the smoke of many fires, and a swarm of men, hard at work despite the cold. They were digging into the frozen earth atop a high bluff overlooking the Hudson. A man in a fur greatcoat held a bundle of plans and talked with the foreman.

"Is this what you brought me to see?" Esther demanded sharply.

"Yes. See that man in the fur coat? That's Rosini—best architect in the country. They talk about Stewart's house—

228

it cost him a measly two million. Well, this one's going to cost five!"

"A house?" Esther whispered. "You're building a house?"

"For her," Pride said gently. "She's got to have the best."

"But, Pride, Father left us a wonderful house. We don't need—"

"I'm not thinking about us. It's for Caprice. And it's no ordinary house—it's a castle."

"A—a castle!"

"Yes. Did you ever see a princess without a castle? Half the crowned heads of Europe are poorer than I am anyhow. Why shouldn't I build a castle? Towers and battlements—maybe even a drawbridge . . ."

"A castle," Esther whispered. "Pride's castle!" Then softly, merrily, she began to laugh.

"What's so funny?" Pride growled.

"You. You're a throwback. You're exactly the sort of man who built castles in the first place. They built them to protect themselves against the people they had defrauded and robbed. And they put them at strategic points where travelers had to pass so they could go on thieving. And ever so often, Pride, the serfs rose up and besieged their liege lord—or an enemy baron decided to take over. Then they died in their castles with an arrow through their hearts . . . or they surrendered and were beheaded. Take your choice, Pride!"

"You think something like that's going to happen to me? Well, it won't. I'm too damned strong. Besides, nothing can kill me—except maybe pride itself . . ."

"That could happen, too," Esther said.

The next afternoon Tim McCarthy walked into Pride's office.

"I found your man Terence waiting for me," he said grimly. "What do you want, Pride?"

"Couple of things. First I want to show you these." He opened his drawer and brought out a heavy sheaf of papers. Wordlessly he passed them over to Tim.

Tim looked at him, a puzzled expression creeping into his eyes. Then silently he began to read. When he had finished he looked up again.

"The ventilators, the hospital, the school and an orphanage. You've gone the whole hog—eh, Pride? Now you lock the stable door!"

"There are other horses besides the ones that have been stolen," Pride said. "Want your job back now?"

"Hell, no!" Tim exploded.

"I thought you wouldn't. Well, there's still the other thing. . . . You know, old man Morrison, of Morrisons brokerage, died last week. I bought the business."

"So?" Tim said.

"It's yours, Tim. I know you won't take it as a gift, so I'll charge you fifty thousand for it—that's a lot less than it's worth."

Tim studied the big man with unconcealed amazement.

"There's just a couple of things wrong with that," he said at last. "I haven't got fifty thousand dollars . . . hell, I haven't got ten. And I don't know a damned thing about the brokerage business."

"You can learn, can't you? Keep young Johns on. He's a boy wonder at investments. Tell him right off the bat you don't know anything: then listen to him and learn. Raise his pay—that'll make him loyal. Give him a title—vice-president or something. That old fool Morrison had a gold mine in that boy and didn't know it!"

"You still haven't told me where I'm going to get the fifty thousand dollars to pay you with," Tim said drily.

"Out of the business, of course! Hell, you'll make more'n that in a month, if you play your cards right. I'm not even going to charge you interest."

Tim's Adam's apple jerked in his muscular throat. Slowly he put out his hand.

"This is mighty white of you, Pride," he choked.

"Forget it. And get it through your thick head that I don't like to see anybody killed. It's just that when you aren't in a place, things don't seem so important to you. I'm sorry it had to happen, Tim—but there aren't any really safe mines. After I put in those ventilators men are going to go right on getting killed."

"But not as many of them," Tim said.

"That's true. Come on, let's go have dinner and a drink."

"Fine," Tim said.

When they reached Delmonico's, the head waiter directed them to a table for three.

"The lady hasn't come yet," he said.

"Is Esther coming here?" Tim asked. "How is she? I hear you've got a kid, now."

Pride frowned.

"Esther's fine," he said. "Yes, we've got a baby daughter. Sweetest, prettiest little thing that ever drew breath. You've got to bring Lucy and Lance over to see her. How about Sunday?"

"Sure," Tim said. "Sunday'll be fine!"

Pride waited silently, fidgeting in his seat. Something's wrong, Tim thought. He's worried about something . . . Then he saw Pride's big head jerk. He half-turned in his seat and gazed toward the door.

Sharon O'Neil stood there, searching the tables with her eyes. Then she saw Pride. She started toward their table, walking swiftly, her face radiant.

"I'm late!" she said gaily. "Oh, darling, I'm so sorry!" Then she saw Tim.

Why did I come? Tim thought miserably. Why did Pride have to invite me on the spur of the moment? Just like him —never thinking further than his nose, except about money. I'd rather have gone hungry than have to see this. Look at the misery and guilt in her poor little face! And she's one of the few people on this miserable earth I had faith in!

Sharon stood quite still looking at Tim, seeing his face bleak and forbidding. But it was too late now—now and forever too late.

She came forward slowly.

"Hello, Tim," she said softly.

"Howdy, Miss Sharon," Tim said. "Glad to see you again."

No, you're not—are you, Tim? You'd rather see me dead than this way. You saved me once—remember? Are you glad now, Tim? Now that you can see for what purpose you saved my life? She blinked her eyes hard to keep back the tears.

"How's Lucy?" she asked. "And Lance?"

"Fine," Tim said. "Just fine."

"Tell Lucy I'm coming to see her," Sharon said impulsively. "It's been so long . . ."

"Yes," Tim said, "it has." He cleared his throat noisily.

"Only—well, Lucy—isn't having visitors just now. She's not so well . . . and we're not fixed up yet."

Sharon stiffened, as though she had been struck.

No, she thought, she's not receiving visitors—is she, Tim? Not visitors like me. A decent man can't permit his wife to be friendly with—with a whore. Oh, God, now all the doors are closing . . . all the doors in the world!

She bowed her head for an instant and mastered her tears. She was capable of doing that now. She had had so much practice at it.

"Pride," she said gently, "I don't think I want dinner after all. . . . I have the vilest headache."

"What the devil!" Pride began.

But Sharon was already standing up.

"Please, Pride," she whispered. "Some other time . . ." Then she turned and fled abruptly, weaving her way between the tables.

Slowly Pride sat down again.

"Now, what on earth got into her?" he wondered.

It was, Tim recalled afterwards, the most wretched meal he had ever eaten in all his life.

The moment he stepped into the door of their dingy little flat, Lucy read his face, as though it were a printed page.

"What is it, Tim?" she asked. "Something's wrong. Did Pride—"

"No," Tim said heavily. "In fact, he was awful good to us. He fixed it so I could take over a business that'll make us rich for life."

"That's wonderful!" Lucy said. "But something's wrong —I can tell."

"Where's Lance?"

"Out looking for a job. Why?"

"I've got something to tell you, Lucy. Something that's not fit for his ears. It's about Sharon O'Neil . . . Pride's keeping her."

"No!"

"Yes. I wish I weren't so sure. Pride and I had dinner together at Delmonico's. The waiter set places for three. I thought for a while that Esther was coming—then I looked up and saw her. She didn't see me at first. Called him 'darling' right there in front of me. And when she did see me, you ought to have seen her face!"

"No," Lucy whispered. "Oh no, Tim—no!"

"She asked for you . . . said she was coming to see you. All I could think of saying was that you weren't well and couldn't have visitors right now . . . But she got it—right between the eyes."

"Tim, you didn't!"

"Yes, I did. She got right up then and made excuses. Said she had a headache. She left the place without eating. . . . Lucy, where're you going?"

"To see her, of course! Don't you know that whatever she's done—or whatever she's doing—it's Pride's fault? Don't you remember how fine she was?"

"But, Lucy—"

"No buts about it! . . . You can get your own supper, Tim McCarthy! And don't expect me back until late!"

When Lucy reached Sharon's shop it was nearly closing time. She went in, shrugging off the manageress' offers of help and walked toward the back where Sharon sat, bent over a cup of black coffee. Her slim body was an eloquent expression of pure despair. Lucy walked slowly over to where Sharon sat, and gently put an arm around her shoulders.

"Hello, child," she said.

Sharon looked up, startled. Then very slowly she came erect.

"Lucy!" she whispered. "You—you came to see me! Oh, Lucy, it was so good of you to come!" Then they both fell, sobbing, into each other's arms.

"Hush," Lucy crooned. "Hush, child—hush, my poor baby—hush . . ."

"You don't know," Sharon said brokenly. "How could you know? You're so good, while I—while I—"

"Hush," Lucy whispered. "Not here—not now. We'll go some other place and you can tell me about it."

"My place," Sharon said. "We'll go to my flat, and—"

"No," Lucy said sternly, "we'll go somewhere else. I'll not put my foot in any place that man . . ."

Sharon looked at her.

"I said *my* place, Lucy," she said with gentle dignity. "Pride doesn't pay my rent—or spend money on me in any way. He doesn't even give me presents. He tried to at first, but I sent them back to him. Whatever I am—I'm not kept, Lucy."

"Bless you, child; I knew you hadn't changed. . . . All right, we'll go to your place then. Will he come there tonight?"

"If he does," Sharon said, "I'll send him away. Wait just a minute until I get my things . . ."

"But your shop?"

"Mathilda'll close for me. I'll only be a second."

"So!" Lucy said an hour later. "I knew it was his fault!"

"The first time, perhaps," Sharon whispered, "but not afterwards. Then the fault was mine."

"The question is what you're going to do now," Lucy said.

Sharon's head came up slowly, and her eyes, looking at Lucy, were clear.

"Nothing," she said quietly.

"Nothing!" Lucy was shocked.

"Yes: nothing. What can I do, Lucy? I love him."

"Then stop loving him! It's a wicked love, Sharon. It'll bring you nothing but shame and sorrow. Just—stop it."

"I can't do that," Sharon said. "I've tried. God and the Blessed Virgin witness how I've tried. But it's no good—no good at all."

"But he's wicked," Lucy protested. "He's brutal and cruel and treacherous and . . ." She stopped, seeing Sharon's face.

"You don't have to read me a catalogue of sins," Sharon said. "I know them all—more of them than you could know. You could have added that he's greedy and selfish— to mention a few more. It wouldn't matter, though. It doesn't matter." She turned her great dark eyes, starry with tears, upon Lucy's face. "Now let me tell you about him— the other side, I mean. The reasons why I love him . . ."

Lucy nodded grimly. "I'm waiting," she said.

"With me, he's very gentle. Yes, Lucy, gentle—even tender. Our love isn't just lust. Though there is that in it too, to be truthful—but it comes as much from me as from him. Often—oh, very often—he comes here and talks to me by the hour, then kisses me good night and goes home —nothing more. He tells me about his hopes and dreams. He—he's a kingly man, bigger than most men in all ways

234

—bigger even in spirit. He doesn't mean to be cruel—it's just that the false gods he worships are cruel gods. He's never wanted anyone hurt or killed. When something like that happens, he broods for days. . . .

"Hear me out, Lucy. I know what you're thinking. Perhaps you're right. Perhaps I am blind with love. . . . There are other times when he comes here and sits and stares into the fire for hours and never says a word. Then I keep silent too—for I know his moods. He tells me he needs me—that I'm truly his wife, the wife he dreamed of. And I believe him. We should have been married before he met Esther Stillworth. I should have insisted upon it then. But he was penniless—and as proud as Lucifer. So I waited . . . and she met him. She dangled her millions of dollars before him . . . and you know Pride."

"I'm beginning to think I don't," Lucy said.

"Nobody could entirely—not even I. He's something that doesn't exist any more. Every time I look at him I think of the passage of Scripture that says: 'And there were giants in the earth . . .' And when he takes me in his arms I remember the other verse, the one that goes: 'And the Angels of God saw the daughters of men—that they were fair . . .'"

"Angels!" Lucy gasped. "Him!"

"Yes—to me."

Lucy stood up, shaking her head.

"God pity you!" she said.

"Amen," Sharon whispered.

CHAPTER TWENTY-ONE—1873

BY THE EARLY SPRING of 1873, Pride Dawson's castle was finished. For a time, among New Yorkers at least, it was the eighth wonder of the world. Rosini was a painstaking and exacting artist. He was, besides, the foremost medievalist of his time. So it stood there now, above the

Hudson—a great, ugly, stone pile of soaring towers, fantastic spires and heavy battlements. There was even a drawbridge, though the steep ascent to the bluff on which it stood ruled out the possibility of a moat. But Pride had to have his drawbridge. It spanned a ridiculously shallow ditch, which ran across only one side of the castle and which had been dug for the sole purpose of providing an excuse for the drawbridge.

When it came to the interior of the place, Pride had some ideas of his own. In vain did Rosini show him pictures and plead that the furnishings be kept in harmony with the period of the structure. But the gloomy medieval interiors displeased Pride. The sparse, simple, beautiful furniture of the Middle Ages seemed naked to him. At last Rosini threw up his hands in disgust and resigned: Pride had his own way with the inside of his castle.

So it was that Pride's castle combined two worlds: the world of Richard the Lion-Hearted and the world of Queen Victoria. The interior was almost barbaric in its splendor. Gilt fretwork and bas-relief covered the walls, massive chandeliers and furniture in red plush crowded the high-ceilinged rooms. There were the inevitable whatnots and ribbons, the Victorian curtains and rubber plants. The heavy gilt-encrusted picture frames, Tim McCarthy was sure, must have been lifted into place with a steam winch.

It is not to be imagined that this outrageous defilement of good taste made Pride the laughingstock of society. In his furnishings he had merely out-Heroded Herod, for the taste of the society of his time was as uniformly bad as his own. Society came, gasped and imitated him. Pride was content.

As soon as the place was in order, Pride gave a grand ball. He invited, among others, Governor Dix of New York, and Mayor Havemeyer of New York City. He recklessly invited such mutually bitter enemies as Daniel Drew, Jay Gould and the Vanderbilts. The old Commodore failed to appear, but many other world-famous figures were among the early arrivals. Fully half of the New York State Legislature and most of the wealthier city aldermen attended.

No wonder that Timothy McCarthy, now head of the firm of McCarthy & Son, Brokers, felt ill at ease. He stood there with his large, red, laborer's hands dangling from the cuffs of his newly purchased formal tailcoat, and stared at the dazzling array that Pride had assembled. Lucy, whose parents had been among the first families of New Orleans' Garden Section, was less nervous than her husband: unlike him, she had no fear of committing a *faux pas* or, to use Tim's less delicate language, "of cutting a hog." Tim needn't have worried. Those assembled at Pride's ball were either the first or second generation of their dynasties: they were still too much engaged in money-getting to have much time for polish. Their speech, more often than not, was typified by Commodore Vanderbilt's famous statement: "The law? To hell with the law! Hain't I got the power?"

Pride, who was a little drunk, personally conducted Tim and Lucy through the vast, rambling structure. Lucy was overwhelmed by the splendor, but Tim, who was a simple man, thought wryly, What good is it? A man can't sleep in but one bed, bathe in but one tub, and eat from but one table . . .

When they reached Pride and Esther's apartment on the upper floor, Tim's jaw dropped. Then, despite himself, he began to laugh. Here were tiger-skin rugs, Moorish furniture and crystal chandeliers set in bronze scrollwork, like something out of the *Arabian Nights*. The rugs were ankle-deep, the beds were enormous. In the bathroom was a gigantic porcelain-lined tub, made to Pride's measure, carefully fitted into a case of light mahogany and inlaid with rosewood and cedar.

Hearing his laughter, Lucy looked at him.

"What ails you, Tim?" she whispered.

"Nothing," Tim chuckled. It was impossible to tell her the source of his ill-timed mirth. Looking at the overblown furnishings of Pride's apartment, Tim had become aware of the growing impression that he had seen most of these things before. Then it had come to him in a sudden flash of memory. Point by point, with absolute fidelity, Pride had copied the *décor* of Hattie Hamilton's notorious establishment in Basin Street, in New Orleans. It was, Tim reflected, probably the most magnificent place that Pride, in his youth, had been able to enter. The next day, when the leading newspapers lyrically described these same furnishings, Tim lost, once and for all, his fears of New York society.

Two things, of course, had commanded the attendance

of the elect: Esther Dawson was a Stillworth and hence one of them; and rumor had credited Pride with being far richer than he actually was. The ball was an unqualified success. Early in the evening someone had discovered that the amber liquid that arched from the mouth of the marble dolphin fountain was actually vintage champagne. Thereafter the party grew lively.

The women stared with frank envy at Esther's gown of heavy blue faille with bowknots, at her pointed train of white taffeta drapery with pearl embroidery, at the white ostrich tips and aigrettes in her pale golden hair, and at the hard blaze of her massive diamond necklace and matching earrings. They clucked and cooed over Caprice, sleeping in her lace, until she awoke and began to scream with fright; then they fled sympathetically downstairs leaving to the nursemaid the task of quieting her again.

Yes, it was a definite success. . . . After that spring night in 1873, whatever society's qualms over this huge southern barbarian, Pride was "in." His name appeared in the pages of the society sheets; his imported coachmen sounded their horns along the Harlem Kill; he engaged in impromptu road wagon races with William Vanderbilt; he and Esther were invited everywhere. And remembering his youth—insults that still rankled, labor in the canals, Negro-driving, contraband running—Pride found it good. . . .

As spring turned to summer, Pride was conscious of a growing feeling of uneasiness in the world of business. There were rumors which a man could never quite pin down of great businesses dangerously overextended. Profits from the mines, mills and railroads fell off alarmingly. Abruptly, early in July, Pride stopped his program of expansion. A week later he began to curtail his activities. Afterwards he called it a hunch, but it was more than that. Early in his career he had learned the value of surrounding himself with brilliant young men who could make up for his own deficiencies. From them he demanded and received frequent and accurate reports. Notable among them was studious young Will Bleeker, who once had been Thomas Stillworth's clerk. To Will Bleeker, Pride represented the personification of a success he could never himself hope to attain, and as a result he served the big man with doglike devotion.

During his years with Stillworth, Will had come to know the world of business inside out. To this knowledge, his natural scholarliness had added much. He had read almost every available book on economics; Adam Smith's *Wealth of Nations* was his bible. He was at present engaged in two writing assignments: a study of American economics and a biography of Pride Dawson. Pride was shrewd enough to see the value of the former and vain enough to like the idea of the latter, so he set no other tasks before the young man and paid him well. There was, Pride realized regretfully, only one man in New York as capable in matters of finance as Will—and that was Elliot Johns, who now worked for Tim McCarthy.

Early in April, Pride sent Will on an extended tour of his holdings. Bleeker visited Pennsylvania, Colorado and Texas, and came back by way of Canada and Massachusetts so that he could inspect Pride's textile mills.

"Look, Mr. Dawson," Will said—nothing on earth could bring him to call his employer "Pride," though Pride had often told him to do so—"the signs are all bad. All the factories and farms have produced far more than people have money to buy. There are miles of railroads running through empty land with no populations to serve. And the public is in an angry mood. There's been too much talk about railroad speculation . . ."

"I see," Pride said thoughtfully. "Go on!"

"By the end of this month, Elliot Johns at McCarthy's office tells me, there's going to be a lot of dumping. Too many investors are short of hard cash and long on securities. Minerals mostly—and copper, tin and oil. That's about all, sir. Do you have any orders?"

"Yes. Those textile mills in Massachusetts," Pride growled. "Sell them!"

"All of them, sir?"

"All. And wire Henkja to cut down production in Millville by half and lay off the men we don't need."

"That's going to cause a lot of hardship," Will mused.

"I don't go in for philanthropy or run charitable institutions," Pride said firmly. "I'm a businessman, Will."

"I quite agree, sir."

"Good! Get in touch with Blake in Texas and tell him to graze the herds for another season. What about the silver mine, Will?"

"That's quite safe, sir. Silver won't decline."

"Good! And get me some of those securities they'll be dumping. Hold them against a slight rise."

"If there is any rise," Will said gloomily. "I'll do that, sir—but if I may make a suggestion, I wouldn't hold them too long. After September first, unless I'm crazy, the bottom's going to drop out."

"You're crazy, all right—crazy like a fox," Pride said. "See what I'm driving at? By buying those stocks, I may be able to create an artificial corner."

"That's the rarest thing in financial history," Will said. "Most corners are accidents, but I believe you could do it this time."

"I know I can! And, Will, go short for me on everything that's going to crash."

"I wouldn't do that, sir. It's too risky to enter a bear market now."

"Why?" Pride roared. "A coming decline is the natural time to sell short!"

"Because, sir, this isn't going to be just a decline—it's going to be a panic. How would you feel if when you tried to deliver the stocks to your customers you found them in the hands of the receiver? Bankrupts can't keep their pledges. No matter how much they promised to pay you for the paper, they couldn't honor their pledges, if they didn't have a dime."

"That bad, eh?" Pride said. "Good boy! I'll get busy—right now!"

The next morning the Massachusetts mills were quietly sold. In Millville hundreds of men found themselves suddenly jobless and drifted away, promising to send for their families when they found work. Hungry children went hungrier still to help protect Pride's millions.

For all his vanity, Pride knew when to keep his mouth shut. He did not speak of his plans even to Tim. Elliot Johns, Tim's financial advisor, had arrived at much the same conclusions as Will; and Tim was very busy, trying to corner the same markets in which Pride's agents were buying efficiently but unobtrusively. Tim had paid back the fifty thousand dollar loan; he himself was worth a modest fortune now, but appetite grows with eating, and Tim had visions of making his family's material future secure.

Pride made only one exception to his rule of "play sharp

and say nothing." That same night when he visited Sharon he asked suddenly:

"How's business?"

"Bad," Sharon said. "Pride, I don't understand it! Nobody seems to be buying any more. Are they all planning to wear their old things another season?"

"Yes. Worse than that."

"What is it, Pride?" Sharon asked. "You know, don't you?"

"I think so. Look, Sharon, you'd better cut down. Right now—fast. Keep your shop, but reduce your staff. Will Bleeker says there's going to be a panic; and I never knew Will to be wrong yet."

"Is he sure, Pride?"

"Sure as shooting!"

"I—I hate to let my girls go. They've been so loyal."

"Look, Shay, when this is over you can hire them back. But you've got to save yourself. In the long run that's their best chance too. If the one who's got the brains and the ability goes down, what chance has the poor devil who's depending on him to come to his rescue later?"

"There's sense in that," Sharon said thoughtfully. "Still—"

"You do what I tell you!" Pride ordered.

Sharon stared at him.

"All right, Pride," she whispered.

"Good! Now come here and kiss me good night, because I've got to go. I'll be up all night putting my affairs in shape to ride this thing through. But my mind's at ease now, knowing you'll be all right. It isn't like you'd let me take care of you . . ."

"Please, Pride—we settled that long ago."

"I know, I know. Only, when I give you something, I'm not paying you. It's my way of showing you how much I love you—how much I need you. Oh, damn! What's the use of talking about it?"

"None," Sharon said gently. "It's just that it makes me feel a little better about us, if we keep it this way. I have my own self-respect to consider, too, darling."

After Pride had gone Sharon lay upon her bed thinking. Why is there no child? she wondered. It was a recurrent nightmare that some day she would bring into the world a child of her shame and sorrow. During the first year of Pride's marriage, she had been somewhat reassured by the fact that Esther had borne him no child, but now there was Caprice. . . .

She suddenly remembered something Lucy had once said—an odd, fleeting remark: "Tim was surprised when Esther had that baby. He says that Pride played around so much in the old days, it's a wonder that there's not something wrong with him . . ."

Well, she mused, if there's any barrenness here, it's mine, not Pride's. And I hope I am! Pray God I have no unhallowed child!

On the first of August, Will Bleeker came into Pride's office, his thin face gray with misery. Pride took one look at him and jumped from his seat.

"Don't tell me you were wrong!" he roared. "We aren't caught, are we?"

"No, sir," Will whispered. "You'll make a profit. Quite a tidy profit—though how much I can't say exactly. It isn't that."

"Then what the devil is it?"

"It's my friend Elliot Johns, sir—and Mr. McCarthy. They went short on the same stocks I told you to buy. I didn't think of that. Of course, with your having so much more money, your men were able to get them. I—I'm afraid Mr. McCarthy's firm will be ruined, sir."

"Jehosaphat!" Pride exploded. "Tim! . . . Will, you get right over there and tell Tim I want to see him. I'll have to fix this—fast."

When Will Bleeker came back with Tim, Pride stood up and faced him soberly.

"Tim," he growled, "damn your hide for a stubborn fool! Don't you ever tell me anything?"

"No," Tim said. "Why should I? I paid you back. It's my business now."

"Like hell it is! More than likely it's the receiver's business. You went short on General Minerals, didn't you? And Amalgamated Copper—and oil? Tim McCarthy, you poor blind fool, I own three quarters of that stuff now! How in hellfire do you think you're going to deliver?"

Tim's face paled, then the red came back, deeper than ever.

"If I'd known you were on this deal, Tim, I'd have kept my paws off," Pride continued. "Now I've got to fix things.

242

Thank God I found out in time. Here's what you have to do. You've got those notes—orders for your clients for later delivery of stock you don't own yet. I'll bet my bottom dollar they're dated for after September fifteenth, because your boy Johns is as smart as my Will. Right?"

Tim nodded grimly.

"Dump those damn notes, Tim! Write letters to your clients—tell 'em you're sick. Then discount those notes to Warren. He'll buy anything—as long as it's discounted. That will leave him holding the bag and you'll be in the clear. Of course, you'll take a slight beating—but you'll still be in business. . . ."

"That," Tim said, "is downright dishonest!"

Pride grinned.

"You could say the whole idea of a bear market is dishonest," he said. "After all, you promise to deliver stuff to folks that isn't yours and that you aren't even sure you can get. And you hold them to the price at which it was quoted at the time you took their notes—even if the bottom's dropped clean out of it since."

"But you lose your shirt if the stocks happen to rise instead of falling," Tim reminded him. "Or if somebody corners 'em—like you . . . It's a gamble, Pride, but the risks are equal on both sides. So I call it an honest gamble. But dumping those notes isn't gambling. That's being a crook and a polecat!"

"Money," Pride said, "can perfume the stink off a polecat. You have no choice, Tim."

"Oh, yes I have! I'm going to buck you, Pride. I'm going to get my hands on enough of that stuff to stay floating, and rebate the rest."

"Tim," Pride said sorrowfully, "you're a fool! I've got two million dollars tied up in this stuff, and much as I like you that's too much money for friendship. You're going to go down."

"But fighting," Tim said. "Fighting hard!"

"Look, Tim—chuck the whole thing. Go out of business now, while you've still got your reputation. I'll tell you what I'll do. You and I prospected together in California. There's not much about precious metals you don't know. I'll make you manager of my Colorado lode."

"You're not going to do any such thing," Tim said.

"Tim, boy, this is the chance of a lifetime."

"It is like hell! Don't you ever get tired of playing God, Pride? I've done your dirty work before. But I'm through now. It's a hell of a lot of fun to make men, then break 'em, isn't it? I'm not going to be at your mercy any more. I'm not going to send any more men down to die while you sit here and dally with your fancy woman! Get somebody else. All right, you'll break me. No hard feelings over that —business, we'll call it, the fortunes of war . . . But you've got too many people in the hollow of your hand now. It's bad enough for Esther and that poor little baby of yours. It's worse for Sharon, who was as fine a lady as ever lived before you got your paws on her."

Pride stepped forward slowly, his breath making a loud rustle in the room.

"Say her name again," he said quietly, "and I'll break your stubborn neck, Tim McCarthy!"

"I'll say what I damn well please!" Tim roared. "Just remember this, Pride Dawson, you're not adding me or Lucy and Lance to the bones piled around your cave!" Then he turned and marched from the room.

"The stubborn jackass!" Pride growled. "Why'd he have to fix it so that I've got to ruin him?"

Then he sat down again behind his desk and stared moodily out into space. It was a fact that Pride could have saved him by selling him enough of the cornered stock at cost to meet his commitments; but it was also a fact that such an idea had never even occurred to Pride.

On the fifteenth of August, Pride gave the signal for the kill.

"Now's the time to sell, son," he told Will Bleeker. "And since it was you who gave me the idea, you do it. Go down to the Exchange and dump all the trash you've made me buy. You can have one percent commission on the profits, if any. If there are no profits, I'm going to have your hide for a lap robe! Now get out of here and get busy!"

"All right, sir," Will said. "I'll go right away!"

Three hours later he was back, his face white and still.

"Don't tell me," Pride groaned. "I know. You've lost my shirt!"

"No, sir," Will whispered. "You've made your profit— about two and a half million. It's just that we've ruined Mr. McCarthy and thrown Elliot Johns out of a job."

Pride growled. "I never did see a longer face on a fellow who'd just made himself twenty-five thousand dollars!"

Will's face cleared, but only momentarily.

"That's right," he said, half to himself, "I did do that, didn't I?"

"You sure did!" Pride grinned. "Now, you go right over and get your precious Elliot Johns. Tell him he's hired at sixty-five hundred a year as your assistant. That ought to wipe the tears out of his eyes."

Will's face at that moment was a study in hero-worship. Pride found the look embarrassing.

"Get out of here!" he ordered. "I've got work to do!"

On September 8, 1873, the New York Warehouse Securities Co. closed its doors. On the thirteenth, Kenyon Cox & Co., in which shrewd old Daniel Drew was a partner, announced its bankruptcy. And rumor had it that George Opdyke & Co. was in danger.

Pride sent for Will Bleeker and congratulated him on his sound judgment.

"Take a week's vacation!" he grinned. "Elliot can take over your work temporarily. But leave that crystal ball of yours here where I can watch it!"

On September seventeenth Jay Cooke was entertaining the President of the United States at Ogontz, his magnificent home near Philadelphia. A servant entered with the yellow square of a telegram in his hand. Cooke excused himself and read it. Then he turned back to his guest with tears in his eyes.

"I'm sorry, sir," he said simply, "but I have to go. There's trouble in New York. My partners are announcing insolvency."

It is difficult to imagine what it was like the day Jay Cooke failed. It was as though the Rock of Gibraltar had suddenly sunk into the sea. Wall Street was full of men, cursing, crying and roaring out their rage.

The rain poured down upon their heads, but they paid no attention to it. On a corner a newsboy shrilled:

"Read all about it! . . . Jay Cooke & Co. fails!"

A policeman, his face black with wrath, stormed out of the crowd and arrested the newsboy.

"I'll teach you to shout such lies!" he said.

But it was no lie. Public confidence melted like snow in

a noonday sun. Every bank in the city was besieged by men hungry for cash to meet the notes that creditors everywhere were suddenly calling in. The banks, of course, could not stand the runs. Their assets were miles of shining rails running through the empty prairies, their holdings were farm lands on which the crops would now rot in the fields, their securities were mines whose rich lodes were no longer worth taking from the bowels of the earth.

On the twentieth, the Stock Exchange closed its doors.

Pride sat back, grinning. He was neither buying nor selling. His assets were in gold or in government bonds, locked in his own big safe.

And still the heads rolled. Fisk and Hatch failed. Lake Shore Railroad failed. The Union & National Trust Co. was forced to suspend.

The day after that happened, Sharon came to Pride's office, her face filled with gratitude.

"Thank you, darling," she said. "I had all the store's funds and my own in the Union & National. I drew them all last month. Here they are. Keep them for me, won't you?"

"Good!" Pride replied. "I'm glad to see you're safe."

"I—I hired Lucy McCarthy yesterday, Pride. She's quite good with the needle—and with Tim gone . . ."

"I see," Pride said heavily. "Reckon that was my fault in a way."

"Lucy says you didn't know. Tim's gone West, Pride— out to California. He intends to prospect and see if he can't make a real strike. Lance is out looking for work."

"I'll hire him," Pride said. "Tell Lucy to send him to me."

"I'm afraid he wouldn't come," Sharon said. "Lance is— a little bitter, Pride."

"So—" Pride mumbled. "Guess I can't blame him much. I'll tell you what I'll do. I'll pay Lucy's salary for you. You don't have to tell her."

"Thanks, Pride—but no. I'll manage."

Then she kissed him lightly on the cheek and walked out. Pride was reminded once more how much of life was not under his control.

Pride Dawson was not the only great capitalist who survived the Panic. All of the bigger ones did. Jay Gould, ousted that summer from the Erie after having stolen some

246

twenty-five millions, went on to ravage the Northern Pacific. And the Vanderbilts picked up the carcasses of their smaller competitors for a song. The actual effect of the Panic was to eliminate competition and to leave the giants towering higher than ever.

And during this period there was no appreciable improvement in the state of the nation's soul. Secretary of the Treasury Richards, in conjunction with B. F. Butler whom New Orleans had cause to remember, farmed out the tax collections of the State of Massachusetts to a man named Sanborn, who was allowed to keep fifty percent. Whether he made a substantial kick-back to Congressman Butler and Secretary Richards has never been revealed. Butler, despite his crossed eyes, knew how to count. In New Orleans, during the war, he had counted silver spoons. . . .

In Washington, Shepherd, along with his cohorts, was found guilty of extravagance, corruption and oppression. As a result, the District of Columbia lost its territorial form of government and passed under Congressional control.

And Carnegie Steel and Standard Oil and Dawson Enterprises grew and grew, buying up their competitors for a song. In New York City the British-controlled house of Drexel, Morgan & Co. took Jay Cooke's place on the top of the heap.

These were the bare bones of the matter. The flesh was quite another thing. The flesh was the mile-long line of men, ill-clad and freezing, shivering before the poorhouse on Randall's Island waiting for a free meal. The flesh was the lines standing before the soup kitchens set up all over the city. It was the eleven thousand homeless children fed by the Children's Aid Society, and the countless other thousands who lived by their wits. It was the dirty, homeless boys who scurried through the streets like rats, robbing, killing, if need be, to stay alive. It was Tim McCarthy lying on the floor of a Chicago police station in the company of a hundred other homeless men, his nostrils filled with the stench of their unwashed bodies, his ears sounding-boards for the wailing of the snow-packed wind.

It was the children who froze to death in the packing boxes during that winter, or survived until spring brought them death in the slower form of disease. It was the tens of thousands turned out on the street for nonpayment of rent.

It was the three thousand infants abandoned on doorsteps in New York City alone. It was the hundred pitiful, shriveled little corpses found in ash barrels, areaways and dumps—left there by mothers too poor to bury them. It was the thirteen hundred New York citizens who died by deeds of violence. It was the one out of every seven New Yorkers arrested for thievery and other crimes inspired by unbearable misery. It was, finally, the girls of thirteen and fourteen who sold half-frozen berries gathered on the Harlem Kill—or themselves, depending upon the mood of the customer.

Yes, the flesh was more. Much more.

CHAPTER TWENTY-TWO
1873–1874

IT WAS DURING the months of November and December in 1873 that the famous Dawson family portrait was painted. For the work Pride employed the celebrated Lucius Rossi. Pride found the whole business of standing still exceedingly irksome, but Caprice solved the problem by sleeping quietly in Esther's arms. After it was completed, Pride was extremely gratified, for not only did the painting show his massive frame in all its dignity, but it managed to capture much of Esther's spirited beauty as well.

Best of all, it displayed the giltwork of the vast hall in which it was hung, the red plush furniture, the rich carpets and draperies. Pride was so impressed with it that he drew Rossi aside and broached the subject of having him do a portrait of "a dear friend."

The dear friend was, of course, Sharon O'Neil. But Sharon politely and firmly refused. Instead she went down to the studio of an immigrant photographer, a German who claimed to have learned his art from Matthew Brady, and sat with her head in a wire frame while the slow wet-plate camera recorded her image. The result was a wonderful picture, beautifully and pitifully revealing.

Sharon came up to Pride one night in the snow as he was leaving the Winslow Hotel, where he had been having a sociable glass with friends, and handed it to him.

Pride tore open the wrappings and stared at it under the street lamp.

"Beautiful!" he breathed. "God, Shay—it's you!"

"Thank you," she said. "I—I felt bad about refusing you the portrait. But I couldn't, Pride. I couldn't sit still with that man's eyes upon me and know what he was thinking. . . . So I give you this. It's a poor thing, but it's yours—like my heart."

Pride bent down and kissed her, under the dim lantern glow.

She drew her face away slowly, and stood looking up at him wistfully.

"Pride," she said, "will you give me one of you? I want something to remember you by, if . . ."

"If, hell!" Pride snorted. "I'm going to be around a long time, Shay."

"I know. But then you may not or I may not. Time and people change. I believe I'll love you forever, but I don't know how long it will be before you grow tired of me."

"Never!" Pride said.

"Never is a long time, Pride. I want your picture. Will you give me one, please?"

"Sure," Pride said. "Sure thing, Shay. I'll have it taken tomorrow. Where's this man's studio?"

"The address is printed on the bottom of the folder," Sharon told him. "Come and walk with me."

Pride strode along beside her in the snow, holding the photograph. Sharon was walking aimlessly, as though the very motion would still the hunger and the grief in her heart. How can I tell him, she thought, that for all his visits, I'm still lonely? Could I make him understand how it is to be without a friend, except for Lucy—and she, too, disapproves of me? He does what he has to in order to fulfill his destiny. And once it's done, he forgets it—no matter how wrong or shameful it is . . .

But I—I cannot. He has no God but Mammon, he idolizes nothing but wealth and power. But he himself is my only idol, because of him God has turned His face away from me. Oh, Pride, Pride—have you never felt the crushing weight of sin? Have you never stood—in shame and sorrow—outside the Church that once illumined your life, and dared not enter?

I have a hunger for God, Pride, I have a thirst for righteousness. Yet, I cannot assuage them—because of you. Were I to go in, the very images of the saints would frown upon me, the smell of incense would stifle my breathing. And She—God's Holy Mother—how dare I lift up my eyes to Her? How can I bare my shame?

You don't understand such things, Pride—or even believe. If only I weren't alone so much! If only I were married to you, so I could at least have the solace of a child. But that, too, is denied me. I am denied all things, Pride: joy, peace and true happiness—all save the anguished joy that I find in your arms . . .

She caught him by the coat sleeve suddenly and leaned against him, shuddering.

Pride looked past her and saw the block-long line of ragged men standing before the door of the soup kitchen, hunched over beneath the whiplashes of the sleet and snow.

"Oh, Pride, let's go!" she said. "I can't bear it!"

"Hush, Shay," Pride tried to comfort her. "Things'll get better."

"Oh, take me home!" Sharon whispered. "Take me home and hold me in your arms!"

They turned back and retraced their steps, but somehow, in the dark and cold, they took a wrong turn. They found themselves in the dismal confines of a street on which neither of them had been before. It was pitch black between the shabby tenements; mounds of frozen garbage impeded their passage. Pride caught at Sharon's arm to guide her, and it was then that they heard the child's moaning.

Pride started forward, his hands outthrust, searching. They closed over the rough edge of a packing box. He gave a push and the box turned over, spilling its contents. From somewhere far below him a small voice shrilled:

"Damn your black soul to hell, you lousy bastard!"

Pride bent down and picked up the child. It was impossible to tell whether it was boy or girl from its nondescript clothing. It seemed to be about six years old, and it was hammering at his face with considerable force.

Pride paid no attention to the blows but strode on, with

Sharon half-running at his heels, until they came to a street light. He held the child up to the light and studied its filth-caked face. Then lifting one big hand, he tugged at the cap. At once a mass of heavy black hair tumbled down and, matted though it was with dirt and straw and feathers, Sharon could see that the child was a girl—an orphan lost as she was lost . . . a waif sent down to her by God.

"Oh, Pride," she whispered, taking the child from him, "I'm going to keep her!"

"It depends on whether she has folks," Pride growled. "Have you, missy?"

The child had recovered somewhat and was staring at them out of round, dark brown eyes.

"You got any folks?" Pride repeated. "Any pa or ma?"

The child shook her head.

"Maw's dead," she said calmly. "Paw beat her with a broomstick and she died. Then he went away. I live—there." She pointed toward the packing box.

"Poor little baby!" Sharon whispered. "Well, you have a mommy now. I'll be your mommy!"

The child studied her with grave eyes.

"You a whore?" she asked simply.

Sharon gasped and almost dropped her precocious burden.

"No," Pride grinned, "she isn't. Why?"

"She's dressed so pretty. Only whore ladies dress like that."

"No, honey," Sharon said gently. "There are other ladies who dress well, too. . . . Come, Pride, we'd better find a cab and take her home."

Finding a cab on such a night proved almost an impossibility. They were more than halfway home before a hansom finally passed them.

In Sharon's flat, the child looked about wonderingly. Clearly, she had never seen such luxury before in her life.

"Pride," Sharon said, "there's some soup in the ice chest. Heat it up, will you, while I give her a bath?"

"Sure," Pride grinned. "I'd like to see what she looks like under all that dirt."

It took two complete changes of water to get the child clean. Her hair grayed innumerable rinsing waters before it was soft and shining. But the child who emerged from under the layers of grime was a creature of bewitching beauty. She was dark, thin, gypsy-like. On her body were innumerable tiny marks, always in pairs—deep little cuts as though made by a double knife.

"I wonder what on earth caused them," Sharon said to Pride.

"Rats," the child said suddenly, unexpectedly. "They bite."

"Oh, my God!" Sharon whispered.

Pride put a big finger under the child's chin and lifted her little face.

"What's your name, honey?" he asked.

"Lil'th," she answered promptly.

"Lilith?" Sharon guessed. "Oh, Pride, what a pretty name!"

"Cute little mite, isn't she?" Pride grinned. "Look, Shay —I got some rights in her, haven't I? After all I did find her. And this isn't like you were taking presents from me . . ."

"What do you want to do?" Sharon asked.

"I want to help take care of her. I want to pay for her schooling, anyhow."

"I think that will be all right. What you do for Lilith is goodness and charity. Yes, I'm sure it'll be all right . . ."

They sat, fascinated, and watched the child noisily devouring the soup. Lilith ate as though she had never eaten before. At last she looked up and said:

"More!"

Sharon refilled the bowl four times, and at last the dark, curly head slumped over the bowl. Sharon sprang up and took Lilith in her arms. She stood there a long time, staring down at the sleeping child.

"Oh, thank you, God!" she said.

"I'll get a nursemaid for her," Pride said, "unless you want to quit work and let me take care of both of you."

"No," Sharon said, "I can't do that, Pride. All right, get a nursemaid to come during the day. The poor little thing! God knows what she must have suffered . . ."

The authorities put no difficulties in the way of Sharon's adopting the child, though she put the word "spinster" firmly after her name. They were overwhelmed with unwanted children. To have one wanted was a gratifying surprise.

Pride was obliged to hire four nursemaids in succession,

before they found one who would stay. Lilith had a fiendish temper and a vocabulary that would have put a veteran sailor to shame. She delighted in wanton destructiveness —tearing Sharon's clothes, spilling her perfumes, smearing powder over everything.

"I can't seem to reach her," Sharon said despairingly. "She's so strange, Pride. She can't seem to bear being loved."

"Give her time," Pride said. "She'll change."

He was right. At last a large motherly German woman, Frau Himpel, arrived and took over. She ignored Lilith's tantrums and swearing, and doggedly fed, bathed and dressed the child. Lilith kicked and screamed, but it had no effect upon this placid mountain of pink flesh. Finally, Lilith gave it up and became almost a model child, but her dark, mysterious little mind was busy . . .

On the other side of town, Lucy McCarthy sat sewing under the gas lights. Her head ached, and it required an effort to focus her eyes upon the fine stitches. But this extra work, this "piecework" as it was known among the needletrades, was the only thing that kept body and soul together. The salary that Sharon paid her was far from adequate, but Lucy recognized the fact that Sharon was making a sacrifice to keep her on at all, and was grateful.

She thought about Tim—lost now, swallowed up in the vast wasteland that lay to the west—and her throat contracted with fear. Too many times she had heard him tell of the blizzards that came sweeping down from the north with winds so fierce that no man could stand against them; or of wagon trains caught out too late in the fall and found only after the spring thaws, the grotesque skeletons of the men still holding the reins. There were the Indians too, still largely unsubdued—and the fierce beasts. . . .

She must not think of these things. She must sit very quietly and do her work and pray. She must not even think too much of Lance, growing thinner and angrier. The jails and the gallows had ended the lives of too many young people who had burned with the same just and terrible anger.

Tomorrow would be Christmas, and here in her house there would be nothing. No gifts, no bright holly, no tree. It had been bad before but never this bad. Quickly, she turned aside her head for fear her teardrops would spot the fine cloth.

The knock at the door sounded several times before she roused herself sufficiently from her brooding to hear it. Then she sprang up and rushed to the door, the thought of Tim flaming in her mind. But it was not Tim. Instead, Stepan Henkja stood there, smiling at her, his beard covered with flakes of snow.

"I had a letter from Lance," he said timidly, almost apologetically, "telling me of your distress. I came to see what I could do."

"Come in," Lucy said. "Come in! Oh, Stepan, I'm so glad to see you!"

Stepan brushed the snowflakes off his greatcoat and came into the dingy little room.

"No word from Tim?" he asked.

"No," Lucy said sadly, "none."

"He'll come back all right," Stepan said. "Then your troubles will be over."

"I hope so," Lucy said fervently. "God knows, I hope so!"

She noticed that he was still standing, awkwardly holding his hat in his hand.

"Sit down, won't you?" she said. "I'll make some tea— I'm afraid there isn't much else."

"Tea will do nicely, thank you," Stepan said. "Where's Lance?"

"Out looking for work—though there never is any. He'll be in soon."

"That's one reason I came," Stepan declared. "I may be able to do something for Lance—at least I hope so."

They had finished their tea when Lance came in. He was blue with cold, and his handsome young face was bleak. But when he saw Stepan, some of his gloom left him.

"Stepan!" he cried. "You here! I'm ever so glad to see you!"

"And I'm glad to see you," Stepan said gently. "Here, have some of your mother's excellent tea, for I'm afraid I must drag you back out into the cold."

"Why?" Lance said.

"The matter of a job, son. I have here, though I never told you before, certain connections. I think they could use such a one as you. But more of this later. Drink your tea."

Lance downed his tea almost at a gulp, and stood up.

"I'm ready," he said.

"Ah," Stepan sighed, "the eagerness of youth! Don't wait up for us, Mrs. McCarthy—we shall be very late."

"All right," Lucy said. "And God bless you, Stepan, for your kindness."

They went out into the street and Stepan hailed a cab.

"Fifty East First Street," he told the driver.

It was a long way. By the time they reached the address, Stepan had parried dozens of questions from Lance as to the nature of their errand.

But as they stood on the sidewalk in front of their destination, Stepan explained.

"This is Justus Schwab's Saloon and Restaurant," he said. "It is the gathering place for all who hold those beliefs that society calls radical. I did not wish to discuss it in the driver's presence—secrecy among us is the price of safety, Lance. Come, we will go in now."

He pushed open the door and they entered. Instantly, the man behind the bar set up a bellow like that of an enraged bull.

"Stepan!" he roared. "You sly old fox! Where have you been?" Then he came rushing forward, his huge hand extended.

"Schwab," Stepan whispered to Lance.

Lance studied Justus Schwab closely. He was magnificently built, with a great tawny beard and a massive head. He looked like a Wagnerian hero—and had the voice to match his appearance. He wore a colored shirt, open at the throat, so that Lance could see his mighty neck.

Now he was pumping Stepan's hand, as though he would break it off.

"Good to see you!" he rumbled, in his Olympian bass. "*Ach, ja*—very good!" Then his gaze fell upon Lance.

"Who's this?" he thundered. "A new recruit?"

He seems, Lance thought, incapable of speaking quietly.

"I think so—yes," Stepan said.

"You think so! Don't you know?"

"He has had the experiences necessary to make a man sympathetic toward our views," Stepan said quietly. "He's seen men die like rats in the mines and mills, to increase one man's wealth. His own father was ruined by that same man—but he lacks indoctrination."

"Then you've been falling down," Schwab roared.

"Oh, I'm a capitalist now," Stepan laughed. "I manage a steel mill!"

"No!" Schwab gasped. "You traitor!"

"You have not asked me how I manage it," Stepan smiled. "A nine-hour day—wages double those paid anywhere else in the industry—hospital care . . ."

"Utopia! Good for you, Stepan . . . Come have a drink —on the house. What's yours, boy? Beer?"

"Yes," Lance said, "I'll take beer."

"Oh, I forgot," Stepan said. "His name is Lance McCarthy."

"Another Irishman, eh?" Schwab laughed. Lance could tell by his tone that he meant no offense. Therefore, he smiled.

"Good boy," Schwab said.

They sat at the bar, sipping drinks.

"Do you think that Heinkel could use him?" Stepan asked Schwab.

"Sure," Schwab said at once. "Be good for the boy, too —he could learn the printer's trade and more about our movement. He seems a likely lad, Stepan."

"Then I'll take him over to Georg now."

"Sit down!" Schwab roared. "There is no need. Georg will be in sooner or later—he always is."

The evening grew merrier. Schwab went to the piano and played and sang the *Marseillaise*, translating it into German, however, as he went along. Then he sang *Uns Fuehrt Lassalle* . . . which, Stepan told Lance, meant Lassalle leads us. His voice was of the finest quality: deep and rich. Lance thought that he could have become famous on the operatic stage. . . .

Then Georg Heinkel came in, and it was done. Lance found himself hired as a printer's devil and call boy, on nothing more than Stepan's recommendation. He was to work on *Der Arbeiter* in its English version, *The Worker*. Later on, it was agreed, he could learn German.

When he left the saloon his head was in a whirl. He had listened to a French revolutionary named Victor Drury describe his visit to Karl Marx in London. He had listened as Drury described the apartment in Soho where Marx lived, the furniture broken and tattered, the rooms untidy, filled with eye-stinging tobacco smoke, and Marx's poor Jenny overworked, exhausted with childbearing, nobly carrying on while her husband scornfully refused to let bourgeois society turn him into a money-making machine.

It was incomprehensible to Lance, this reverence accorded to what seemed to him churlish and unkind behavior.

Later, soberly and patiently, in an all-night session, they explained the articles of their revolutionary faith to him: their own dazzling interpretation of the religion of envy, of the faith of defeated men everywhere, who, despairing of attaining success by the application of their own brains and abilities, sought their place in the sun by leveling the structure above them.

Lance, who had seen men suffer and die under private enterprise, was almost convinced. Almost—but not quite.

The next day he began to learn the printing trade; he set type and inked the presses and distributed the wet bundles to the news vendors. And slowly, painfully, he began to learn the German tongue. But he was not convinced. He might never have been convinced, but for Tompkins Square . . .

Lance stood with Georg Heinkel on January 14, 1874, and watched the crowds gathering to listen to the speakers in the Square. His throat was taut with worry, for only last night Justus Schwab had been escorted down to the Mulberry Street Station and given a warning. The police captain had leaned over the desk and looked at the big German.

"Heard tell you're planning to burn the city," he growled. "Maybe toss a few bombs about. Well, Heinie, this ain't Paris. We got the City Hall, the Post Office and the Archbishop's house guarded—and we got plainclothesmen stationed in the Square. And they ain't been ordered to arrest you—oh, no! Look, you dirty anarchist, if one shot is fired, you leave that party feet first!"

What the people wanted was very simple. They wanted work—public work, if necessary, to save them from starvation. They wanted an order forbidding evictions during the cold months. But the Communists had seen in this human misery the perfect opening for a propaganda war. And they had taken over. They had flooded the city with tracts; they talked darkly of dynamite, razings, burning, assassination.

The daily press had become alarmed. The words "Commune" and "Revolution" appeared in the headlines. Nast, in *Harper's*, drew a skeletal figure labeled "Communist," seducing an American worker.

The stage was set, Lance knew, for tragedy. What Lance didn't know—and what ninety-nine percent of those present didn't know—was the fact that the Park Commissioner had withdrawn the permit for the meeting. The New York City Safety Committee, named after its dread predecessor of the French Revolution, had simply hidden the permit.

Lance looked at Georg. The mild-mannered Bavarian was serene. Already the speeches were beginning, in French, German and English, and the polyglot crowds listened. It was ten-thirty in the morning and, looking up, Lance could see that hundreds of uniformed police had surrounded the huge iron fence that encircled Tompkins Square. Through their ranks, broken to let it pass, marched a delegation bearing a banner which read: *Tenth Ward Union Labor*.

They came from Avenue A, and the police followed them. At first there was no word, no outcry, no flinging of stones: just the dull crack of the clubs against the skulls of the crowd. Then the people fled shrieking in all directions, and behind them the police came, swinging their billies in deadly earnest.

Lance caught Georg by the arm and the two of them ran down Eighth Street. Suddenly, Georg stopped and pointed back. Mounted police were charging down the street, rising in their saddles to strike down at the people. There were men and women in the street who didn't even know that a meeting was being held in Tompkins Square—a meeting whose purpose was to beg for the relief of the starving. But they were beaten with the rest. Lance and Georg plunged into an areaway to escape the clubs and the hoofs of the horses. Lance saw a baby carriage smashed by the iron-shod hoofs; the baby rolled out into the snow, squalling at the top of its lungs but miraculously unhurt.

A gray-haired old woman went down and lay moaning. Lance saw a short, powerful man leap into a cellar door. Afterwards he was to learn it was Samuel Gompers.

"This is not Europe!" Heinkel wept. "Those are not Cossacks! This is America, Lance, America!"

All day long, that fourteenth day of January, 1874, in

lower New York, the police charged whenever they saw a crowd of shabbily dressed people. The hospitals were filled to overflowing. And Lance McCarthy, a mild Socialist in the morning, went home that night a full-fledged Communist-Anarchist—a believer in force.

CHAPTER TWENTY-THREE—1876

THERE WAS NOBODY in the world, four-year-old Caprice Dawson was convinced, quite so nice as her daddy. Not only did he bring her a new and exciting toy almost every time he entered the house, but he knew so many different ways of having fun. He would get down on all fours and let her ride on his back. He would toss her up almost as high as the big chandelier in the hall, and catch her as she fell, breathless and squealing. He took her sailing on Long Island Sound on his yacht; and he bought her the most beautiful bang-tail pony harnessed to a wicker cart.

Sometimes it seemed that Mommy didn't love him as much as she, Caprice, did. How could she be so cross with him? The other day Daddy had taken her over to play with Lil'th. (How pretty Lil'th was! A real big girl, nine years old, Daddy said.) Caprice had sat on Auntie Sharon's knee and eaten ice cream. Auntie Sharon was nice too, not so pretty as Mommy but nicer. But when Daddy had brought Caprice home Mommy had been very angry.

"Oh, Pride, how could you?" Mommy had said.

There had been a lot of other talk that she hadn't understood, but part of it she did understand; for when Mommy had started talking about leaving Daddy flat and taking Caprice with her, she, Caprice, had started to cry. . . .

"You see!" Daddy had said to Mommy.

They talked a lot more, but she had been so sleepy. The last thing she had heard was Mommy saying something about fixing Daddy. . . . Was Daddy broken? She looked at him anxiously to see if one of his arms or legs had come loose—as her dolly's did when she pulled at them too hard —but Daddy had been all right. He was too big for anybody to pull loose.

Now they were going away to a place that Caprice couldn't remember—to a kind of fair. Daddy had explained it to her. It was because the country was now one hundred years old.

"Are you a hundred years old, too, Daddy?" she had asked him, and he had told her solemnly that he was two hundred. But people couldn't be that old. Auntie Sharon had told her that only elephants and turtles grew that old. She wondered whether if she ate a lot she could grow into an elephant. Daddy was almost an elephant already, he was so big.

But she was very glad to be going away to the place with the long name, if only because of that man. That other man—"Joe," Mommy called him. He came to the house sometimes when Daddy wasn't home, but he teased Caprice too much and pinched her cheeks. He looked like such a nice man, but he wasn't—not like Daddy. He never brought her anything, and he was always holding Mommy's hands and talking to her so quietly that Caprice couldn't hear what they were saying. Caprice didn't like him. He wasn't big like Daddy and his hair was yellow like Mommy's—only a little darker. . . .

Anyway, they were going away from that Joe now, and she wouldn't have to worry about him any more. She had meant to tell Daddy about him, but most times when Daddy would come home he would have his hands behind his back, hiding the present he had bought for her, and she would get so excited she would forget. . . . Ah, there Daddy was now! And as her tiny feet flew down the hall, Caprice wondered what he had brought her.

Esther, too, was relieved when Pride announced that he was taking them down to Philadelphia for the great Centennial Exposition. She had discovered at last that there was no sense in even hoping that she could force Pride to abandon Sharon O'Neil. She had played her trump card and had lost. For when she had threatened to take Caprice away from him, the child had cried so bitterly that even she was shocked.

"Just try it," Pride had said grimly. "I'll buy up the

whole damn Pinkerton Agency and set them on your trail till I find you. Then I'll have you committed to a lunatic asylum—and don't say I couldn't do it!"

Esther was afraid that he might be right. Any woman who would leave a man as rich and powerful as Pride Dawson was sure to be considered mad by legions of envious women, as well as a benchful of seedy judges. No, she'd just have to bide her time, and plot the nature and magnitude of her revenge.

The first thing that Esther insisted upon seeing when they reached Fairmount Park was the art exhibition. To her surprise, she found that Pride was actually eager to go too—as eager as she was herself. No man could live the life that Pride Dawson lived without gaining a little culture despite himself. She had noticed that his speech was improving, and since the completion of the Rossi portrait, he had acquired a genuine interest in art.

At the exhibit, however, Esther was disappointed. None of the Continental artists had considered American taste worth the effort. But the British had sent paintings by Gainsborough, Reynolds, Millais, Holman Hunt, Turner and Alma-Tadema. It was the first time in the nation's hundred years of existence, now being celebrated, that the public had seen really good art.

The American artists, too, were not to be sneered at. There were such early painters as Gilbert Stuart, Copley, Allston, Rembrandt Peale, and the newer, younger men: Winslow Homer, Alden Weir, Thomas Moran and Eastman Johnson. Johnson had painted Esther's good friends, the Hatch family of New York, at a thousand dollars a head, and gained an additional fee when a baby had been born during the period of months-long sittings.

Pride, however, was instantly taken with Rothermel's "Battle of Gettysburg"—a gory atrocity of stupendously bad taste. It was all Esther could do to keep him from buying it on the spot. Finally, he bought a piece of sculpture which was only slightly less hideous.

But Esther came to realize, while in the English handicrafts and manufacturing exhibit, what an extravagant horror Pride's castle really was. The English were undergoing a renaissance in which simplicity and good proportions were being rediscovered. There were Lambeth faïence, Eastlake furniture, Minton tiles, and cabinet work in the style of the Jacobean and Queen Anne periods. For the first time, Esther realized that furniture did not have to be overwhelming in order to be good; it could also be small and simple and beautiful.

She exclaimed over the German porcelain and the exquisite French textiles. She was delighted with the bronzes, porcelains, ceramics and lacquerware from Japan.

Pride was pleased with these things, too; but what really impressed him was the tremendous Corliss stationary engine in Machinery Hall. As tall as a three-story house, this gleaming steel and brass monster turned out a full sixteen hundred brake horsepower, and shook the whole building when it ran.

In the women's pavilion, Esther saw the new sewing machines, and gleefully pointed out a wide range of exhibits from the hands of women, extending from textiles designed by women trained at the Massachusetts Institute of Technology to a complete Materia Medica from the Women's Medical College of Philadelphia. Here, she told him scornfully, was a refutation of his scoffing at her feminism and suffragette sentiments; but Pride only grinned complacently and said:

"Exceptions prove the rule!"

But at one last exhibit Esther was brought up short with a new and serious idea in her head. Here were the kindergartens of Belgium, Germany and Switzerland. The more she studied them, the more she was aware of how pitifully inferior American education was. She asked questions and took names and addresses. Pride, when he found out what she was doing, agreed with her. If these schools were better than the New York schools, he would import one! Caprice had to have the best. . . .

When Manfredi Carloni, a Swiss professor who combined the German, Italian and French culture of his trilingual land in his one small, fastidious person, stepped off the boat two months later, he found his school awaiting him—complete with pupils, hovered over by the most bejeweled collection of mothers and grandmothers he had ever seen. Esther had recruited his young scholars from the wealthiest families of New York.

Life was going very smoothly for Pride Dawson now. The country was slowly recovering from the depression.

The lines before the soup kitchens were shorter, and now and then a Help Wanted sign appeared. Pride's railroads were barely breaking even, but his mines, mills and shipping lines were pouring gold into his vaults. Out West there was a hint of trouble to come. Here and there the first of the squatters were building their sod huts on the prairies, and laying down their lines of fences. The fences—that was the trouble! With the squatters closing the range, it was becoming more and more difficult to drive the herds from Texas to the shipping corrals near the railroads in the North.

His foreman wrote him long, complaining letters. Pride read them and wired back: "Do something about it!"

That was all. He never ordered people killed or houses burned. Just: "Do something!"

So in the West bands of horsemen rode hard through the night and revolvers cracked in the darkness. Miles of fences were torn down. Patiently, doggedly, the squatters rebuilt them, and continued to turn up the grazing land with their plows. Pride and other cattle barons—few of them absentee owners like him—struck back with increasing fury. The squatters' houses burned, and men died of gunshot wounds over the handles of their plows. Nobody, of course, told Pride of this war that flamed from the northern borders of Texas almost to the plains of Montana. His foreman reported merely that satisfactory progress was being made. Pride grinned and was content. . . .

"Content—" Sharon O'Neil was thinking. "Ah, I shall never be content. I shall never be strong enough not to flinch at the whispers. . . ."

"Look," Mathilda interrupted in a whisper, "it's the Randolphs."

Sharon stood up and patted a stray wisp of hair back into place. The Randolphs had been rich so long that people had forgotten when it was that they did not have money. Peter John Randolph, the first of the line, had amassed a fortune in colonial times. One branch of the family had turned its back upon the crudities of American life and had become British subjects. There was a Viscount Randolph now, and the American branch of the family shuttled back and forth across the Atlantic.

Sharon walked forward to meet the Misses Grace and

Patricia Randolph, a smile on her face. To acquire the Randolphs as clients was almost like making a patron of the Queen herself: New York society, many of whose members already had followed Esther Stillworth into the shop, would now break down the doors.

The Misses Randolph, Sharon decided at once, were going to be difficult customers. They had lived so long in England that they had acquired the English cast of countenance—which, to Sharon, represented a certain vertical elongation of feature, like the face of a horse displeased with his paddock.

But the young man who accompanied them was quite different; it was only after Sharon had come much closer that she could see that he too was a Randolph. His face, much less equine than that of his sisters, was undeniably handsome. He had curly, brown hair, and blue eyes shaded by lashes that were shockingly long for a man. The sideburns were as curly as the hair on his head and even lighter in hue, being almost blond.

It was a nice face, Sharon thought, but weak. . . . Then she was bowing gracefully to the Randolph sisters.

"So good of you to come," she murmured. "I had no idea that you'd be back from England so soon."

This last was pure salesmanship, designed to let the Randolphs know that they were recognized.

But the Misses Randolph were used to being recognized. They showed their large, yellow teeth fleetingly in mirthless smiles.

"Caroline told us about your place," Patricia Randolph said, "and showed us some of the frocks you made for her. Very nice."

Caroline? Sharon searched her memory. Oh yes—that was the youngest of the Astor girls, William Waldorf's daughter. It paid to keep track of such things.

"Yes," she said, "I've made a number of things for her. Misses Helen and Emily, too, and—" She caught herself in time. She had been about to add Charlotte Augusta to the list. But Charlotte Augusta had been divorced. Adding her would be no recommendation to the Randolphs, even if she was an Astor.

"Would you mind showing us some of your things?" Grace Randolph said abruptly.

They had acquired, Sharon saw, the English habit of

being curt with persons whom they considered their inferiors. Oh, well, she could put up with that. The Randolphs, at the moment, were worth their weight in gold to her.

"Delighted," she murmured, and raised her hand to Mathilda.

As she did so she looked full into young Randolph's face. He was staring at her with unconcealed interest. Quickly, Sharon turned aside.

Mathilda hurried out, carrying a large number of dresses. Some of them had been made as samples and others were gowns ordered by one or another of Sharon's clientele, but not yet delivered.

Grace and Patricia Randolph examined them all, their long faces impassive. But Sharon could see a glow in their eyes, for all their English-trained habit of self-control. Young Randolph, however, was not at all impassive.

"Beautiful!" he said. "I tell you, Miss O'Neil, they don't make gowns like this—not even in Paris!"

"Oh, hush!" Patricia Randolph said fretfully. "What do you know about clothes?"

"I know what I like. And coming from a man, that ought to be the ultimate judgment. Or don't you dress to please men?"

"No," Grace said flatly, "we don't. Men will like anything—once they get used to it. We dress to make other women envious."

That, Sharon reflected, was God's own truth—though it was rather disconcerting to hear it expressed so baldly.

"However," Grace went on, "your dresses are beautiful, Miss O'Neil. I think I'll want six. Might we see some designs?"

Sharon brought out a portfolio of her sketches.

"You realize," she said, "that once I make a dress from these sketches, I destroy the sketch. Only one of a kind—no duplicates. I assure you, Miss Randolph, that you'll never meet yourself coming down the street."

"You must be quite expensive," Patricia Randolph said.

"I am," Sharon said firmly.

"Hang the expense!" her brother said. "Where else will you get clothes like these?"

Patricia Randolph shot him a reproving look. Then she turned back to the sketches and her face became alive and eager.

"Six," she repeated. "The wine, the mauve, the blue . . ."

Grace Randolph also took six. Sharon's pencil flew over her notebook, recording the selections. But when they were leaving the unexpected happened. For, instead of merely murmuring "Good day" as his sisters had done, young Randolph impulsively put out his hand.

"It's been nice meeting you, Miss O'Neil," he said.

"Thank you," Sharon said quietly, noting the shocked expressions upon his sisters' faces. Then she bowed them out.

That evening, as she locked the door of the shop, she was aware of a figure lurking in the shadows. She knew it could not be Pride, for this was not his evening to call. She moved off, walking very quickly, hearing footsteps behind her. She was badly frightened. There was no one else in sight—no policeman, no passers-by. She did not want to run, but the footfalls were gaining on her. Then she saw a hansom cab.

She raised her parasol to summon it, though she knew that this was an extravagance; but a voice from behind stopped her.

"Miss O'Neil!" it called. "Oh, Miss O'Neil—wait a bit, won't you?"

Sharon lowered her parasol and turned.

"Why, Mr. Randolph!" she said, in surprise.

"I beg your pardon, Miss O'Neil," he said. "Please forgive me—I just had to see you."

"Why?" Sharon asked directly.

"Why? That is a poser, isn't it? You were hailing that cabby, there. Come, let's ride about a bit and I'll try to explain . . ."

"No," Sharon said.

"No?" Randolph's face was filled with astonishment. Clearly he wasn't used to being rebuffed. Especially not by the lower orders, Sharon thought grimly.

"No, thank you, Mr. Randolph. I'm on my way home—and after all we haven't been properly introduced . . ."

"Oh!" Randolph said. "Very well, I'm Courtney Randolph, at your service, ma'am. And you're Miss Sharon O'Neil—a lovely name, by the way. Now we're properly introduced. May I take you riding?"

Sharon started to shake her head, but the humor of the situation struck her with irresistible force. She and Pride hadn't been properly introduced either. Who was she to stand on ceremony? Besides, Courtney Randolph seemed a thoroughly likeable young man—that ridiculous British accent of his excepted.

"All right," she smiled, "for a little while. I'm very tired. We'll ride around the square until you explain why you accosted me on the street. Then you'll take me home."

"That," Courtney said, once they were settled in the cab, "is very easy to explain: I didn't know how else to get in touch with you. I didn't mean to be rude, truly I didn't— you must believe me!"

"I do believe you," Sharon said gently. "But that only brings us to the main question of why you wanted to get in touch with me in the first place."

Courtney sat very still, looking at her.

"Because," he said sadly, "I'm afraid I've fallen hopelessly in love with you. Oh, yes . . ."

Sharon stared at him incredulously.

"Now, really, Mr. Randolph," she began, "you don't expect me to believe that. Up to this morning, you'd never seen me before in your life."

"How long is it supposed to take?" Courtney said, almost angrily. "I walked into your shop and—presto!— there it was. It's something that has never happened to me before. Oh, no—quite the contrary. But you—you're so different. Strangely and delightfully different. 'Courtney,' I said to myself, the moment after I heard your lovely voice, 'you must see her again—you must!' "

"Please," Sharon said, "please don't! You can't know what you're saying—it's impossible!"

"Impossible? Hardly that. Let us say: difficult. First I have to convince you that I'm sincere, that I mean you neither harm nor dishonor. That *is* difficult. Unfortunately, men of my class have made it so. All I'm asking, my dear Miss O'Neil, is the opportunity of calling upon you."

"Please take me home now," Sharon said. "I—I'm all confused."

"Good! At least I have some effect on you. I was beginning to despair. What's your address?"

Sharon told him. Then she sat back and listened to his gay platitudes until they had reached her house.

"I must go now," she said. But Courtney caught her hand.

"Wait," he said. "You haven't told me whether or not I may call."

Sharon thought quickly, wildly. He's so nice. Oh, why didn't I meet him long ago—before Pride—oh, yes, before I was destroyed by Pride. . . .

"Please," Courtney Randolph whispered.

Why not? Sharon reflected. I'm not bound to Pride. Must I remain forever the prisoner of my weakness and my love? I—I could marry this boy, perhaps, and then I would be—free! Oh, Pride, why is it that I must love you so?

"Please," Randolph said again.

"Yes," Sharon said at last, "you may call. But not on Thursday nights—I'm always busy then."

"Oh, thank you—thank you!" Courtney Randolph said, and leaping from the cab, helped her down. "This is the most wonderful day of my life!" he declared.

Or the most unfortunate, Sharon thought. Then she said "Good night" and fled upstairs. . . .

CHAPTER TWENTY-FOUR—1876

IN JULY a band of Plains Indians surrounded the two hundred and seventy-seven troops led by General Custer and killed every man.

Reading about it in the papers, Lucy McCarthy wept. In the three years that Tim had been gone, only a scattered letter or two had trickled back out of the West. They told of jobs held and lost, they enclosed money, and they always ended on a note of hope. But for the last year there had been no letters, no word sent back by returning travelers—nothing. Bowing her head over the newspaper, Lucy had horrible visions of a bloody savage bending over Tim's prone form, knife in hand . . .

The doorbell shrilled suddenly. Lance? Lucy wondered. Ever since Lance had taken that job as a reporter, she nev-

268

er knew when he was coming home. Lucy grieved over Lance. It was not that he was wild. She was quite sure that he drank little beyond an occasional glass of beer, and she was even surer that he was not in love. In this, she was wrong. The dream was his love. The Socialist Utopia for which he worked was a demanding mistress. But what troubled Lucy's sleep was the fact that for three years Lance had not entered the doors of a church, and now declared baldly: "There is no God!"

As she walked toward the door, Lucy thought: "It's a wonder I don't go mad!" Then she twisted the knob and opened the door. Tim was standing there in the hall, grinning down at her.

The corners of her mouth worked, but try as she would she could not say his name. Tim stood there a long time, looking at her, his rough weather-beaten face filled with tenderness. Then he put his arms out to her. Lucy surged forward all at once, and buried herself in them, whispering over and over: "Oh, thank God! Thank God!"

"Don't cry, Lucy," Tim said. "It's all right now. Everything's fine!"

Lucy pushed him away from her tenderly, holding him at arm's length.

"Just let me look at you!" she said. "Just let me look!"

"Not much to see," Tim said. "I'm a little older—a bit more tired—but much richer, Lucy! That's the main thing! I've got my stake."

"I don't care about that," Lucy said. "Having you back is as much as a body can stand at the moment. It's not good to pile up joys."

They had come into the room now and Tim's eyes wandered about it, seeing its grim poverty. His heart swelled with joy.

"No more of this!" he said. "You're going to have everything! Before I'm through, you're going to dress better than Esther Dawson. And it's a sure thing you're going to have a better-looking house than that ugly rockpile!"

"Still thinking about Pride, Tim?" Lucy murmured.

"Yes—and no. I forgave him long ago for what he did to me. It's not that. I'm kind of grateful to him for showing me that a man can come up if he has enough guts and determination. I'm going up, Lucy, but I'm not going to use his dirty methods."

"Good!" Lucy said. "I'm glad of that, Tim. Let me get you something—some tea or coffee? We'll have to shop for something to eat. There isn't a thing in the house."

And there hasn't been in a long time, Tim thought grimly, noting how thin she had become. "No, Lucy," he said aloud. "Nothing right now. Afterwards, we'll go out and eat. We've got to celebrate. Sit down and listen: I've got to tell you about it."

"Yes," Lucy said, "do."

There's something on her mind, Tim thought. Something's not right. But he pigeonholed the thought for later consideration and launched into his story.

"Remember I told you that Pride and I first come East after the sale of a low-grade gold mine? Well, it was that mine that turned the trick."

"But you sold it, Tim," Lucy protested. "How could you—"

"Hold your horses, Lucy, I'm getting to that. Reason we couldn't get rich on that mine was because the vein was so poor it wasn't hardly worth taking out of the ground. . . . I didn't go right to it at first. I prospected around, and didn't find a blamed thing. Reckon I was kind of hoping for a miracle, but it looks like the world's run plumb out of miracles. A man don't get himself out of a hole by luck. He's got to do it with brains. . . .

"So, after I saw I wasn't going to dig any millions out of the ground, I thought about that mine. I went out to see it. It was a-sitting there, high and dry—abandoned. Four or five men had owned it since Pride and I sold it. Sunk shafts and dug out the ore, and even built sluice runs, so they could pan out the gold; but it wasn't any good. They never even got back what they put into it.

"I went up to the claims office and looked for the last owner, thinking I'd make him an offer. I had a few dollars saved from my last job. But he was dead, killed in a barroom brawl down Denver way. So I just stuck in a claim and got back that mine for nothing. They laughed at me at the claims office. Told me that place was called Sullivan's Jinx—Sullivan being the man who bought it from Pride and me. But I've got no respect for jinxes. I went back down to Denver and got in touch with a fellow named Norton. That Norton is a genius with machinery. He and his pa used to

270

own a shoe factory back in Massachusetts before the crash —and that boy's got himself an engineering degree from the Massachusetts Institute of Technology. So I got Charlie Norton and took him up to the mine and showed it to him. I told him I'd cut him in for half if he'd tell me how to get gold out of it. Took one look at it and said, 'Isn't much here, but what there is, we'll get.'

"Then we went down to Frisco and floated ourselves a loan, on the strength of the claim papers. Couldn't of done it in Denver, because they knew too much about the mine. But in Frisco they'll plunge on anything that smells of gold. So we come back with some mighty peculiar machinery: steam pumps that could put water under terrible pressure, and gates and sluices. That there Charlie was a whiz. We put those big hoses on the side of that bank and washed it plumb away. Inside of six months, the vein gave out completely—but we had paid for the machinery and made almost a hundred thousand dollars besides. So we split the money and come East. Charlie's up in Boston reopening his pa's old plant, and I'm going in with him. We're going to make the best shoes in the East. And you, Lucy, aren't never going to be poor any more!"

"That's simply wonderful!" Lucy said.

"Sure is!" Tim grinned; then: "Where's Lance?"

"Out," Lucy said. "Out working. He's a reporter on a newspaper."

"Good for him! Which one? The *Times?*"

"No—" Lucy faltered. "It—it's called the *Socialist.* . . ."

Tim's big jaw dropped.

"Don't tell me," he said, "that that kid of mine got mixed up with radicals!"

Miserably, Lucy nodded her head.

"I'll fix that!" Tim roared. "I'll have his hide, if . . ."

"No, Tim," Lucy said. "That's not the way to do it. You see, we were very poor and the Socialists were the only people who—or so Lance thinks—seemed to care. He became very interested in their program. He wants to improve the condition of the workingmen and the poor. It's a noble idea in a way. Only, I'm a pretty good judge of people. I don't think the men Lance goes around with are really interested in the poor. It's power they want: terrible power, Tim. And they'll use misery and discontent to get that power. They aren't really good people. If they were, why should they insist upon making an atheist out of Lance?"

"Lance—an—an atheist?" Tim growled. "You mean he doesn't believe in God any more?"

"Yes," Lucy whispered. "That's what I mean, Tim."

"That's bad. That's very bad. Didn't you have Father Shannon talk to him?"

"Of course. But Lance talked about the Church being a vested interest, owning property and keeping the people poor, until Father Shannon left, saying he'd put Lance in the hands of God. God, he told me, would bring him around in His own good time. . . . Only, it's terrible waiting for it to happen."

"I'm going to talk to that boy," Tim said grimly. "Come on, let's you'n' me get a bite to eat."

And talk he did, all through a painful session that lasted the entire night. Lance was polite but firm. No, he no longer believed in God. Besides, any God Who would allow such suffering to fall upon the innocent must be a diabolical monster, and he wanted no part of Him. Yes, it was wonderful that his father had recouped his fortunes, but he didn't want a job in the shoe factory—not as manager, worker or even janitor. His life was pledged to the fight against private ownership of property: he preferred to fight other men, not his own father, which he would have to do if he took work in Tim's new plant.

Tim lost his temper finally, and swore at his son. But Lance stood there with pitying calm and refused to budge one inch from his stated position.

"Look, son," Tim said at last. "I'm going to take your ma up to Boston to live. The day you change that stubborn mind of yours, you come up there. I'll have a home waiting for you, and a job. But don't come before you can get down on your knees again, and say your 'Hail Mary,' and 'Our Father.' You're no son of mine."

"Very well, Father," Lance said.

In a corner, Lucy wept.

"Do you like Courtney?" Sharon inquired of Lilith.

"Very much," Lilith said soberly. "He's ever so much nicer than Pride. Besides, I need a daddy. Don't you think so, Auntie Sharon?"

272

Sharon stared at this strange child whom she had adopted. Lilith, at nine, was tall for her age and very slender. There was something indefinable about her beauty. Something smoldering, Sharon thought—something sensual? But how could a nine-year-old child be sensual? There was, Sharon decided, at least a promise of the qualities that might bring Lilith to the same fate which she herself had suffered. She would have to take good care of the child. She must guard her well. . . .

That brought up another aspect of the problem. Lilith was growing up. Always remarkably alert, she had become even more so in the past year. She was beginning to ask questions about Pride. How long could she conceal the truth from her, she wondered. She had never lied to Lilith. The child knew, for instance, that she was adopted. It was she who had chosen to call her "Auntie Sharon," rather than "Mother." Sharon had been troubled by this choice, but she had said nothing. . . .

Courtney was coming tonight. He would take Sharon riding or to the theater, or anywhere she wanted to go. He had been very patient. And I do like him, Sharon thought, truly I do!

The trouble is, she said to herself, I still love Pride. Nothing—no, nothing at all—seems to make the slightest difference in that. Nor would anything ever. But was she sure? If she were to go away—far away—and settle down with a man who was gentleness itself, might she not forget Pride? Was it not, after all, her duty to Lilith, to herself and to God, to forget Pride? She put her hands to her head. It ached so. Yet she must think. She must decide once and for all which way to go. It really was so simple. All she had to do was to say "Yes" to Courtney. Even the difference in their religions was of no importance. Courtney, in order to win her, would gladly become a convert to her faith. He had said as much.

She could go to Father Shannon and confess her years of sin. God, after all, had forgiven much blacker trespasses when repentance was sincere. And all the rest of her life, she would know real peace. . . .

It was so simple on the face of it. Only . . . Pride's big fingers had but to touch her hand and the wild sweet madness started. He could kiss her casually, unthinkingly, his thoughts far away, and she went down fathoms deep in

273

tenderness and rose to leaping flame. It was like that. Mother of God, it was like that! If he was silent, she was silent. If he was sad, she felt like crying; when he was gay, laughter bubbled up from her throat.

Dear God, she thought, I am nothing apart from him. . . .

Well, she would end it, if she could. If her own deep weakness did not betray her, if all her lust and longing, and the fire in her flesh and the tenderness that melted her very heart, did not betray her. If the rebellion of her very being against what should be, in favor of what was, did not betray her. If, in the end, she were not by all of these undone . . .

She heard the bell now, sounding clearly in the hall. "I'm coming, Courtney," she called. . . . Oh, yes, tonight at last, I'll come to you.

She threw open the door, and stood there in the dull glow of the street lamp, her face flushed and eager so that, seeing it, Courtney was powerless to move.

"Sharon," he whispered. "Oh, my dearest . . ."

"Come in," she said gently. "We won't go out tonight. I —I want to talk to you."

He followed her mutely up the stairs, his eyes filled with such doglike devotion that she could feel it though she did not look at him.

"Sit down," she said. "Would you like some wine?"

"No—yes! God knows I need some. You were so lovely there in the doorway, Sharon. There was something in your face that unnerved me. I don't know what it was."

"I do," Sharon said. "I think you saw that I've come to a decision—about us."

"Oh, God!" he breathed. "Don't say it's over, Sharon. Please don't say we're finished."

"Don't be alarmed, Courtney," she said slowly. "That wasn't what I was going to say. . . ."

He was on his feet now. Then with a gesture that was absurd and touching at the same time, he dropped to his knees.

"Sharon," he whispered, "you don't mean—Oh, dearest, dearest . . ."

Sharon stopped suddenly, the hand she was about to put out to him half-withdrawn. The tenderness upon his face was beautiful to see. It was a deep and honest emotion—

clumsy and without grace, as such things usually are—but very real. And what she had been about to do was the worst of all betrayals: she was about to accept a man under false pretenses. Unthinkingly up to now she had been about to allow him to wed a woman whom he did not know, whom he believed to be virginal and pure. But now she could not do it. There had been too many lies—too many betrayals. She knew at that moment, with terrifying certainty, that if she did this thing she would ensure her damnation in the eyes of God.

She lifted her fine head proudly. And, even as his heart sank, Courtney was sure that never again would he see anyone so beautiful.

"Yes," she said at last, "I was going to say that. I was going to tell you I'd marry you. But I cannot. I'd have to lie in order to do it—and you are far too good for lies."

"I don't understand, Sharon. Put it a bit more simply, won't you? Lies? How could you lie? . . . No, I don't believe that. I've never seen anyone so good and fine. . . ."

Sharon bent forward suddenly, her pride gone as though it had never been.

"Please, Courtney—please go," she said. "Don't make me tell you any more. Don't make me, please!"

Courtney scrambled clumsily to his feet.

"There isn't anything," he said stoutly, "that could make a particle of difference in the way I feel about you."

"Are you sure, Courtney?" Sharon whispered.

"Absolutely!"

"Very well," she said, looking straight into his face. "I've been Pride Dawson's mistress for nearly five years. I am neither good nor fine. How can I become your wife?" She stood there, seeing his face contorted with grief, the pain in his eyes so naked and pitiful, that even to look upon it was shameful.

Then she bent down with her characteristically angular grace and picked up his hat.

"Good-bye, Courtney," she said.

He did not answer her. She held the door open for him, and watched him as he reeled drunkenly through it. Then, very quietly, she closed it behind him.

The morning came graying in. Courtney Randolph ran a hand over his jaw, feeling the bristles that had sprouted during the night. He was aware, too, that his feet were masses of lead, without feeling, impossible to lift. He had no idea how far he had walked after leaving Sharon's house. He could not even remember the streets through which he had passed.

Surely, no man had ever been called upon to bear anything like this. There was a thing called mercy. He remembered how when his fine chestnut hunter had broken her forelegs in a nasty spill in England, he himself had sent for his revolver and shot the poor animal. The chestnut's eyes had been bulging and rolling with pain, and he had stilled it. Was there no one to stop this far greater hurt? Must he go on daily knowing this—this debasement of his idol?

He looked up suddenly and saw the gossamer tracery of the still incomplete Brooklyn Bridge in the distance. The first morning sunlight caught in it, making of it a long web of silver, soaring across the East River. It was very high, and a single footpath ran across the void which the great span would presently surmount. One could mount that footpath, he knew. For the sum of fifty cents or a dollar, he could not remember which, one was permitted to walk across the dizzily swaying catwalk to the other side.

A dollar! A cheap enough price for mercy: bargain rates for surcease from unbearable pain. He quickened his steps, walking toward it.

It took him more than an hour to reach it, for he had been far uptown when he glimpsed the span. Then, unhesitatingly, he mounted the runway to the narrow catwalk, and put a bill in the hand of the sleepy attendant.

He started out, feeling the wind on his face. On the river, far below, a few tugs hooted and butted their way upstream. The sun, beyond the Brooklyn shore, spilled gold over everything. There was a feeling of freedom, of treading on the air itself—nothing between him and the river but the rope-slung handrail, nothing really between him and peace.

But the loveliness of it caught him. He stood quite still in the middle of the bridge and breathed in the clean, cool air. He could feel the pain leaving him and the stunned cells of his brain coming to life.

She said she'd marry me, he thought, but I would not have her. How is it then that I'm here seeking death in preference to losing her, when losing her is a matter of my

choice? I love her. What kind of love is it that has no forgiveness in it? In what way is she damaged? How, actually,
is she soiled? Because she loved the wrong man? Because
she was led or forced into error? Dear God, I've bought
women in Piccadilly Circus. . . . Who am I to condemn
her?

He stared down from the dizzy height toward the black
water below. I could save her from this thing, he reflected.
Am I going to abandon her forever to that rotter? He's
married, too. What hope is there for Sharon, except to die
broken and castoff and alone? I've been thinking about
mercy. Is this the way I show it? Isn't Sharon—whatever
she has done, whatever she is doing—worth my life? My
whole life—all the joy I can bring her, all the peace, all the
tenderness?

He turned and walked back to the Manhattan side. At
the foot of the ramp, he hailed a passing cab and told the
driver to take him to Sharon's house. It never occurred to
him that Sharon had probably gone to her shop already.

But in this, at least, fortune favored him. As the cab
drew up before the house, he saw her coming down the
steps. He jumped down, signaling to the driver to wait, and
raced toward her.

Sharon saw him coming. She stood still, her dark eyes
somber and questioning, until he came up to her.

"Sharon, I—" Courtney began.

"Yes?" she said quietly. "Yes, Courtney?"

"I've been a fool! Forgive me. Say you'll forgive me,
darling, and never again as long as I live will I—"

Sharon's brows rose sharply.

"*I* forgive *you*? For what?"

"For behaving so badly. For making you think my love
so small a thing. It isn't, you know. You told me about
your past. Well, that's dead now. It died last night—but I
didn't have the sense to know it. Let's leave it buried, shall
we? Let's go on as though nothing—as though it had never
been. . . ."

She stood there looking at him, her eyes widening and
darkening in her fine face.

"You made a mistake," he went on hurriedly. "Granted.
But I'm not God. It isn't my duty to judge you or punish
you. All I can do is love you and help you forget—if you
can. Can you, Sharon?"

Slowly she shook her head.

"No," she whispered. "Does it matter?"

"No!" he said emphatically. "It doesn't. Nothing matters but the fact I love you. Nothing counts, except that I'm going to marry you, if you'll have me. Will you, Sharon? I'd be most humbly grateful."

She did not move. Her face was as still and white as though it had been carved from stone; her eyes were wide, staring at him, their expression unchanged except that now they filled up slowly with tears. He stood there in the silent street, listening to the sound of his own breathing. The cab horse brought his foot down upon the cobblestones. The clang of the iron shoe was deafening—Courtney jumped at the sound.

The teardrops brimmed in Sharon's eyes, spilling over her lashes and making slow streaks down her cheeks. Courtney remembered a face of Our Lady of Sorrows he had seen in Spain. Sharon's face was like that now, illumined with tenderness, the corners of her wide, sweet mouth trembling.

"You'd 'be grateful,' " she whispered. "You'd be grateful —for saving my life. For taking away all my shame and all the self-torment I've lived with all these years. No, Courtney, it's I who must be grateful."

He put out his arms to her and she came to him gladly.

"No more of that," he said gruffly. "Forget it. If you weren't good, I couldn't love you. But you are good—good all the way through. The ones who are bad, aren't sorry. I've a feeling you've paid a thousand times over in remorse for what you've done. Remorse is heavy coin, Sharon. It adds up in God's scales. They've struck a balance, now."

"You think so, Courtney?" she said.

"I do, Sharon. Now kiss me, quickly. I've things to do. I've a ring to buy, remember?"

Sharon kissed him softly, then hung back against the circle of his arms, looking at him.

"And the Instructions in the Church, Courtney? You'll do that for me?"

"For you I'd become a Turk. And your faith is beautiful. I think I shall enjoy finding out what has made you what you are. One more thing, Sharon—when?"

"As soon as you've finished the Instructions," Sharon

said. "I'm afraid to wait too long—something might happen."

"Nothing will happen now! Nothing could."

"You're very sure, aren't you?" Sharon sighed. "Very well. But I've got to tell you something else, Courtney. I don't want any lies between us. I don't love you. I wish I did. But the—other has done too much to me. I'm a little numb, I think. I'm very grateful to you—honestly grateful. It's a great honor to become your wife. I want you to be patient with me, because when I do start to love you—and I will, Courtney, I will!—I shall love you very much. . . ."

"That's all I ask," Courtney said.

Sharon smiled at him softly.

"I'm afraid I'm going to begin demanding things of you already," she sighed, "but I can't go to the shop today. Will you drive down there and tell the girls I won't be in? I'll go with you part of the way. I want you to drop me off at the Cathedral. I—I have to talk to Father Shannon."

"Gladly," Courtney said.

The sky was blue above the Cathedral, and in the wash of sun there were fleecy wisps of cloud. Even the heavy oaken doors had lost their forbidding look. One of them stood ajar, and through it Sharon could see the dancing flames of the candles clustered about the feet of the Holy Mother. There was joy in her heart now, a wild, sweet joy. She got out of the cab and ran toward the door of the Cathedral, but before reaching it she turned aside and went up the path that led to the Rectory.

Watching her go, Courtney Randolph said a short and simple prayer. "Forgive her, God," he murmured. "I can—and it ought to be so much easier for You. . . ." Then he lifted the little trap and signaled the driver to go on.

Inside the Rectory Father Shannon stood up as Sharon entered. She fell to her knees before him and covered his hands with kisses, sobbing so hard she could not speak.

"Hush, child," he said gently. "I've been expecting you. God, in His own good time and in His own way, always brings His chosen home. Come, there's a place for these things." Then, taking her by the hand, he raised her from the floor and led her through a passageway into the Cathedral, where the confessional box waited. Through its wicker sides many a torment, many a grief, and many,

many sins had been lifted up to God. . . .

Going home through the busy noonday streets, Sharon's steps were as light as thistledown, though she knew that the heaviest of her tasks still lay before her. She must send for Pride and tell him what she was going to do. This was a proud thing, not something to be accomplished like a theft in the night. It was going to be very bad, telling him. He would do everything in his power to stop her. Before, she would have been afraid of that. She would have been unsure of her own strength. But today she had no fear. Her love for Pride was a thing of terrible force, encompassed with flame. But what was even such a fierce love before the all-embracing love of God? Let Pride do what he would, he could not stop her now.

She sent a note to him by special messenger and settled down to wait. It would not take long, she knew. But she was unprepared for how little time it actually took. A scant half-hour later, her bell was ringing madly.

She went down the stairs and opened the door. Pride stood there, trembling all over with fury.

"You!" he roared. "You lying little—"

"Hush, Pride," she said quietly. "Come inside, please. This is our affair. There's no cause to discuss it with the world."

Inside her flat, she turned quickly to Hilda and told her to take Lilith out for a walk—a long walk. What must be said now was not for the ears of a child.

Hilda and the child were not halfway down the stairs before Pride turned to Sharon.

"So," he sneered, "you're marrying the Randolph millions! What's the matter—wasn't my money good enough for you? You wouldn't take a penny from me. How come you think it's any different to take it from that pup? Tell me!"

"It's vastly different, Pride," she said. "And you know it. I shall be Courtney's wife. There's nothing standing between us—as there was between you and me. Did you believe I liked what I was doing? Didn't you realize I'd jump at the chance to hold up my head again and look people in the face and not be ashamed?"

"But you love me!" Pride growled. "Me!"

Sharon sighed. "It's a very wicked love, Pride. I've often wished I didn't."

"And marrying him isn't wicked? Standing up in the church in the bride's white which you have no right to, isn't a sin? Fooling him isn't either? Only, you're not going to marry him, Shay—you know why?"

"No," Sharon whispered, "why?"

"Because I'm going to go to him and tell him the truth! I'm going to let him know he's taking my leavings. When I get through with you, the girls down at Horseface Harry's are going to look like plaster saints alongside you! Then what becomes of your pretty wedding, Shay? Think he'll have you then?"

"I know he will," Sharon said simply.

"Then you're a fool! There isn't a man on earth who would—"

"Except Courtney," Sharon said quietly. "Except the kind of man that a selfish beast like you could never understand. . . . Go to him, Pride, and hear him tell you that I've told him about us already. Go and look at a man whose heart is big enough to forgive even that. It'll do you good. It's time you found out that all the world isn't made to your measure. Oh, yes, Pride—go to him!"

"You—you told him?" Pride whispered. "All about us?"

"All."

"And it didn't make any difference? Hell, Shay, he's no man!"

"Not your kind of a man, thank God!"

Pride studied her, his brow furrowed in a frown.

Now, Sharon knew, he was going to change his tactics. He was going to plead with her. . . .

"Look, Shay," he said humbly, "you can't do this to me. I made a bad mistake in not marrying you right off. When I tried to fix things up by getting a divorce, you wouldn't let me. How can you stand there and hurt me so? Don't you know how I love you—can't you understand how much I need you?"

"You don't need anybody!" Sharon said coldly.

Pride walked toward her, his eyes dark in his big face.

"I'll show you how I need you!" he snarled, and pulled her into his arms. Sharon twisted her face away from his kisses.

"I don't want to fight you, Pride," she said. "But if you try—that—I shall die first. Look at me, Pride. Look into my eyes and you'll see I mean what I say. I tell you I'll die first. Do you understand that? Now let me go!"

She could feel his grip loosening slowly, until at last he stood back, looking at her. His face looked so baffled and beaten that for one moment she was sorry for him. Then she hardened.

"Good-bye, Pride," she said calmly, and put out her hand.

Slowly, clumsily, he took it. He stood there holding it a long time. Then, suddenly, he let it drop.

"You'll be seeing me," he said and, turning, went through the door and downstairs.

Sharon stood there a long time after he had gone. I will not cry! she told herself, I will not! But a moment later she was a small and broken figure, sobbing against the chair.

CHAPTER TWENTY-FIVE—1877

SHARON'S GAZE rested briefly upon the face of her husband. Then she looked upward again toward the dirty gray of the curtains. That was only one of the many things she did not like about Pittsburgh. But she had no grounds for complaint, for it was her suggestion that they come here shortly after their marriage. Her decision had been based in part on the fact that a portion of the mighty Randolph fortune was in steel, so that it would be easy for Courtney to obtain a position in one of the family mills; but more important was her belief in the compelling necessity to get as far away from Pride as possible.

What's happened to us? she thought miserably. I've tried so hard—so hard. . . .

She had an impulse to lean across the breakfast table and take Courtney's hand. But one glance at his face was enough to stifle that impulse completely. In less than a year of marriage, Courtney Randolph had aged visibly. There was no youth in his eyes now, no light, no gaiety. He stared at Sharon now with owl-like gravity, his whole expression that of a man who sat eternally in judgment and yet was powerless to pass sentence.

Those letters, Sharon told herself for the thousandth time, those damnable letters! But knowing the reason for his unhappiness was of no value, when the knowing did not provide a remedy. She could not go to Courtney and say, "Don't think about it, my darling; it's nothing—forget it for my sake." Not any more. She had said those words and others like them too many times. And with no effect. Courtney would have believed her, if he could; but he could not. His sickness, a terrible disease in any man, was for a man of his temperament incurable. And mortal, Sharon realized suddenly. If he doesn't get over his jealousy, he'll very likely die of it. Look at his hands, how the bones show through: he must have lost twenty pounds in the last two months.

She looked at the food untouched upon his plate.

"Courtney, please," she whispered.

"Eh—what? Oh, my breakfast. So sorry, my dear; but I'm really not hungry. . . ."

"You always say that," Sharon declared. "But you must eat, darling—you must! And this business of never sleeping —how many times have I awakened to find you gone from me? Roaming about the house like a ghost. . . . Oh, Court —why can't you forget it? Why can't you believe in me?"

He leaned forward suddenly and took her hand.

"I do, Sharon," he said. "It's myself that I don't believe in. Of course, it was a shock to discover that you'd conceal anything from me."

"Court, Court . . ." Sharon whispered. "You know why! Pride wrote me and I never answered him. I thought he would give up after a time, though I should have known him better than that. It was just because I didn't want you to worry that I never told you. That day you came into the house with one of his letters in your hand, I knew I had been wrong. But was I, Court? Wouldn't you have worried just the same, if I had told you?"

"Yes," Courtney said honestly, "I suppose I would have. There's only one way you could stop me from worrying, Sharon. You know what that is?"

Slowly, Sharon shook her head.

"No, Court," she said.

"It's very simple, really. All you have to do is look into my eyes and say, 'I don't love him any more, Court' . . . and mean it. Rather an easy thing. Only you have to mean it, for I'll know if you're lying."

He looked at her and his eyes were imploring, begging for a word, a mere breath of comfort.

I should do it now, Sharon thought. In this world there are no absolutes, and the sin of lying would be outweighed by the kindness which prompted it.

She lifted up his face and gazed full into his eyes. They were very blue and clear. But there was something else in them now: the quality of quiet, the look of almost impassively exact judgment. Courtney was right; he would know if she lied. Slowly, she bowed her head.

The silence stretched itself between them, rearing up like a wall.

"I see," Courtney whispered. "It's that way still."

"Yes," Sharon said miserably. "But not for always, Court! I promise you—not for always!"

He stood up and she came to him, but he did not kiss her. Instead, he looked down somberly into her eyes.

"Don't promise, Sharon," he said gently. "Promises should be based on more than the will; before making them, you should also have the means . . ."

"Oh, Court," Sharon whispered. "Court . . ."

"Hush," he said. "Don't cry."

Sharon blinked back her tears.

"There's something I wanted to talk to you about," she said, "but between us we've spoiled the morning. It will have to wait now."

"No," Courtney said. "Let's have it out. I'd rather not spend the day at the office wondering."

"I—I suppose you're right," Sharon said faintly. "It's just that I have to go to New York."

"No!"

"Look, Court, be reasonable. Mathilda has finally found a buyer for my shop, but he won't come to terms with anyone but the actual owner. So I have to go. Don't you see, darling—it's a good thing? After this, I'll have no further connections with New York."

"But what about—him?" Courtney said ominously.

"New York is a huge city," Sharon said. "Why should

Pride try to find me—since he will not even know that I am there?"

Courtney measured her with his eyes.

"He won't know?" he said.

Sharon's answering gaze was cool and serene.

"He won't know," she said.

Before the conviction in her tone, Courtney bowed.

"When do you have to go?" he asked.

"That's just the trouble. I should go today, but I'll wire Mathilda to put it off until tomorrow."

Courtney glanced at his watch.

"No, don't," he said. "There's a train leaving at eleven o'clock. I'll put you on it. They can spare me at the office for one morning. In fact—"

"No, Court," Sharon interrupted him, "there's no need for you to go with me. I'll be quite all right. Besides, you've done so well at the office that I don't want anything to spoil it. Your father was awfully nice the last time he was here."

"Credits you with making a man of me. He's right, too. Oh, well—I guess I'll survive until you come back. Only, don't be too long, dear. Promise me?"

"I promise," Sharon said cheerfully. "Now I have to rush! It's only two hours till eleven!"

After he had kissed his wife good-bye and watched the train pull out, Courtney Randolph stood for a long time upon the platform. And, try as he would to ignore them, the nagging little demons continued to push their pikes into his consciousness.

"No, Court," he repeated her words in the darkness of his mind, "there's no need for you to go with me . . ." No need at all. Perhaps, you poor cuckold, you might even see too much. You might interfere with a most rapturous reunion. Did you *see* the letter from Mathilda? Why didn't she show it to you? Why else but because there wasn't any letter? Oh, fool, fool! Even this very morning she hadn't denied that she loved him. And how quickly she spoke up before I even finished suggesting that I might go along with her! I've borne this thing long enough! Love letters in every mail—though she tells me she destroys them. . . . All right—but before or after answering them? This time I won't stand for it. . . .

He had reached the ticket window by this time and was

hammering upon the counter with his hand.

"Eh?" the ticket seller said apathetically. "What's your hurry?"

"New York!" Courtney shouted. "The next train!"

"It don't leave till seven o'clock tonight," the ticket vendor said calmly. "So you might as well keep your shirt on."

"There aren't any before then?" Courtney groaned.

"Nary a one. Well, speak up: do you want a ticket, or don't you?"

"Yes," Courtney said wearily. "New York—round trip."

When Sharon arrived in New York she went at once to Mathilda's lodgings and spent the balance of the night with her shop manageress. She regretted having to wake Mathilda so late at night, but she knew there was nothing else she could do. (In those days not a single respectable New York hotel would receive an unescorted woman as a guest after six o'clock in the evening.) She took pity on Mathilda's half-shut eyes and incessant yawning and refrained from questioning her about the details until the next morning.

"To tell the truth," Mathilda told her over coffee, "I don't know much. I haven't even seen this man. Talked to his lawyer, a fellow by the name of Bern—Bernstone—Bernstein—something like that, I never could pronounce those names. Anyway, this man is quite willing to buy, but he wants to discuss terms with you. I'm not worried any more, for this young lawyer said he was quite sure his client would keep on the same staff."

"Good," Sharon said. "That's a weight off my mind. I only hope that this doesn't take too long—Courtney's upset at the idea of my being away."

"Lucky girl!" Mathilda said. "All that money and him so handsome, too! Wish I were in your shoes."

"Who knows?" Sharon said. "When this new boss of yours starts coming around . . ."

"Bless you!" Mathilda said, "but no man in his right mind would take a second look at me."

"I'm no prize myself," Sharon said. "But here we are. Funny he wanted to meet us at the shop instead of his offices."

"Awfully mysterious man, if you ask me," Mathilda declared. "He sure doesn't believe in showing his hand ahead of time."

They went into the shop and all the girls sprang up to greet Sharon with glad cries. They exclaimed over her looks and her clothes, and hinted mischievously at the possibility of another Randolph heir. That, Sharon thought soberly, would probably be the ideal solution; but she had no time to finish her thought, for Robert Bernstein was coming through the doorway with his briefcase in his hand —and behind him strode Pride Dawson!

"You!" Sharon said.

"Yes," Pride grinned, "me!"

"I should have known," Sharon whispered. "Of all the low, contemptible tricks . . ."

Robert Bernstein looked at her with some astonishment.

"Now, really," he began. "This is a perfectly ordinary business deal. I see nothing unfair or illegal about it. In fact, my client is prepared to be quite generous—yes, quite . . ."

Sharon turned to the lawyer, her cheeks flushed with wrath. But one look at his face, and she stilled the hot words on the tip of her tongue: it was quite apparent that young Bernstein knew none of the ramifications of the affair.

"I'm afraid you don't understand, Mr. Bernstein," she said quietly, "but Mr. Dawson knew quite well that I wouldn't sell my shop to him if he were the last man on earth. He also knew that I would not have left my home to come here and discuss the matter—that's why he was so careful to conceal his identity. So, if you have any other business to attend to, or other clients waiting, I'd suggest that you go back to your office! There will be no business transacted here today!"

Robert Bernstein looked from Sharon to Pride in helpless astonishment.

"All right, Bob," Pride said. "Reckon we'll have to put this off till some other time. Mrs. Randolph doesn't seem to be in the right frame of mind . . ."

"And you," Sharon said, seeing that Pride was lounging calmly in the doorway, "go with him! I've nothing to say to you, Pride Dawson—nothing at all!"

"But I have things to say to you," Pride grinned. "Now, if you had your choice, would you rather I said 'em right here in front of all these nice little gals of yours—or would you rather go riding around the park where I can say them kind of privately?"

"Oh, you!" Sharon exploded, but Pride did not move.

"Come along, Shay," he said gently. "It won't take long. And I'll be good—I promise you."

There was, Sharon realized, sincerity in his tone. Besides, there could be no real harm in a quiet conversation with an old friend. The term, oddly, fitted Pride. He had been her lover, true enough; but he had been a companion in a way that Courtney could never be, for in addition to their lovemaking there had been the far more numerous times they had spent together in slow restful talk, or in the deep peace of each other's presence.

"All right," she said curtly, "but you'll have to be brief —I haven't much time."

"You're going to be surprised how brief I can be," Pride said gruffly.

He took her by the arm and led her out to the sidewalk. Beside it, his road wagon waited, with Prince and Emperor tossing their silky manes and pawing the cobblestones impatiently.

He lifted her up and climbed in beside her. Then he cracked the whip sharply and they moved off. Sharon got a fleeting glance at Mathilda's face as they whirled away; it was filled with disapproval. Ah, well, Sharon thought, Mathilda would never understand. . . .

Pride half-turned and looked at her.

"I said I'd make it short," he growled, "and I will. I can say all I want to say in one sentence. . . . Are you happy, Shay?"

How easy life would be, Sharon thought miserably, if only I could lie! Then she lifted her head and faced him.

"No," she said quietly, "I'm not."

"I thought so. If you had said yes, that would have been all I was going to say. Now I can say more. When are you coming back to me, Shay?"

"Never," Sharon said.

"That's one hell of a long time," Pride said grimly. "Longer than you can figure. Longer than anybody can. You aren't happy, I'm not happy, Courtney isn't happy— and Esther isn't, either. Why? Because you've been trying to play according to the rules. I'm not asking you to come back as my mistress—I know how that hurt you. As my wife—the same as I asked you seven years ago, before money and power got in the way. Esther won't mind giving me a divorce; she can marry Joe Fairhill day after tomorrow. He's still hanging around mooning after her. And I don't think she loves me any more—I've hurt her too many times now.

"Not marrying you right off the bat was the worst mistake I ever made. Now when I have the chance to fix things up, you won't let me. . . . But we could straighten it out, Shay—truly we could."

Sharon turned toward him and put her hand on his arm.

"No, Pride," she said, "we couldn't. Life is too terribly simple for you. It consists of what you have and what you want. But for me there are other considerations: what is right and decent and acceptable in the sight of God."

Pride growled, "God sure messed things up for us!"

"No! We muddied the waters ourselves! I said I wasn't happy. You know why, Pride? Because Courtney found a letter from you, which I was too weak or too stupid to destroy. Now he's eaten up with jealousy—and it's making our life a hell."

"You—love him?" Pride demanded.

Sharon bent her head and stared at the toes of her shoes.

"No," she whispered, "I don't."

"Then what's so honest and fine about it?"

"I told him before we were married that I didn't," Sharon said softly, "but that I'd try to learn to . . . And I have tried, Pride—God knows I've tried! But I—I can't."

"Because you love me?" Pride murmured.

Sharon straightened up and looked him full in the face.

"Yes," she said quietly, "because I love you—God help me!"

Pride put out his great arms and drew her to him. She lay against his chest without motion, but her whole body was rigid, with no surrender in it.

"No, Pride," she said.

Slowly, quietly, he released her.

"I'm not going to argue with you, Shay. I did that once. . . . When you left me, I came to you and talked loud and mean and dirty. I'm ashamed of that. There never was anything like that between us. No meanness or dirt. It was a good love, wasn't it? Except for somebody mumbling the words over the book, it was just like being married, wasn't it? I had the words with Esther, you had them with Courtney—and that didn't make a marriage, did it? It takes love for that: someday, nothing or nobody'll stand in our way any more. I keep wishing that someday I'll put out my arms and you'll come running—without shame, without fear. Oh, hell, let's go somewhere and get something to eat. I'm wasting my time and yours. Only, it's kind of wonderful to see you again, Shay—"

"Oh, Pride," Sharon sobbed. "Pride . . ."

"Hush, Shay. I'm not worth crying over, and you know it. Come on now—they've got some Portuguese Madeira over at Delmonico's that'll make you forget all your troubles."

But you are worth crying over, Sharon thought. You always were. Oh, yes, Pride, you're worth all my tears. And you're right about the rules. They don't apply to you. If—only they didn't apply—to me. . . .

The first thing she noticed when she got back to Pittsburgh was the fact that the bed had not been slept in. Poor Court, she thought, he's been having a bad time of it. But I'll make it up to him. We can be happy, if we work at it. . . .

But when dinner was ready she looked up at the clock, and realized that it was long past the time that Courtney usually came back from the mill. She sat quite still, waiting. The hands crawled around the dial with agonizing slowness. What's happened to him? she thought. Oh, my God— I wonder if . . .

She was up now, and running toward the closet where she kept her wraps. Then she set out toward the mill, riding the horsecars and later in a cab. When she got there the watchman at the gate greeted her pleasantly.

"No, ma'am, Mr. Courtney ain't been here—not in two, three days. Wondered about it a bit myself seeing as how he always stops a while for a word with me."

"But where is he?" Sharon cried. "Haven't you any idea?"

"No'm. But you can go in there and ask some of the bosses. They'll know."

"Thank you," Sharon whispered. Then she went into the mill.

But here, too, she got no information. Courtney's associates were genuinely surprised to learn that he had not been at home with her.

"Thought he was sick," they said.

There was nothing to do now but go home and wait. Sharon entered the house and sat down in a chair in the living room. It was a thing she did not often do. Yet today there was a certain rightness in sitting alone in the room usually reserved for the entertainment of their infrequent guests. Today she sat listening to the silence. . . .

The light spilled over the rim of the world, the late sun drowned in mill smoke, and the darkness was shot through with tongues of flame. Sharon sat very still with the flame-glow from the stacks of the distant blast furnace flickering across her face; but she made no move to rise and light the gas jets. The intermittent red from the coking ovens and the yellow-white from the Bessemer converters came through the dusty windowpanes and transformed her staid, Victorian sitting room into a scene out of the *Inferno*.

Sharon waited. The morning came in gray, the sun fighting its eternally losing battle with the fine soot, mill smoke, and haze that forever hid the sky over the steel city, until finally Sharon could stand it no longer and rose stiffly from her chair. She was conscious of being hungry and thirsty, and thought wryly of how oblivious the body's needs are of disaster. But when she tried to eat, she could not.

He's dead, she thought wildly. Oh, my God, he's dead! Then she ran into the bedroom and flung herself across the still unrumpled bed.

After a day or two, she got used to waiting. She knew that she should have gone to the police long ago, but somehow she could not bring herself to do it. What if they asked her whether there were any reasons for her husband's leaving home? What could she tell them except the truth—and that was beyond bearing, for the truth was a very private matter between Courtney and herself.

On the afternoon of the fourth day she heard the heavy tread of the postman on the veranda. She got up and walked toward the door, her face heavy with frowning. Oh, Pride, she thought, you promised not to write any more! Why must you continue to torment me?

But the letter, when she picked it up, was in Courtney's delicate hand.

It was a long time before she could control her trembling fingers enough to open it. But once she began to read it, phrases flew up at her, blinding in their terrible simplicity.

"I'm in New York," Courtney had written. "I arrived here shortly after you did—in time to witness your leaving the shop in the company of Pride Dawson. Later you dined at Delmonico's; after that I hadn't the heart to follow you any more.

"This is, of course, good-bye. It is far better this way, Sharon. I have made provisions so that you will never again know want. Beyond that, what can I say? That I trusted you and you lied to me? You know that. That I believed in you and you betrayed me?

"I keep telling myself that I am wrong—that there is some other explanation for what I saw. But there cannot be. In closing, permit me to say that I love you still with all my heart, that you have my forgiveness fully, freely given. Yet, I cannot come back to a life of doubt and mistrust. Therefore, my little Sharon, farewell—and all my love, always. Court."

Sharon stood there holding the letter in her hand. Her fingers closed over it slowly, crumpling it into a tight ball. Then she flung it from her and ran toward the closet where her clothes hung. She threw a few necessities into a bag, put her hat firmly down upon her dark, soft-curling hair, and ran from the house.

When the cab drew up before the station she was astonished to find that the ticket window was closed. She put her bag down, and ran along the platform, seeking someone, anyone from whom she might learn how to reach New York. After a moment, she saw the men, gathered into tight little groups, talking quietly, ominously.

"Please," she gasped, "the train for New York! Has it gone? I must catch it—I have to go! I've got to!"

They looked at her quietly, almost pityingly. One of the older men cleared his throat.

"Sorry, ma'am," he said. "There ain't no trains running out of Pittsburgh. Not to New York—not to anywheres. Ain't you heard about the strike?"

"Strike?" Sharon echoed blankly. "What strike?"

"The railroads, ma'am. Nearly every one in the country.

They cut our wages for the third time—and we got children that has to eat same as anybody. There's a few trains still coming in—but none going out. I'm sorry, ma'am."

"You're sorry!" Sharon cried. *"You're* sorry!" Then, more quietly: "Forgive me. It's not your problem, really. . . ."

She turned and went back to where her baggage stood in a forlorn little heap upon the platform. Then she picked it up and walked from the station, her dark eyes blank and unseeing.

CHAPTER TWENTY-SIX
1877–1879

WHERE AND WHEN it actually started, no man afterwards could rightly say. But Allan Pinkerton, the detective, was not too far wrong in calling it a revolution. The history of many a great nation has been permanently changed by battles of lesser extent than the United States experienced during the great strike of 1877.

Lance McCarthy, riding on the train to Pittsburgh with the labor agitator Victor Drury, knew more about the background of the strike than most. He was in a position to know. As a reporter for the Marxist papers, he was aware of the faintest stirring of labor troubles. It was the fixed policy of the Socialists, Communists and Anarchists to take advantage of these uprisings wherever and whenever they occurred. That by so doing they did a grievous disservice to the cause of labor never occurred to Lance. He was a true believer; such minor considerations could not bother him. He had seen the Internationalist Workingman's Party change first to the Social Democratic Workingman's Party and then to the Workingman's Party, as the leaders slowly discovered the American worker's abiding distaste for the words "socialist" and "internationalist." Even the English-language weekly for which he worked, *The Socialist*, had changed in August, 1876, to the *Labor Standard*, without deviating one iota from its fixed editorial policy of promoting class warfare and world revolution.

Lance's sympathy for the strikers was very real. Since the debacle of 1873, their wages had been cut three times from a sum which in the beginning had not been enough to keep body and soul together. And lately the railroads had added the last straw by introducing the practice of double-headers—trains of thirty-two cars instead of sixteen—and forcing the crew to take care of the extra cars without adding men, thus enabling the roads to lay off hundreds of workers.

He knew, too, that it was still possible to estimate a switchman's length of service by the number of fingers he had lost, and that brakemen were daily thrown beneath the wheels while setting the exceedingly dangerous hand brakes. He had heard Lorenzo Coffin speak, making his futile plea for the introduction of airbrakes and automatic couplers, which had been invented some time ago; but in 1877 less than one tenth of the roads employed these proven devices.

It made Lance a little sick to listen to Victor Drury's exultant estimate of the advantages that would accrue to the party, as a result of the strike. He had in his pocket the clippings from Baltimore and Martinsville. There were twelve men dead in Martinsville, Maryland, now, shot down by the militia, as they attempted to halt trains that were leaving the village. Lance had seen men die, but he still had no stomach for murder. Try as he would, the idea of using men's deaths for political advantage still seemed to him a shameful thing.

There were on that same train two other men to whom the strike was an irresistible magnet, drawing them to Pittsburgh. In a car near the middle of the train rode Pride Dawson, prompted by the strike to look after his marshalling yards and, if possible, to protect Sharon; and in the last car, nervously biting his nails, was Courtney Randolph.

Despite his avowed intention of leaving her, Courtney, half-insane with fear and jealousy, had not been able to bring himself to stay away from Sharon, now that the clicking wires hourly poured their tales of death and disaster into the New York newspaper offices.

They all saw Pittsburgh burning a full hour before they reached the city. A little later they could hear the booming of the dynamite, and later still, the harsh crackle of rifle fire. Now and again, the quick stutter of Gatling guns punctuated the din. Pride reached into his pocket and drew out the "Virgin's Pistol." It was a beautiful little weapon, heavily engraved and embossed with silver. On the barrel, the name "Sharon" had been engraved.

The pistol was in itself a kind of madness—if one did not know Pride—, but his love for the flamboyant had grown with the years. Before leaving New York he had hastily sought a gunsmith's shop for a pocket pistol to give to Sharon for her own protection, in the event she refused to return with him from the terror-racked city. In the store his eye had fallen on the little gun, and he remembered that it was of a type carried by the women of Louisiana in former years to protect their chastity—notably against Carpetbaggers and Negroes, though Pride honestly doubted that the list could be so sharply limited. His real folly had been his decision to wait for the old German to engrave Sharon's name upon the barrel. This had cost Pride two full hours and had almost made him miss the train. Not that he regretted it—such gestures were almost a part of him now. . . .

The train stopped near the station, which was a scene of utter chaos and which was burning like so much tinder. Groups of passengers, isolated from one another by the smoke and confusion, made their way into the city on foot. Soon they were bruised, dirty and torn, for they had to fight their way through howling, frenzied mobs intent on no other object than loot.

Lance and Victor Drury walked together and the closer they came the worse it grew. There were bodies in the street now, for the most part women and children trampled underfoot by the mobs. When they reached the roundhouse they stopped, and watched in amazement as the people of Pittsburgh dragged two bronze cannon into position and aimed them to answer the fire of the Gatling guns manned by the militiamen trapped in the roundhouse. Lance stood there, his stomach turning over, as women ran past, their arms loaded with bolts of cloth. There were other men and women carrying stolen hams, smoked meats, fruit and foodstuffs of all sorts. Still others had liquor.

Grinning, Victor Drury pulled up a packing box, and mounted it.

"Men of Pittsburgh!" he cried. "To arms! The day of vengeance is at hand!"

"You tell 'em, brother!" someone shouted; but the rest of Drury's speech was lost in a rattle of Gatling fire. Lance saw the would-be cannoneers reel from their weapons and sprawl grotesquely on the grass. Then others appeared, pushing a haycart. They poured oil and liquor over it, and a man applied the torch. Then they shoved it down the grade so that it crashed into the roundhouse. The flames leaped up, bloodying the sky. . . .

Are these the people, Lance thought bitterly, for whom I have fought so lovingly? These depraved, thieving monsters! What if I have been wrong! What if there is evil in the hearts of the Marxists too as well as in the hearts of the masters? The people! Mobs, rabble, brigands—no better than the men they fought. . . . Oh, God, God. . . .

He stopped, aghast. He had called upon the non-existent. He had prayed to the Deity he had so long denied!

He turned in time to see a burly workman busily engaged in pushing his head into the barrel from which the firebrands had obtained the liquor to ignite the haycart. The man with the torch saw the workman too and brought it downward into the barrel. The flames came up with a gigantic whoosh and the workman fell back, on fire from head to heel. Then he ran off, screaming, trailing five-yard-long curtains of flame behind him. The Hardscrabble boys threw back their heads and roared with laughter.

Lance turned and saw two beefy German women engaged in a tug of war over a bolt of cloth. They had ripped away each other's clothing to the waist, and their huge, pendulous breasts were covered with bloody scratches. Behind them the battle went on.

Lance looked toward the marshalling yards of the Pennsylvania Railroad, seeing the locomotives that burned there, overturned like gigantic beetles by the charges of dynamite the strikers had put under them. Now the explosions were coming faster than he could count.

Then, very slowly, he kneeled in the street, oblivious of the gunfire that rattled about his head.

"Dear God," he prayed, "I have been wrong. Forgive me for my folly and my sins, and forgive them, too, for they know not what they do. . . ."

Pride, when he got off the train, did not even attempt to reach the small marshalling yards that the Pennsylvania Railroad had leased to him; one look at the destruction in the Pennsylvania's own yards was enough to convince him that it was useless. . . . Instead, he made his way on foot toward the house where he knew Sharon lived.

Sharon sat behind her windows, digging her fingers into her ears to shut out the sound of the gunfire. Then she saw Pride outside and ran to the door. The next instant she was in his arms.

"Hush, Shay," Pride murmured. "It's all right. I came for you. You'll go back with me now, won't you?"

But with a last flash of resistance, Sharon shook her head.

"Oh, no!" she cried. "Oh, no, Pride! I've got to find Courtney! He's here somewhere—he wired me he was coming."

"Courtney, hell!" Pride spat. "You've got to come with me. Your life isn't safe here."

Sharon was quieter now. Though she trembled all over, she was regaining control of herself.

"I couldn't leave him, Pride," she whispered. "He's my husband, who married me in good faith. . . ."

Pride stood there looking at her a long time. Then slowly he put out his hand with the beautiful little "Virgin's Pistol" in it.

"Here," he growled, "take this. Use it if you have to. Now what about Lilith? You'll let me take her back home, won't you?"

"Lilith? She's not here, thank God! Mathilda's been keeping her for me in New York. I—I wasn't sure I was going to like Pittsburgh, so Mathilda's been keeping her until I was really settled. Only—I never did get really settled, Pride. . . ."

Pride stood there looking at her. Then he said, his voice endlessly deep and tender:

"I may never see you again, Shay. Will you kiss me good-bye—for old time's sake?"

Sharon surged forward and buried herself in his arms.

"Pride," Sharon whispered. "Oh, Pride . . ."

"Hush, Shay," Pride murmured.

"But this is wrong," she whispered. "Don't you understand? This is wrong."

But Pride had lifted her from her feet now, and was walking quietly back into the darkened house. . . .

Outside in the street, Courtney Randolph had seen everything. He fell to the ground now, and belabored the sidewalk with his fists. Then he lifted his head and howled. He got to his feet clumsily and began to run away from the house—back toward the sound of the gunfire.

Lance McCarthy noticed the stumbling, half-crazed figure turn the corner and start in the direction of the burning roundhouse. He shouted to him, but the man kept on, straight for the silent muzzles of the militiamen's guns. Others started screaming at him and one of the men fired a rifle over his head.

At once the guns in the roundhouse opened up. Lance saw the man stumble as the bullets hit him, but he kept on, until finally one of the soldiers turned the crank of the Gatling gun, and the ugly weapon set up its furious stutter. The man stopped short as though he had run up against an invisible wall. Lance saw his body jerk again and again as the torrent of slugs tore into him. Then he crumpled slowly like an actor taking a bow, and went down upon the earth, and still the Gatling gun poured bullets into him, shaking his pitiful corpse with the repeated impact of its fire. Then all the guns were still.

Unbelievingly, Lance saw the flag of truce raised above the roundhouse. Then he began to run toward the torn figure on the ground. Others were just behind him. He heard a voice, awed and incredulous, saying:

"Why, it's Mr. Randolph!"

Then the men were gathering Courtney up, and one by one they took off their hats. Lance watched them bearing the body away. He had neither the heart nor the inclination to follow.

Like a hero Courtney Randolph was borne to his house. Sharon stood beside Pride Dawson and bit her underlip in such agony that the blood ran down her chin.

"He died brave, ma'am," they said, "fighting to the last!"

Sharon buried her face against Pride's sleeve and sobbed. And none of them could know how many were the tears of shame, and how few the tears of grief.

"I'll take care of everything," Pride mumbled. "Don't you worry your head. . . ."

Two days later the strike was over. The Federal troops had arrived and put down the rioting, thus ending the greatest danger of revolution since the states of the South had revolted against the Federal Government. It had cost scores of lives and millions in property damage. It had flared from city to city throughout most of the central part of the nation. But it had done some good, too—for in the future, when Labor spoke men listened, and conditions slowly improved for those who worked with their hands. . . .

After Courtney's funeral, Sharon had gone back to New York with Pride. He stood now in the lobby of the hotel to which he had brought her, and held her hands in his.

"Will you come back to me?" he murmured. "Not right off—let some time go by. . . . But you'll come back, Shay?"

Sharon stared at him, her eyes very wide and dark.

"I—I don't know," she said slowly. "It would be very simple to say no. And simpler to say, 'Yes, my darling, I'll fly back to your arms.' Because the two halves of me are saying both of those things—and saying them at the same time."

"Follow your heart," Pride urged. "Follow your heart!"

"Even *it* is divided, Pride. One part of it loves God and goodness. The other part loves you—the wicked part . . . the hot, rebellious part. The part that can forget poor Courtney lying there and make me turn to kiss your mouth."

"Oh, hell," Pride groaned, "I know just what you're building up to!"

"Then you know more than I do. I think what I want is a change. I want to go far away from you, Pride—I want to see if I can stay away. You see, I'm putting nothing positively as I would have once. Then I would have said goodbye, remembering Courtney—remembering that we defiled his house while he lay dying in the street!"

"Don't cry, Shay!" Pride begged. "Not here—not in front of all these people!"

"What do I care about these people!" Sharon said suddenly, fiercely. "No, I'm wrong. This is a very private matter—between you and me and Courtney and God. Wait here. I'll come down in a minute, and you can take me

299

driving, while we talk it out. All right?"

"All right," Pride said.

They sat in the cab for a long time without speaking, then Sharon leaned over and took Pride's hand.

"My mind's made up," she said gently. "I'm going away, Pride."

"No!"

"Yes, Pride. I don't know how much or how little we had to do with Courtney's death—but however little it was, it was still too much."

"Shay, please!"

"Hear me out. I've loved you very much. I do still—more than I ought. And I've been loved more than any woman has any right to. I'm very grateful for that. But now I need to be alone. I—I have so much to atone for. . . ."

"You've got nothing to make up for!" Pride said fiercely. "All you ever got out of life was a hard row. My fault, too —all I ever brought you was misery. But don't make this good-bye, Shay. Go away if you want to and set your mind at ease. Then come back to me."

"Pride," Sharon whispered, "I must tell you the truth. I'm going to try to stay away from you forever. I hope I can. It would be the right and best thing. I'm ashamed that I cannot say, 'I'm going to,' instead of just 'I'm going to try.' But I have to be honest with myself. I know that as long as you're alive and in the same world with me, the danger exists that I will someday come running back to you."

"Where are you going?" Pride demanded.

"To Paris. I've some money saved. Enough to keep Lilith and me comfortably. There's so much I can learn there. I can send back gowns and sketches to my shop. And the shop will keep us going while we live abroad."

"I could—"

"No, Pride—nothing from you. I've never accepted anything from you while we were together. Why should I now that we're far apart?"

"No reason, I guess. But, Shay, think it over. Don't just go running off from me like this!"

"I'll think it over," she said. "Now take me back to the hotel, Pride."

That night Sharon sent for Robert Bernstein, Pride's

lawyer, and signed a document in which she waived all claim to the money that Courtney had left her. Then she took Lilith from Mathilda and spent several hours packing their bags. Two days later, they boarded a ship for France. Pride made no move to stop them. In fact, he came down to the pier to see them off and filled their cabin with flowers.

The Randolphs received Sharon's waiver in stunned silence. It was half a day before they recovered sufficiently to call their lawyer and instruct him to drop the case they had already been preparing to contest Courtney's will.

Pride Dawson merely kept still and waited. . . . Two entire years passed . . . and then one day, unable to endure the separation any longer, he boarded a fast steamer.

When Sharon saw him standing in the doorway of her modest pension, she did not say a word. Instead, she stood quite still and looked at him while the silence between them stretched out to the boundaries of forever.

Then, slowly, she started to walk toward him, her footsteps echoing hollowly in the dark little hall. Pride watched her come, holding his breath hard in his throat. Then the tight-held band of silence burst and she was running toward him, her arms outstretched, to nestle finally in his arms.

They came back to New York a month later, leaving Lilith in the care of a French family of the strictest traditions. Though it grieved Sharon once more to leave the child, she knew it was better that way. After they had arrived in New York, Pride bought a plot of land in lower New York. Upon it he built a brick Georgian house whose chaste lines and simple beauty were a far cry from the flamboyant ugliness of his castle.

Sharon accepted the house. She was worn out with fighting Pride, tired of endlessly resisting her love for him. Her surrender now, at long last, was complete.

CHAPTER TWENTY-SEVEN—1888

LIFE IS A FERMENT of years: Pride Dawson knew that now. Already, though he was still in his middle fifties, he was conscious that the lines were blurring. He could remember Caprice as a child of four—an infant sprite, all pink and white and silvery gold—and look up to see her now, a girl of sixteen, and catch his breath at the thought of how brief had been the period of change. Only the feeling was the same—the aching, clumsy, almost bearlike tenderness.

He raised his big hand, seeing the hair on its back mingled with white now, and snapped on the electric lights. Though he had done this many times since he had had them installed the year before, he never lost his feeling of surprise that they worked. Truly this was an age of miracles! Pride remembered how the whole town had laughed at Edison's experiments in his Pearl Street laboratory. But by 1883 the offices of the New York *Times* had been equipped with them and the chuckles gave way to openmouthed awe. Pride, after one visit to the *Times* office, had tried to have his castle similarly equipped, but for a long time it was impossible; he lived too far uptown.

However, he had them now, and also an even stranger invention that made it possible for him to remain away from his office for weeks at a time. He had only to go over to the wall, turn a crank, and he could talk to men miles away. He had owned his telephone even longer than the lights, for Hilborne Roosevelt had formed the New York Telephone Company in 1877, just a year after Dom Pedro, Emperor of Brazil, had dropped the instrument from his hand at the Philadelphia Exposition with the cry, "My God! It talks!" There had been only seventeen subscribers at first, but now there were hundreds of telephones in New

York City. There was one in Pride's home, another in his office, and still another at Sharon's house.

Today a man could ride all the way up to Harlem on the elevated railways—though Jay Gould had until lately blocked the use of electric cars, common in Chicago and elsewhere. The city was growing.

The city and the nation and the world were growing—and dying. Pride did not like to think of that. It made him feel old. In a short space of years Commodore Vanderbilt and two of his sons had died—and that great fortune was now in the hands of men who had been children when Pride had come to New York. Strange! Pride remembered how Cornelius J. Vanderbilt had died, with a pistol clutched in his fist and a hole in his temple. That memory nagged at him. How did it happen that a man chose such a death? What griefs, what pains, what fears drove him to such an end? Pride shook his head, his big face tightening.

Ever since Grant and Ward had failed in 1884, he had known the pressure of fear. He had lost heavily in that debacle because his faith in the ex-President had been absolute. And his cattle ranch was gone too, sold at a three-million-dollar loss; the squatters had won at last and the range was closed. The strikers of '77 had burned his marshalling yards; steel was down to sixteen dollars a ton instead of the one hundred and thirty-eight it had sold for in 1868; the Greenbackers were screaming for a currency unbacked by silver. He could, conceivably, die a poor man. If that happened, would he like gay young Cornelius Vanderbilt take a pistol and . . . ?

Wryly, he shook his head. It was not good to think about such things. Better to avoid all the troubles and confusion that hammered at him through the newspapers. Forget Chicago, where the memory of the Haymarket bombing still rankled. Forget East St. Louis where deputies had killed five men and one woman at a crossing—to discover later that only one of them had been a striker.

Forget them . . . and remember the pleasant things, such as the time Albert Edward, Prince of Wales, visited New York and stayed two nights at Pride's castle. Pride now wore the new double-breasted frock coat, christened the "Prince Albert," that His Highness had given him as a mark of esteem. . . . Remember the genuine emotion he had felt at the unveiling of the Statue of Liberty that same year, or the thrill at the memory of the dark figure of Steve Brodie plunging from the now-completed Brooklyn Bridge. Remember the swift drives behind his four-in-hand under the reins of a masterly whip, with the horns winding. He had been a member of the Coaching Club since 1875, and one of his thoroughbreds had been awarded a ribbon at Gilmore's Garden in 1885, at the first Horse Show ever held in New York. . . .

Remember Sharon's face, aglow with tenderness. Remember Caprice, dancing spritelike across the grass courts as she played the new game of tennis, or rode her new bicycle with the drop frame and the equal-sized wheels which had been invented only this year. How lovely his daughter was! (I've spoiled her something awful, he thought, but it doesn't seem to have done her harm.)

Yes, remember the pleasant things; remember them and forget Esther's face with its habitual expression of cool, amused contempt. (I wonder if she's really carrying on with little Joe? And if she is, I wonder why she thinks I give a damn?)

He looked up to see Malcolm entering the room. Malcolm tried hard to walk erect, but he was bent far over with the weight of his years. (Why, Pride realized suddenly, he must be near seventy!)

"A gentleman to see you, sir," he said.

"Who is it?" Pride asked reluctantly. He had gotten into the habit of spending much of his time by himself. It had been over two weeks since he had visited Sharon, and tonight Pride was in no mood for visitors.

"A young gentleman, sir," Malcolm added. "He said his name was McCarthy."

"McCarthy?" Pride mused. Tim? But Malcolm had said a young man. Tim would be pushing sixty by now. Hardly young. What about Lance? That was it—Tim's son. Little Lance McCarthy, a young gentleman by now. How the years had flown!

"Show him in," Pride growled. "Show him in!"

"Yes, sir," Malcolm said.

Then he was back, leading Lance McCarthy, and Pride started upright in his Morris chair. He had been prepared for a young gentleman, but not for a young prince. Yet that was what Lance seemed to be. He reminded Pride suddenly of Joseph Fairhill in his youth, though Lance was as

304

dark as Joseph was fair. He brought back to Pride the old, familiar feeling of gracelessness, reminding him of his big hands and feet, his thick arms and thighs.

Lance wore a Prince Albert—His Highness' styles were all the rage—and his fawn-colored gloves flapped gracefully between his slender fingers. His clothes were perfect, avoiding excesses of either fashion or conservatism, Pride decided, and turned once more to his undeniably compelling good looks. There was an exotic quality about them— Latin, anyone would have guessed at once, Spanish after a moment: a young Grandee, but lately come from Spain. The haughtiness of his bearing seemed to emphasize this: his dark eyes, meeting Pride's over the proud arch of his Roman nose, were utterly cold.

Pride got clumsily to his feet.

"Well, Lance," he said. "I'm mighty glad to see you. It's been a long time."

"Eighteen years," Lance said, and took the hand that Pride offered him.

"A long time," Pride mused. "Why, you must be almost—"

"Thirty," Lance finished for him, "in another month."

"Married?"

"No. Frankly, I haven't seen the girl who interests me enough. Besides, I'm much too busy."

"Sit down, son. You'll have some brandy, won't you? And a cigar?"

"The brandy—yes. I prefer a pipe. You are well, sir?"

"Well enough, though I've been feeling my age lately. How's Tim—and Lucy?"

"They're fine. Mother looks better now than she did when she was younger. It's the easy life, I think—having servants to do for her at last. It's worked wonders."

"That's right," Pride agreed. "I heard that Tim was one of the richest men in Boston—that so?"

"No, it isn't. But we've done well. That's what brings me here. I suggested to Father that it would be a good idea to have an outlet for our ladies' shoes in New York, and Mother suggested Mrs. Randolph's shop. I'm here to see her."

"So. It's a good idea, son. Sharon's got all the best folks now. But you'll have to talk to her yourself. I can't do you any good there."

"I know. I didn't come to ask you to help me, sir. Father

305

asked me to pay his respects. . . . This is rather good brandy."

"The best." Pride looked at Lance shrewdly. "Would you have come," he said soberly, "if your pa hadn't asked you?"

One of Lance's thin lips curled slightly.

"Truthfully, no," he said.

"I gave your father a raw deal, didn't I? But he's willing to forgive and forget, while you—"

"It's not my affair, sir. But I'm less generous than Father."

"I see. It appears to me he had a lot to forgive you for, if I heard right."

"You mean my former associates? The folly of youth, sir. After all, I was less than twenty. I manage the factory now and take Mother to Mass. Father's satisfied."

"Good," Pride said.

Lance stood up.

"I'd better be going," he said, and put out his hand.

Pride took it, but before he could say good-bye Caprice ran into the room.

"Daddy!" she began; then she saw Lance. She stood quite still, her blue eyes becoming round and enormous.

"I—I'm sorry," she said. "I didn't know . . ."

"It's all right," Pride said gruffly. "Caprice, meet Lance McCarthy—Tim's boy, you know. And Lance, this is Caprice, my daughter."

"Delighted," Lance murmured smoothly and put out his hand. Caprice took it without saying a word, but there were great pink roses, suddenly blooming, in her cheeks.

My God, Lance thought, what a beauty! Too bad she's so young. Why, in another year or two. . . . Then he recovered.

"I was just saying good night to your father," he said gently. He turned once more to Pride. "Good night, sir. You must be extremely proud of such a daughter. . . . Good night, Miss Dawson."

"Good night," Caprice whispered.

Lance turned then and went through the doorway. Caprice looked at Pride.

"Oh, Daddy," she said, "what a perfectly stunning young man!"

Pride gazed at her soberly, thinking: My little girl's

growing up. I'm going to lose her soon—to some slicked-up young pup like that one! He was surprised at how bitter the thought was.

Caprice sat down in his lap and playfully ruffled his thick, graying hair.

"Buy him for me," she teased.

"Caprice!"

"Why not? You've bought me everything else."

"I can't buy men, and I wouldn't if I could—not for you. I aim to keep you, Cappie—I aim to keep you a long time."

Caprice snuggled deeper into his arms and rubbed the pink tip of her nose against his cheeks.

"You're nice," she laughed. "Much nicer than anyone else. I'm never going to leave you—not even when I get married. I'll bring my husband right here to this house, and you can bounce your grandchildren on your knee. Won't that be nice?"

"No," Pride said gruffly. Then: "How's the safety?"

"Wonderful! It goes so fast. And it's so low that even when I fall off I don't get hurt. It's the best bike ever. Thank you for it."

"I'm glad you like it."

"Tell me, Daddy—is he coming back?"

"Is who coming back?"

"That young man. Lance. Lance—what a divine name!"

"I hope not," Pride said.

"I do. I'd like to see him again. Maybe he'd take me bike riding—or roller skating. That would be fun."

"Look, Cappie, forget that boy."

"Why? I think he's nice."

"He's too old for you. He's thirty—"

"But I like older men. For instance, I like you."

"That's different. . . . Besides, he's a stiff-necked young fool—like his father before him. And there's bad blood between the McCarthys and myself. So forget him, Cappie."

"No," Caprice said. Then: "Daddy, why didn't you marry Auntie Sharon instead of Mother?"

"Caprice!"

"That's the second time tonight you've said 'Caprice!' like that. Why didn't you? She's ever so much nicer—and she loves you so much."

"Things," Pride muttered, "got in the way . . ."

"Things like money," Caprice said clearly. "I'll never marry for money—only for love. Is Auntie Sharon your mistress, Daddy?"

"Cappie—I swear—!"

"The servants say she is. And they always know everything."

"I'm going to fire every one of 'em! Talking about things like that in front of you!"

"Is talking about them any worse than doing them, Daddy?" Caprice said seriously. "Didn't you know I'd find it out sooner or later? And if you fire them, I'll be very angry with you."

"All right, all right! I won't fire them, still—"

"Daddy, you don't love Mother, do you?"

"I did before you were born. I might have loved her again by now—but she wouldn't let me. She was so all-fired jealous of Sharon."

"Can you blame her?"

"No, I can't say that I can. Only, if she had handled the thing a little differently, it all would have turned out all right."

"If *you* had handled it a little differently, Daddy. Poor Mother! What a life she's had!"

"She's bearing up," Pride growled.

"I guess she is. But what about Auntie Sharon? It must be terrible to have people always whispering about you, and never be able to go anywhere and—"

"It is," Pride said grimly.

Sharon sat before the fire in her living room and looked at Lilith. Lilith lounged upon the sofa, smoking a cigarette. It was a habit she had acquired in France. She had acquired so many things in France—all of them wrong, Sharon thought bitterly. Like that false beauty spot pasted to her cheek, and that feline way of walking.

But there was nothing Sharon could do. The first time, since her return a week ago, that Lilith had lit a cigarette, Sharon had glared at her in horror and said:

"Lilith! Take that thing out of your mouth!"

And Lilith had turned to her slowly, trailing twin streamers of smoke through her exquisite nostrils, and asked calmly:

"Why? I like to smoke."

"It's—it's unladylike," Sharon had said. "No decent girl would dare . . ."

"I think," Lilith had said cruelly, "that you're hardly in a position to talk about decency, Mother."

"Oh!" Sharon had faltered, but only for a moment. Then she had returned to the attack. "Precisely what do you mean?" she had demanded.

"Precisely what I say," Lilith repeated. "That Pride Dawson's mistress can scarcely expect to instruct me in morality."

Sharon had bent her head, her face white and still.

"I see," she murmured. "So—you know . . ."

"I've known all along. A child with my background would, you know. I'm only surprised that it has lasted so long. These things seldom do—at least not in France."

"Oh, damn France anyhow!" Sharon had exploded. "Why on earth did I ever leave you there!"

"Necessity, I'd say. But don't feel bad, Mother dear." (Why has she stopped calling me "Auntie Sharon"? Sharon thought wildly; it was she who invented the name.) "Pride is rather charming, in a crude sort of way. If you ever get tired of him, let me know. I'll take over myself. It should be—fun." Then she had ground out her cigarette against a saucer, and kissed Sharon's cheek lightly.

Looking at her now, Sharon thought: I've mothered a viper. But such a beautiful viper! she added quickly. Lilith was beautiful—darkly, stunningly beautiful. But it was a beauty without tenderness, a hard, flamelike beauty—utterly provocative.

No man will ever love her, Sharon thought suddenly, but all men will want her. My God, how dreadful that is!

Lilith put up her slim fingers and pushed them through the heavy deep-curling masses of her dark hair.

That's lip rouge on her mouth! Sharon realized. It is! And her cheeks are painted, too!

The bell shrilled.

Lilith stood up—though to describe the motion thus was a vast understatement. Rather, she swayed erect—her body a tropic palm trunk, caressed by the lightest breeze.

"I'll get it, Mother," she said. Then she walked toward the door, with that gait that was calculated provocation—practiced so long that it was second nature now.

She turned the knob and opened the door.

Lance McCarthy stood looking at her, his jaw dropping foolishly.

"My God!" he whispered.

"I agree," Lilith said. "Only, I would have said 'Thank God!' Come in, won't you? The light's better in here, and I want to see if you're real."

Sharon sat back slowly, as Lance came into the room.

"Auntie Sharon!" he began. "I mean—Miss O'Neil—I mean—"

"Mother, dear," Lilith said admiringly, "you really are good! Introduce me, won't you? Who is he? He's much too handsome to believe . . ."

"My daughter, Lilith," Sharon said, "for whose horrible manners I freely apologize. Mr. McCarthy—Lance, I'm awfully glad to see you. You look fine. Lucy must be so proud."

"Thank you," Lance murmured. "I—I'm sorry I called so late. I came on business, really. Only, I stopped by to say hello to Pride."

"I see," Sharon said steadily.

"I—I'll come back again—some other time. I didn't know . . ."

"Don't mind me," Lilith said. "You and Mother have your little talk. I'll wait until you have finished."

Lance glanced at her uneasily. Then he launched into his project, blurting it out awkwardly, forgetting completely the careful approach he had planned.

"It's a good idea," Sharon said thoughtfully. "It should be successful. But your shoes will have to be the very finest —better than the ones that Worth imports from Paris."

"They are," Lance said stoutly. "They'll wear ten times as long!"

"That's no selling point at all to the clientele I deal with. Are they prettier? Are they fussier and smarter?"

Lance sat there looking at Sharon with dawning respect in his eyes.

"You know," he said, "I never thought of that." Then he added, truthfully: "No—they aren't."

"Could you make them so?" Sharon demanded.

"I—I think so. We could make them any way at all—if we only had the designs. Our designer is a Bostonian—and, well—conservative."

Sharon turned to Lilith.

"Get me my pencils and my sketch pad," she said quietly.

Lilith, surprisingly demure, got up and left the room. A moment later she was back. Sharon took pencil and paper from Lilith's hands and went to work. Her pencil raced. Lance was amazed as exquisite designs grew like magic under her hand. Finally, she was done.

"These will do, I think," she said crisply. "When can I see some samples?"

"Beautiful!" Lance breathed. "It's fantastic—you're a real genius, Auntie Sharon."

"Thank you. But I'll need some samples right away."

"In about a month," Lance said. "Is that soon enough?"

"Quite."

"We'll make a fortune out of these shoes!" Lance exulted. "How I wish you worked for us!"

"Make me an offer," Sharon said drily. "You may be surprised."

"I'll speak to Father about it. Would you really?"

"I might. Tell Tim to write me."

Lance stood up.

"I'll take the train for Boston tonight," he said, then he felt the soft fingers on his arm.

"You will not," Lilith said calmly. "Next week will do as well. And sit down. You've talked business with Mother quite enough. It's been very dull—and I don't think you're dull, really. In fact, you look quite exciting. Now you're going to talk to me. You have Mother's permission to call —hasn't he, dear?"

"Of course," Sharon said, "if he wants it."

"But I do want it!" Lance said. "Your daughter, Auntie Sharon, is one of the loveliest girls I've ever seen."

"On your own head be it," Sharon said. "I'm going to bed. I think I can trust you, Lance. If she annoys you too much, just call."

"You won't, will you?" Lilith whispered after Sharon had gone upstairs.

"I won't what?"

"Call Mother if I annoy you. I'm afraid I might. You're much too handsome, Lance McCarthy!"

Lance laughed gaily.

"You're the strangest girl I've ever known," he said, "and one of the prettiest."

Lilith frowned.

"That's the second time you've said that," she declared. "One of the prettiest. I don't like being one-of-the-anything. I must be the best. You know someone prettier than I am?"

Now it was Lance who frowned. You *can* be annoying, he thought.

"Yes," he said. "Today, I met a girl much prettier than you."

"Who?" Lilith demanded.

"Caprice Dawson—Pride's daughter."

"Caprice! She's like a doll of Dresden china. Besides, she's much too young for you."

"Perhaps, but I'm only fourteen years older than she is. My father's ten years older than my mother. I agree she's too young now. Later, she mightn't be."

He was conscious of a feeling of surprise at his own words. Why, he thought, that's true! When she's twenty, I'll only be thirty-three—nearer thirty-four than -three, though. It's funny how much closer twenty is to thirty-four than sixteen is to thirty—and I do believe that she liked me!

"You are going," Lilith said, "to forget that child."

"Why?" Lance asked.

"Because I'm going to make you. Come—let's walk in the garden."

"No," Lance said, "it's too cold. Let's stay here."

"Very well. When are you going to get around to kissing me?"

Lance looked at her and a hard glint appeared in his dark eyes.

"Now," he said grimly. "Right now!"

But it was he who broke free of the embrace.

"My God!" he whispered.

Lilith laughed throatily.

"What's the matter, Lance?" she said. "Is it too warm in here?"

"Much!"

"I told you to come out into the garden, but you wanted to stay here. Oh, well . . ." Then she leaned forward again.

"You're very sweet," she whispered finally. "Very good and very sweet. I like that. I think you'll make me a grand husband, Lance."

"Husband!" Lance gasped.

"Yes—husband. What did you think I meant—that I'd become your mistress?"

"I—I—no!" But that was exactly what he had thought. There was nothing about Lilith that suggested domesticity. But Lilith was looking at him gravely.

"I probably wouldn't mind," she said simply. "Only, it would be a mistake. I'm not talking about ethics, Lance. It's just that I've seen how Mother has suffered with Pride. I shouldn't like to be so helpless. I've had a number of such —propositions in France. I've refused them all. You will find me quite as virginal as your little Caprice, Lance—and for better reasons."

The heat rose out of Lance's collar and beat about his face in waves. These were modern times, God knew. This was the year of Our Lord 1888. Only, there were words that nice girls simply did not use.

"You say the most shocking things!" he declared.

"Do I? I'm sorry. It's just that I'm very simple and very direct. Honest, too. Those are usually considered admirable traits—except in women."

"Except in women," Lance echoed.

"Yet a man should value them in a woman—because he would know then that such a woman as I am would never lie to him or trouble him or betray him in any way. That should be a comfort."

"It is," Lance said.

"Good. We're going to be very happy together."

"But," Lance spluttered, "I haven't said . . ."

"I know you haven't—but you will. Take your time, darling. I want your mind to be quite made up. I'm going to work at it. Hard. It won't be as difficult as you think—now, will it?"

Lance looked at her, seeing her hair, black, deep-curling, her lips wine-red and a trifle full, her eyes dark-smoldering beneath a heavy curve of brows, and her figure, revealed by the tight bodice of her Parisian gown, utterly maddening.

"No," he said miserably, "it won't be."

"Good. Now kiss me again. I like the way you kiss. You're so gentle. I feel—so safe with you."

That, Lance reflected, was hardly a compliment. She takes me for one of these namby-pamby New Englanders with ice-water in his veins. I'll show her! Whereupon he did.

"I think," Lilith said clearly, "you'd better go now."

At once Lance was abject.

"I'm sorry," he whispered.

"I'm not," Lilith said. "I'm glad you have some spirit. But this is getting dangerous. I want them to say, 'Mrs. Lance McCarthy,' not 'young McCarthy's fancy woman' out of the sides of their mouths in whispers. So I won't take chances—not with you or with myself. Good night, Lance. I'll see you tomorrow?"

"Perhaps," Lance muttered. "I don't know. I—I've things to do. . . ."

"I shall expect you at eight," Lilith said. . . . I'll catch the first train for Boston in the morning, Lance thought. But the next morning was March 11, 1888, and New York was in the grip of a blizzard that was not to be equaled for another sixty years.

CHAPTER TWENTY-EIGHT—1888

ESTHER CAME into the house with the snowflakes still clinging to the gray fur of her bonnet. Joseph Fairhill was only a step behind her.

"Hello, darling," she said to Pride, and bent over to kiss his cheek. Then she straightened up, smiling.

"It's wonderful!" she said. "Nothing is moving. No elevateds, streetcars, hacks—nothing. New York is completely paralyzed. You've never seen anything so beautiful—or so still. We had to walk for miles."

"She means plow," Joe grinned. "The snow was up to our waists. . . . Order us something, Pride, that will thaw the blood! I'm frozen all the way through."

Pride put up his hand and pulled the bell cord.

"Whiskey," he told Malcolm when the old butler had creaked into the room. "And you, Es? Sherry?"

"No, thank you. I'm afraid I'll be unladylike and take whiskey, too. Or brandy. Sherry is far too mild tonight."

Pride looked at Joe with grim amusement.

"What brings you way up here, Joe?" he demanded. "Don't tell me you struggled all the way from downtown just to bring Esther home."

"Partly. I'm the gallant type. Esther missed a lot by marrying you instead of me. Oh, well . . ."

" 'Partly,' " Pride grinned. "What's the other part, little Joe?"

"Business. But it will take half this bottle to get me to a state where I can discuss it."

Pride glanced at Caprice, who was curled up in a big chair with a book.

"Run along, Cappie," he said. "We've got things to talk about."

"Oh, let her stay," Joseph said. "It's nothing that she can't hear." His eyes, looking at Caprice, were sad. . . .

Poor devil, Pride thought, he should have married, instead of wasting his life mooning over Esther.

Joseph put down his glass with a great sigh.

"A-a-a-h!" he said, "That was good!"

"Have another," Pride said, "then start talking, because I've got to go out."

He's going to see Sharon, Esther thought bitterly. Strange that it still bothers me. It shouldn't, not now, not any more.

"Very well," Joseph said. "You know what a beating I took when Grant and Ward went down. For that matter, you took one yourself—right?"

"Right," Pride said.

"Only, you survived—while I almost lost my shirt. Well, I've a chance to recoup. The catch is—I haven't the means. I didn't want to come to you, but Esther suggested it. Here's the point: I've pretty definite information that the Bland-Allison Act is going to be repealed."

Pride sat bolt upright.

"The hell you say!" he roared.

"Yes. I know you have big stakes in silver—that's why Esther thought you'd be interested. If they repeal that silver-purchasing act, how much will your mine be worth?"

"Not a nickel," Pride groaned. "And it's the only damned thing I've got that's keeping me afloat. Even with

315

it, I just break even. It takes all its profits these days to keep the rest of my stuff going."

"Pride," Joseph said, "why don't we go short on silver? Plunge big! Then even when the Government stops buying silver, we'll have made our pile. You could sell that mine beforehand."

"I don't know," Pride said thoughtfully. "I've been having bad luck with politics. First we get Garfield, who was right for business—and that damned fool had to go and shoot him. Then Chester Arthur, who anybody'd have thought would have been on our side since he's rich himself—and damned if he didn't start a reform government and put some of my best friends in jail!"

"The Star Route Frauds," Joe murmured. "I remember."

"I thought we'd whip Cleveland in '84—especially with that business about the kid . . ."

Caprice suddenly burst into song:

> 'Ma! Ma!
> Where's my pa?
> Gone to the White House,
> Ha! Ha! Ha!'

"Cappie!" Pride roared.

"But, Daddy," Caprice protested, "you used to sing that song yourself."

"I don't care if I did! Now, you get out of here!"

"She's growing up," Joseph said.

"Yep—still I don't want her singing songs about anybody's yard children—even if Grover is President."

"A rather exalted type of bastard, I'd say," Joe grinned. "Oh—forgive me, Esther."

"It's all right," Esther said. "It's too bad that you two aren't in public life so that the sins of your youth could catch up with you!"

"The trouble is," Pride said, "I'm in kind of deep in this business of getting Ben Harrison elected. There's more than four million of hard money floating around in his behalf—and a lot of it's mine!"

"What's the matter, darling," Esther drawled, "are you getting cold feet?"

"Hell, no!" Pride spluttered, "only—"

"Only, you used to say that you were going to become

316

the richest man in America. Now look at you. I doubt that you could call even a million dollars your own. Everybody's outstripped you: Gould, Vanderbilt, Carnegie . . ."

"That's enough!" Pride roared. "How much do you want, Joe?"

"Could you lend me a million? At any rates you want. I'm that sure."

"Hell, I'll lend you two! And I'm going in on this thing five more for myself! Cold feet, eh? I'm still going to be top dog!"

"Good for you, Pride," Esther said quietly.

Pride stood up.

"I've got to go now," he growled. "You and little Joe entertain each other. Tell Malcolm to give him the south bedroom, there's no need of him trying to get home in this storm tonight."

Joseph put out his hand.

"Thanks, Pride," he said.

"It's nothing. Good night."

Caprice saw him leave the house, but she continued to sit in the music room, her fingers moving idly over the keys of the grand piano.

Daddy's angry, she thought. And whatever it is that Mother's got him to do is wrong for him. I know that. She probably teased him into it. He can't stand her making fun of him.

She sat there a long time, feeling the room gradually growing cold. It was long past her bedtime, but she didn't expect to be bothered. That was one of the advantages of being sixteen. Nobody bothered you very much. Except for the rare occasions that Esther remembered her, she was allowed to stay up as late as she pleased. Tonight she intended to stay up very late. She wanted to think about Lance. It was clear that he considered her a mere child. The thought rankled. She was entirely grown. There were girls her age who were married and had children. And one of the girls in her class at school . . .

She blushed scarlet, suddenly. She wasn't even supposed to think about things like that, but Louise had been expelled for mysterious reasons—and the whispers had circulated that she was going to have a "fatherless" child.

Why "fatherless"? That was ridiculous. Obviously, the child had to have a father—whether Louise was married to

317

him or not. What messes people made of their lives! She'd have to be careful. Caprice was going to be very, very careful.

But Lance was so handsome. What if he was thirty? She'd be twenty soon. She wondered if Lance still would look on her as a child then?

I'm no child! she thought bitterly. . . . She was conscious that her feet were cold—terribly cold. But before she could get up, her mother came into the music room with Joseph Fairhill.

"Oh," Esther said sharply, "you're in here! In the name of common sense, Caprice, don't you ever go to bed?"

"Yes, Mother," Caprice said sadly. "I'm going now."

She got up stiffly, thinking: Mother wants me out of here. She wouldn't have come in, if she had known I was here. It's true what the servants say—it is, it is! Mother and Joe are betraying Daddy right under his nose. Can't he see it? I can—though everybody thinks I'm a child. All that business of talking about it in front of me in nonsense syllables and disguised allusions . . . I guess Daddy's so proud that he'd never guess that Mother would—or could —deceive him. But she is. Oh, I hate her for this!

As she passed the spot where Joseph was standing, he put out his arms to her.

"Come and give an old man a kiss, Cappie," he said.

Caprice looked at him.

"No," she said coldly, then she fled through the doorway. But she did not go to her room. Instead, she went to the big window and, cradling her face between her hands, stared out at the drifting snow. Suddenly, she stiffened, then pressed her nose against the cold glass, shading her eyes with one hand so that the reflections would not hinder her view.

"It is!" she breathed. "It *is* Lance!" Then she ran through the great hall and out into the snowy courtyard where Lance McCarthy stood, staring at her window.

She came up to him very quietly and took his arm.

"Hello, Lance," she said. "Come in, won't you?"

"Oh!" Lance gasped. "I—I—er—" But it was impossible for Lance to explain what he was doing outside Pride's castle on such a night. The truth of the matter was that he didn't know himself. His mind was terribly confused. He knew how badly he wanted Lilith—and he knew that he

318

did not love her. What he needed, his subconscious mind must have told him, was an antidote. And no better antidote for Lilith's sensual beauty existed than Caprice Dawson. . . .

"Come in," Caprice said again. "It's cold out here." She held him gently by the arm and led him back into the great hall. Inside the hall a fire smoldered feebly in the great fireplace. Caprice released Lance, who poked at the embers. Then, little by little, he added wood until the fire was blazing and throwing out an intense heat. Caprice sat before it and looked at him with great, wondering eyes.

"What were you doing out there?" she asked him softly.

"I don't know," Lance answered truthfully. "I think I was hoping to see you again."

"Were you? Oh, Lance—I'm so glad!"

"Are you really? Then I'm glad too." He stopped abruptly. For the life of him, he couldn't think of anything to say. They sat still for a long time, brooding before the fire. The firelight flickered its reflection over Lance's lean, handsome face, and the dreams that glowed half-hidden in his eyes were slow and deep.

Caprice looked at him. She did not want to talk, nor even for Lance to do so—talking would break the spell. There was an enchantment here—a suspension of the borders of space, of time and of reality. It was possible, under it, for her to forget her mother's ugly act of betrayal and vengeance that had been going on for God knew how many years. She knew all about that now. Incidents from her childhood came flooding back: words, inflections of the voice, gestures between her mother and Joseph which now told their damning tale. She pushed the pain from her heart and looked at Lance. How wonderful he is! she thought.

But then Lance spoke.

"You said you were glad I came to see you," he said. "Why, Caprice?"

Caprice gazed at him, her blue eyes soft and tender.

"Because I like you," she whispered. "Because I've dreamed about somebody like you all my life."

"But you're so young!" Lance protested.

"I know. It's not my fault. And I shan't be young always. I don't feel young. Tonight—I feel old, terribly old."

"Why?" Lance demanded.

"Because you're here. I feel like that princess in the tower who awakened after a hundred years. Do you—do you love me, Lance, like that fairy princess?"

Lance looked at her wonderingly as though he saw her for the first time. The firelight danced, throwing leaping reflections across the silvery gold of her soft, shining hair. In her eyes the reflections were starlight, suddenly.

"Yes!" he groaned. "God help me, yes!"

"I'm glad," Caprice said very simply. "I'm very glad. Because, you see—I love you, too."

"Love!" Lance said harshly. "What can a child like you know of love?"

"Everything there is to know. That it can be a terribly cruel thing—hurting people like Auntie Sharon has been hurt. Or—like Mother. Or even like Daddy is going to be some day soon. And it can be very fierce, making people do foolish, wicked things—things that will destroy them, finally. Or it can be like ours is going to be, Lance. . . . Very sweet and gentle, like Daddy says: a kind of being together in all ways—in mind and in spirit and in body. That kind lasts. The day I die, I shall be loving you, just as I do now. . . ."

Lance gazed at her wonderingly.

"You're very wise," he murmured. "Now, tell me one other thing: what will we do—about us?"

"I'll be eighteen in two years. Then I'll marry you. And we'll have children, the most beautiful children on earth!"

"Suppose," Lance hesitated, "your father objects?"

"He won't—not when I tell him I want you. He's never yet failed to let me have what I really wanted. Lance . . ."

"Yes, Caprice?"

"It's all right for you to kiss me now, isn't it? Now that we're engaged?"

"Yes," Lance said. "Oh, yes!"

She lay back very peacefully against his shoulder.

"You know," she said, "that's the first time any man has ever kissed me—except my father. It was nice. Do it again, please."

"No!" Lance said in a half-strangled voice. "For God's sake, no!"

"You needn't be afraid, Lance. We won't do anything wrong. I won't and I won't let you. So kiss me one more time."

Lance kissed her and her sigh was soft with contentment. . . .

CHAPTER TWENTY-NINE—1888

"Yes, PRIDE," Sharon repeated, "I think we should call it
quits now."

"Why—it's worked all these years . . . ?"

"No, Pride," Sharon said gently, "it hasn't. You're
strong—I'm not. Things that don't bother you at all have
broken my heart into a million pieces. Things like having
women stare at me and not even bother to drop their eyes
when I look at them. Things like having women whom I
know only slightly, get up when I sit beside them on the
cars—or like being baited about my conduct by my
Lilith. . . ."

"So Lilith knows, eh? Funny thing—so does Cappie."

"No! Oh, no, Pride!"

"Yep. She mentioned it to me only this morning."

Sharon put her face down into her hands suddenly.

Pride growled, "You act like it's worse for Cappie to
know than for Lilith."

"It is!" Sharon whispered. "Oh, yes—it is!"

"Why?"

"Caprice is so sweet, and she has loved me so much. It's
been one of the things that has sustained me so long. Now
she'll hate me, too!"

"No, she doesn't. She seems to think I'm to blame. It's
funny that you care so much about her opinion and so little about Lilith's."

"Caprice is an angel, while Lilith—"

"Is a product of her ancestors and her upbringing," Lilith finished for her. "Right, Mother?"

Pride looked up to see her lounging in the doorway, with
one eye squinting against the smoke of the cigarette that
dangled from a corner of her sensual lips.

My God! he thought. What a creature!

Then he stood up, towering above her, and his big hand moved out with amazing quickness, his fingers closing about the cigarette and yanking it out of her mouth. Then he half-turned and threw it into the fire.

"You show some respect!" he growled.

Lilith laughed—a cool, amused sound.

"For my elders and betters, I suppose? Very well, Pride —I'll be humble in the future."

"Yep—for your elders and your betters. For people who are older than you and a hell of a lot wiser. We made our mistakes, all right. But it's not your place to judge them. You aren't God—and from the looks of you, you aren't the Virgin Mary either!"

Sharon looked up with amazed joy. Nobody could master Pride. Certainly not this impious slip of a girl.

Lilith was smiling now.

"No, Pride," she said. "I'm not the Virgin Mary. Too bad it was Mother who had to run afoul of you. I could have done much better."

"What the devil do you mean?"

"Mother's too soft. And too good. I am neither. I could have handled you because I'm just like you. By now I'd have been mistress of that monstrosity you call your castle. Only, I'd have made you sell it or tear it down."

"Would you, now?" he laughed.

"Don't be too sure of yourself, Pride. I'm as hard as you are. It would have been interesting. You're quite a man. You're ugly as sin, and yet you're very attractive."

"Suppose," Pride said grimly, "you get the hell out of here so I can talk to your mother!"

"You see?" Sharon said after Lilith had left the room.

"I see, all right," Pride growled. "I see somebody ought to take a razor strop to that brat of yours!"

"The foundation of any home is respect, Pride. How do you expect me to be able to control her—under the circumstances?"

"Is that why you want to quit me—again?"

"Partly. And partly because now I think I can and make it stick. 'For at your age,' she quoted suddenly, 'the heyday in the blood is tame, it's humble, and waits upon the judgment . . .'"

"What's that?"

"Shakespeare. *Hamlet*. Later on he says: 'Rebellious hell, If thou canst mutine in a matron's bones, To flaming youth let virtue be as wax, And melt in her own fire.' There's Lilith, Pride—and Caprice. What could you say if Cappie came to you and said: 'Father, I'm in trouble . . .'?"

"Damn! You know how to stick me where it hurts, don't you?"

"Yes. We've set them a poor example, Pride. But that's not all. There are people who are born rebels—who delight in overturning conventions. I'm not one of them: I suffer. And I don't think Our Father cares very much for deathbed repentances made out of the immediate fear of hell. I'm thirty-eight years old, Pride. I should like to make my peace with God and spend the rest of my days making up for the sins of my youth. . . ."

"I see. What do you plan to do?"

"Tim wants me to come to Boston and design shoes for his plant."

Pride leaned forward, frowning morosely into the fire.

"I knew it would come to this, sometime," he said. "I knew some day I'd lose you. All right, Shay. Only, you don't have to run away. This house is yours—registered in your name. Just a minute! I gave it to you because I love you. It's not a payment for anything. There's nothing on God's green earth—all the money, all the treasures—that could pay for one hour I've spent with you. Consider it your home and let me come sometimes as a visitor—an old friend with whom you don't mind sitting in your parlor and talking about old times. . . ."

His hand went into his pocket suddenly and came out with a key ring. He fumbled with it a moment until he had it open, and took off one of the keys. Sharon recognized the key at once. It was the key to her house.

"Here," Pride said. "When I come now, I'll ring the bell like anybody else. At about ten or eleven o'clock, I'll go home. Is that the way you want it?"

"Yes, Pride," Sharon whispered, "that's the way I want it. And Pride . . ."

"Yes? Yes, Shay?"

"Thank you. Thank you very much. You may not know it or believe it; but this is the nicest thing you've ever done."

Pride got clumsily to his feet. Slowly, he put out his big

323

hand. Sharon hesitated before she took it. She had the impulse to kiss him good night—just this once, just one more time in parting. But she did not. Instead, she took his hand very gently and whispered:

"Good night, Pride."

Good night, Pride. Good night, my lost love. Now and forever, good night. . . .

CHAPTER THIRTY—1891

THREE YEARS HAD PASSED and it was now the fall of 1891. Joseph Fairhill had been wrong. Congress not only did not repeal the Bland-Allison Act; it adopted the Sherman Silver Purchase Act, causing the price of silver to soar. As the owner of one of the richest silver mines in the country, Pride should have made a fortune. Instead he lost the shirt off his back. He had gone short so heavily that everything he owned, including the mine itself, had to be sold to meet his obligations. This September night, when Caprice came into the study leading Lance by the hand, Pride was back where he had been in 1870—virtually penniless. He was not too much troubled by it, however, beyond the hurt to his pride. Caprice's future was secure, for Esther was still worth over twenty million dollars in her own right. He, thank God, had never touched that. He had been down before and had come up again. Still, it would not be too easy this time. . . .

He looked up into the radiant face of his daughter and the gloom left his countenance.

"Yes, Cappie," he said gruffly, "what is it?"

It was Lance who spoke, his handsome young face brick-red.

"I—er—we—we'd like to be married, sir—with your permission."

Pride stiffened in his chair and his face was bleak suddenly. Bleak and fierce. Lose Cappie? Lose the most priceless of his treasures to this young fool? His whole being cried out against it. Sharon was gone. His money, too. And now—Cappie? The very idea held him speechless. With Sharon's renunciation, half his heart had gone. The loss of his fortune had hurt too, but that was minor. But Cappie! Why, Cappie was his life—all his life!

"So," he said helplessly. "I thought something like this was in the wind. Well, I don't know . . ."

But Caprice came to him quietly, and when she was close he could see that her heart was in her eyes.

"Please, Daddy," she whispered.

Lost, he thought bitterly, lost. In all her life I've never been able to deny her anything. And now she wants him. Oh, Jesus—God . . .

"Well, Cappie," he said heavily, "what about it—you want this young scamp?"

"Yes, Daddy," Caprice breathed. "Yes—oh, yes!"

"Hmmn," Pride said. He was fighting for time, and he knew it. "It still calls for some thinking. Lance, how old are you, son?"

"Thirty-three."

"And Cappie's only nineteen." He turned to his daughter. "Look, Baby, I don't suppose you'd consider waiting another year—until you were twenty, say . . ."

"A year!" Caprice gasped. "Oh, Daddy!"

"I see," Pride said sadly. "We-l-l—a husband ought to be older than his wife; the reins will get out of his hands otherwise. Look, son, you know I'm broke—Cappie can't expect to get a nickel from me?"

Lance stiffened.

"I'm asking you for Caprice, sir—not your bank account!"

"Good boy! I like spirit. You still think I'm a horny-handed old pirate?"

"Yes, sir," Lance answered stoutly. "Only, I don't care any more. Your business ethics are your concern, sir, not mine."

"Spoken like a man," Pride said, a glint of amusement appearing in his eyes. "You two sit down. I want to think about this thing for a minute. It's not good business to answer things like this too fast."

Caprice and Lance sank into nearby chairs, studying his big face apprehensively.

Lose her, Pride was thinking, I'm going to lose her! I

325

can't stop her—it's normal for a girl to fall in love and want to marry. I knew it would happen sometime. Only, why did it have to be now? First Sharon, then the money and now Caprice. My sins are finding me out, I guess— "the mills of the gods," Ma always used to say.

Cappie, my little Cappie! . . . Then he straightened up and faced them.

"All right," he said gruffly. "All right, you two—I'm willing."

"Oh, Daddy!" Caprice cried and, throwing both arms about his neck, covered his face with kisses.

"Thank you, sir!" Lance said fervently, and put out his hand.

"I'll see you tomorrow?" Caprice whispered, as she stood in Lance's embrace.

Lance frowned.

"No," he said shortly, "I'm afraid not. There's something I have to do . . ."

"What is it, Lance?" Caprice demanded.

"Nothing that concerns—us."

"Secrets already, Lance?"

"Yes. Jealous?"

"Horribly. If it's another girl, I'll scratch her eyes out!"

"You have nothing to worry about," Lance murmured.

But *I* have, he thought, as he left the house. This business of telling Lilith of his engagement was going to be difficult. Difficult? That was the world's prize understatement. It was going to be damned near impossible. For three years now he had been dividing his time between Caprice and Lilith. And though there had never been any doubt in his mind as to what the outcome would be, he had been unable to shake himself free of the exasperating, maddening effect of Lilith's charm. Her kisses were endlessly promising, hinting of unequaled delights; and giving nothing—nothing at all. He wanted her. God, how he wanted her! But he had sense enough to realize that being married to Lilith would be pure hell. So the break had to be made now. At once. . . .

Lilith came into the house and threw her wraps carelessly upon a chair. She was humming to herself, and her cheeks were flushed. Sharon looked up at her with a frown.

"Where have you been?" she demanded.

"Out riding with Pride," Lilith said.

"Again?"

"Yes, Mother—again. Any objections?"

"Yes. It's not at all becoming."

"Why not? You gave him up. He's a fascinating man, and he's fabulously wealthy. Since he's inclined to be nice to me, why shouldn't I?"

"He's fifty-seven years old and—"

"And you're still in love with him. That's it, isn't it, Mother?"

"No. That's not it. Loving Pride is something I can't help. But letting you repeat my mistakes is something I can help, and I will!"

"How? It seems to me that the matter is a little beyond your control."

"That remains to be seen. If I were to go to Pride and tell him I don't like your going out with him, he'd give you up in an instant."

Lilith yawned.

"Are you so sure, Mother dear?" she drawled.

"Why, you little . . ."

"Don't be common, Mother. It doesn't become you. Wasn't that the bell? Don't bother, I'll get it."

Oh, my God, Sharon prayed silently, haven't I suffered enough? And now this—this! Oh, Pride, Pride, I never would have believed this of you!

But Lilith was coming back now with Lance close behind her.

Maybe it would be better, Sharon thought, if Lance were to marry her. Only, I'm much too fond of Lance to wish Lilith on him. She'd drive him insane in a year.

"You can go to bed now, Mother," Lilith said calmly. "Lance and I have things to talk about."

"Thank you, I will," Sharon said. "Good night, Lance."

"Good night, Auntie Sharon," Lance said miserably.

Lilith lay back on the sofa and stretched up her arms to Lance.

"Oh, darling," she whispered, "it's been so long . . ."

But Lance remained standing, safely out of reach.

"Lilith," he said hoarsely, "I—I came to tell you—"

"Yes, Lance? Yes, darling?"

"Good-bye," Lance blurted.

"Good-bye? You're going somewhere?"

"No. It's—it's just that Caprice and I are going to get married next month."

It was out now. He had said it.

Lilith didn't answer him. She sat very still on the sofa and her mouth tightened slowly into a hard line. Lance realized that she was not going to cry—that there would not be any scene. But this silence was infinitely worse.

Then, ever so slowly, Lilith stood up. With deliberate grace she reached down and picked up her furs. Then she stood before the mirror and draped them carefully about her shoulders.

Lance ran his tongue over dry lips.

"Where are you going?" he demanded.

"To Pride," Lilith said simply.

"You don't understand," Lance said. "He's already given his consent."

"I know. My congratulations, Lance. I'm not going to discuss you—I'm going away." She turned and looked Lance full in the face. *"With* Pride," she added softly.

Lance stood there foolishly holding his hat in his hands. The crash of the door, as Lilith slammed it, awakened him from his reverie. Then he put his hat on his head and went out, too, under the silent stars.

It was almost morning before Lance realized what he should have done. But once the idea came to him, he acted immediately. He hailed a cab and drove back to Sharon's house.

He had no difficulty in awakening Sharon. In fact, she was not asleep.

She sat very still, looking tiny and frail in her quilted robe and absurdly young for all her forty-one years. And she listened quietly, while Lance poured out his sorry tale. When he had finished, she stood up calmly.

"Thank you, Lance," she said.

"What are you going to do?" Lance demanded.

"I'll take care of Lilith—and Pride," she said. "Don't worry, I'll take care of it."

After he had gone she went upstairs and dressed herself without haste. Then she went to a cabinet and opened a drawer. She stood there very still for a long time—then she put in her hand and drew out the pistol.

It gleamed dully in the light of the gas jets, polished silver, embossed with leaves and tendrils, and among them her name spelled out in exquisite scrollwork. Her pistol. The "Virgin's Pistol" Pride had given her long ago in Pittsburgh—to protect her life or, ironically, her honor.

Her hands moved slowly, breaking it open. Yes, it was loaded. There were bullets in each of the two barrels. Two. Just enough. One for each life that now was forfeit . . .

She came out into the graying dawn and, because there were no hansom cabs clopping through the streets at this hour, walked over to Sixth Avenue and climbed the stairs to the elevated. The little steam engine that pulled it, snorted and puffed uptown, drawing a fine tracery of soot upon her face.

Malcolm opened the door for her.

"I'd appreciate it," she said, "if you'd awaken Mr. Dawson for me. It's very important. That is—if he's here."

"Yes, Madame," Malcolm said. "He's here. And I don't have to awaken him. He's in the study. Truth to tell, I don't think he went to bed."

Pride was sitting in his big chair before a dying fire. His hair was tousled, and his eyes were red from lack of sleep.

"Hello, Shay," he rumbled, "what brings you here?"

"Where is she?" Sharon snapped.

Pride's jaw dropped a little.

"Where's who? What the devil ails you, Shay?"

"Lilith," Sharon said grimly. "Where is she?"

"Damned if I know," Pride said calmly.

"Don't lie to me! She said she was coming here! She told Lance that she was going away with you. I've forgiven you many things, Pride Dawson; but this is one thing that not even I can forgive!"

She put her hand into the bag and took out the little pistol. When she spoke again, her voice was very quiet.

"Where is she, Pride?" she said.

Pride stood up.

"So you came here to kill me," he said. "That little gun isn't much good—way over here you might miss. I guess I'd better come a little closer."

He walked toward her calmly, until the twin muzzles were inches from his chest. He took a half-step forward, until they touched him. "Go on," he said quietly, "shoot!"

Sharon hesitated, looking up at his great, calm face.

"I want to see if you can do it," he said. "I'd like to see if you've stopped loving me enough. If you have, life is no good anyhow. Well—what are you waiting for?"

Slowly, Sharon's hand wavered and came down. The next moment, she was in his arms.

"Oh, Pride!" she cried.

"Hush, Shay," he grinned. "Didn't you know you couldn't kill me? Here, give me that." He took the "Virgin's Pistol" and dropped it into the pocket of his smoking jacket.

"Lilith . . ." Sharon sobbed.

"I know. She was here last night. I sent her packing. Everything she says is a lie. Look at me, Shay. Could I run off with Cappie? Well, that kid of yours is almost as much mine, too. I found her, remember? I've been sending her things and doing for her all her life. She was hurt—hurt bad—over this business about Lance. So she had to hurt back. And smart little trick that she is, she figgered out the best way to do it. Only, she didn't know—me."

"I'm—I'm so ashamed," Sharon whispered. "Please forgive me. I don't know what made me believe such a thing."

"You love me," Pride grinned, "and you're a jealous woman, Shay. There's nothing on earth blinder than that. Come on, let's have some coffee. Then you go home and rest. I'll find that brat of yours for you. And when I do, I'm going to take her over my knee, big as she is!"

"Good!" Sharon said grimly. "I hope you do."

Again, after the coffee, Sharon felt the impulse to kiss Pride. But she only put out her hand and said good-bye.

Pride ran his hand over the iron-gray bristles on his massive jaw. I need a shave, he thought. A bath, too. A little later, though—right now, I just want to sit here and think.

He pulled the bell cord and after some time Malcolm appeared.

"Tell Mrs. Dawson," Pride said, "when she comes in, that I want to see her."

"Yes, sir," Malcolm said.

Poor Malcolm, Pride thought, as the butler creaked out, he's an old man now. But then—who isn't? I'm fifty-seven—fifty-eight in another month. God! How times flies!

He settled back in the chair, feeling the stiffness in his limbs. Yet for some reason he had no desire to get up. I'm tired, he thought, too blamed tired. . . . There's so much to do. I've got to come back. Yes—I'm right back where I was when I hit this town. I'll have to start all over again—and I'm fifty-seven years old. I've half a mind to chuck the whole thing. . . . Esther's got all that money Black Tom left her. Even Sharon's well off, with her shop. And Cappie . . .

(Cappie! Even to say the name was like a cry in the darkness of his heart.) Cappie has Lance. She doesn't need me any more—either. (That was the worst thing. He had to be wanted by someone—he had to be needed. All his fierce energies had resolved into this one thing finally; all his tremendous pride had been centered upon Caprice's small and shining head . . .)

He sat there brooding—remembering. There had been a day when she was small—nine, she was, he thought—that he had taken her sailing in his yawl on the Sound. He had sat at the tiller and made the swift boat obey his lightest touch; but his eyes had kept straying to her small face, flushed with delight at the motion. She had turned and seen him finally, and she had said:

"You—love me very much, don't you, Daddy?"

"Yep," he had said gruffly, his throat tight suddenly, "very much!"

"Why?" she had whispered. "Because I'm your little girl?"

"Yes. Because you're mine. And because you're good and pretty and sweet. You're the only thing your old daddy's got, Cappie, that's really worth having."

"And you've always loved me, Daddy?"

"From the minute you were born. I thought I couldn't love you any more than I did then—but you sort of grew on me, Cappie . . ."

"I grew on you, Daddy? How?"

He had looked out over the blue waters and then back at her small form. When he spoke again his voice was deep and tender.

"Like a little tree on a rock. I'm the rock, Cappie—and you're the tree. The rock thought he was very strong—that there weren't any cracks in him anywhere. But there was—one tiny little crack. And a seed fell in that crack, and put down its roots and grew. It's a little tree now, but it'll be a big tree. And the roots will keep pushing the crack wider and wider apart until . . ."

"Until what, Daddy?"

"Nothing," he had growled. But the answer was obvious —the roots of this love he bore her would some day split his heart. Like now, he thought miserably . . . like now!

Now nobody needs me any more. Not a soul. The rock is almost split and hanging there on the mountainside, getting ready to fall. There's really not much for me to live for. I'm tired—so damned tired . . .

He brought his big head up and stared at the door.

This isn't like me. I'm Pride. I'm big Pride Dawson who never knuckled under. I can't now. I've got to live up to that name. Oh, Ma—when you gave it to me, did you ever stop to think whether it was really worth it? . . . Esther'll be home soon. All I have to do is to ask her to lend me the money. A couple of million will be enough. I'll buy back the Millville holdings and make them pay. I've never paid enough attention to them before. I'd like to get that silver mine back, but that's out of the question. There's not enough money in the world to pay for it now, with the Government buying silver like crazy. . . .

He stiffened suddenly, hearing the light patter of Esther's feet in the hall, and the tired quaver of old Malcolm's voice. Then there was the sound of the doorknob turning.

He sat very still and waited.

Esther came into the room and stood there looking at him, her lovely face as cold and still as death.

"Yes?" she said.

"I suppose you know . . ." he mumbled.

"Yes. You've lost your money. So has Joe . . . I was with him when it happened," she added coolly.

"So—" Pride said heavily, "you *have* been carrying on with him."

"Yes, Pride," Esther said. "I have. For years. What else could you expect?"

"Nothing, I guess. I asked for it. Funny. Ten years ago —or five—I'd be reaching for my gun. But now—no. I don't suppose I care, really. We're even. So now we can call it quits. Just one thing, Esther. I'll need some money. I have to get started again. Could you lend me . . ."

"No," Esther said. "I couldn't."

"Dear God, Es! I'll be finished if . . ."

Esther bent forward a little, her soft lips smiling.

"That is precisely what I want, Pride Dawson! You see,

we're not even. You made me suffer too long and hurt me far too much. Even Joe couldn't fix that. No lover could. I —I thought being in his arms would be revenge enough. But it wasn't. I want more. Much more."

Pride looked at her, and smiled with grim mockery.

"I'll get the money somewhere else," he said. "Sorry I can't oblige you . . ."

Outside the door Caprice paused with her hand on the knob, hearing the voices coming through. She turned and looked questioningly at Lance. "No," he said, "I wouldn't go in—not now."

"I don't think," Esther continued, "you'll get the money anywhere, Pride. I don't think you'll even want to."

"Why not?"

Esther sat down on the edge of the desk.

"What do you need money for now?" she asked.

"There's Cappie," Pride said. "I want to leave her well-fixed."

"Cappie," Esther said clearly, "is no concern of yours."

"What?" Pride roared, half-rising from his chair. "What the devil do you mean, Esther?"

"Precisely what I say. Caprice is no concern of yours." She leaned forward, looking into his face. "Oh, you great vain fool!" she said bitingly. "How could you have believed all these years that you fathered her! You, you great sterile ox! Look at her, Pride—look at her face. Have you never really seen her? Can't you see that she's Joe's? Don't you realize no child of yours would have half that beauty— half that grace? I've waited for this—oh, yes, Pride, I've waited. Her eyes, her mouth, even her lashes—his, all his! What have you to work for now, Pride Dawson? What, I ask you?"

Pride sank back into the chair, his face ashen, his mouth working, shaping words that never came out.

"You lie!" Pride finally bellowed, then his big voice broke. "You lie, Esther," he got out. "Say that you lie. Tell me it's not so. . . . Tell me, Es. For the love of God, tell me!"

"You'd have me lie to save your pride?" Esther said. "No, even that business about her being a premature child was untrue. When she was conceived—you were in Colorado . . ."

"Cappie . . ." Pride whispered. "My little Cappie."

"She's not anything—to you!" Esther said cruelly. Then she got up from the desk and walked toward the door. In the doorway she turned.

"Go to Sharon," she said. "Go to her, Pride—and tell her to replace the child you've lost!"

She opened the door and went out. As she stepped out into the hall, she heard the swift clatter of Caprice's feet as she raced up the stairs. Turning, she looked into Lance's stricken face.

"She—she heard?" Esther whispered.

"Yes," Lance said. "Yes—she heard. And damn your wicked soul to hell, Mrs. Dawson!" Then he, too, spun on his heel and marched through the door.

Inside the study, Pride slumped in his chair. The roots had gone in too deep, now—and the rock was split. There was nothing about him that moved—neither his lips nor his eyes, nor his hands hanging like lumps of broken clay over the arms of his chair. Then slowly, mechanically, his hands came up. He groped in the box on the desk and took out a cigar. His fingers fumbled helplessly in his pockets searching for a match. They did not find one. Instead, they closed on something else—something hard and cold. He drew it out and sat there looking down at it, seeing the exquisite scrollwork, the name "Sharon" engraved upon the barrel, the swift, curved triggers needing only the lightest pull. He hefted it delicately, feeling its weight, its perfect balance.

To him, at that moment, it seemed the most beautiful thing in all the world. . . .

CHAPTER THIRTY-ONE—1891

SHARON PUSHED OPEN the casement windows and looked across the green sweep of the lawn toward the hedgerows. The asters were clustered around the pool and, from a break in the mossy surface of the rocks, the water fell in a tiny silver cascade, making a noise like laughter. The willow bent low over the unruffled surface of the water, like a sorrowing woman trailing her hair after her; and the hollyhocks stood along the rough-hewn surfaces of the stone wall. There were lilacs, slim-stalked, standing in clumps here and there amid the rocks, and between them there were roses. The whole thing had that air of studied unconcern which betrayed the fact, after a time, that here was a masterly defeat, that the whole garden had been planned to give the impression of an utter naturalness which it always missed in small, indefinable ways.

Sharon wondered about this. God knew, Pride had spent time and money enough upon her garden. The gardener had been brought all the way from England; the stones had been carted fifty miles from the district about Lake Mahopac, and the willow had traveled from a plantation in Virginia. You could not see, Sharon knew, that the silver water tinkled from a pipe of the finest softest copper: it seemed to bubble up from the earth itself. Yet the sound it made was faintly derisive. It was as though, looking up suddenly, she half-expected the whole thing to vanish, to see again the livery stable that had occupied the spot on which Pride had built her garden, to smell the harsh nostril-stinging odors of horses, wet straw and steaming hair. She shook her head, as if to clear it. The garden would not vanish. False though it was, it was permanent.

Her hand reached out and gripped the casement to close it, but the motion was arrested abruptly, as she peered toward the gate in the hedgerows. A girl had come through the opening in the hedges, a tall girl with silvery blond hair piled high on top of her head.

"Caprice!" Sharon murmured. "Ah, Caprice!" She and Caprice had been seeing much of each other lately. Now Sharon leaned forward, half through the window, all her being caught up in a wild surge of love for the slim girl walking through her garden, for this fairy princess who should have been her daughter but was not: Caprice—Pride's child, not hers. So different from Lilith, Sharon thought; so many miles and ages and aeons different from my dark tumultuous Lilith, my eternal foundling—a stranger and a changeling from the hour of her birth. . . .

Caprice came toward Sharon, walking slowly, with a state-liness totally unlike the spring dance of her usual gait. Caprice, at nineteen, still ran, still skipped; she was mer-curial and virginal, as pure as a wild woods creature, a lit-tle beyond comprehension, so that, watching her, Sharon's coldly critical faculty suspended judgment, while what was left of youth in her looked upon Caprice with joy.

But now, today, there was no joy. Caprice's small feet moved slowly, and her small head was bent. Sharon never knew how the feeling of terror started. But suddenly it was there—like the hand of winter in her garden, like the weight of death upon her heart. She leaned out now, far out of her window, and called.

"Caprice!"

The girl's head came up. There was something awful in the deliberation of the motion. Her blue eyes caught Shar-on's gaze in a shaft of utter finality.

"Auntie Sharon," she said, her voice clear and toneless. "Auntie Sharon, I came to tell you—"

Sharon settled her weight upon her thin arms, and stared at Caprice.

"Come in, child," she said gently. "Please, come in."

Sharon walked back from the window, put her hand on the knob and opened the door.

Caprice stood there, her face colorless and still, her eye-lids moving rapidly in an effort to blink back her tears.

"Yes?" Sharon whispered. "Yes, Caprice? What is it you've come to tell me?"

"Pride's dead. He shot himself."

Sharon stared at Caprice, her own mind off on oblique, idiotic paths. (Once I saw Bernhardt receive news like this in a play. Her grief was unbearable to watch. But I—I feel nothing and there are no words for me to say. . . . I'm not crying. I'm quite sure I'm not going to faint. Is it because, at times like these, we have no means of expressing a grief which is actually beyond expression?)

Then she put out her arms. Caprice walked into them. (How many times have I held her thus? Her, the lost and the loved, neither bone of my bone, nor flesh of my flesh, but truly the child of my heart's blood and my rebellious spirit.)

"Auntie Sharon," Caprice said. "Don't cry. Pride

336

wouldn't like it. I haven't cried. I'm not going to."

Wildly, Sharon shook her head.

"I won't," she promised. "But how—why? I saw him yesterday; he wasn't sad. He laughed at me. Why, Caprice, why?"

"Mother," Caprice said.

"Your mother?"

"Yes. I came home last night with Lance. When we got into the hall, we heard voices—Mother's mostly. She was screaming at Daddy. Like—like a fishwife. She said the most dreadful things . . ."

"What?" Sharon whispered. "What did she say?"

"You know that Daddy lost his money? He told you, didn't he? Well, he must have asked Mother to lend him enough to get back on his feet. She refused. But it wasn't that . . ."

"Then what was it?"

"You know how Daddy loved me?"

"Yes—oh, yes!"

"Well, Mother told him I was not—his child."

"Caprice!"

"Yes. She told him that Joseph Fairhill has been her lover for years. She said I was not a seven-months baby—that I was conceived while Daddy was away. And you know what, Auntie Sharon . . . ?"

"No, child?"

"She told the truth. I—I sent Lance away then, and went and looked in my mirror. Auntie Sharon—oh, Auntie Sharon, I look just like Joe! I do! I do!"

That was it, Sharon realized suddenly, the thing that has eluded me all these years! Caprice was the image of Joseph. . . .

"I've known about Mother and Joseph all these years," Caprice went on in her slow, controlled tone, "but I never told Daddy. I didn't want him to find out. But it wasn't that, finally. I don't think he really cared—it was finding out that I, whom he loved so much, was not his. He could have borne everything else. The money—even Mother's cheating—"

She shook her head violently, fighting for control.

"Mother came home this morning and went straight to her room. She doesn't know yet. I haven't told her."

"You," Sharon whispered, spacing the words one after the other with great pauses in between, "have not told Esther?"

"No."

"But why, Caprice?"

"Pride loved you, Auntie Sharon—not Mother. I think he'd want you to know first."

Sharon looked up to the ceiling, where the gas lights were sputtering, their gauzelike filaments glowing white though it was barely dusk; then she looked back at Caprice's still face.

"You know," she said flatly, "this is dreadful. You should have told Esther first."

"Dreadful?" Caprice's voice had the first thin note of hysteria in it. "What isn't dreadful in this world? Wasn't it dreadful for Daddy to know you first, to love you from the hour he set eyes on you, and yet to marry Mother just because she was rich? Wasn't it dreadful for me to live in that big, empty castle, where there is no love, with a mother who has been tortured into a thing of hatred? Wasn't that dreadful?"

"And what I did?" Sharon whispered. "Wasn't that dreadful?"

"No. Pride belonged to you. Mother should have given him up."

"Caprice!"

"I'm sorry. And now I've lost Lance, too."

"Lance? Why?"

"I couldn't expect him to marry me now—under the circumstances. . . ."

"Why don't you let him decide that," Sharon said, and pointed to the telephone.

Caprice got up slowly, like a sleepwalker, and turned the crank. Sharon heard her give the number, wait, then whisper into the mouthpiece. Even from where she sat, she could hear the staccato bark of Lance's reply, and see the happiness pouring into Caprice's face.

"It's all right, isn't it?" she asked when Caprice turned from the phone.

"Yes," Caprice whispered. "Yes, oh yes! I'm going to him, now. But you must be ready, Auntie Sharon. I came here to tell you that. You're going to be troubled—more

338

troubled than Mother or me, or anybody else. God, but Daddy was a cruel man!"

"Caprice, you don't know!"

"I do know! There are going to be journalists, Auntie Sharon! I don't want them writing about you. Pride Dawson's mistress—that's what they'll say! And it wasn't like that. It wasn't like that at all."

"No," Sharon said slowly, "it really wasn't like that. But the papers know nothing of me. Who'll tell them?"

"Mother, maybe," Caprice said flatly. "Who knows? Besides," the blue eyes measured Sharon's brown ones, "Father shot himself with a little pocket pistol that has your name engraved on the barrel. It—it was still in his hand when I saw him . . ."

Sharon could feel the anguish inside herself now. She remembered how Pride had gained possession of that pistol; how he had taken it from her own nerveless fingers when she had meant to kill him. He had laughed at her then, saying: "You can't kill me. No one can." What he really had meant was, "You can't kill Pride. Only Pride can kill himself!" All these years he had borne within himself the seeds of his own destruction. . . . And suddenly the recognition of the reality of his death was too much for Sharon: she felt the slow upsurge of a tremendous wave of pain but, before she could indulge in the blessed relief of giving way to it, she looked into Caprice's eyes.

The girl was staring at her, the high, white courage in her face crumbling into splintery planes and angles of grief. "I tried to take it away," she whispered, "but I couldn't! He'd gripped it so tight and held it so long . . ." She swayed forward suddenly, and Sharon caught her to her breast, feeling through the warm and trembling flesh, the cold, sick movement of the girl's anguish. There was nothing she could do, no words of comfort she could say, being herself comfortless, so she rocked Caprice back and forth in her arms like a child, murmuring wordless, ancient mother-things. Caprice's sobs died into a low whimpering, then into silence. Finally, she looked up at Sharon.

"I wasn't very brave, was I?" she whispered. Her small pink mouth brushed Sharon's thin face. "Good-bye, Auntie Sharon, I have to go now." She stood up, dabbing at her eyes with a wisp of handkerchief. "You'll be ready, won't you?" she asked anxiously. "They'll be here soon."

Sharon got up and put her arm about the girl's slim waist.

"I'll be ready," she said, and together they walked out into the garden.

When Sharon pushed open the door and reëntered the house, she found the maid waiting for her.

"Oh, ma'am," the woman began, "there's some gentlemen . . ."

"Waiting for me," Sharon finished for her. "Representatives of the press. Well, did you show them in?"

"Didn't have to," the woman complained. "Fair stuck their feet in the door and shouldered me out of the way. You want to see them? I can tell them you got a headache —or something."

Sharon put up a tired hand and pushed back a dark lock from her brow. With an effort, she managed a smile.

"I'll see them," she said.

The maid shrugged, a heavy peasant gesture.

"They ain't nice," she grumbled. "If it was me, I'd show 'em the door."

"I'll manage," Sharon said, and went into the drawing-room.

The reporters stood up as she entered—a little slowly perhaps, as though they were making the gesture unwillingly. Yet as Sharon waited there in the doorway, the last of them got clumsily to his feet.

Sharon looked from one to another of them, her brown eyes resting at last upon the big man who had not removed his hat. Her gaze was serene and without censure, but it held level until at last his hand came up and took off the battered derby. It was only then that Sharon greeted them.

"Good afternoon, gentlemen," she said. "What can I do for you?"

They looked at one another a little sheepishly, each waiting for his neighbor to speak. Almost as clearly as though it were printed upon their foreheads, she read the reasons for their hesitation: to them she was Pride Dawson's kept woman. . . . But now, at least for the moment, she had given them pause.

Plainly, she was something outside their previous experiences with rich men's mistresses: her voice was soft-spoken, quiet, controlled, entirely lacking in affectation. Her dress was conservative to the point of being old-fashioned, and her bearing and mannerisms were those usually associated with generations of wealth and culture. Most puzzling of all was the fact that this woman who faced them with so much composure was utterly plain. Sharon's hair, they saw at once, was neither red nor golden nor vivid black. It was, instead, merely dark brown. How were they then to describe her in their stories, this woman who had enthralled a financial Titan for twenty years? ("The auburn-haired beauty who . . .") This small, graceful woman with dark brown hair, and eyes the color of old pennies; this face with its freckles plainly showing above the short upturned nose. . . . This woman whose mouth was large ("wide-lipped," they might have said, "generous"—but that would have called for imagination and they had none), whose fine-cut bones showed plainly through the tight-drawn flesh of her face, who was all planes and angles and hollows, with nothing about her suggesting the voluptuous?

It was disappointing and more. Pride Dawson's mistress (but now, seeing her, was she? How could she have been?) should have been blond and painted, noisy and vulgar . . . and Sharon was none of these.

Nelson, of the *Herald,* cleared his throat.

"Excuse me, ma'am," he began, glancing uneasily over his shoulder at his fellows, "but have you heard about Pride—Mr. Dawson, that is?"

Sharon inclined her head the barest fraction of an inch. When she spoke, her voice was lower still.

"Yes," she said, "I've heard." Then, "Won't you be seated, gentlemen? You look so uncomfortable, standing there."

They reddened. This was skill, they realized, feeling the quick verbal thrust, timed with precision to throw them off balance so that the advantage could not for an instant pass into their hands.

Slowly, they sank into the overstuffed chairs, the massive, horsehair furniture that filled the large room.

"Well," Nelson went on, while the others poised their pencils and waited, "seeing that it's pretty widely held that you're a friend of his—a very good friend—we thought we might get some explanation of why . . ."

Sharon smiled from the depths of the big chair in which she had seated herself. She realized now that she need not have feared them. If they expected her to rise to so clumsy a bait, they could be managed with ease.

"Why, yes," she said, "Mr. Dawson was a friend of mine, though I haven't seen him in many years. I'm afraid I can't shed much light on his death. I've heard he was having financial difficulties . . ."

The fat man in the corner snorted. It was Hendricks of the *Police Gazette*.

"Some house," he said, looking about him. "No financial difficulties here—at any rate."

"No," Sharon said very quietly. "No difficulties—of any sort."

Nelson turned a frowning face at Hendricks. This woman, he knew now, was not to be bullied. If she was to make any disclosures, she must be trapped into them. He had the feeling she was playing with them with quiet and skillful contempt.

He turned back to her.

"Your given name, ma'am, is Sharon, isn't it?"

Again that quick, graceful nod.

"Well, Mr. Dawson killed himself with a pistol that had 'Sharon' engraved upon the barrel. I was wondering . . ."

Sharon studied him coolly.

"Yes, the pistol was mine." The pencils raced now, scratching avidly over the paper.

"Mr. Dawson gave it to me many years ago during the riots of 1877. I was living in Pittsburgh then with my husband . . ." The pencils stopped abruptly, then started again. "Courtney Randolph. You know the Randolphs, of course."

They knew well enough, and again the picture they had formed of her was becoming distorted. So this pleasant but hardly beautiful woman had not only captivated Pride Dawson, but had married a Randolph! They waited, their eyes glistening and eager.

"My husband and Mr. Dawson were close friends," said Sharon and smiled softly to herself before continuing. "During those terrible days when half the town was burned and the locomotives dynamited in the depot, Mr. Dawson

342

came to Pittsburgh to protect certain interests of his—the marshalling yards of his railroad."

Sharon closed her eyes and a grimace of pain crossed her face.

"When he arrived," she continued, "he discovered that my husband had disappeared. Later we learned that he had been killed by the rioters. Mr. Dawson wanted to stay to protect me but, of course, I couldn't permit that. So, as an alternative, he bought that pistol and gave it to me. Some of you gentlemen knew him, no doubt. Then you must know how he loved the magnificent. It never occurred to him that just *any* weapon could have served. No, he wasted hours and perhaps endangered my life, searching for that beautiful little pistol and then having my name engraved upon it. . . ."

"Because," Hendricks snarled, "he loved its beauty?"

Sharon's glance was candid, even humorous.

"Obviously!"

"Then," Nelson suggested heavily, "there was no romantic attachment between you and Mr. Dawson?"

Sharon's brown eyes lifted and came level, holding Nelson's gaze.

"You must never have seen Mrs. Dawson!" she said quietly. "Pride Dawson insisted upon beauty in everything that surrounded him. Would you call me beautiful? Esther Dawson is—ravishing."

Nelson nodded, the puzzled look deepening about his eyes. He had seen Esther Stillworth Dawson many times. That was the final thing, now that Sharon mentioned it, which jolted his preconceived notions. Esther Dawson's beauty had exhausted the adjectives of the society editors. He knew she was one of the loveliest women in New York. Why on earth then, if the rumors were true, would Pride Dawson turn to this thin, plain creature? He had known Pride Dawson well—the man had been lavish, grandiloquent, magnificent. A woman like Jim Fisk's Josie might have turned his head, but this little stick—never.

"One thing more," he said. "How did Mr. Dawson get that pistol, if he gave it to you?"

"I gave it back to him. I returned to New York a week after the riots. That pistol reminded me too much of—of what had happened. So I sent it to him by a messenger the day I arrived. I haven't seen it since. Why Mr. Dawson had to use that particular weapon to end his life is something I shall never understand." She paused and lowered her eyes, staring down at her small well-shod feet.

"Dreadful, wasn't it?" she whispered. "I wish I had thrown that pistol away."

"He would have used another," Hendricks said brusquely. Sharon looked at him.

"Another," she said clearly, "would have been much better, as far as I'm concerned. For then, sir, I would have been spared meeting you."

She stood up then with that angular grace that was so much a part of her and reached for the bell cord. It was no help to Hendricks' disposition that few of them could resist at least a chuckle at Sharon's parting thrust.

She turned her head and looked at them over her shoulder.

"You'll have brandy, gentlemen, before you leave?" she murmured.

Nelson stood very still, watching her, the thoughts in his mind moving with ponderous slowness. Intelligence, that's what it is, he decided. It dominates her whole face. . . . She knows what a man's thinking before he half does himself. She'd wind a man like Dawson about her little finger —and make him like it. After a while she'd make him forget she wasn't pretty. In a year he'd swear that she was lovely. And, by God, she is! It's what's in her that's beautiful, not her face or figure. . . .

"No, thank you, ma'am," he said gently. "We've got to get back to our papers . . ."

They filed out then—all but Hendricks. He stopped before her, red and perspiring, his little black eyes glinting evilly in his round face.

"You fooled them," he grinned. "But not me. Not old Bob Hendricks. If you ever want somebody to kind of rally around—and take Pride's place—just turn the crank on that telephone and call the *Gazette*. I'll skip right over."

Sharon could feel her palm itch with the desire to strike him. She could almost hear the sound that the slap would make, exploding against his fat jowls. But she stood quite still, and her gaze moved over him with slowness and deliberation, having in it exactly the same quality he had often seen in the eyes of a visitor to the zoo, examining some curious beast—safely behind stout bars.

"Good day, Mr. Hendricks," she said quietly and, turning, walked back to the big chair.

It was very quiet after they had gone. Sharon sat very still and gazed into the blackened and empty fireplace. It was far too warm for a fire, but Sharon felt cold. I shall never feel warm again, she thought, never warm, or wanted or loved. . . . Oh, Pride, Pride, why did you leave me behind? I would have gone with you. . . . Ah, yes, my love, how gladly would I have gone.

She stared into the fireplace with unseeing eyes. They'll lie, she thought. No—not lie . . . They'll say cruel things— all true, but for the wrong reasons. They don't know the real reasons, Pride—and I couldn't tell them. They never heard you say: "I was poorer'n dirt, Sharon, and I didn't like it!" . . . And they never heard you say: "Ever eat clay —red mud, to stay alive? Have you ever been made to come in the back door with the serving blacks? Did you ever dig canals with the sun boiling your brains and the stink getting into your nose, so that you still smell it thirty years after?" . . . Have they ever tried to kick down a man who had no servility in him—a man like you, whose pride exceeded Lucifer's? "My ma," you used to say—"she named me Pride so I wouldn't forget to have it!"

And you didn't forget, did you, darling? You never forgot though it made you ravage the world, taking, taking, taking—until every man's hand was against you, and only I could see the grandeur in you. . . . For I did love you, Pride—more than you knew, or believed, or understood. Not for what men called you, but for what you might have been and sometimes were—with me.

Then, bowing her head, she loosed the tears that had run all day through the dark and secret places of her heart. They were better out of her. Held in, they might have destroyed her.

SHARON PUT ON her hat and coat and gloves, and went out into the street. Then she hailed a cab and drove to Pride's castle.

She knew it was not the wisest thing to do. It could conceivably reopen the old wounds of a scandal; but she had to go. This much she owed Pride—this much she owed the love she bore him.

Esther herself opened the door. She stood still, looking at Sharon. Then she whispered:

"Come in."

Sharon slipped into the big hall, and Esther guided her into the great salon where they had placed him. Sharon stood there looking down at Pride, holding tight reins on the wild, unceasing grief that tore her.

"Cry!" Esther said, suddenly, harshly. "It's better that he has someone to weep for him."

Sharon turned and looked at Esther, seeing with surprise that her still lovely face was ravaged by grief, the hurt rising unbearably in her eyes.

"Why," she whispered, "you love him! You love him still!"

"You think that Joe could take his place?" Esther said. "That was revenge—nothing more. And now I've killed him. I—who loved him so!"

"Say rather that we killed him," Sharon murmured gently. "You and I and the world—and perhaps even the hand of God. Don't blame yourself too much, Esther."

"Don't blame myself?" Esther whispered. "Don't blame myself? God knows I shall never know another peaceful night!"

"What about Joseph?" Sharon asked. "You'll marry him now?"

"I don't know," Esther said. "I don't know. . . ."

As if in answer to the name, Malcolm came into the salon and announced in a whisper: "Mr. Fairhill's here."

Joseph Fairhill came into the room, walking very stiffly. And in his still-young face the image of Caprice stood out like a damning cry.

Silently, he crossed over to Pride's bier and glanced down. Then he looked at Esther. She started toward him, walking swiftly. When she was close he drew back his hand suddenly, and slapped her across the mouth.

Oh, my God! Sharon wept, you might have spared me this. . . .

Then she turned to flee but Joseph already was gone, walking like a mechanical toy toward the door; but Esther still hung there, the prints of his fingers vivid against her pale skin.

There was nothing else for Sharon to do, so she put out her arms. And Esther came to her, whimpering like a whipped child.

Afterwards—long afterwards when Sharon came back into the house that Pride had given her—she found the fire had been lit and the house straightened, which was strange, for she had given the maid the day off.

She stood looking around her; then Lilith came from behind the curtains. She held a package of cigarettes in her hand. Her face looked different. Then Sharon saw what it was. It was clean—clean and shining. Every trace of paint had been scrubbed off, and her lips were their own natural pink. Her dark hair was brushed back from her forehead very simply.

Then while Sharon watched, slowly, ceremoniously, Lilith threw the package of cigarettes into the fire.

"I—I've always hated those things," she whispered.

For the second time that day Sharon put out her arms.

"Come to me, child," she said. . . .

Later she sat in the great chair before the fireplace, where she had sat so many times before with Pride, and gazed into the fire. Lilith nestled beside her on the floor, her head resting in Sharon's lap. From time to time Sharon's hand moved, stroking Lilith's soft, shining hair.

Lilith was all right now, she knew. Whatever the sickness in her heart and mind and soul had been, whether it was born of insecurity, or want of love, or fear—it was gone. And it would not come back.

Only she, Sharon, was alone now. In his great, ugly stone pile of a castle, Pride Dawson lay dead. No, not dead —not ever dead . . . never could that tremendous vitality be forever ended. Not while she lived and memory had its seat in her.

No, she thought. No, Pride. The days of my years will be but a time of separation. . . .

Frank Yerby's

magnificent historical novels have
enthralled millions around the world . . .

Don't miss these bestsellers—

BESTSELLERS
FROM DELL

fiction